I0586389

IN THE

YULE-LOG GLOW

CHRISTMAS TALES FROM
'ROUND THE WORLD

"Sic as folk tell ower at a winter ingle"

Scott

EDITED BY

HARRISON S. MORRIS

THREE VOLUMES IN ONE.

Book I.

WILDSIDE PRESS

Copyright, 1891, by J. B. LIPPINCOTT COMPANY.

PRINTED BY J. B. LIPPINCOTT COMPANY, PHILADELPHIA.

THE THRESHOLD.

IF, gentle reader, you will step across this threshold, now, as the moon rises in the keen Christmas air, and will find a place by the ruddy ingle within-doors, you may hear, if you will, a Babel of voices from many lands, telling over the adventures of the road and falling into the good-fellowship of the happy Christmas season.

Here from the north, with his ample furs thrown back, sits the Russian in friendly talk with a gay little wanderer from Sicilian valleys. There, with elbow crooked by a foaming tankard, leans the German, narrating his perils and pleasures to a gallant Frenchman and a sunbrowned Spaniard who smoke and chatter together as now and then Mynheer stops for a pull at his pipe.

A Swede, Norwegians, an Englishman or two, and even a happy-go-lucky American, are clustered about the Yule-log; for the place you have entered is the common-room of the wide world.

As you slip the latch and take your seat, some traveller calls out: A Merry Christmas! Another cries: A story, a story! and so they fall to, each from his own scrip taking forth a native tale,—and so they sit the midnight out listening and talking in turn; while the good cheer goes round in endless abundance and laughter and song make interludes for the varied narratives.

CONTENTS OF BOOK I.

PAGE

THE THREE KINGS OF COLOGNE 9
A modern version of an old English Chronicle.
By Harrison S. Morris.

THE THREE CHRISTMAS MASSES 47
From the French of Alphonse Daudet.
By Harrison S. Morris.

A RUSSIAN CHRISTMAS PARTY* 63
By Count Léon Tolstoï.

TWO CHRISTMASES 103
From the German of Georg Schuster.

A TALE OF A TURKEY 121
By Harrison S Morris.

A STILL CHRISTMAS† 173
By Agnes Repplier.

THROND 193
From the Norwegian of Björnson.

CHRISTMAS IN THE DESERT 211
By Matilda Betham Edwards.

---

* By courtesy of Messrs. W. S. Gottsberger & Co.
† By courtesy of "The Catholic World."

ILLUSTRATIONS, BOOK I.

THE YULE-LOG GLOW . . . . Frontispiece.

SONIA . . . . Page 82

THE CAVALIER FROM FRANCE. . . . . " 182

MY LITTLE SISTER MARY . . . . " 224

A Tale Spoken by a Graybeard Out of the East.

> "Gracious powers! Perhaps you *are* a hundred years old, now I think of it! You look more than a hundred. Yes, you may be a thousand years old for what 1 know."
>
> *Thackeray.*

THE THREE KINGS OF COLOGNE.

A CHRISTMAS TALE FROM AN OLD ENGLISH CHRONICLE.

(Written by John of Hildesheim in the Fourteenth Century.)

Here followeth the manner and form of seeking and offering; and also of the burying and translations of the three Holy and Worshipful Kings of Cologne: Jaspar, Melchior, and Balthazar.

Now when the Children of Israel were gone out of Egypt and had won and made subject to them Jerusalem and all the land lying about, so that no man durst set against them in all that country for dread that they had of them; then was there a little hill called Vaws, which was also called the Hill of Victory, and on this hill the ward of them of Ind was ordained and kept by divers sentinels by night and by day against the Children of Israel, and afterward against the Romans; so that if any people at any time purposed with strong hand to enter into the country of the Kingdom of Ind, anon, sentinels of other hills about, through tokens, warned the keepers on the hill of Vaws. And by night they made a great fire and by day they

9

made a great smoke, for that hill Vaws passeth
the height of all other hills in all the East.
Wherefore, when any such token was seen, then
all manner of men made ready to defend themselves from the enemy that approached.

Now in the time when Balaam prophesied
of the Star that should betoken the coming of
Christ, all the great lords and all the other
people of Ind and in the East desired greatly
to see the Star of which he spake, and gave
gifts to the keepers of the hill of Vaws, and
moreover hired them with great rewards, that,
if it so were, they saw by day or by night, far
or near, any light or any star in the air other
than was seen beforetime, anon they should
show and send them word. And thus was it
that for so long a time the fame of this Star was
borne through all the lands of the East; until,
of the name of the hill of Vaws, arose up a
worshipful and a great kindred in Ind, which
is called the progeny of Vaws even unto this
day; and there is not a more mighty kindred in
all the kingdoms of the East; for this worshipful kindred came first from the King's blood
that was named Melchior, that offered gold to
our Lord, as ye shall hereafter learn.

In the year of our Lord 1200, when the city
of Acon, that in this country is called Akers,
flourished and stood in virtue, joy, and pros-

perity, and was inhabited richly with worshipful princes, and lords, and divers orders of men
of religion, and all manner of men of all nations
and tongues, so that there was no city like unto
it in nobility and might; then, because of its
great name and of the marvels that were there,
the greatest of birth that were of the progeny
of Vaws came out of Ind unto Acon; and when
they saw there all things more wonderful than
in Ind; then, because of delight, they abode
there and made a fair and strong castle for any
king or lord. And they brought with them out
of the East many rich and wonderful ornaments and jewels. And among all other jewels, they brought a diadem of gold arrayed with
precious stones and pearls, and about its edge
stood letters of Chaldaic, and a star made like
after the Star that appeared to the Three Kings
of the East when they sought God, with a sign
of the cross, beside. And that diadem was
Melchior's, the king of Nubia and of Araby,
that offered gold to the Babe in the manger.
And afterward the master of the Order of
Templars received this same diadem of gold
and many other precious jewels; but when that
Order was destroyed the diadem and precious
ornaments were lost, and have never been found
unto this day. Wherefore there was great sorrow made in all the country for a long time after.

But these same princes of Vaws brought
with them out of Ind books written in He-
brew and Chaldaic, concerning the life and deeds
of these three blessed Kings, which books were
afterward translated into the French tongue:
and so, from these books, and from hearsay, and
sight, and also from sermons and homilies out
of divers other works, the story here written
hath been brought together into one book.

And you shall understand that the old kindred
of Vaws beareth always in its banner, unto this
day, a star with a sign of the cross, made after
the same manner as it appeared to the three
blessed Kings.

Now it so happened that after Balaam had
prophesied of this Star, the more it was sought
for the more its fame increased through the
land of Ind and Chaldee, and all the people desired to see it.

So they ordained twelve of the wisest and
greatest clerks of astronomy that were in all
that country about, and gave them great hire to
keep watch upon this hill of Vaws for the Star
that was prophesied of Balaam. And the cause
that there were ordained twelve men was, that
if one man died another should be put in his
stead; and also that some should keep watch at
one time and some another—nevertheless the
people looked not only after the Star, but after

the Man who was betokened by the Star, the which Man should be Lord of all folk.

And they of Ind and Chaldee who came often into Jerusalem because of merchandise and also for disport—the which, for the most part, be learned in astronomy—said that in Ind were many stars in the firmament that might not be seen by night in Jerusalem; but, specially on this hill of Vaws in clear weather, were seen many and divers strange stars that at the foot of the hill were not seen. Yet this hill of Vaws hath no more breadth than a little chapel is made upon, the which the three worshipful kings did build of stone and timber, And there be about this hill, many steps upon which men go up to the chapel on high, and also there grew many good trees and herbs and divers spices all about the hill—for else men might not well go upon this hill because it is so high and so narrow. There is also a pillar of stone made above this chapel, of wondrous height, and in the head of the pillar standeth a great star, well made of gilt, and which turneth with the wind as a vane: and through the light of the sun by day, and of the moon by night, this star gives light a great way about the country. And many other marvels are spoken of this hill of Vaws, the which were long to tell.

Now when the time of grace was come, that

2*

God would have mercy on all mankind, in which
time the Father of Heaven sent down his Son
to take flesh and blood and to be born a man
for salvation of all the world: in that time
Octavianus, that was Emperor of Rome, sent
out a commandment that all the people within
his empire should be counted and taxed; and
every man went forth from his dwelling-place
into his native country. Then came Joseph up
from Nazareth unto Bethlehem the city of
David, because he was of the household and
race of King David, and with him came Mary
that was his wife, and also great with child.

And you shall understand that Bethlehem
was never of much reputation, neither a place
of great quantity. It hath a good site and
good ground, for there be many caves and dens
under the earth thereabout; and it is distant
from Jerusalem but two little miles; and it is
but a castle, but is called a city because King
David was born there. And in that town was
sometime a house which belonged to Isai, the
father of David, where David was born and
anointed into the kingdom of Israel by Samuel
the prophet. And in this same dwelling was
the Son of Heaven born of Mary.

And this same house was at the end of a street
that was in that time called the Covered Street,
because, to keep out the great heat and burn-

ing of the sun, this street was canopied above
with black cloths and other things,—for such
is the use in that country always. And here
was wont to be great bargaining, or a fair
once a week of old clothes; and specially of
trees or timber, by the little house which stood
before a den under the earth, made and shaped
like a little cellar, where Isai and others that
dwelt there after him put certain necessaries
that belonged to the household, against the
heat of the sun. It is also the manner in all
that country that there be certain houses, the
which be called there *alchan*, that we call hos-
telries, and in these houses be mules, horses,
asses, and camels always ready, that, if so
that any merchant or any man that travelled
by the way, be it far or near, need any beast
for himself, or for his merchandise, then he
goeth to such a house and there he may hire a
horse, or what beast that he will, for a certain
price. And when he hath such a beast then he
goeth from that city to another, where to abide
and rest him for a time. Then he dischargeth
his beast of his burden, and so sendeth him to a
house called there also *alchan;* and the master
of the house giveth his beast meat, and, when
he may, he sendeth it home to the same place
that it came from.

And such a house was, before the birth of

Christ, in the place where Christ was born, but, about the time of the Nativity, that house was all destroyed, insomuch that there was nothing left but broken walls on every side, and a little cave under earth, and a little unthrifty house before the cave: and there men sold bread on the same ground; for it is the usage in all that country that all the bread that is sold shall be brought unto a certain place.

Now when Octavianus had sent out a commandment as it is aforesaid, then went Joseph and Mary riding on an ass, late in the eventide, toward the city of Bethlehem, and because they came so late, and all places were occupied with pilgrims and other men, and also because they came in poor array and went about the city, none would receive them, and specially, men say, because that Mary, a young woman, sitting upon an ass, heavy and sorry, and full weary of the way, was near to the time of bearing of her child. Then Joseph led his wife into this shed that none took keep of, down into the little dark house, and there our Lord, Jesus Christ, the same night was born of the Virgin, without any disease or sorrow of her body, for salvation of all mankind.

And in that house, before the cave of old time, was left a manger of the length of a fathom, made in the wall; and to that same manger was an ox of a poor man tied, that none might harbor. And beside that ox Joseph tied his ass, and in that same manger Mary wrapped her blessed Son in cloths and laid Him on high before the ass and the ox,—for there was none other place.

And shepherds were fast by in the same country keeping their sheep in the night, and an angel of Heaven came and stood beside them with a great light, wherefore they were in much dread. And the angel said to them, " Be not afraid, for I tell you a great joy that shall be to all people, for this day is born to us our Lord, Christ, in the city of David, and this shall be to you a token : Ye shall find a young child wrapped in cloths and put in a manger." And then suddenly there came a great multitude of angels of Heaven praising God, who said : " Joy be to God on high and peace in earth to men of good will."

Now the place where the angel appeared to the shepherds that night when Christ was born is but half a mile from Bethlehem, and in that same place David, when he was a child, fed sheep and kept them from the bear and the lion.

Some books say that the shepherds in that country, twice in the year, are wont to keep

I.—*b*　　˝　2*

their sheep in the night, and, therein, times be
when the day and the night are both of one
length. And you shall understand that the
land about Bethlehem is all mountainous for
the most part, so that in some places a man
shall not well know winter from summer, and
in some places it is right cold, and some it is
both winter and summer at one time, and sometimes on the mountains, in parts of the East,
men shall find snow in the month of August,
and that snow is gathered by them that dwell
about, and put in caves, and afterward it is
borne to the market, where the great lords of
the country will buy it, and take it to their
houses, and set it in a basin upon their board to
make their drink cold.

In September and October, when the sun
cometh a little low in that country, then seeds
and all manner of herbs commonly begin to
wax in the fields, as in this country herbs begin
to grow in March and April; also in some parts
of the East they reap corn in April and in
March, but most in May, as in some places the
ground is higher, in some places lower; but
beside Bethlehem are many more places of good
pasture and of flat ground than elsewhere: insomuch that at Christmas-tide barley beginneth
to ear and to wax ripe; and then men send
thither, from divers countries, their horses and

mules, to make them fat : and that time we call among us Christmas, they call, in their language, the time of herbage. And forasmuch as when Christ was born, peace was in all the world, and betwixt Bethlehem and that place where the angel appeared to the shepherds was but half a mile and a little way more, and also there was no great cold thereabout, therefore the shepherds, all that winter night and day, now in one place, now in another, dwelled there with their sheep, and so they do yet to this day.

Now when Christ was born of the Virgin Mary for salvation of all mankind, then His Star, that was prophesied of Balaam and long awaited and looked for by the twelve astronomers on the hill of Vaws, at that same night and at that same hour, began to arise in the manner of a sun, bright shining ; and so after, in the form of an eagle, it ascended above the hill of Vaws. And all that day in highest air it abode without moving, insomuch that when the sun was most hot and most high there was no difference in shining betwixt them.

But when the day of the Nativity was passed, the Star ascended up into the firmament, and it was nothing like to stars that be painted in divers places, for it had right many long streaks and beams, more burning and lighter than a

brand of fire ; and, as an eagle flying and beating
the air with his wings, right so the streaks and
beams of the Star stirred it about.   And it had
in itself the form and likeness of a young child,
and above him a sign of the holy cross, and a
voice was heard in the Star, saying : " This day
is born to us the King of Jews that folk have
awaited, and Lord is of them.   Go and seek Him
and do Him worship !"

Then all the people, both man and woman, of
all the country about, when they saw this wonderful and marvellous Star and also heard the
voice out of the Star, were greatly aghast and
had wonder thereof; but yet they knew well
that it was the Star that was prophesied by
Balaam, and long time was desired of all the
people in that country.

Now when the three worshipful Kings who
in that time reigned in Ind, Chaldee, and Persia
were informed, by the astronomers, of this Star,
they were right glad that they had grace to see
the Star in their days.   Wherefore these three
worshipful Kings, though each of them was far
from the other, and none knew of the other's
purpose, yet in the same hour the Star appeared
to all three, and then they ordained and purposed them, with great and rich gifts and many
rich and diverse ornaments that belong to a
king's array, and also with mules and camels

and horses charged with treasure, and with a
great multitude of people, to go seek and worship the Lord and King of the Jews that was
new born, as the voice of the Star had commanded. And furthermore they arrayed themselves the much more honestly and worshipfully,
because they knew well that he was a worthier
King than any of them was.

And you shall understand that there be three
Indias, of which these three lords were kings;
and all the lands for the most part are islands,
and there are also there great waters and wil-
dernesses full of wild and perilous beasts and
horrible serpents, and there grow also reeds so
high and so great that men make thereof houses
and ships. And these isles are divided every
one by itself far from the others, so that only
with great travail shall a man pass from one
kingdom to another.

Now, in the first Ind was the land of Nubia,
and therein reigned King Melchior, in the time
that Christ was born. Therein also is the land
of Araby, in which is the hill Sinai : and a man
may lightly sail by the Red Sea out of Egypt
and Syria into Ind. In this land is found gold
wonderfully red, like thin and small roots, and
that gold is the best that is in the world.
Herein is also a hill called Bena, where is found
a precious stone, called smaragd.

In the second Ind was the kingdom of Godo-
lia, of which Balthazar was king when Christ
was born; and this Belthazar offered incense to
the Babe; for in this land many more good
spices grow than in all the countries of the
East, and especially incense, more than in all
places of the world; and it droppeth down out
of certain trees in the manner of gum.

In the third Ind was the kingdom of Thaars.
Of that kingdom was Jaspar king at the birth
of Christ. And Jaspar offered myrrh to the
young Child, and in this land is the isle of
Egrisoulla, where groweth myrrh more plentifully than in any place of the world, and it
waxeth like ears of corn that are burnt with
the weather, and right thick; and when it is
ripe it is so soft that it cleaveth to men's clothes
as they go by the way.

Now when these three worshipful Kings were
passed forth out of their kingdoms, the Star
evenly went before each King and his people,
and when they stood still and rested the Star
stood still, and when they went forward again
the Star always went before them in virtue and
strength, and gave light all the way. And, as
it is written before, in the time that Christ was
born there was peace in all the world, wherefore in all the cities and towns which they went
through there was no gate shut neither by

night nor by day : and all men of the cities and towns that these worthy Kings went through in the night were wonderfully aghast and passingly marvelled thereof, for they saw kings and vast multitudes go by in great haste ; but they knew not what they were, nor whence they came, nor whither they should go. On the morrow the way was greatly befouled with horses' hoofs, whereof they were in much doubt what it might mean, and great altercation was among them for a long time.

Furthermore, these Kings rode forth over hills, waters, valleys, plains, and other divers and perilous places without hindrance or disease, for all the way seemed to them plain and even, and they never took shelter by night nor by day ; nor ever rested ; nor did their horses or other beasts ever eat or drink till they had come to Bethlehem ; and all this time seemed to them but a day.

And thus, through the mercy of God and the leading of the Star, they came unto Jerusalem and Bethlehem the thirteenth day after Christ was born, at the uprising of the sun, whereof is no doubt : for they found Mary and her son in the same place where the Child was born, and laid in the manger.

But when the three blessed Kings, with their host and company were almost come to Jerusa-

lem, saving but two miles, then a great and
dark cloud held all the earth, and in that dark
cloud they lost the Star. And Melchior with
his people was come fast by Jerusalem beside
the hill of Calvary, where Christ was afterward crucified ; and there the King abode in a
cloud of fog and in darkness.

At that time the hill of Calvary was a rock
of twelve degrees high, where thieves and other
men for divers trespasses were put to death ;
and there was beside this hill a place where
three highways met together. But because of
the darkness of the cloud, and also because they
knew not the way, they abode there, and went
no further at that time.

And next came Balthazar, and he abode under
the same cloud, beside the Mount of Olives in
a little town that is called Galilee.

Then, when the two Kings were come to these
places, the cloud began to ascend and wax clear,
yet the Star appeared not. But when they saw
that they were near to the city of Jerusalem,
knowing not each other, they took their way
thither with all their folk ; and when they came
where the three ways met, then also appeared
King Jaspar with all his host. And so these
three glorious Kings, each with his host and
burdens and beasts, met together in the highway beside the Hill of Calvary. And, notwith-

standing that none of them ever before had seen the other, nor knew him, nor had heard of his coming, yet, at their meeting, each one with great reverence and joy kissed the other. And though they were of diverse language, yet all, to their seeming, used the same tongue.

So, afterward, when they had spoken together and each had told his purpose and the cause of his journey, and the cause of all was learned to be the same, then they were much more glad and more fervent. And so they rode forth, and suddenly, at the uprising of the sun, they came into the city of Jerusalem. And when they knew that this was the city which the Chaldeans of old time had besieged and destroyed, they were right glad, expecting to have found the King born in that city. But Herod and all his people were greatly disturbed at their sudden coming, for their company and beasts of burden were of so great a number that the city might not receive them, but for the most part they lay without the gates all about, whereof Isaias prophesied : " The strength of folk cometh to thee—that is to say, to the City of Jerusalem—great plenty of camels shall do thee service, and dromedaries of Madyan and Effa shall come to thee. All men shall come from Saba, bringing gold and incense and showing praise to God."

B
3

So, these three worshipful Kings, when they were come into the city, asked of the people concerning the Child that was born; and, when Herod heard this, he was troubled and all Jerusalem with him, and he gathered together all his princes and priests and asked them where Christ should be born, and they said : " In Bethlehem of Judea." Then Herod privily summoned to him these three Kings, and learned of them the time that the Star appeared, and so sent them forth unto Bethlehem, saying : " Go and inquire busily of this Child, and when you have found Him, come and tell me, that I may go and do Him worship."

Now when these three Kings were informed of the birth of Christ and of the place where He was born, and so were passed out of Jerusalem, then the Star appeared to them again as it did erst, and went before them till they came to Bethlehem. And fast by that place were the shepherds to whom the angel appeared with great light, showing them the birth of Christ. And the three Kings spake with them, and when the shepherds saw the Star they run together and told how the angel had appeared to them, and furthermore all that the angel had spoken to them. And the Kings were wondrous glad, and with good cheer heard and took consideration of the shepherds' words; and so from witness, and from the words of the shepherds and from the voice of the angel that was heard out of the Star, they had no doubt of the thing. Then anon, when they knew that they were come to Bethlehem, they got down from their horses and changed all their array, and clothed themselves in the best and richest that they had, as kings should be clothed—and always the Star went forth before them.

Now the nearer the Kings came to the place where Christ was born the brighter shined the Star, and they entered Bethlehem the sixth hour of the day. And then they rode through the covered street till they came before that little house. And there the Star stood still, and then descended and shone with so great a light that the little house and the cave within were full of radiance, till anon the Star again went upward into the air, and stood still always above the same place, yet the light ever remained in the house where Christ and Mary were. So as it is said in the Gospel: "They went into the house and found the Child, and fell down and worshipped Him, and offered to Him gifts of gold, myrrh, and incense."

Of this example came afterward a usage, that in all the countries of the East no man should go into the presence of the Sultan, but he brought gold or silver or somewhat else in his

hands; and, also, ere he spoke to the Sultan he
should kiss the ground, and this is a custom
which is used in all the countries of the East
to this day. But the Franciscan friars, when
they approached the Sultan, offered to him
only pears or apples, for they might not touch
gold nor silver; and these offerings were received by the Sultan with all reverence and
meekness.

Now on the day that the three Kings sought
Christ and worshipped Him, He was a little
child of thirteen days old, and He was somewhat fat, and lay wrapped in poor clothes in the
hay of the manger up to His arms. And Mary,
His Mother, as it is written in divers books, was,
in person, fleshy and somewhat brown. In the
presence of the three Kings she was covered
with a poor white mantle, which she held close
before her with her left hand. Her head was
concealed altogether, save her face, with a linen
cloth; and she sat upon the manger and with
her right hand held up the young Child's head.
And the Kings worshipped Him and kissed His
hand devoutly and laid their gifts beside His
head.

But what was done with these gifts, ye shall
learn hereafter.

Now Melchior, that offered gold to the Holy
Child, was the least in stature and person of

the three Kings. Balthazar, that offered incense, was of a medium stature; and Jaspar,
that offered myrrh, was most in person; whereof
is no doubt, for the prophet saith: "Before
Him shall fall down Ethiops, and His enemies
shall lick the earth. They shall come to Thee
that betrayed Thee, and they shall worship the
steps of Thy feet." And having regard to the
stature of men of that time these Kings were
right little of person, insomuch that all manner
of people marvelled at them. And this showed
well that they were come from far out of the
East, for the nearer toward the uprising of the
sun that men be born, the less they be of
stature and be feebler and more tender.

And you shall understand that these three
Kings brought out of their lands many gifts
and rich ornaments which King Alexander left
in Ind, in Chaldee, and in Persia; and all the
ornaments which Queen Saba found in Solomon's
temple, and divers vessels that were of the
king's house and the Temple of God in Jerusalem, which, in the time of its destruction, were
borne into their countries by the Persians and
Chaldeans, and many other jewels, both gold
and silver, and precious stones, brought they
with them to offer to Christ. But when they
found our Lord laid on high in the manger and
in poor cloths, and the Star that gave so great

light in all the place, that it seemed as though they stood in a furnace of fire, then these Kings were so sore afraid that, of all the rich jewels and ornaments they brought with them, they chose nothing, when their treasury was opened, but what came first to their hands, for Melchior took a round apple of gold, as much as a man might hold in his hand, and thirty gilt pennies, and these he offered to our Lord. Balthazar took out of his treasury incense; and Jaspar took out myrrh, as it came first, and that he offered, with weeping and tears.

And the Kings were so aghast and so devout and fervent in their oblations, that to all the words that Mary said they gave but little consideration, save only that to every King as he offered his gifts she bowed down her head meekly, and said, " *Deo gracias :*" that is to say, " I thank God."

When these three Kings had thus performed their way and will, and done all things that they came for, then, as mankind asketh and would, they and all their men and beasts began to eat, and drink, and sleep, and betook them to rest and sport all that day in Bethlehem. For, as is said before, they had neither eaten nor drunk during thirteen days. And then they meekly told to all men in that city how wonderfully the Star had brought them thither from the furthest part of the world.

Now, as the Evangelist saith: A command came to these Kings in their sleep that they should not return again to Herod, and so, by another way, they went home to their kingdoms. But the Star that went before them, appeared no more. And so these three Kings, that suddenly met together at the Mount of Calvary, rode home together with great joy and honor, and rested by the way as men should do.

And they rode through the provinces that Holofernes of old time had traversed with all his hosts, and the people supposed that Holofernes had come again, for as they journeyed into any town they were meekly and worshipfully received, and evermore they told what they had seen, done, and heard, so that their name and praise were never after forgot. But the way that before had taken only thirteen days, through leading of the Star, they found now to take two years, which was ordained, that all men should know what difference is between God's working and man's.

Now, when Herod and the scribes heard that the Kings were gone home again, and came not to him as he had bade them, then, of much envy and malice, he pursued them a great way; and always he found the people bless them, and

praise them, and tell of their nobility. Wherefore Herod burnt and destroyed all the land
that was under his power where the Kings had
ridden, and especially Tharsis and Cilicia, for he
charged them that they had suffered the three
Kings privily to pass across the sea in their
ships. And Herod's envy was great when he
heard how marvellously the Kings had come
out of their lands in thirteen days through
leading of the Star, and how, afterward, they
went home again, without the Star, through
guides and interpreters,—yet no man could tell,
for wonder, how night and day they passed by;
and for this reason the paynims, who had no
knowledge of Holy Writ, nor of the birth of
Christ, called these three Kings *Magos;* that is
to say, Wise Men of the East.

Now, when the Kings were come with great
travail to the Hill of Vaws, they made there,
as is aforesaid, a fair chapel in worship of the
Child they had sought. Also they made a covenant to meet together at the same place once
in the year; and there they ordained their
burial. Then all the princes and lords and
worshipful knights of their kingdoms, hearing of the return of these three Kings, anon
rode forth to them with great solemnity and
met them at the place aforesaid, and with meekness and humility received them. And when

they heard how wonderfully God had wrought
for their Kings, they held them in more reverence, love, and dread forever after.

So, when the Kings had done what they
would, they took leave of each other, and each
one, with his people, rode home to his own land
with great joy.

And when they were come into their own
realms, they preached to all the people what
they had seen and done on their journey; and
they made in their temples a star after the likeness of that which appeared to them, wherefore
many paynims left their errors and worshipped
the Holy Child.

And thus these three worshipful Kings dwelt
in their kingdoms in honest and devout conversation until the coming of St. Thomas, the
apostle.

Now, after the three Kings had gone forth
from Bethlehem, there began to wax, all about,
a great fame for Mary and her Child, and for
the Kings of the East. Wherefore, Mary, in
dread of persecution, fled out of the little house
where Christ was born, and went to another
dark cave and there abode; and divers men and
women loved her and ministered to her all
manner of necessaries. But when she went
out of the little house, Mary forgot and left
behind her her smock and the clothes in which

I.—*c*

Christ was wrapped, folded together and laid in the manger; and there they were, whole and fresh, in the same place to the time when St. Helen, the mother of Emperor Constantine, came thither, long after.

Anon so great was grown Mary's fame that she durst not abide longer there for dread of Herod and the Jews, and an angel appeared to Joseph, saying: " Arise, and take the Child and His mother and flee into Egypt, and tarry there till I summon thee, for it is to come that Herod shall seek the Child to slay Him." Then Joseph arose and took the Child and His mother and went into Egypt in the night, and there he remained until Herod died. And Mary and her Son dwelt in Egypt seven years.

And it is told that by the road which Mary journeyed thither and came back again, grew roses, which are called the Roses of Jericho, and they grow in no other place. The shepherds of that country, in following their sheep, gather these roses in their season, and sell them to pilgrims, and thus they be borne into divers lands. And the place where Mary dwelt is now a garden where groweth balm, and to every bush a Christian man, among the Sultan's prisoners, is assigned to protect it and keep it clean; for when a paynim keepeth them, anon the bushes wax dry and grow no more. And this balm hath many virtues the which were long to tell; but all men in the East believe truly that the place bears such a virtue of growing balm because Mary dwelt there seven years, and washed and bathed her Son in its wells of water.

And as to the gifts which the three Kings gave to Christ: the thirty gilt pennies of Melchior were made of old by Thara, father of Abraham, and Abraham bare them with him when he went on pilgrimage out of the land of Chaldee into Ebron, which was then called Arabia, and there he bought with them a burial-place for himself, his wife, and his children, Isaac and Jacob. In exchange for the same thirty pieces Joseph was sold by his brethren to merchants of Egypt. Afterward, when Jacob died, they were sent to the land of Sheba to buy divers spices and ornaments for his sepulture, and so they were put into the king's treasury of that land. Then by process of time, in Solomon's reign, the Queen of Sheba offered these thirty gilt pennies, with many rich jewels, in the Temple at Jerusalem; but in the time of Roboam, King Solomon's son, when Jerusalem was destroyed and the Temple despoiled, they were carried to the King of Arabia, and were put into his treasury with other spoils from the Temple.

And Melchior offered these same thirty pieces to Christ, because they were of the finest gold, and the best that he had. But when Mary went into Egypt she lost all the gifts of the three Kings by the way, bound all in one cloth together. And it happened there was a shepherd who had so great an infirmity that no leech might heal him, and all that he had he paid to the leeches to be whole,—yet it might not be. But, on a time, as he went into the fields with his sheep, he found these thirty gilt pennies, with incense and myrrh, bound all in a cloth together, and he kept them privily to himself, until, hearing tell of a holy prophet that healed all men of their infirmities by a word, he came to Christ and prayed Him for grace and help ; and, being healed, he offered the gold, and incense, and myrrh to Him with good devotion. And when Christ saw the thirty gilt pennies and precious herbs He knew them well, and bade the shepherd go into the Temple and offer them upon the altar.

Now, when the priest saw such oblations laid upon the altar he marvelled much, and took all three things and put them in the common treasury. And afterward, when Judas Iscariot came into the Temple to make covenant with the Princes of the Law to betray his master, they gave him for his pay the same thirty pieces of gold, and for them Judas sold his Master. And after Christ was crucified, then Judas repented, and went to the Temple and cast down to the Princes of the Law the thirty pieces. And with fifteen of these gilt pennies the Jews bought a field of burial for pilgrims; and the other fifteen they gave to the knights who kept the sepulchre of Christ.

And the reason these thirty gilt pennies were called silver in the Gospel, notwithstanding they were fine gold, is, that it is the common usage in that country so to call them, as men in this country call gold from beyond the sea scutys, motouns or florins; moreover in the East the same print is made in gold and silver and copper, and the print on the thirty pieces is this: on one side is a king's head crowned, and on the other are written letters in Chaldaic, which men now cannot read. And many marvels are told of these pieces of gold which were long to tell.

Now when Our Lord was ascended into heaven, then he sent St. Thomas, his apostle, into Ind, to preach there God's word. And as St. Thomas went about in the temples he found a star in every one, painted after the manner of the Star that appeared to the three Kings when Christ was born, in which Star was a sign of the Cross and a Child above. And when

4

St. Thomas saw this he asked of the bishops what it was, and they told him that such a Star of old time appeared on the Hill of Vaws in token of a Child that was born who should be king of the Jews, as was heard spoken out of the same Star.

And when St. Thomas had preached and taught the people the understanding of this Star and of the Cross and the Child, then he went to the kingdoms of the three Kings, and he found them whole of body and of a great age. And St. Thomas christened these three Kings and all their people, and the Kings began anon to preach with the Apostle, and when they had converted the people to the law of Christ he ordained them to be Archbishops. And after this St. Thomas was slain, and in all that country where he was martyred both men and women have visages shaped like hounds, yet they be not hairy—and they are so unto this day.

Now under the Hill of Vaws St. Thomas and these three Kings had made a rich city and called it Sewill, and this city is the best and richest city in all the country of Ind to this day ; and therein is the habitation of Prester John that is called lord of Ind, and there dwelleth also the Patriarch of Ind who is called Thomas, in worship of St. Thomas and for an everlasting memorial. And when all things were disposed by these three Kings they went to the city of Sewill, and there they lived twelve years.

And a little before the feast of Christ's nativity, when these years were drawn to an end, there appeared a wonderful star above this city and the Kings knew that their time was nigh when they should pass out of this world. Then of one assent they ordained a fair and large tomb for their burial in the church they had made in the city ; and in the feast of Christmas they did, solemnly, God's service.

And in the feast of the Circumcision, Melchior, King of Araby, laid him down before all his people and without any disease yielded up his spirit, in the year of his age one hundred and sixteen. Then in the feast of Epiphany, five days thereafter, Balthazar, King of Godolie and Saba, died in the year of his age one hundred and twelve. And then Jaspar the third king, the sixth day after was taken into everlasting joy, and they were all buried in the same tomb that they had ordained ; and the Star that appeared over the city before their death, abode always till their bodies were translated unto Cologne, as they of Ind tell.

Now after much time had passed, Queen Helen, the mother of the glorious Emperor Constantine, began to think greatly of the bodies

of these three Kings, and she arrayed her with
certain people and went into the land of Ind.
And she had much praise among the people because of the finding of Mary's smock and the
cloths that Christ was wound in in his childhood; and seeing that she was worshipped of all
people, the Patriarch Thomas and Prester John,
took counsel of other lords and princes and
gave her the bodies of King Melchior and King
Balthazar. But the Nestorines had borne the
body of the third king, King Jaspar, into the
isle of Egrisoulla. And these Nestorines were
the worst heretics of the world. For the most
part they were black Ethiops, who painted
Christ and His Mother Mary and the three
Kings in their churches all in black, and the
Devil all white, in despite of all other Christian
men. But because Queen Helen wished not
that the three Kings should be parted, she
made many prayers and gave great gifts to the
chief lords of the isle of Egrisoulla, and thus
anon did she get the body of King Jaspar.

And you shall understand that after she had
found the bodies of all these three Kings,
Queen Helen put them into one chest and
arrayed it with great riches, and she brought
them unto Constantinople with joy and reverence, and laid them in a church that is called
St. Sophia; and this church King Constantine

did make—and he alone, with a little child, set up all the pillars of marble.

Now after the death of this worshipful King Constantine and Queen Helen aforesaid, there began a new persecution of heresy against the Christian faith, and of death against them that would maintain the law of Christ. The Greeks forsook the Church and chose a Patriarch for themselves, whom they yet obey until this day.

Now in this persecution the bodies and the relics of the three holy Kings were put at no reverence, but utterly set at naught. For the Saracens and Turks at this time won with strong battle the lands of Greece and Armenia, and destroyed a great part of these lands.

Then came an Emperor of Rome who was called Mauricius, and through the help of them of Milan he recovered all these lands again, and, as is said among men in that country, through counsel of this Emperor the bodies of the three Kings were carried unto Milan, and they were there laid with all solemnity and worship in a fair church which is called after St. Eustorgio, because he had asked the bodies from the Emperor, and being granted them had sent them unto Milan.

Then afterward by process of time, it happed that the city of Milan began to rebel against the Emperor, who was called Frederick I., and

4*

this Emperor sent to the Archbishop of Cologne, who was called Rainald, for help. Then this Archbishop, through help of divers lords of the land of Milan, took the city of Milan and destroyed a great part thereof. And the chief men of the city took the bodies of the three Kings and hid them privily in the earth.

Now among all others there was in Milan a lord named Asso, and the Emperor hated him more than all the rest of its people. So it happed that in the destruction of the city the Archbishop won Asso's palace through strong hand, and lived therein a great while, for Asso was taken and put into prison.

Then, anon, Asso sent privily by his keepers to the Archbishop of Cologne and prayed him that he would come and speak with him, and it was granted that Asso should go to the Archbishop. And when he was come to him, he prayed him that, if he would get him grace of the Emperor and his love and the restoration of his lordship, he would give him the bodies of the three Kings.

When the Archbishop heard this, he went to the Emperor and prayed for Lord Asso, and got him grace and love. And when this was done, Asso brought, secretly, the three bodies of the Kings to the Archbishop of Cologne.

Then the Archbishop sent the bodies forth,

by private means, a great way out of the city
of Milan, whereupon he went to the Emperor
anew and prayed him that he would grant him
these three bodies, and the Emperor did so with
good will. Then the Archbishop openly, with
great solemnity and procession, brought the
three holy Kings unto Cologne, and there put
them in the fair church of St. Peter, worshipfully; and all the people of the country, with
all the reverence they might, received these
holy relics; and **there** they are kept and be-
holden of all manner of nations unto this day.

Thus endeth the translation of these Three
Worshipful Kings: Melchior, Balthazar, and
Jaspar.

A French Yeoman's Legend.

> "He laughed fit to make the
> plates rattle, his little brown
> eyes twinkling all the while."
>
> *Erckmann-Chatrian.*

THE THREE CHRISTMAS MASSES.

I.

"Two truffled turkeys, Garrigou?"

" Yes, reverend Father, two magnificent turkeys stuffed with truffles. There's no mistake, for I helped to stuff them myself. The flesh almost cracked as they roasted, it was so tight—so——"

" Holy Virgin! and I, who love truffles as—— Hurry; give me my surplice, Garrigou. And what else besides the turkeys; what else did you see in the kitchen?"

"Oh! all sorts of good things. Since noon we've done nothing but pluck pheasants, pewits, wood-hens, and heath-cocks. Feathers are scattered thick. Then from the pond they've brought eels and golden carp and trout, and——"

" What size are the trout, Garrigou?"

" Oh, as big as that! reverend Father. Enormous!"

" Heavens, I seem to see them! Have you put the wine in the flasks?"

" Yes, reverend Father, I've put the wine in

the flasks. But what's a mouthful or two as
you go to midnight Mass! You should see the
dining-hall in the château, full of decanters that
sparkle with wine of every color. And the
silver dishes, above all the ornamented ones;
the flowers; the candlesticks! I never saw
anything to equal it. Monsieur the Marquis
has invited all the nobility of the neighborhood.
You will be at least forty at table, without
counting either the bailiff or the notary. Ah!
it will make you very happy to be there, reverend Father. Why, only to smell the delicious
turkeys—the odor of truffles pursues me even
yet. Muh!"

"Come, come, Garrigou, you must guard
against the sin of greediness, and especially on
the night of the Nativity. Quickly, now, light
the candles and sound the first bell for Mass;
midnight is very near, and we must not be
late."

This conversation was held on Christmas
night, in the year of grace sixteen hundred and
sixteen, between the reverend Dom Balaguère,
formerly prior of Barnabites, now chaplain in
the service of the Sires de Trinquelague, and
his clerk Garrigou; or at least what he supposed was his clerk Garrigou, because you will
learn that the devil had that night taken on
the round face and wavering traits of the

young sacristan, the better to tempt the reverend Father to commit the dreadful sin of gluttony. Now, while the supposed Garrigou (hum! hum!) rung, with all his might, the bells of the seignorial chapel, the reverend Father put on his chasuble in the little sacristy of the château; and, his mind already becoming troubled by the gastronomic descriptions he had heard, he repeated to himself:

"Roasted turkeys; golden carp; trout as large as that!"

Outside, the night wind blew, scattering the music of the bells, and one by one lights began to appear in the shadows about the flanks of Mont Ventoux, upon the summit of which rose the ancient towers of Trinquelague. These lights were carried by the farmers on their way to attend midnight Mass at the château. They climbed the paths in groups of five or six, the father leading, lantern in hand, the women enveloped in their big brown mantles, where their infants nestled for shelter. . In spite of the hour and the cold all these honest people marched cheerfully on, sustained by the thought that when they came out from the Mass they would find, as they did each year, tables spread for them below in the kitchens. Now and again on the rough ascent, the coach of some seigneur, preceded by torch-bearing porters, reflected in its glasses the cold moonlight; or, maybe, a mule trotted along shaking his bells, and in the light of the lanterns covered with frost, the farmers recognized their bailiff and saluted him as he passed:

" Good-evening, good-evening, Master Arno- ton."

" Good-evening, good-evening, my children."

The night was clear, the stars were polished with cold, the wind stung, and a fine sleet, which glistened on the clothes without wetting them, kept faithfully the tradition of Christmases white with snow. Raised there aloft, the château appeared like the goal of all things, with its enormous mass of towers and gables, the belfry of its chapel mounting into the blue- black sky, and a crowd of small lights that winked, went and came, twinkled at all the windows, and seemed, on the sombre background of the building, like sparks running through the cinders of burnt paper. Once past the drawbridge and the postern, it was necessary, in order to gain the chapel, to traverse the first courtyard, full of coaches, of valets, of sedan- chairs, and bright with the flare of torches and the fires of the kitchens. There was the click of the turnspits, the crash of stewpans, the noises of glass and silver preparing for the dinner. From below, a warm vapor, which smelt of roasting meat and the strong herbs of curious sauces, whispered to the farmers, to the chaplain, to the bailiff—to all the world :

" What a revel we are going to have after Mass !"

II.

Drelindin din! Drelindin din! Midnight Mass is about to begin. In the chapel of the château, a miniature cathedral with arches intercrossed and a wainscot of oak mounting as high as the walls, all the hangings have been arranged, all the candles lit.

And what a host of people! And what toilettes! First, seated in the sculptured stall which surrounds the choir, behold the Sire de Trinquelague in a suit of salmon-colored taffeta ; and next to him all the invited nobles. Facing these, on a prie-dieu trimmed with velvet, is the old dowager Marquise in her robe of fire-colored brocade, and the young Dame de Trinquelague, surmounted by a huge head-dress of lace, made in the latest fashion of the French court. Further down, dressed in black, with vast pointed perukes and shaven faces, are the bailiff, Thomas Arnoton, and the notary, Master Ambroy, two grave objects among the flowing silks and figured damasks. Then come the fat majordomos, the pages, the grooms, the attendants; dame Barbe, all her keys suspended at her side on a ring of thin silver. At the bottom of the hall, on the benches, are the servants, the yeomen with their families; and lastly, beyond, all about the doors as they open and shut discretely, are the scullions, who steal in, between two sauces, to get a little of the Mass, carrying an odor of the revelry into the church, all in its gay attire and warm with so many burning candles.

Is it a glimpse of their little white caps that distracts the celebrant of the Mass? Or, it may be the clangor made by Garrigou's bells, that pulsating sound which shakes the altar with an infernal vibration and seems to say all the time:

"Hurry up, hurry up. We'll soon be done; we'll soon be at table!"

The fact is, that each time it sounds—that peal of the devil—the chaplain forgets his Mass and thinks of nothing but the coming revel. He pictures to himself the uproar of the kitchens; the furnace heated like a blacksmith's forge; the vapor of opening trenchers, and in that vapor two magnificent turkeys, buttered, tender, bursting with truffles.

Or, perhaps he saw pass the files of little pages bearing dishes enveloped in tempting

steam, and, with them, entered the grand saloon
already prepared for the feast. O deliciousness!
behold the immense table all set and sparkling;
the peacocks in their plumes; the pheasants
with their open wings of reddish-brown; the
ruby-colored flagons; the pyramids of fruit
peeping from green branches; and those marvellous fish of which Garrigou told (ah! well,
yes, Garrigou!) held aloft on a bed of fennel,
the mother-of-pearl scales as bright as when
they came from the water, with a bouquet of
odorous herbs in their monster-like nostrils. So
distinct is the vision of these marvels, that it
seems to Dom Balaguère as if all the wonderful dishes are served before him on the embroid-
eries of the altar-cloth; and two or three times,
in place of *Dominus vobiscum*, he is surprised to
find himself repeating the *Benedicite*. Saving
these slight mistakes, the holy man does his
office very conscientiously, without skipping a
line, without omitting a genuflexion; and all
goes well enough as far as the end of the first
Mass; because, you know, on Christmas night
the same celebrant must repeat three consecu-
tive Masses.

"One!" said the chaplain, with a sigh of relief; then, without losing a minute, he made a
sign to his clerk—or the person he believed to
be his clerk, and——

5*

Drelindin din! Drelindin din!

The second Mass begins, and with it begins also the sin of Dom Balaguère.

"Hurry, hurry, let's get done," cries the thin voice of Garrigou's bell, and this time the unlucky priest, abandoning himself to the demon of gluttony, rushes through the missal, devouring its pages with all the avidity of an overcharged appetite. Frantically he bows; arises; makes the signs of the cross, goes through the genuflexions, abbreviates all his gestures, the sooner to be finished. Scarcely does he extend his arms to the Gospel, or strike his breast where it is required. Between the clerk and him it is a race which shall jabber the faster. Verse and response hurry each other, tumble over each other. The words, hardly pronounced, because it takes too much time to open the mouth, become incomprehensible murmurs.

Oremus ps—ps—ps—
Meâ culpâ—pâ—pâ—.

Like hard-working vintagers pressing grapes in a vat, both wade through the Latin of the Mass, splashing it on all sides.

"*Dom—scum!*" says Balaguère.

"*Stutuo!*" responds Garrigou, and all the while the damnable chime sounds in their ears, like those little bells put on the post-horses to

make them gallop more swiftly. Believe me,
under such conditions a low Mass is vastly ex-
pedited !

"Two !" said the chaplain, all out of breath ;
then without taking time to breathe, red, per-
spiring, he tumbled down the stairs of the
altar.

Drelindin din ! Drelindin din ! The third
Mass begins.

Only a step or so and then the dining-hall !
but, alas, the nearer the revel approaches, the
more the unfortunate Balaguère is seized with
the very folly of impatience and greediness.
His vision accentuates it ; the golden carp, the
roast turkeys are there. He may touch them—
he may—Oh, Holy Virgin ! the dishes steam ;
the wines send forth sweet odors ; and shaking out its reckless song, the bell cries to him :

"Hurry up, hurry up ; still faster, still
faster !"

But how can he go any faster ? He scarcely
moves his lips, he pronounces fully not a single
word. He tries to cheat the good God altogether of His Mass, and that is what brings
his ruin. By temptation upon temptation, he
begins to jump one verse, then two. Then the
epistle is too long—he does not finish it ;
skims the Gospel, passes by the creed without even entering, skips the pater, salutes from

afar the preface, and by bounds and jumps precipitates himself into eternal damnation, always following the infamous Garrigou (*vade retro, Satanas*), who seconds him with marvellous skill; tucks up his chasuble, turns the leaves two by two, disarranges the music-desk, reverses the flagons, and unceasingly rings the bell more and more vigorously, more and more quickly.

You should have seen what a figure all the assistants cut. Obliged to follow, like mimics, a Mass of which they did not understand a word, some rose when others kneeled, or seated themselves when others stood, and all the actors in this singular office mixed themselves on the benches in numberless contrary attitudes.

The star of Christmas, on its journey through the heavens yonder by the little manger, paled with astonishment at the confusion.

"The Abbé's in a dreadful hurry : I can't follow him at all," said the aged dowager, shaking her head-dress with bewilderment. Master Arnoton, his great steel spectacles on his nose, searched in his prayer-book where the deuce the words could be. But, after all, that gallant host, which itself was thinking only of the feast, was far from being vexed because the Mass rode post; and when Balaguère, with beaming countenance, turned toward the assembly crying with all his might, *Ite missa est*, with a single voice they returned, *Deo gratias*, so joyously, so fervently, that one might have thought them already at table responding to the first toast of the night.

III.

Five minutes later the crowd of seigneurs was seated in the grand dining-hall, the chaplain in the midst of them. The château, illuminated from top to bottom, echoed with songs, cries, laughter, uproar, and the venerable Dom Balaguère planted his fork in the wing of a woodhen, drowning the remorse of his sin under floods of wine of the Pope and the sweet juices of the meats.

So much did he eat and drink, that the poor holy man died in the night of a terrible attack of sickness, without having even time to repent. Then near the morning he arrived in heaven with all the savor of the feast still about him and I leave you to imagine how he was received:

"Retire from my sight, evil Christian!" said the Sovereign Judge, "thy fault is dark enough to efface a whole life of virtue. Ah, thou hast robbed me of a Mass to-night. Thou shalt pay

me back three hundred in its place, and thou
shalt not enter into Paradise unless thou shalt
have celebrated in thy proper chapel these three
hundred Christmas Masses in the presence of all
those who have sinned by thy fault and with
thee."

This, then, is the true legend of Dom Balaguère
as they tell it in the land of olives. To-day the
château of Trinquelague is no more, but the
chapel still stands erect on the summit of Mont
Ventoux, in a grove of green oaks. The wind
beats its disjointed portal; the grass creeps
across its threshold ; the birds have built in the
angles of the altar and in the embrasures of
the high windows, whence the colored panes
have long ago vanished. But it appears that
every year at Christmas, a supernatural light
runs about these ruins, and that, in going to
Mass or feast, the peasants see the chapel illuminated by invisible candles which burn brightly
even through the wind and snow.

You may laugh if you will, but a vine-dresser
of the neighborhood named Garrigue, without
doubt a descendant of Garrigou, has assured me
that one Christmas night, finding himself a
little so-so-ish, he became lost on the mountain
beside Trinquelague, and behold what he saw !
At eleven o'clock, nothing. All was silent,
dark, lifeless. Suddenly, toward midnight, a

chime sounded up above from a clock, an old, old chime which seemed six leagues away. Pretty soon, on the ascending road, Garrigue saw lights trembling in the uncertain shadows. Under the porch of the chapel somebody walked, somebody whispered:

" Good-evening, Master Arnoton."

" Good-evening, good-evening, my children."

When the whole company was entered, my vine-dresser, who was exceedingly brave, approached stealthily, and peeping through the broken door saw a strange spectacle. All those who had passed him were ranged about the choir, in the ruined nave, as if the ancient benches still existed. Beautiful dames in brocade with coifs of lace; seigneurs bedizzened from top to toe; peasants in flowered jackets like those of our grandfathers,—everything with an ancient air, faded, dusty, worn-out. Now and then the night-birds, habitual dwellers in the chapel, awakened by all these lights, winged about the candles, whose flames mounted straight and vague as if they burnt behind gauze. And what amused Garrigue most was a certain personage with great steel spectacles, who shook at each instant his high black peruke, on which one of the birds had alighted and entangled itself, silently beating its wings.

At the farthest end, a little old man of boyish

size, on his knees in the midst of the choir,
pulled desperately at the chimeless and silent
bell; while a priest attired in ancient gold, went
and came before the altar reciting orisons of
which one heard not a single word. Surely,
that was Dom Balaguère in the act of saying
his third low Mass.

A Love-Passage from a Wandering Cossack.

> "Dressed in his everlasting blue
> frock, he sat near the fire play-
> ing cards."
>
> *Turgenieff.*

A RUSSIAN CHRISTMAS PARTY.

Count Rostow's affairs were going from bad to worse. He was of a warm, generous nature, with unlimited faith in his servants, and hence was blind to the mismanagement and dishonesty which had sapped his fortune. The possessor of a handsome establishment at the Russian capital, Moscow, the owner of rich provincial estates, and the inheritor of a noble name and wealth, he was nevertheless on the verge of ruin. He had given up his appointment as *Maréchal de la Noblesse,* which he had gone to his seat of Otradnoë to assume, because it entailed too many expenses; and yet there was no improvement in the state of his finances.

Nicolas and Natacha, his son and daughter, often found their father and mother in anxious consultation, talking in low tones of the sale of their Moscow house or of their property in the neighborhood. Having thus retired into private life, the count now gave neither fêtes nor entertainments. Life at Otradnoë was much less gay than in past years; still, the house and domain were as full of servants as ever, and twenty persons or more sat down to dinner daily. These were dependants, friends, and intimates, who were regarded almost as part of the family, or at any rate seemed unable to tear themselves away from it : among them a musician named Dimmler and his wife, Ioghel the dancing-master and his family, an old Mlle. Bélow, former governess of Natacha and Sonia, the count's niece and adopted child, and now the tutor of Pétia, his younger son ; besides others who found it simpler to live at the count's expense than at their own. Thus, though there were no more festivities, life was carried on almost as expensively as of old, and neither the master nor the mistress ever imagined any change possible. Nicolas, again, had added to the hunting establishment ; there were still fifty horses in the stables, still fifteen drivers ; handsome presents were given on all birthdays and fête days, which invariably wound up as of old with a grand dinner to all the neighborhood ; the count still played whist or boston, invariably letting his cards be seen by his friends, who were always ready to make up his table, and relieve him without hesitation of the few hundred roubles which constituted their principal income. The old man marched on blindfold through the tangle of his pecuniary difficulties, trying to conceal them, and only succeeding in augmenting them; having neither the courage nor the patience to untie the knots one by one.

The loving heart by his side foresaw their children's ruin, but she could not accuse her husband, who was, alas! too old for amendment; she could only seek some remedy for the disaster. From her woman's point of view there was but one: Nicolas's marriage, namely, with some rich heiress. She clung desperately to this last chance of salvation; but if her son should refuse the wife she should propose to him, every hope of reinstating their fortune would vanish. The young lady whom she had in view was the daughter of people of the highest respectability, whom the Rostows had known from her infancy: Julie Karaguine, who, by the death of her second brother, had suddenly come into great wealth.

The countess herself wrote to Mme. Karaguine to ask her whether she could regard the match with favor, and received a most flattering answer. Indeed, Mme. Karaguine invited Nicolas to her house at Moscow, to give her daughter an opportunity of deciding for herself.

Nicolas had often heard his mother say, with tears in her eyes, that her dearest wish was to see him married. The fulfilment of this wish

I.—*e* 6*

would sweeten her remaining days, she would
say, adding covert hints as to a charming girl
who would exactly suit him.   One day she took
the opportunity of speaking plainly to him of
Julie's charms and merits, and urged him to
spend a short time in Moscow before Christmas.
Nicolas, who had no difficulty in guessing what
she was aiming at, persuaded her to be explicit
on the matter, and she owned frankly that her
hope was to see their sinking fortunes restored
by his marriage with her dear Julie !

"Then, mother, if I loved a penniless girl, you
would desire me to sacrifice my feelings and my
honor—to marry solely for money ?"

"Nay, nay; you have misunderstood me,"
she said, not knowing how to excuse her mer-
cenary hopes.   "I wish only for your happiness !"   And then, conscious that this was not
her sole aim, and that she was not perfectly
honest, she burst into tears.

"Do not cry, mamma; you have only to say
that you really and truly desire it, and you
know I would give my life to see you happy;
that I would sacrifice everything, even my
feelings."

But this was not his mother's notion.   She
asked no sacrifice, she would have none; she
would sooner have sacrificed herself, if it had
been possible.

" Say no more about it; you do not understand," she said, drying away her tears.

" How could she think of such a marriage ?"
thought Nicolas. " Does she think that because
Sonia is poor I do not love her ? And yet I
should be a thousand times happier with her
than with a doll like Julie."

He stayed in the country, and his mother did
not revert to the subject. Still, as she saw the
growing intimacy between Nicolas and Sonia,
she could not help worrying Sonia about every
little thing, and speaking to her with colder
formality. Sometimes she reproached herself
for these continual pin-pricks of annoyance, and
was quite vexed with the poor girl for submit-
ting to them with such wonderful humility and
sweetness, for taking every opportunity of
showing her devoted gratitude, and for loving
Nicolas with a faithful and disinterested affection which commanded her admiration.

Just about this time a letter came from Prince
André, dated from Rome, whither he had gone
to pass the year of probation demanded by his
father as a condition to giving consent to his
son's marriage with the Countess Natacha. It
was the fourth the Prince had written since his
departure. He ought long since to have been
on his way home, he said, but the heat of the
summer had caused the wound he had received

at Austerlitz to reopen, and this compelled him
to postpone his return till early in January.

Natacha, though she was so much in love
that her very passion for Prince André had
made her day-dreams happy, had hitherto been
open to all the bright influences of her young
life; but now, after nearly four months of
parting, she fell into a state of extreme melancholy, and gave way to it completely. She
bewailed her hard fate, she bewailed the time
that was slipping away and lost to her, while
her heart ached with the dull craving to love
and be loved. Nicolas, too, had nearly spent
his leave from his regiment, and the anticipation
of his departure added gloom to the saddened
household.

Christmas came; but, excepting the pompous
high Mass and the other religious ceremonies,
the endless string of neighbors and servants
with the regular compliments of the season,
and the new gowns which made their first appearance on the occasion, nothing more than
usual happened on that day, or more extraordinary than twenty degrees of frost, with brilliant
sunshine, a still atmosphere, and at night a
glorious starry sky.

After dinner, on the third day of Christmas-
tide, when every one had settled into his own corner once more, ennui reigned supreme through-

out the house. Nicolas, who had been paying
a round of visits in the neighborhood, was fast
asleep in the drawing-room. The old count had
followed his example in his room. Sonia, seated
at a table in the sitting-room, was copying a
drawing. The countess was playing out a
"patience," and Nastacia Ivanovna, the old
buffoon, with his peevish face, sitting in a
window with two old women, did not say a
word.

Natacha came into the room, and, after leaning over Sonia for a minute or two to examine
her work, went over to her mother and stood
still in front of her.

The countess looked up. " Why are you wandering about like a soul in torment? What do
you want?" she said.

"Want! I want him!" replied Natacha,
shortly, and her eyes glowed. " Now, here—
at once!"

Her mother gazed at her anxiously.

" Do not look at me like that; you will make
me cry."

" Sit down here."

" Mamma, I want him, I want him! Why
must I die of weariness?" Her voice broke
and tears started from her eyes. She hastily
quitted the drawing-room and went to the
housekeeper's room, where an old servant was

scolding one of the girls who had just come in breathless from out-of-doors.

"There is a time for all things," growled the old woman. "You have had time enough for play."

"Oh, leave her in peace, Kondratievna," said Natacha. "Run away, Mavroucha—go."

Pursuing her wandering, Natacha went into the hall; an old man-servant was playing cards with two of the boys. Her entrance stopped their game and they rose. "And what am I to say to these?" thought she.

"Nikita, would you please go—what on earth can I ask for?—go and find me a cock; and you, Micha, a handful of corn."

"A handful of corn?" said Micha, laughing.

"Go, go at once," said the old man.

"And you, Fédor, can you give me a piece of chalk?"

Then she went on to the servants' hall and ordered the samovar to be got ready, though it was not yet tea-time; she wanted to try her power over Foka, the old butler, the most morose and disobliging of all the servants. He could not believe his ears, and asked her if she really meant it. "What next will our young lady want?" muttered Foka, affecting to be very cross.

No one gave so many orders as Natacha, no

one sent them on so many errands at once.   As
soon as a servant came in sight she seemed to
invent some want or message ; she could not
help it.   It seemed as though she wanted to try
her power over them ; to see whether, some fine
day, one or another would not rebel against her
tyranny ; but, on the contrary, they always
flew to obey her more readily than any one
else.

"And now what shall I do, where can I go ?"
thought she, as she slowly went along the corridor, where she presently met the buffoon.

"Nastacia Ivanovna," said she, "if I ever
have children, what will they be ?"

"You!   Fleas and grasshoppers, you may
depend upon it !"

Natacha went on.   "Good God! have mercy,
have mercy !" she said to herself.   "Wherever
I go it is always, always the same.   I am so
weary ; what shall I do ?"

Skipping lightly from step to step, she went
to the upper story and dropped in on the Ioghels.
Two governesses were sitting chatting with M.
and Mme. Ioghel ; dessert, consisting of dried
fruit, was on the table, and they were eagerly
discussing the cost of living at Moscow and
Odessa.   Natacha took a seat for a moment,
listened with pensive attention, and then jumped
up again.   "The island of Madagascar !" she

murmured, " Ma-da-gas-car !" and she separated
the syllables.   Then she left the room without
answering Mme. Schoss, who was utterly mys-
tified by her strange exclamation.

She next met Pétia and a companion, both
very full of some fireworks which were to be
let off that evening.   " Pétia !" she exclaimed,
" carry me down-stairs !"   And she sprang upon
his back, throwing her arms round her neck ;
and, laughing and galloping, they thus scram-
bled along to the head of the stairs.

" Thank you, that will do.   Madagascar !" she
repeated ; and, jumping down, she ran down the
flight.

After thus inspecting her dominions, testing
her power, and convincing herself that her
subjects were docile, and that there was no
novelty to be got out of them, Natacha settled
herself in the darkest corner of the music-room
with her guitar, striking the bass strings, and
trying to make an accompaniment to an air
from an opera that she and Prince André had
once heard together at St. Petersburg.   The
uncertain chords which her unpractised fingers
sketched out would have struck the least experienced ear as wanting in harmony and musical accuracy, while to her excited imagination
they brought a whole train of memories.   Leaning against the wall and half hidden by a cabi-

net, with her eyes fixed on a thread of light
that came under the door from the rooms
beyond, she listened in ecstasy and dreamed of
the past.

Sonia crossed the room with a glass in her
hand. Natacha glanced round at her and again
fixed her eyes on the streak of light. She had
the strange feeling of having once before gone
through the same experience—sat in the same
place, surrounded by the same details, and watching Sonia pass carrying a tumbler. "Yes, it
was exactly the same," she.thought.

"Sonia, what is this tune?" she said, playing
a few notes.

"What, are you there?" said Sonia, startled.
"I do not know," she said, coming closer to
listen, "unless it is from 'La Tempête';" but
she spoke doubtfully.

"It was exactly so," thought Natacha. "She
started as she came forward, smiling so gently;
and I thought then, as I think now, that there
is something in her which is quite lacking in
me. No," she said aloud, "you are quite out;
it is the chorus from the 'Porteur d'Eau'—
listen," and she hummed the air. "Where are
you going?"

"For some fresh water to finish my drawing."

"You are always busy and I never. Where
is Nicolas?"

D   7

"Asleep, I think."

"Go and wake him, Sonia. Tell him to come and sing."

Sonia went, and Natacha relapsed into dreaming and wondering how it had all happened. Not being able to solve the puzzle, she drifted into reminiscence once more. She could see him —*him*— and feel his impassioned eyes fixed on her face. "Oh, make haste back! I am so afraid he will not come yet! Besides, it is all very well, but I am growing old; I shall be quite different from what I am now! Who knows? Perhaps he will come to-day! Perhaps he is here already! Here in the drawing-room. Perhaps he came yesterday and I have forgotten."

She rose, laid down the guitar, and went into the next room. All the household party were seated round the tea-table,—the professors, the governesses, the guests; the servants were waiting on one and another—but there was no Prince André.

"Ah, here she is," said her father. "Come and sit down here." But Natacha stopped by her mother without heeding his bidding.

"Oh, mamma, bring him to me, give him to me soon, very soon," she murmured, swallowing down a sob. Then she sat down and listened to the others. "Good God! always the same

people! always the same thing! Papa holds
his cup as he always does, and blows his tea to
cool it as he did yesterday, and as he will to-
morrow."

She felt a sort of dull rebellion against them
all; she hated them for always being the same.

After tea Sonia, Natacha, and Nicolas huddled
together in their favorite, snug corner of the
drawing-room; that was where they talked
freely to each other.

"Do you ever feel," Natacha asked her
brother, "as if there was nothing left to look
forward to; as if you had had all your share
of happiness, and were not so much weary as
utterly dull?"

"Of course I have. Very often I have seen
my friends and fellow-officers in the highest
spirits and been just as jolly myself, and suddenly have been struck so dull and dismal, have
so hated life, that I have wondered whether
we were not all to die at once. I remember
one day, for instance, when I was with the
regiment; the band was playing, and I had
such a fit of melancholy that I never even
thought of going to the promenade."

"How well I understand that! I recollect
once," Natacha went on, "once when I was a
little girl, I was punished for having eaten some
plums, I think. I had not done it, and you were

all dancing, and I was left alone in the school-
room. How I cried! cried because I was so
sorry for myself, and so vexed with you all for
making me so unhappy."

"I remember; and I went to comfort you
and did not know how; we were funny children
then; I had a toy with bells that jingled, and I
made you a present of it."

"Do you remember," said Natacha, "long before that, when we were no bigger than my
hand, my uncle called us into his room, where
it was quite dark, and suddenly we saw——"

"A negro!" interrupted Nicolas, smiling at
her recollection. "To be sure. I can see him
now; and to this day I wonder whether it was
a dream or a reality, or mere fancy invented
afterwards."

"He had white teeth and stared at us with
his black eyes."

"Do you remember him, Sonia?"

"Yes, yes—but very dimly."

"But papa and mamma have always declared
that no negro ever came to the house. And the
eggs; do you remember the eggs we used to
roll up at Easter; and one day how two little
grinning old women came up through the floor
and began to spin round the table?"

"Of course. And how papa used to put on
his fur coat and fire off his gun from the balcony.

And don't you remember——?" And so they went on recalling, one after the other, not the bitter memories of old age, but the bright pictures of early childhood, which float and fade on a distant horizon of poetic vagueness, midway between reality and dreams. Sonia remembered being frightened once at the sight of Nicolas in his braided jacket, and her nurse promising her that she should some day have a frock trimmed from top to bottom.

"And they told me you had been found in the garden under a cabbage," said Natacha. "I dared not say it was not true, but it puzzled me tremendously."

A door opened, and a woman put in her head, exclaiming, "Mademoiselle, mademoiselle, they have fetched the cock!"

"I do not want it now; send it away again, Polia," said Natacha.

Dimmler, who had meanwhile come into the room, went up to the harp, which stood in a corner, and in taking off the cover made the strings ring discordantly.

"Edward Karlovitch, play my favorite nocturne—Field's," cried the countess, from the adjoining room.

Dimmler struck a chord. "How quiet you young people are," he said, addressing them.

"Yes, we are studying philosophy," said

7*

Natacha, and they went on talking of their dreams.

Dimmler had no sooner begun his nocturne than Natacha, crossing the room on tiptoe, seized the wax-light that was burning on the table and carried it into the next room; then she stole back to her seat, it was now quite dark in the larger room, especially in their corner, but the silvery moonbeams came in at the wide windows and lay in broad sheets on the floor.

"Do you know," whispered Natacha, while Dimmler, after playing the nocturne, let his fingers wander over the strings, uncertain what to play next, "when I go on remembering one thing beyond another, I go back so far, so far, that at last I remember things that happened before 1 was born, and——"

"That is metempsychosis," interrupted Sonia, with a reminiscence of her early lessons. "The Egyptians believed that our souls had once inhabited the bodies of animals, and would return to animals again after our death."

"I do not believe that," said Natacha, still in a low voice, though the music had ceased. "But I am quite sure that we were angels once, somewhere there beyond, or, perhaps, even here; and that is the reason we remember a previous existence."

"May I join the party?" asked Dimmler, coming towards them.

"If we were once angels, how is it that we have fallen lower?"

"Lower? Who says that it is lower? Who knows what I was?" Natacha retorted with full conviction. "Since the soul is immortal, and I am to live forever in the future, I must have existed in the past, so I have eternity behind me, too."

"Yes; but it is very difficult to conceive of that eternity," said Dimmler, whose ironical smile had died away.

"Why?" asked Natacha. "After to-day comes to-morrow, and then the day after, and so on forever; yesterday has been, to-morrow will be——"

"Natacha, now it is your turn; sing me something," said her mother. "What are you doing in that corner like a party of conspirators?"

"I am not at all in the humor, mamma," said she; nevertheless she rose. Nicolas sat down to the piano; and standing, as usual, in the middle of the room, where the voice sounded best, she sang her mother's favorite ballad.

Though she had said she was not in the humor, it was long since Natacha had sung so well as she did that evening, and long before she sang so well again. Her father, who was talking

over business with Mitenka in his room, hurriedly gave him some final instructions as soon
as he heard the first note, as a schoolboy scram-
bles through his tasks to get to his play; but as
the steward did not go, he sat in silence, listening, while Mitenka, too, standing in his presence, listened with evident satisfaction. Nicolas
did not take his eyes off his sister's face, and
only breathed when she took breath. Sonia was
under the spell of that exquisite voice and
thinking of the gulf of difference that lay between her and her friend, full conscious that she
could never exercise such fascination. The old
countess had paused in her "patience,"—a sad,
fond smile played on her lips, her eyes were full
of tears, and she shook her head, remembering
her own youth, looking forward to her daughter's future and reflecting on her strange prospects of marriage.

Dimmler, sitting by her side, listened with
rapture, his eyes half closed.

"She really has a marvellous gift!" he exclaimed. "She has nothing to learn,—such
power, such sweetness, such roundness!"

"And how much I fear for her happiness!"
replied the countess, who in her mother's heart
could feel the flame that must some day be fatal
to her child's peace.

Natacha was still singing when Pétia dashed

noisily into the room to announce, in triumphant tones, that a party of mummers had come.

"Idiot!" exclaimed Natacha, stopping short, and, dropping into a chair, she began to sob so violently that it was some time before she could recover herself. "It is nothing, mamma, really nothing at all," she declared, trying to smile. "Only Pétia frightened me; nothing more." And her tears flowed afresh.

All the servants had dressed up, some as bears, Turks, tavern-keepers, or fine ladies; others as mongrel monsters. Bringing with them the chill of the night outside, they did not at first venture any farther than the hall; by degrees, however, they took courage; pushing each other forward for self-protection, they all soon came into the music-room. Once there, their shyness thawed; they became expansively merry, and singing, dancing, and sports were soon the order of the day. The countess, after looking at them and identifying them all, went back into the sitting-room, leaving her husband, whose jovial face encouraged them to enjoy themselves.

The young people had all vanished; but half an hour later an old marquise with patches appeared on the scene—none other than Nicolas; Pétia as a Turk; a clown—Dimmler; a hussar —Natacha; and a Circassian—Sonia. Both the

I.—*f*

girls had blackened their eyebrows and given themselves mustaches with burned cork.

After being received with well-feigned surprise, and recognized more or less quickly, the children, who were very proud of their costumes, unanimously declared that they must go and display them elsewhere. Nicolas, who was dying to take them all for a long drive *en troïka*,* proposed that, as the roads were in splendid order, they should go, a party of ten, to the Little Uncle's.

"You will disturb the old man, and that will be all," said the countess. "Why, he has not even room for you all to get into the house! If you must go out, you had better go to the Mélukows'."

Mme. Mélukow was a widow living in the neighborhood; her house, full of children of all ages, with tutors and governesses, was distant only four versts from Otradnoë.

"A capital idea, my dear," cried the count, enchanted. "I will dress up in costume and go, too. I will wake them up, I warrant you!"

But this did not at all meet his wife's views. Perfect madness! For him to go out with his gouty feet in such cold weather was sheer folly! The count gave way, and Mme. Schoss volun

---

* A team of three horses harnessed abreast.

teered to chaperon the girls. Sonia's was by
far the most successful disguise ; her fierce eyebrows and mustache were wonderfully becoming, her pretty features gained expression, and
she wore the dress of a man with unexpected
swagger and smartness. Something in her in-
most soul told her that this evening would seal
her fate.

In a few minutes four sleighs with three
horses abreast to each, their harness jingling
with bells, drew up in a line before the steps,
the runners creaking and crunching over the
frozen snow. Natacha was the foremost, and
the first to tune her spirits to the pitch of this
carnival freak. This mirth, in fact, proved
highly infectious, and reached its height of
tumult and excitement when the party went
down the steps and packed themselves into the
sleighs, laughing and shouting to each other at
the top of their voices. Two of the sleighs
were drawn by light cart-horses, to the third
the count's carriage horses were harnessed, and
one of these was reputed a famous trotter from
Orlow's stable ; the fourth sleigh, with its rough-
coated, black shaft-horse, was Nicolas's private
property. In his marquise costume, over which
he had thrown his hussar's cloak, fastened with
a belt round the waist, he stood gathering up
the reins. The moon was shining brightly, re-

flected in the plating of the harness and in the
horses' anxious eyes as they turned their heads
in uneasy amazement at the noisy group that
clustered under the dark porch. Natacha,
Sonia, and Mme. Schoss, with two women servants, got into Nicolas's sleigh; Dimmler and
his wife, with Pétia, into the count's; the
rest of the mummers packed into the other
sleighs.

"Lead the way, Zakhare!" cried Nicolas, to
his father's coachman, promising himself the
pleasure of outstripping him presently; the
count's sleigh swayed and strained, the runners,
which the frost had already glued to the ground,
creaked, the bells rang out, the horses closed up
for a pull, and off they went over the glittering,
hard snow, flinging it up right and left like
spray of powdered sugar. Nicolas started next,
and the others followed along the narrow way,
with no less jingling and creaking. While they
drove under the wall of the park the shadows
of the tall, skeleton trees lay on the road,
checkering the broad moonlight; but as soon
as they had left it behind them, the wide and
spotless plain spread on all sides, its whiteness broken by myriads of flashing sparks and
spangles of reflected light. Suddenly a rut
caused the foremost sleigh to jolt violently, and
then the others in succession; they fell away a

little, their intrusive clatter breaking the supreme and solemn silence of the night.

"A hare's tracks!" exclaimed Natacha, and her voice pierced the frozen air like an arrow.

"How light it is, Nicolas," said Sonia. Nicolas turned round to look at the pretty face with its black mustache, under the sable hood, looking at once so far away and so close in the moonshine. "It is not Sonia at all," he said, smiling.

"Why, what is the matter?"

"Nothing," said he, returning to his former position.

When they got out on the high-road, beaten and ploughed by horses' hoofs and polished with the tracks of sleighs, his steeds began to pull and go at a great pace. The near horse, turning away his head, was galloping rather wildly, while the horse in the shafts pricked his ears and still seemed to doubt whether the moment for a dash had come. Zakhare's sleigh, lost in the distance, was no more than a black spot on the white snow, and as he drew farther away the ringing of the bells was fainter and fainter; only the shouts and songs of the maskers rang through the calm, clear night.

"On you go, my beauties!" cried Nicolas, shaking the reins and raising his whip. The sleigh seemed to leap forward, but the sharp air that cut their faces and the flying pace of

8

the two outer horses alone gave them any idea
of the speed they were making. Nicolas glanced
back at the other two drivers ; they were shouting and urging their shaft-horses with cries and
cracking of whips, so as not to be quite left behind ; Nicolas's middle horse, swinging steadily
along under the shaft-bow, kept up his regular
pace, quite ready to go twice as fast the moment
he should be called upon.

They soon overtook the first troïka, and after
going down a slope they came upon a wide
cross-road running by the side of a meadow.

" Where are we, I wonder," thought Nicolas ;
" this must be the field and slope by the river.
No—I do not know where we are ! This is all
new and unfamiliar to me ! God only knows
where we are ! But no matter !" And smack-
ing his whip with a will, he went straight
ahead. Zakhare held in his beasts for an instant,
and turned his face, all fringed with frost, to
look at Nicolas, who came flying onward.

" Steady there, sir !" cried the coachman, and
leaning forward, with a click of his tongue he
urged his horses in their turn to their utmost
speed. For a few minutes the sleighs ran equal,
but before long, in spite of all Zakhare could do,
Nicolas gained on him and at last flew past
him like a lightning flash ; a cloud of fine snow,
kicked up by the horses, came showering down

on the rival sleigh ; the women squeaked, and
the two teams had a struggle for the precedence,
their shadows crossing and mingling on the
snow.

Then Nicolas, moderating his speed, looked
about him ; before, behind, and on each side of
him stretched the fairy scene ; a plain strewn
with stars and flooded with light.

" To the left, Zakhare says. Why to the
left ?" thought he. " We were going to the
Mélukows'. But we are going where fate directs
or as Heaven may guide us. It is all very
strange and most delightful, is it not ?" he said,
turning to the others.

" Oh ! look at his eyelashes and beard ; they
are quite white !" exclaimed one of the sweet
young men, with pencilled mustache and arched
eyebrows.

" That I believe is Natacha ?" said Nicolas.
" And that little Circassian—who is he ? I do
not know him, but I like his looks uncommonly !
Are you not frozen ?" Their answer was a shout
of laughter.

Dimmler was talking himself hoarse, and he
must be saying very funny things, for the party
in his sleigh were in fits of laughing.

" Better and better," said Nicolas to himself ;
" now we are in an enchanted forest—the black
shadows lie across a flooring of diamonds and

mix with the sparkling of gems. That might be a fairy palace, out there, built of large blocks of marble and jewelled tiles? Did I not hear the howl of wild beasts in the distance? Supposing it were only Mélukovka that I am coming to after all! On my word, it would be no less miraculous to have reached port after steering so completely at random!"

It was, in fact, Mélukovka, for he could see the house servants coming out on the balcony with lights, and then down to meet them, only too glad of this unexpected diversion.

" Who is there ?" a voice asked within.

" The mummers from Count Rostow's ; they are his teams," replied the servants.

Pélaguéïa Danilovna Mélukow, a stout and commanding personality, in spectacles and a flowing dressing-gown, was sitting in her drawing-room surrounded by her children, whom she was doing her best to amuse by modelling heads in wax and tracing the shadows they cast on the wall, when steps and voices were heard in the ante-room. Hussars, witches, clowns, and bears were rubbing their faces, which were scorched by the cold and covered with rime, or shaking the snow off their clothes. As soon as they had cast off their furs they rushed into the large drawing-room, which was hastily lighted

up. Dimmler, the clown, and Nicolas, the marquise, performed a dance, while the others stood
close along the wall, the children shouting and
jumping about them with glee.

"It is impossible to know who is who—can
that really be Natacha? Look at her; does
not she remind you of some one? Edward,
before Karlovitch, how fine you are! and how
beautifully you dance! Oh! and that splendid
Circassian—why, it is Sonia! What a kind and
delightful surprise; we were so desperately
dull. Ha, ha! what a beautiful hussar! A
real hussar, or a real monkey of a boy—which
is he, I wonder? I cannot look at you without
laughing." They all shouted and laughed and
talked at once, at the top of their voices.

Natacha, to whom the Mélukows were devoted, soon vanished with them to their own
room, where corks and various articles of men's
clothing were brought to them, and clutched by
bare arms through a half-open door. Ten minutes later all the young people of the house
rejoined the company, equally unrecognizable.
Pélaguéïa Danilovna, going and coming among
them all, with her spectacles on her nose and a
quiet smile, had seats arranged and a supper
laid out for the visitors, masters and servants
alike. She looked straight in the face of each
in turn, recognizing no one of the motley crew

—neither the Rostows, nor Dimmler, nor even her own children, nor any of the clothes they figured in.

" That one, who is she ?" she asked the governess, stopping a Kazan Tartar, who was, in fact, her own daughter. " One of the Rostows, is it not ? And you, gallant hussar, what regiment do you belong to ?" she went on, addressing Natacha. " Give some *pastila* to this Turkish lady," she cried to the butler ; " it is not forbidden by her religion, I believe."

At the sight of some of the reckless dancing which the mummers performed under the shelter of their disguise, Pélaguéïa Danilovna could not help hiding her face in her handkerchief, while her huge person shook with uncontrollable laughter—the laugh of a kindly matron, frankly jovial and gay.

When they had danced all the national dances, ending with the *Horovody*, she placed every one, both masters and servants, in a large circle, holding a cord with a ring and a rouble, and for a while they played games. An hour after, when the finery was the worse for wear and heat and laughter had removed much of the charcoal, Pélaguéïa Danilovna could recognize them, compliment the girls on the success of their disguise, and thank the whole party for the amusement they had given her. Supper was served for the company in the drawing-room, and for the servants in the large dining-room.

" You should try your fortune in the bath-room over there ; that is enough to frighten you !" said an old maid who lived with the Mélukows.

" Why ?" said the eldest girl.

" Oh ! you would never dare to do it ; you must be very brave."

" Well, I will go," said Sonia.

" Tell us what happened to that young girl, you know," said the youngest Mélukow.

" Once a young girl went to the bath, taking with her a cock and two plates with knives and forks, which is what you must do ; and she waited. Suddenly she heard horses' bells—some one was coming ; he stopped, came up-stairs, and she saw an officer walk into the room ; a real live officer—at least so he seemed—who sat down opposite to her where the second cover was laid."

" Oh ! how horrible !" exclaimed Natacha, wide-eyed. " And he spoke to her—really spoke ?"

" Yes, just as if he had really been a man. He begged and prayed her to listen to him, and all she had to do was to refuse him and hold out till the cock crowed ; but she was too much

frightened. She covered her face with her
hands, and he clasped her in his arms; luckily
some girls who were on the watch rushed in
when she screamed."

"Why do you terrify them with such nonsense?" said Pélaguéïa Danilovna.

"But, mamma, you know you wanted to try
your fortune too."

"And if you try your fortune in a barn, what
do you do?" asked Sonia.

"That is quite simple. You must go to the
barn—now, for instance—and listen. If you
hear thrashing, it is for ill-luck; if you hear
grain dropping, that is good."

"Tell us, mother, what happened to you in
the barn."

"It is so long ago," said the mother, with a
smile, "that I have quite forgotten; besides,
not one of you is brave enough to try it."

"Yes, I will go," said Sonia. "Let me go."

"Go by all means if you are not afraid."

"May I, Madame Schoss?" said Sonia to the
governess.

Now, whether playing games or sitting
quietly and chatting, Nicolas had not left
Sonia's side the whole evening; he felt as if he
had seen her for the first time, and only just
now appreciated all her merits. Bright, be-
witchingly pretty in her quaint costume, and

excited as she very rarely was, she had completely fascinated him.

"What a simpleton I must have been!"
thought he, responding in thought to those
sparkling eyes and that triumphant smile which
had revealed to him a little dimple at the tip
of her mustache that he had never observed
before.

"I am afraid of nothing," she declared. She
rose, asked her way, precisely, to the barn, and
every detail as to what she was to expect, waiting there in total silence; then she threw a fur
cloak over her shoulders, glanced at Nicolas,
and went on.

She went along the corridor and down the
back-stairs; while Nicolas, saying that the heat
of the room was too much for him, slipped out
by the front entrance. It was as cold as ever,
and the moon seemed to be shining even more
brightly than before. The snow at her feet was
strewn with stars, while their sisters overhead
twinkled in the deep gloom of the sky, and she
soon looked away from them, back to the gleaming earth in its radiant mantle of ermine.

Nicolas hurried across the hall, turned the
corner of the house, and went past the side
door where Sonia was to come out. Half-way
to the barn stacks of wood, in the full moonlight, threw their shadows on the path, and

beyond, an alley of lime-trees traced a tangled
pattern on the snow with the fine crossed lines
of their leafless twigs. The beams of the house
and its snow-laden roof looked as if they had
been hewn out of a block of opal, with iridescent
lights where the facets caught the silvery moonlight. Suddenly a bough fell crashing off a tree
in the garden; then all was still again. Sonia's
heart beat high with gladness; as if she were
drinking in not common air, but some life-giving
elixir of eternal youth and joy.

"Straight on, if you please, miss, and on no
account look behind you."

"I am not afraid," said Sonia, her little shoes
tapping the stone steps and then crunching the
carpet of snow as she ran to meet Nicolas, who
was within a couple of yards of her. And yet
not the Nicolas of every-day life. What had
transfigured him so completely? Was it his
woman's costume with frizzed-out hair, or was
it that radiant smile which he so rarely wore,
and which at this moment illumined his face?

"But Sonia is quite unlike herself, and yet
she is herself," thought Nicolas on his side,
looking down at the sweet little face in the
moonlight. He slipped his arms under the fur
cloak that wrapped her, and drew her to him,
and he kissed her lips, which still tasted of the
burned cork that had blackened her mustache.

" Nicolas—Sonia," they whispered ; and Sonia put her little hands round his face. Then, hand in hand, they ran to the barn and back, and each went in by the different doors they had come out of.

Natacha, who had noted everything, managed so that she, Mme. Schoss, and Dimmler should return in one sleigh, while the maids went with Nicolas and Sonia in another. Nicolas was in no hurry to get home ; he could not help looking at Sonia and trying to find under her disguise the true Sonia—his Sonia, from whom nothing now could ever part him. The magical effects of moonlight, the remembrance of that kiss on her sweet lips, the dizzy flight of the snow-clad ground under the horses' hoofs, the black sky, studded with diamonds, that bent over their heads, the icy air that seemed to give vigor to his lungs—all was enough to make him fancy that they were transported to a land of magic.

" Sonia, are you not cold ?"

" No ; and you ?"

Nicolas pulled up, and giving the reins to a man to drive, he ran back to the sleigh in which Natacha was sitting.

" Listen," he said, in a whisper and in French ; " I have made up my mind to tell Sonia."

" And you have spoken to her ?" exclaimed Natacha, radiant with joy.

"Oh, Natacha, how queer that mustache makes you look! Are you glad?"

"Glad! I am delighted. I did not say anything, you know, but I have been so vexed with you. She is a jewel, a heart of gold. I —I am often naughty, and I have no right to have all the happiness to myself now. Go, go back to her."

"No. Wait one minute. Mercy, how funny you look!" he repeated, examining her closely and discovering in her face, too, an unwonted tenderness and emotion that struck him deeply.

"Natacha, is there not some magic at the bottom of it all, heh?"

"You have acted very wisely. Go."

"If I had ever seen Natacha look as she does at this moment I should have asked her advice and have obeyed her, whatever she had bid me do; and all would have gone well. So you are glad?" he said, aloud. "I have done right?"

"Yes, yes, of course you have! I was quite angry with mamma the other day about you two. Mamma would have it that Sonia was running after you. I will not allow any one to say—no, nor even to think—any evil of her, for she is sweetness and truth itself."

"So much the better." Nicolas jumped down and in a few long strides overtook his own sleigh, where the little Circassian received him with a smile from under the fur hood; and the Circassian was Sonia, and Sonia beyond a doubt would be his beloved little wife!

When they got home the two girls went into the countess's room and gave her an account of their expedition; then they went to bed. Without stopping to wipe off their mustaches they stood chattering as they undressed; they had so much to say of their happiness, their future prospects, the friendship between their husbands:

"But, oh! when will it all be? I am so afraid it will never come to pass," said Natacha, as she went toward a table on which two looking-glasses stood.

"Sit down," said Sonia, "and look in the glass; perhaps you will see something about it." Natacha lighted two pairs of candles and seated herself. "I certainly see a pair of mustaches," she said, laughing.

"You should not laugh," said the maid, very gravely.

Natacha settled herself to gaze without blinking into the mirror; she put on a solemn face and sat in silence for some time, wondering what she should see. Would a coffin rise before her, or would Prince André presently stand revealed against the confused background in the shining glass? Her eyes were weary and could hardly distinguish even the flickering light of

the candles. But with the best will in the
world she could see nothing; not a spot to sug-
gest the image either of a coffin or of a human
form. She rose.

" Why do other people see things and I never
see anything at all? Take my place, Sonia;
you must look for yourself and for me, too. I
am so frightened; if I could but know !"

Sonia sat down and fixed her eyes on the
mirror.

" Sofia Alexandrovna will be sure to see something," whispered Douniacha; " but you always
are laughing at such things." Sonia heard the
remark and Natacha's whispered reply: " Yes,
she is sure to see something; she did last year."

Three minutes they waited in total silence.

" She is sure to see something," Natacha repeated, trembling.

Sonia started back, covered her face with one
hand, and cried out:

" Natacha !"

" You saw something? What did you see?"
And Natacha rushed forward to hold up the
glass.

But Sonia had seen nothing; her eyes were
getting dim, and she was on the point of giving
it up when Natacha's exclamation had stopped
her; she did not want to disappoint them; but
there is nothing so tiring as sitting motionless.

She did not know why she had called out and hidden her face.

"Did you see him?" asked Natacha.

"Yes; stop a minute, I saw him," said Sonia, not quite sure whether "him" was to mean Nicolas or Prince André. "Why not make them believe that I saw something?" she thought. "A great many people have done so before, and no one can prove the contrary. Yes, I saw him," she repeated.

"How? standing up or lying down?"

"I saw him—at first there was nothing; then suddenly I saw him lying down."

"André, lying down? Then he is ill!" And Natacha gazed horror-stricken at her companion.

"Not at all; he seemed quite cheerful, on the contrary," said she, beginning to believe in her own inventions.

"And then—Sonia, what then?"

"Then I saw only confusion—red and blue."

"And when will he come back, Sonia? When shall I see him again? O God! I am afraid for him—afraid of everything."

And, without listening to Sonia's attempts at comfort, Natacha slipped into bed, and, long after the lights were out, she lay motionless but awake, her eyes fixed on the moonshine that came dimly through the frost-embroidered windows.

A Wayfarer's Fancy.

" A felicitous combination of the
German, the Sclave, and the
Semite, with grand features,
brown hair floating in artistic
fashion, and brown eyes in spectacles."

George Eliot.

TWO CHRISTMASES.

I.

It was the time of the great war. Germany was desolated. Towns and villages were destroyed by flames. Order and law had given way to savage power; and from the walls of many a ruined house of God the wooden image of the Saviour looked down with a face of anguish on the horrors of the degenerate times.

The terrified citizens of towns that were still untouched by war, hid themselves within their narrow walls, awaiting, in tremulous fear, the day on which their homes must also fall a prey to plundering soldiers. If any one were obliged to go beyond the boundaries, he would glance anxiously at the bushes on either side of the road; and when night came on, he would be forced to look with horror and sorrow at the reddened horizon, where a little village or lonely hamlet was burning to ashes.

But who is it cowers there in the ditch by the highway? A dried-up little man with deathly-pale countenance, and clad in a black coat!

Flee, Wanderer! let him not gaze at you with his piercing gray eyes! Beware! for that old man is the Plague-man!

The heart of the Wanderer sinks within him. Horrified he rushes away, and thanks heaven when, in the gray of the morning, he sees again the towers of his native town. Enraptured by the sight of home he believes these towers with the dear, well-known faces can protect him; but the old cripple has been quicker than he. Before break of day he has knocked at the town-gate, and the gate-keeper, on opening it, has scarcely looked into his gray eyes before he sank down as though some one had felled him with an axe.

Then the gray old man begins his terrible work. Like a bat he slips into all dwellings; no gate and no bolt is an obstacle to him. Right up into the lofts he climbs and opens the most secret chamber. That threshold he passes is doomed to the Black-death.

It had happened thus to a little town in Franconia, where but a few houses remained untouched by the terrible plague. In this town there lived a poor, honest couple with their child, a boy of nearly three years. Their cottage lay on a small hill, and was divided from the road by a little garden. People ascribed it to this that the awful spirit for a long time had left their home untouched. But at last he seemed to have found his way to even this out-of-the-way place.

A few days before Christmas the boy fell sick, and on Christmas morning he lay motion-less in bed, so that the poor parents thought the plague had taken their child from them. The father wanted to bury the body at once, but the mother showed him the rosy cheeks of the dead child, and said that a death that looked so like sleep could do them no harm. Thereupon she went into the little garden and cut box-tree leaves from under the snow, and made a wreath for the dead darling. She placed the wreath on his curly head and moved his bed into the middle of the room, where she set candles burn-ing around it, just as we do in quieter times for a dear departed one. Then she went into the wood, cut down a small Christmas-tree and placed it, all decorated with lights, nuts, and bright tinsel, next to the coffin, in order that the dead child might also have his Christmas pleasure.

This was the only Christmas-tree that the poor stricken town lit up! People passing along the road looked with secret jealousy at the ·illuminated window, wondering how they could still rejoice in such bitter times. But no gladsome sounds from the window reached the

street, where flake after flake was whirling
down from the gray heavens, covering everything in its white cloak. And unceasingly, as
flake after flake sank down to earth, so in the
little chamber the tears of the poor woman
rolled down her cheeks till the lights of the
Christmas-tree burned low, the fire in the stove
died away, and sleep closed the streaming eyes
of the mother. Then all was quiet, very quiet,
in the little chamber.

But at the gates of Heaven it was very noisy
that evening. Countless hosts were crowding
up the broad stairway, young and old, rich and
poor: a mixed and motley crowd. There the
patrician elbowed the tailor who had made his
coat; the general the lowest sutler; and a
ragged beggar was even next to a king, who
drew his purple closer around him in order not
to be contaminated. All were pushing towards
the great, light gate, and many a one, who on
earth had only beaten and jostled others, received here in the crowd his own first jostling.
At the gate stood a beautiful, tall angel, who
sprinkled each one with water out of a golden
vessel. The touch of this water obliterated at
once all remembrance of the past.

St. Peter, who considered the noise and bustle too much of a good thing, was of the opin-

ion that mankind had none of the bother of
dying, all the work falling on him; and he was
accordingly grumbling to himself. Suddenly he
saw a little fellow, clad only in a shirt, standing
before him, shivering all over, and regarding
him with innocent, childish eyes, as if asking
whether he might enter. St. Peter, unwilling
that such little folks should cause delay in business, said, roughly, "In with you!" The little
frightened fellow rushed, thereupon, so quickly
through the gate that the angel did not have
time to sprinkle him with the waters of oblivion.

Now, as children of two years have but short
memories and very harmless pasts, the angel
smilingly let him slip by. Once inside, little
Hans was seized by a host of flying angels and
whirled away to Paradise, which was more
beautiful than the fairest garden on earth.
Rare plants with big, magnificently colored
blossoms filled the air with spicy odor. Here
dwelt the tiny children who had left earth
before they knew anything of it. Here they
could dream on forever; and their breath swept
softly over every bud. Large butterflies with
silken wings were bathing in the clear ether,
and floating entranced from bud to bud. The
heavens glittered and lightened as though composed of millions of diamonds; yet the sun did
not blind the eye, nor the warmth rise to sum-

mer heat. Eternal spring had banished from
these regions battle and death, tempest and
decay, and far away below in misty distance lay
all the sorrows of tormented creation. Amongst
the flowers wandered blissful forms, absorbed in
the beauty of surrounding harmony.

The boy curiously observed all this splendor,
peered into the dewy buds of the flowers, examined the wings of his heavenly playmates,
and was not a little rejoiced on observing that
two wings had also grown on him, with which
he could fly like a bird. "If neighbor Liesel
could only see me!" thought Hans, and he felt
quite proud at the thought. For, notwithstanding all the splendor about him, the picture of
his parents' home presented itself constantly to
his little mind. He had an excellent memory
of the much despised earth, which soon with
magnetic power drew all his thoughts towards it.
At the sight of the wonderful flowers of Paradise,
such as the earth never produces, he could think
of nothing but the violets, and crocuses, and
tulips which curled up in spring-time out of the
black earth of his father's garden. The golden
fruits on the trees reminded him of the gilded
ones of the Christmas-tree, and seemed to him
even brighter; and although the Paradise of
heaven, with its eternal clearness, was a thousand times more beautiful than the changing

air below, yet the little heart felt a dim yearning for the beloved earth, the griefs of which
he had not yet learned to measure ; and, amidst
all this angelic beauty, he only felt an uncontrollable longing for the plain, human countenance of his mother. Then there came an end
to his enjoyment. He began to cry, and, finally,
to roar lustily. The other little angels gathered
astonished around him, staring at the strange
playmate who had dewdrops in his eyes and
made such awful faces. Such a thing did not
generally occur in heaven, where all were good
and quiet. But just then St. James came
along and, on seeing the crying angel, he spoke
pleasantly to him, and finally took him up in
his arms in order to comfort him. But a great
surprise lay in store for the Saint ; for it would
have been easier for him to convert a thousand
heathens than to quiet the little unruly fellow,
who commenced kicking and wriggling, and
made such a terrible outcry that the angels
fluttered away in consternation. There stood
the Saint with the child in his arms, and did
not know what to do ! At last he concluded to
show the strange being to the Lord Himself,
and went with the little one before His throne.
Then the Lord Almighty smiled, and all the
angels around His throne smiled, when they saw
St. James, who certainly did not seem very well

adapted for nursing children, and in whose arms little Hans, regardless of all surroundings, continued to roar unmercifully. But the merciful Lord opined that the greatest squallers often turned out the best men, and He ordered an angel to carry the little one back to dear earth.

And this was done. With mighty strokes of his pinions the heavenly messenger floated back to earth, which came nearer and nearer with its mountains, lakes, and rivers, and with the old, lifeworn town, and from out the town rose up the gabled roof of the parents' home with a cap of snow upon it.

The boy in the coffin opened his eyes, and with a cry of joy his mother pressed him to her heart. Among the boughs of the Christmas-tree there was a soft rustling and whispering.

Methinks the tree remembered that winter is only a deep sleep, and was dreaming of spring.

II.

The years of misery and war were over. In the streets of the old town, where only a few years ago the roll of the drum resounded, and where the plague, in deathly silence, had spread its black wings, there, the stork on the town-hall heard, to his great satisfaction, merry shouts of children,—the ringing laugh of peace.

A group of boys chased each other noisily over the market-place, playing at war. War! which had desolated so many of their homes. Oh! the fresh, merry laughter of childhood! how like unto ivy it climbeth over all ruins and findeth at last the sunshine!

But there was one not amongst the noisy group, and that one was Hans. His parents perceived with anxiety that the little noisy child had grown into a silent, shy boy, who avoided the games of his comrades and dreamingly went his own way. For hours he sat in the garden on the bench near his mother's flowers, and gazed dreamingly at the busy bees and butterflies, or lay in the woods near by and stared up through the branches of the beech-trees at the blue sky.

"What are you thinking of?" his mother would ask at times; then he would start up like one awakened from sleep, the thread of whose dreams are broken by awaking. "He is ill," the mother would think, anxiously. But folks would shake their heads suspiciously when, on speaking to the boy, they received no other answer than a shy, questioning look. "There is something wanting," said some, with an unmistakable gesture. "He is a fool," murmured others.

Thus a boy fares who has peeped too early

into Paradise. The children of his own age
made fun of him, and poor Hans would have
been quite forsaken if Liesel from next door
had not taken his part. She was quite the
opposite to him,—merry and high-spirited.
Whilst he sat dreaming, she was romping about,
singing and laughing. But the children kept
together, and the parents thought they might
some day be a pair. The boy's reserved nature
vexed the father, and, being of the opinion that
man's hand cannot learn too early to handle
and knead the tough clay of existence, he ap-
prenticed him to a potter, in the hope that time
would change the character of his son. He
was mistaken, however; the boy grew up a fine,
handsome youth, but in character he remained
the boy of former days. If he looked up from
his work it was not in order to gaze, like other
journeymen, after a young girl who maybe was
tripping past; but to stare up at the sky, which
shone so blue between the houses, or to follow
with his eyes the great white clouds sailing
away,—who knows whither? In his free time
he did not go like others to the market-place,
but would mount the ramparts at the back of
his parents' house and gaze into the valley
below, where the river was bearing its silvery
wavelets into the far distance. What might
not be in the far distance? Far, far away

yonder must be the place where the dream of his childhood was realized! How astonished, then, was his father, when one fine sunny spring morning his son stood before him, with knapsack and staff, in order to bid him farewell before setting out on his travels. Who would ever have thought he would want to travel! The father rejoiced in the belief that the son would seek work according to the custom of journeymen workmen, and gave him his blessing, and much good advice besides. But he hardly even heard the words and advice of his father; there was a singing in his ears and a mist before his eyes, so that he felt like one intoxicated. Yes, he was a fool! Nor did he see the tears his mother and Liesel were shedding at his departure: he only thought of that far-off land, of the dream of his childhood. What mattered to him their tears! He wanted only to travel to find his Eden. And he travelled. With each rising sun he arose and thought, " To-day you will find what you seek;" and when he laid himself down tired at night, he thought, " To-morrow I shall reach my goal;" and, happy in this thought, he would fall asleep. No mountain was too steep for him, no path too stony, no forest too dense; he thought of his Eden, and minded not the thorns that tore his flesh. Yes, he was a fool!

I.—*h* 10*

Far behind him, forgotten, lay his home in the dim distance!

No living creature could tell him where his Paradise lay! The birds of the forest went on with their song; the deer gazed at him astonished; the brooks babbled on monotonously and sought the way to the ocean. People he asked only laughed, and they looked back at the strange lad, shaking their heads.

Quickly the time flew by; the spring faded, summer and autumn passed, and still he wandered on. His path, that once lay before him green and fair, was now covered with snow. He, however, heeded it not, and journeyed on. It must come at last, the long-sought goal! At last he reached a mighty snow-covered mountain range, so mighty that he said to himself, "Beyond this it must surely lie," and in glad hope passed forward. A whole day he ascended over snow and ice: his feet were sore and bruised, and he was shivering from the cold, and yet no hut was to be seen that might offer him shelter. The sun went down in crimson behind the ice-armored mountains, leaving behind a bitter coldness, so great that the stars in the heavens shivered with frost.

Then it occurred to tired Hans that it was Christmas, and for the first time on his journey he thought for a long while of home, where the

Christmas-tree was now lighting up the warm room, and the dear ones were assembling around it. But what mattered the Christmas-tree to him; he was seeking Paradise!

Suddenly he saw on the roadside an old man. He was sitting on his bundle, and leaning his head on his hands. He must have been very old, for his face was furrowed like the bark of an oak, and his snowy beard hung nearly to the ground.

Then tired Hans rejoiced, greeted him, and asked how far it might be to the nearest habitation of man.

"To-day you can no longer reach it," replied the old man. "Whither are you journeying?"

"I seek Paradise," answered Hans: "nearly a year have I wandered over the earth, and yet have not found it."

Thereupon the old man arose, laid his hands upon Hans's shoulder, and said, "Turn back and go home! I have wandered for more than a thousand years on earth, and sought Paradise, and have not found it. Know, then, I am Ahasuerus, doomed to everlasting wandering as a penance. Wherever I go I am persecuted; where I knock the gate is locked; and nowhere have I a home. Stones are my bed, and my bundle is my pillow. Go, poor fool! return to the place of your birth. There, some day, they will dig a grave for you, wherein you may sleep peacefully. Go back to your home, where a Christmas-tree is lit up for you, and where you are loved, and leave to me all wandering and seeking: to me, the poor, old, accursed man!"

Then Hans was very sad: he threw down his bundle, sat down in the snow, and wept bitterly. However, he was so tired from the long journey that he soon forgot all his misery, and fell into a deep slumber. The old man spread his cloak over him to protect him from the cold, and then listened to the deep-drawn breathing of precious sleep, that drowns all cares. The youth lying there could sleep, and die, and forget! but he himself must keep awake, and live, and wander!

Upon the face of Hans a smile was playing; he was dreaming! Did he see the long-sought Paradise? He saw in his dream a house with snow-covered gable and little windows; a small house, closely encircled by other houses, a garden in front. In a room inside sat his parents round a cheerful fire. The spinning-wheel whizzed, and the cat purred in comfort in front of the fire. Softly there fell, now and again, a needle from the Christmas-tree. A resinous, pine-tree odor filled the room. From the next house a clear, maiden's voice was singing the old, old Christmas carol,—

" A rose has bloomed
   From a tender root,
   Our fathers have sung :
   Out of Jesse it came."

And the crackling of the fire, the whizzing of
the spinning-wheel, and the maiden's song
seemed to the dreamer fairer than a thousand
Edens. An indescribable homesickness overcame him.

When he awoke, the east was radiant with
the blush of morning. He sprang up and seized
his staff. Scales seemed to fall from his eyes.
"Home, home!" a thousand voices seemed to
echo within him.

But up the mountains, outlined by the red
of the morn, he saw the old man wandering on
his comfortless path.

A Yarn Spun by a Yankee.

> " A white-haired, thin-visaged,
> weather-worn old gentleman in
> a blue. Quaker-cut coat."
> *Hawthorne.*

A TALE OF A TURKEY.

I.

THE shutters of a little spur of warehouses
which breaks out into mountainous stores and
open valleys of streets around the corner, but
which itself overlooks no fairer view than a
narrow, muddy alley of a thoroughfare scarcely
broad enough to admit two drays abreast, and,
by actual measurement,—taken with persistent
diligence by the adjacent office boys,—just two
running-jumps from gutter to gutter; the shutters of this, in its own eyes, important little
trade centre, were up, and a great clattering
they had made in getting up on a clear, tingling
night before Christmas, eighteen hundred and
—no matter what.

The porters had come out in their faded great-
coats, bandaged right and left in woolly mufflers,
and more than usually clumsy in padded gloves,
and had been bitten and tossed about by the
wind with such unbecoming violence that even
a porter felt it necessary to hurry and bustle.

Taking the shutters by assault from the foe's embraces, they had thumped, and banged, and hammered, and scolded them into place, and, in undignified haste, had betaken themselves, steaming warm breath through their fingers, into their proper and respective places by the counting-house fire.

The magic—so it seemed in its effects—tolling of a deep-toned bell in the neighborhood would not allow them to doze long in their warm nooks, but, like the jealous monster in the fairy-tale, kept its captives always going, going, going, for its sixth stroke had not died away before they began to appear again, this time with the addition of fur, hats and little dinner-baskets, and with no perceptible noses—unless the existence of watery eyes above their mufflers argued the missing features to be in their proper places below—and with an accelerated gait— also an act of enchantment.

William, of No. 6, bawled as loud as his worsted gag would permit across the street (so termed by a figure of rhetoric) to James, of No. 7:

"Hello, Jim! Cold as blazes, ain't it?"

James, of No. 7, assenting, Thomas, of No. 4, would like to know "How blazes can be cold, now?"

William, of No. 6, would say "as thunder,"

if that would suit him any better; and as it appeared to do so they, with half a dozen others, breasted the wind and trudged out into the blustery streets beyond.

The merchants, too, had locked their doors, and tried their knobs, and looked up at the faces of their stores as if to say, " Merry Christmas to you, and I wish you a pleasant day tomorrow !" but in reality to see that all was fast, and perchance to indulge in a comfortable survey of their snug little properties—and the complacent tread with which they followed the porters gives color to the suspicion—and draw from it momentum for the enjoyment of the morrow's holiday.

The shutters, then, were up—stop, not all up! One, as you may see by the shaft of gas-light that has just fallen across the pavement near the top of the court, is still down.

The little square window through which the light eddies on the bricks is supported on either side by a heavy door, and all three, the two doors and the window, are in turn crowned and anointed on the head, as it were, by a very bold sign containing very brazen—in every sense of the word—letters which announced pompously, like some servants of similar metallic qualities, the name of their master.

Emanuel Griffin —the tongue uncontrollably

adds Esquire—was the name, and there, if you had looked through the window, in a deep funnel of a room, at a desk near the fire, head behind the open leaves of a ledger, and feet beneath the warm recesses of the stove, sat its possessor.

Outside the railing which formed a barrier between Emanuel Griffin, Esq., and the business world, and encompassed with a less elaborate railing, sat, on a high stool in a cold corner, the little, blackish-green (perhaps the color gas-light imparts to faded black) clerk of Emanuel Griffin, Esq. Whether David Dubbs, such was he called, derived the power of writing from his mouth ; or whether the gentle excitation of moving his lips over toothless gums assisted thought; or whether, as some said, he chewed tobacco, a position which nobody ever held long, as nobody ever proved him to have expectorated during his whole life; his mouth—always closed— moved up and down, up and down, with the motion of his pen. Hair he had none, that is, none to speak of ; there were some few isolated white locks behind his ears and at the back of his head, but he made no pretensions to have any, and openly acknowledged himself bald— and very candid of him it was to do so.

Chroniclers have told us how, after fierce battles that have raged from dawn till nightfall, the moon has come calmly up from the horizon and shone peacefully and serenely over the field of strife and death. So arose a beneficent smile ever and anon over the wrinkled and careworn face of the old clerk; but still he wrote on, Faithful Dave! and if pleasant thoughts swept through him they avoided the business that occupied his hands and did not interrupt it.

They had long sat in quietness, only broken by the noise of turning leaves and crackling coals,—but, in truth, if David Dubbs's eye, in its course to and from the clock, had not, like the world, worked silently on its axis, there must have been continual creaking—when a noise like the name of David emanated from the ledger, and following it—for it was near-sighted —the head of Emanuel Griffin, Esq., lifted itself to an erect posture and repeated in a less muffled tone, " David!"

" Yes, sir," answered the old clerk, in a weak little voice, and climbing down to the floor from his perch.

" You may lock up, David. Ten thousand and odd. Ten thousand's a good year, David; a very good year. Very—good—in-deed! But go and lock up," and then Mr. Griffin took a glance at the clock. " Half-past six! Why it's surprising how time does fly, and Christmas Eve,

too. Well, well! But hurry up with the shutters, David, and we shan't be long——"

Before Mr. Griffin had fully delivered himself
of these remarks the little person of David
Dubbs was out in the cold, was in and out
among the screws on the door, had put up the
shutters, and simultaneously with the last word
stood in the half-opened door and, all unseen by
his employer, waved his hand to some one at the
corner of the court. He then walked as quickly
as his little, bent legs—parabolic were they in
outline, but, as this is not a geometric treatise,
it is of no particular consequence—would permit
him up the long aisle in the centre of the room,
and sent off timid little echoes of his steps to
ramble away among the bales of crockery—for
it was crockery that Emanuel Griffin, Esq., dealt
in—and rattle among the piles of plates.

Having reached again his little cage of an
office, he took down from its accustomed peg
an old, threadbare coat, and, with much exertion and outstretching of arms, finally got it on,
turned up the collar, tied about his ears a not
very robust scarf, and laid thereon, as the cope-
stone of his apparel, a dingy high hat that had
undergone, in point of nap, as many reverses as
its wearer in point of fortune. Thus attired,
he tipped his hat to his employer, all ready, like
himself, to depart, and started out.

Before he reached the door, a cry from Mr.
Griffin arrested him, and he came hastily back;
for, although it would have required a thumb-
screw to have made him confess it, yet he had all
day long looked forward to the time of parting,
when he half expected Emanuel Griffin, Esq.,
contrary to his custom though it was, would
offer him some little gift out of the increased
profits of a business he had done no little to
advance. But no such design had Mr. Griffin
conceived, or if he had it was very soon suppressed as entirely unworthy of a man of purely
business habits, and all he had to say was,—

"I know, David, there is something I was to
have told you to do. Mrs. Griffin impressed it
on me this morning, but,"—here he stood thinking for a moment,—"no matter," he resumed.
"I guess it was nothing very important, so
good-by, David, and a—good-by!" He was
going to say "and a merry Christmas;" but for
a man of purely business habits to unbend so
far and become cheerful—why, it's subversive
of all business discipline, and so he thought to
himself.

David, doubly disappointed, turned and passed
out, and his old eyes must have been extremely
sensitive to the wind, for they ran with something very like tears that he wiped away with
his glove as he muttered,—

"So, no Christmas, after all. Poor girls! Poor girls!" Mr. Griffin was not long behind his faithful old clerk. He extinguished the lights with great care, and then, with the key in his hand, felt his way to the door, banged it after him, and locked it with the satisfaction of a miser over a casket of treasures. His journey home led him to the opposite end of the court from that which David had passed through, and he therefore did not overtake him.

And if he had, would this hard, business-encrusted heart have been less cold than the bitter winds that assailed it? Would the sight which made David Dubbs forget the fierceness of night have penetrated the chilly place where it rested and warmed it in pitying activity? Would the tender impulses, which the unsifted morals of barter extinguish, as they extinguish much of the nobility in man, have enkindled anew and brightened this misery? Not if dollars would have done it; nay, not if even a word would have done it, would Emanuel Griffin have relaxed from the demeanor which purely business habits imposed upon him. He felt it due to his position in business society to maintain rigidly its maxims, the chief of which, "Do unto others as they would do unto you, if they could," he practised to the letter.

slight—and lifted her to his lips, and then, throwing one side of his own scanty coat about her and holding it there with an affectionate hug, he said, " Come, come, little daughter, it's too bleak for a little body like you to be out. It's cruel, cruel, but I dared not tell him it was so late. What does he know or care for my poor little faithful, Loving Scout ?"

" Your Scout couldn't miss Christmas Eve, father, if it was ever so cold."

" And does she ever miss ? No, no, she's a dutiful Scout, winter and summer, rain and shine, morning and night, and what should I ever do without her !"

So, talking and fighting the wind by turns, they walked on, the bent and shuffling old man and his Little Scout, as he had named her and as they all affectionately called her, through dark streets where, ever and anon, a car or belated dray shivered by, as if the cold had touched even its insensibility, and made the tracks re-sound and the paving blocks rattle in the clear air; through deep cisterns of streets, between lofty stone banks—as stern almost as their governing boards, for, although boards are chiefly wooden, a supplication will quickly petrify them ; through rows of illuminated stores like walls of Arabian Night visions, with traceries of frost on their windows richer in design than

the gems within them; through clustering
crowds that entered or left continually the
swinging doors of saloons and hotels; past
waiting carriages; past swearing men; past
laughing ladies, and past beggars, wearier, and
colder, and lonelier than themselves. So they
travelled, scarcely heeding what they saw in
their speed until, on the margin of all the din,
by a turn through a dark street, they reached
a darker alley, and, passing down it, at last
stopped before their own homely door.

The building had once been a warehouse,—
David liked it the better for that, he said.
"Why, all my life has been spent in trade, and,
you see, I've sort a become attached to anything that smacks of it, though I've little reason
to feel so, the Lord knows!" he would exclaim
to his friends. Up above, over a long door in
the top story—you can scarcely make it out in
the uncertain light—jutted a weather-beaten
crane, with a long disused pulley dangling at its
point, cracked, and rusted, and abandoned, and
no less cracked and abandoned, shot out from
the second floor a moss-covered platform that
had been intended for the reception of bales of
stuffs that had never arrived. The mortar had,
here and there, been wrenched from between
the bricks by savage weather and age, and the
doors, too, had shrunk before their united ma-

lignity. How such a house had drifted to such
a locality is unaccountable, unless—as is often
the case—some navigator of real estate had
thought he descried a port, where was only a
shoal that left his venture high and dry among
newer and costlier craft.

However, the nearest approach it had made
in the last twenty years or so—so David said—
to fulfilling its commercial place in the world
was in opening its doors to a gentleman in the
carpentering line. This gentleman, Mr. Jacob
Tripple by name, occupied the ground floor, and
all around it were scattered evidences, in the
shape of window-frames, and wooden-horses,
and props, and old lumber, of a thriving business. He, with all his men, had departed long
ago and left the place dark, and still, and cold.

It had lain in this stupor of silence for more
than an hour, waiting against hope to be resus-
citated by any stray echoes that should drop in
from the neighboring hubbub and waken it up,
when it caught among its bleak angles the
cheery voice of David's Little Scout, and revived
—as some old men do under the charm of gentle
words—to a more respectable opinion of itself.
So immediately it seemed refreshed, that if it
were possible for such a decrepit—not to say
inanimate—old structure as that even metaphorically to prick up its ears, it metaphorically

did as the sound of Dolly's—her proper name
—cheery welcome home echoed round it.

"Here we are once more, father," she cried,
breaking away from him to have the door open
when he plodded up to it. "Once more, and a
welcome home, and a merry Christmas to you!"

"Always on duty, Little Scout! Always on
duty!" he called after her. (The wind was
keen and drew water to his eyes again, and
again he brushed it away.) "Always on duty,"
he went on repeating, with a doleful effort at
cheerfulness.

She was up-stairs by that time, and, opening
the door above, had called in, "Here's father!"
then ran back to meet him, which she did at
the door below.

What these unusual proceedings meant, David
Dubbs might have guessed or might have known
traditionally, they being of an annual nature,
but whether he did or not, or whether his ignorance was also traditional, he gave no sign, and
walked feebly up-stairs, guided by the Little
Scout, just as if it were not Christmas Eve at
all.

What the proceedings did mean was that a
steaming pot of coffee at the given signal was
lifted from its warm corner and tilted into a
cup that held a conspicuous place at the head
of a little white spread table. On its right

hand sat, in the position of an honored and
seldom present guest, a juicy-complexioned, but
not corpulent beefsteak; opposite to it, inviting
death by explosion, rested a bowl full of steaming potatoes in their native jackets, and the
centre was fully occupied by a huge loaf with a
large family of slices.

Around this collation—aroused by the signal,
for they had been idly waiting before—moved
two pairs of hands with loving attention. The
cloth was resmoothed, the knives and forks
straightened, a brace of mealy potatoes was
emptied on the two plates that awaited them,
and at last a ruddy slice of beefsteak was
deposited beside and oozed through them its
savoriness. This last climax was reached just
as the door opened, and the two pairs of hands
speedily transferred themselves to the duty—
no very arduous one—of helping David and
Dolly out of their wraps.

And then, with many caresses and kisses and
cries of "Take this side, father, where the coals
are bright!" or "Put your feet here and get them
good and warm, poor Little Scout!" then, when
thick flying questions and travellings to the one
end of the room for things that were not wanted,
and excursions to the other end of the room for
things that were wanted; when the chairs were
drawn up; when the grateful old man and his

little daughter, with those tender hands over their mouths to stifle the gratitude they struggled to utter, were duly seated at the table, and when the kettle was singing its approval in the corner, then, only,—when all these preliminaries were gone through with,—did the possessors of the hands that devised them seat themselves on a low wooden settee opposite the table and enjoy the zest and delight they had ministered to.

Good nature and tender hearts, pale faces and cheerful eyes, honest red hands and neatly bound-up hair have never been faithfully reproduced in a state of print and paper, much less in imagination, and, indeed, how can anything so buxom and comely, even if the plainest in dress, be expected to be? It is, therefore, needless to say that the twin daughters of David, namely, Molly and Polly Dubbs, being all that is here set down, should have been seen in all their kindliness to be truly known, and no other form of introduction would do them full justice.

Molly was the counterpart of Polly in all respects save height. She was a very little taller than Polly, and a fortunate thing it had been for all concerned that she was so. Else, consider the vexation of the measles and other diseases essential to youth. Why, in their quandary which to begin on, they almost missed the twins altogether as it was. Consider the complexity of young lovers who should pour into the ears of Polly passionate adjectives intended solely to captivate the heart of Molly; and, most important of all, consider the conflict of choice which would have disquieted the soul of Mr. Jacob Tripple and at last driven him to the alternatives of suicide or bigamy.

But all these dangers had been averted by the provisions of Nature, and the twins, who had supped, for economic reasons, earlier in the evening, sat beaming on while David and little Dolly heartily devoured the supper.

David, looking up now for the first time, in the interval of a mouthful swallowed and a mouthful threatened, espied a bowery wreath of holly that hung around a picture of General Washington in the act of crossing a dark, green river Delaware in a court dress of red and breeches of yellow, surrounded on all sides by ice and officers in rainbow uniforms, and, as this was the only adornment of a rather bare room, it is no wonder it caught his eye.

" Why, who's been a-brightening up the gen-'ral so Christmas-like ?" he exclaimed.

" We did, father! Leastwise it was Polly's present," said Molly.

" And who may be a-sending presents to Polly now ?" asked David, with a twinkle in his eye

that had seen better days but none kindlier.
" It wasn't young Cuffy over at the baker's, nor
Jake Tripple, now, was it?"

He looked at Polly for an answer, whereat
she stretched her arm along the back of the
settee and let fall her hand on Molly's shoulder
with a punch which was intended as punishment for the giggles her sister struggled to con-
fine in her mouth with both hands; but which,
in spite of her, bubbled over and attacked David,
and then, with a blush, Polly muttered,—

" It wasn't young Cuffy at all, and I hate his
loafy, little face, and I hate——"

"Not Jacob Tripple! No, no, not good Jake
Tripple?" said David, reprovingly.

" I didn't say that, father!" she exclaimed.
" He's your good old friend, and how could I
hate him? He came in just before leaving for
the day, and asked for you—what made him
think you were home I can't tell, for it was
long before your time—and asked for you, and
left the wreath for—for—me."

The hem of her long checkered apron then
needed close scrutiny and folding for some unknown purpose, and this duty diverted her
thoughts from the subject, but she turned to
Dolly, who enjoyed this banter in her own quiet
little way, which seldom rippled into a loud
laugh, for her own quiet little face was too

pale and too pinched to invite such freebooters. "Come, come, Little Scout," she said. "Is she warm now, and were the rations good, and did she meet Kriss Kingle on his cold journey (with a caress of her pale little cheeks) with heaps of warm dresses, and heaps of pretty dolls, and heaps of sweetmeats too big to carry himself, so he asked her to carry some home to help him! Did she? (with another caress.) And would our Little Scout be sorry if he didn't come himself to look after them and——"

"Ah, that reminds me!" said David, quite audibly for him, and rising from the table with knife and fork still in hand.

"What reminds you, father?" asked the twins, in chorus.

"Why, coming home!" said David, not very intelligibly.

"What coming home?" again from the chorus, in expectant attitude.

"Why, Tom, I told you!" which he hadn't done at all, but as by this time he was deep in the cupboard, where his overcoat hung, and as his voice was a little more muffled than usual, it was useless to argue the point, so the chorus loudly exclaimed,—

"Tom?"

"Yes, yes, yes!" from David, faintly and rather testily, as he had groped through his old coat, and had successively dropped the knife and fork, reeking with gravy, into the inside and outside pockets.

"To be sure! Tom coming home and I clean forgot it, what with the cold and the surprises," he said again, emerging with the knife and fork in one hand and a letter in the other. "Here it is. He'll be home to-morrow, he says, God willin', and eat our turkey with us. Poor Tom, poor boy! He's been away so long he's forgot Griffin and hard times, or he wouldn't say that!"

"Tom! Be home! and to-morrow?"—interruption of chorus as it reaches for the letter, opens and reads it aloud—Dolly being lifted in the sturdy arms of Molly to look over.

David, meanwhile, overcome by the toothsomeness of beefsteak, falls to again, while the others dance a sort of fandango, and turn up the rag carpet, and rattle the dishes on the dresser, and lift Dolly high in the air to the improvised tune of "Tom's coming home! Tom's coming home! Tom's coming home to-morrow!"

"It's another mouth to feed, but it's hard to wish the poor boy back to Californy again," huskily said David; then he exclaimed, as the noise increased, "Hey dey! Why, you'll spill the coffee next, and cave in the walls, too, in a minute, and then there'll be no home for Tom to come to!"

This was good humoredly added as the final swing was given to the dance, which brought the twins holding Dolly aloft in their arms laughing and panting on the settee.

"But tell us, father, is he coming home for good? He don't say so in the letter," asked Dolly, and all leaned forward to hear his answer.

"Coming home for good?" mused David. "Yes, he's coming home for good, I hope; but I'm fearful he'll find little beside the good in his sisters' hearts."

"Poor Tom," said Dolly, with far-away eyes, "he's had a weary life of it in the mines, I guess, poor fellow."

"Yes, yes," said David, "and that's what makes it harder that we can't greet him with a good Christmas to-morrow. Well, well, it'll be a delight to see my poor boy again, hard times or no hard times, and we'll be as cheerful as we can be and are now, thanks to my good girls;" and here he arose from the table, and, seating himself at the fire, opened a morning paper that he had found in the waste-basket in Mr. Griffin's counting-house (and very worthless it must have been to be found there!) in which, through the kind offices of a massive old pair of spectacles, he was soon absorbed.

And now, while the Little Scout—in fulfilment of her established character—plays the spy on sundry crumbs that slink from notice under the table, and while the twins, too busy to talk, wash the dishes and dispose them in a glistening row along the dresser, and, while David opens the paper and plods up and down it, column by column, like a ploughman furrow by furrow up and down a field, and with almost as much toil; and while the ancient clock on the shelf over the stove and under the motley General Washington ticks loud enough to be heard above the clinking dishes and simmering kettle; and while the table, divested of its cloth and exhibiting a stained and blistered old back, is glad enough to avoid attention by being stowed away in the corner; while the pleasant spirits of domesticity that come only at the call of good men, and good wives, and good sons, and good daughters, but resist the imperious beckonings of the wealthiest hands, and wing on over their roofs to lowlier, and scantier, and purer habitations—while the pleasant spirits of domesticity and kindliness throng invisibly into the room, and David Dubbs reads stray scraps from his paper to his daughters, grouped near the fire at his feet, we must softly withdraw and leave them to the care of coming Christmas dreams.

III.

Christmas morning had opened brightly with David Dubbs. The sun, preceded down the court by hustling winds that knocked at every citizen's door and demanded admittance for their oncoming master, had left at each house a gift of golden cheerfulness. The sky above was so blithe and blue that it smiled down at even so insignificant a crack as David Dubbs's court must have appeared to it; and the cold was a jolly and snappish cold.

The twins and David's Little Scout were as merry as the Christmas chimes they lingered and listened to, and not the daintiest dinner that Mr. Cuffy (and that gentleman held the subject somewhat in mind, too, on Polly's account) could have delivered at their door would have added one jot of happiness to their abundance. David's poor old back bent under the stress of poverty that would permit him no indulgences for them—all the more dear on that day; but, used to loving self-denial, they never missed what they so little desired, and so far were they from giving it a thought, that if David had spoken out what he so wilfully turned over and over in his mind, that would have given them far more pain and anxiety. Mr. Tripple was early in his shop, presumptively

to attend to some forgotten duties, but, as he
did not pay very active attention to anything
but carefully tying up a square box in white
paper, and as he did pay very active attention
to what went on up-stairs, at the same time
exhibiting no hurry to get home to dinner,
David, who had, towards noon, gone around the
corner with Polly to make some little purchases
of groceries before the stores closed, dropped in
on his way back and invited Mr. Tripple up-
stairs. Mr. Tripple at first firmly refused, and
said, " Very much obliged, Dave, but couldn't
think of it. Indeed not. They'd 'spect me at
home, ye know, Dave." Whereupon Miss Polly
added her entreaties, and said he needn't expect
anything very much, but if he would walk up
they would be very happy to have him. Mr.
Tripple would have walked up—and, indeed,
wanted very much to walk up—at first, but his
extreme awkwardness, aggravated by holiday
clothes of a tight cut and by a paper collar bent
above his coat like a scimetar, and almost as
sharp and glistening as that weapon, impelled
him to do violence to his wishes in order to
appear calm—under *her* eyes—and to deceive
them politely as to his real desire. But now,
lured on by the siren voice of Polly, he consented
to go up " a little while" (which meant all the
afternoon), and taking the white box under his

arm he locked the shop-door and followed them
up the creaking stairs.

Arrived in the room and relieved of hat and
coat, Mr. Tripple bowed mysteriously to Dolly,
and, intrusting her with the box, whispered,—

"Go and hand that to sister Polly, little un."

Polly, receiving it from her, exclaimed in
surprise,—

"For me, Mr. Tripple?"

"Yes, miss," he replied, growing red and
smiling broadly, "a little something for Christmas, that's all."

Polly opened the box and extracted a paste-
board plane with some artificial shavings pasted
upon it, which, when lifted apart, discovered
a heap of sweetmeats. Dolly and Molly, looking on, exclaimed, "Why, Mr. Tripple, what a
surprise!" and Polly blushingly added, "So very
unexpected!"

Mr. Tripple grew redder and nervously crossed
his legs, saying, "I thought 'twould be kind a
appropriate to the trade, you know, and so I
just fetched it up, and——"

Then Polly, seeing his embarrassment, called
on David and the rest to come and help themselves, and there was good humor and laughing
until the twins darted away to get dinner, which
was soon prepared, for there was little enough
to get, and all invited to sit up to the table.

All were duly in their places, and David had, in accordance with Christmas custom, offered grace. Mr. Tripple and the girls were slowly raising their bowed heads, when a loud knock announced a visitor, and hastened the raising of heads to an unseemly hurry.

" Tom !" all exclaimed.

Molly hurried down-stairs, and the rest rushed to the stair-landing, where, in a moment, they received, not Tom, but a large, square basket, that emitted a very fragrant smell of roasted fowl, in the arms of the returning Molly. Once in the room, the lid was off in a twinkling, and out came a sizable plate, enveloped in dainty, clean napkins, which, being removed in layers, exhibited, in all its brown deliciousness, a huge turkey, just done to a turn.

The party gathered around in pleased wonder, and as Molly threw the napkins into the basket a card fell on the floor. She picked it up and, astonished, read, " Emanuel Griffin."

" What !" said David, snatching it and reading it aloud to himself, " Emanuel Griffin. So it is, and no mistake !" and then he burst out, " Hurrah ! hurrah for Griffin ! I knew he couldn't forget us this year !" His poor old face was almost young again, and his voice,—why, it could actually be heard as he ran on : " Why, there never was such a year for the china trade,

Tripple, and how could he forget me? Jacob
Tripple, your hand! A kiss, Little Scout!
Why, your old father's 'most young again, and
his good girls shall dine like other good girls,
after all! How very thoughtful of Griffin to
send it in the nick of time, too. Come, sit up
again before it gets cold, and I wish we had
something as hot to drink Griffin's health in.
Why, I believe I could sing a song again if we
had something hot. I do, indeed!"

So he ran on in his childish delight at the
thought of being remembered, and at the far
more grateful thought that his beloved daughters were to share the gift with him.

When he had ceased, all turned to Molly and
asked in one breath who had left it. When the
clamor slackened, she replied, " Why, young
Cuffy from the baker's, and all he said was,
' David Dubbs,—to be sent—card inside,' and
then kissing his hand, and crying ' Love to her,'
meaning I don't know who," with a smirk at
Polly, " he jumped aboard his wagon and flew
away down the court."

Never was a turkey enjoyed so much, and
never had a turkey better deserved it.

Mr. Tripple grew bland and talkative under
its juicy influence. He even winked at Polly
occasionally, and one time actually chucked her
under the chin. She sat next to him, remarking

that if he had his way she should live forever
on turkey and sugar-plums. David ventured to
say that that course of diet would be pretty
indigestive, whereupon Mr. Tripple fondly suggested, as he gazed into her eyes, " How would
love do for a substitute, then?" implying that
"his way" would supply that abstract edible in
equally large doses.

David dryly added " Starvation," and thereupon Polly covered her face with her hands,
but left open a laughing eye at Molly, and Mr.
Tripple looked boldly around the board as a
man who had said a very bright thing indeed,
after which survey he broke out into a not very
comfortable laugh. All the rest laughed, too,
then, and such good humor prevailed that
nothing seemed amiss, and Mr. Tripple's inex-
perience was kindly overlooked.

But now the turkey was fast becoming skele-
tonized, and the good company was fast becoming the reverse. The jollity was increasing
and the serious intentions of Mr. Tripple were
impending and ready to fall into open profession
on the slightest encouragement. The Little
Scout's pinched and pale face—sweet and uncomplaining, even through hunger and want—
smiled gently and less sadly as it leaned in
Molly's arms, and, looking up, she said,—

" Poor father! How quiet you were last

night when we were walking home. I knew
you were thinking about to-day and the poor
dinner. How kind it was of good Mr. Griffin.
I'd like to thank him myself, father!"

"And so you shall, Little Scout," said David,
gayly, bending over and kissing her with boyish
contempt of aged bones; "and so you shall,
and I make no doubt he'll be glad to see you,
too, Deary."

The clock in a neighboring steeple, simultaneously with its ancient kinsman on the shelf,
and followed by incoming echoes of a score of
others, struck one; but the company little
heeded that, and the conviviality was far from
diminishing when another summons rattled the
street door, and again all exclaimed "There's
Tom!" and crowded to the landing as before.

Polly this time tripped down and came back
in a moment with only a letter, saying,—

"A young man, father, with this letter for Mr.
Griffin. It's addressed to his store, but he said
it was important, and, knowing you lived here,
he depended on you to deliver it at once."

"Has he gone?" said David, grasping it.

"Yes, father," replied Polly, "right off."

Here was a pitiable state of affairs indeed.
David Dubbs, aroused from the joyful celebra-
tion of his Christmas dinner and from the midst
of this cosey party and sent off across the river

to his master's house with a miserable letter and
by a miserable young man (and if delivering
letters when every other well-intentioned man
is eating his turkey isn't miserable, why what
is it?). Sent off on a graceless errand for
nothing, perhaps. But his kind employer, who
had done so much for his comfort and joy that
very day, must not suffer by his neglect, and
off he must post; that was imperative. Mr.
Tripple offered his services when David had
started down-stairs, and when there was no
chance of his turning back, but David said,
" No, no, Tripple; you just stay and keep the
girls company till I get back, and that'll be
enough for you to attend to. Good-by, girls.
Good-by, Little Scout; if it wasn't so cold, she
should go too." And off he trudged, as patient,
and cheerful, and proud of his master's attention and of his mission, too, now he had fully
set out, as many a younger and better dressed
man would have been.

IV.

When Emanuel Griffin, Esq., leaving the
dark little street wherein stood his warehouse
and wherein very much of his life and very
little of his money was spent—which latter

fact had, however, no merely local application but was of a general nature—when, to resume, Emanuel Griffin, Esq., buttoning up his overcoat and, leaving the dark little street, turned the next corner among the mountainous stores and looked vexedly around for a car to bear him to his home across the river, and rattled his keys in his pocket, and nearly hummed a tune in his impatience, suddenly, as the car appeared like a new planet, and with the easy-going motions of a planet in its ascent had nearly reached him— suddenly a thought of something forgotten flashed through his mind, and the violence of its reaction turned him completely around and sent him in a precipitous hurry in the opposite direction, namely, in that which David Dubbs and his little daughter had pursued but a short time before.

"Pshaw!" he muttered, and looked as if he would like to add something a great deal stronger. "That's what I forgot to tell David; but Mrs. G. 'll never forget it, nor forgive it, either, if I don't attend to it before I get home." So he turned up his collar, and rubbed his ears, and hurried on to keep warm.

His destination proved to be a fancy bakery in the neighborhood of David Dubbs's house. The pavement in front of it at that hour and season, owing to holiday orders, was sending up warm steam from the oven beneath, and a fragrant and appetizing smell of hot bread and browning cakes pervaded the street. It was a large establishment of the kind, and besides its legitimate line of bread-baking, took charge of the cooking and preparing of dinners for ladies of limited domestic conveniences in fashionable life. Heedless of the delicious scents which had attracted several men with greedy eyes to linger at the window and devour in fancy—a process which left them hungrier than ever—the heaps of loaves and cakes on the counter within; heedless of the supplicating looks the men turned on him, and of the confidential attempts of one or two at a begging whisper (but his hurry was in nowise chargeable with that inattention); heedless of everything but finishing his errand and getting home, Mr. Griffin pushed through the crowd in the store, and, reaching the counter, beckoned to a light-haired, light-eyed, and red-cheeked youth, in a blue tie and black waistcoat that, through constant friction with loaves and flour-barrels, had become of a light pepper-and-salt pattern, and hurriedly said,—

"I want a turkey, Cuffy, of about fifteen or twenty pounds, cooked and sent to my house by one o'clock to-morrow."

"Can't do it, Mr. Griffin," said the young

man, who knew him and had bowed as he came up.

"Can't do what?" exclaimed Mr. Griffin, with surprise and dismay.

"Can't send it out," returned the young man, firmly.

"Oh!" said Mr. Griffin, relieved; "I thought you meant that you couldn't prepare it!"

"No, sir," commenced the young man. "You see, sir, Mr. Griffin, it's so late in the day that all our teams is ordered fur to-morrow at that time, and so is our boys, but——"

"Well, I'll soon fix that, Cuffy, said Mr. Griffin, opening his coat and taking out a card. "There, just pin that on the turkey when it is ready, and carry it over here to Dubbs's— David Dubbs is my clerk. He will understand the card, and bring the turkey out to my house. I shouldn't be so particular about it if Mrs Griffin had not impressed it on me this morning. I almost forgot it, too."

Then asking the price, and answering,—

"That is very high, Cuffy;" to which that young man replied,—

"I know it is, sir, Mr. Griffin, but then, you see, the demand is werry great, sir."

Mr. Griffin paid the bill and hurried out, took a car at the next corner, and, after a long, cold ride, got home to allay the anxiety of Mrs.

Griffin by assuring her that the turkey was
ordered, and would be sent home promptly to-
morrow by David Dubbs.

Christmas morning was, among the Griffin
household, which consisted of Mr. and Mrs.
Griffin and a superannuated servant, a very
busy morning indeed, for the reason that Mrs.
Griffin had, according to annual custom, invited
more guests to dine than she could conveniently
provide for. Their house was a cottage in the
suburbs, pretty enough in summer and no thanks
to its mistress or the superannuated servant
either, but to the unaided impulse of nature,
which climbed, in the form of bowery vines,
wherever a vine could find clinging room ; but
now, in the midst of winter, bright though the
day was, the skeletons of so much green gayety
looked bare, and inhospitable, and cold. The
house was approached by a long path that
started at the iron gate and led up to the porch.
It was far from a large house, and looked inconvenient, and famished for paint, and it was
no less inconvenient than it looked, a fact,
indeed, which necessitated the purchase of a
cooked turkey, for the oven was small, and the
stove in the crazy little kitchen needed all the
surface it could afford for the vegetables, oysters,
and other viands which then only, throughout
the year, it blazed and glowed under.

The morning wore on and twelve o'clock
arrived. The big table in the little dining-room
was duly dressed and adorned with Mrs. Griffin's
miscellaneous silver; and after a heated debate
between that lady and the Superannuated, it
was decided that when the company were all
in the parlor the dining-room door should be
left open, and at the bottom of the table, which
now projected against the door, an additional
chair for Mr. Griffin should be inserted. Mrs.
Griffin said of course the company must squeeze
in, but they understood all that, and were glad
enough to get in by any means, to which Superannuated readily assented.

One o'clock, and now the company were all
arrived. Mrs. Griffin was duly excused by Mr.
Griffin, who received them, on the plea of
domestic duties. They were mostly in the
parlor, which contained, beside them, a set of
red velvet furniture and a shining piano, on
legs which emulated the unsteadiness of Superannuated's own, and which, in huskiness of
voice, also resembled that person; a portrait of
Mr. Griffin in rigid broadcloth, and a companion
portrait of Mrs. Griffin in low neck and volumes
of lace; and last, a very pimply-looking carpet,
which seemed to suffer from a severe rash.

Mr. Griffin had occupied the space between
the folding-doors as the company arrived and

suavely—as suavely, by the way, as his wincing
at the cost of it all would admit of—received,
introduced, and seated them. The first arrival
was a single gentleman, whom he saluted as
Fred. He was short, and bald, and spasmodic,
—so much so that his pantaloons were never
straight, and his collar, through much moisten-
ing of its raspy edges, was soiled. After him,
a lady and gentleman drove up to the gate in a
carriage, and, alighting, the lady swept up the
path, in a double sense, while her husband up-
braided the driver for the muddy condition of
the carriage, and then, loudly, " At ten, William!" To which William as loudly replied,
" Can't do it, sir. Got another order; but I'll
send you another man."

The gentleman answered more quietly, with
a careful look at the house, where Mr. Griffin
awaited him on the porch,—

" Very well, driver;" and also swept in, and
was introduced to Fred as Mr. Abbert.

Now came a pair who walked, and were addressed and handed around by the host as " My
dear friends, Mr. and Mrs. Dripps;" and then
the volume of newcomers became quite abun-
dant; so much so that a number of gentlemen
with no apparent use for their hands were
forced to lean about the hall and sit on the
stairs, which they did up to the very top one.

When the company had simmered down a good
deal, and only a few very bold gentlemen ventured to launch remarks into the unanswering
silence, and when everybody was wondering
what everybody else was going to do next, and
all were, as they reported the next day, " enjoying themselves immensely," there was a stir
above stairs, a rustling of dresses, and then the
gentlemen on the stairs, like a row of falling
bricks, were driven down before the gracious
smiles and bows of the transformed hostess.

Tripping down after them and falling at last
into the extended arms of her husband—rather
unsteady under the weight—while the stiffly
polite gentlemen formed a compact crowd out
to the door, Mrs. Griffin was led, with no little
difficulty, through the seated guests, bestowing
bows, and smiles, and " Glad to see you, my
dear Mr. Dripps," and " How well you're looking, my dear Mrs. Abbert," and " Welcome,
gentlemen," (whereat a murmur ran through
the crowd and all shook their heads and tried
to turn round and bow, but utterly failed,) and
" Oh! here's my old Fred," and sundry other
bewitching remarks that led the crowd of gentlemen to murmur again something like " Charming, be Gad!" and grow uneasy.

But now the bell was rung by Superannuated,
who had duly inserted the chair, and Mr. Abbert.

receiving the hostess from the arm of her husband and in turn delivering his smiling wife to Mr. Griffin, led off the throng to dinner.

When they arrived at the protruding table, by a preconcerted arrangement Mrs. Griffin handed Mr. Abbert to the one side and squeezed herself through the other—an action which was imitated by the rest of the company, who were finally seated close up to the door—all but Mr. Griffin, who was to occupy the extra chair, and, as he was already inside, and there was no other means of exit, he was obliged to pass through the kitchen and around the house. He soon appeared again through the front door and the dinner began.

Mrs. Griffin, who had long before left Superannuated to finish while she perfected her toilet, now rang the bell, and, on her appearance, whispered in her ear. Superannuated whispered in her mistress's ear. Mrs. Griffin thereupon uttered a little cry and looked at Mr. Griffin. Mr. Griffin, in consternation, cried, "My dear!" and attempted to squeeze between the chairs, but failed. Then he looked wildly about him, and at last ran through the front door. He soon reappeared at the side of his fainting wife, who revived enough to say,—

"I shall never, never forgive you! Oh, the humiliation! the agony!" then fainted again.

14

" What is it ?" " What's the matter ?" " She's fainted !" and confused screams of the ladies came from all sides. Mrs. Dripps passed along her salts bottle. Mrs. Abbert held Mrs. Griffin's head, and Fred applied water. Under the strong influence of these restoratives she soon revived, and whispered to her husband something which caused him also to start and look despairingly at her.

She then said to him, loud enough for all to hear, " You must tell them it was your fault. Oh, the humiliation !" Here she burst out again, with her handkerchief to her eyes, and Mrs. Abbert soothingly said, " Oh, never mind him, my dear. I wouldn't mind him !" This was growing invidious, and all the gentlemen at the bottom of the table were looking scornfully at him.

He therefore said, in a loud voice,—

" The turkey has not arrived,—that is all."

" That is all," whimpered Mrs. Griffin, mockingly. " That is all, he says ; and isn't it enough, sir, to have all your domestic failings exposed to the world ?"

Mrs. Griffin alluded to cooking facilities, and grew very bitter, while " the world" simpered and exchanged looks.

Mr. Griffin then, in desperation, explained the whole matter,—how he had left the card for

David Dubbs, and paid for the turkey, and come unsuspectingly home. " As," he added, " I have done year after year, for——"

Here Mrs. Griffin checked him with symptoms of another faint, and he stopped short.

Mr. Abbert then said it was all that rascally clerk, and he ought to be discharged at once.

" I know 'em," he added violently and with deeply implied wisdom, which, by the way, was the only species of wisdom he ever attained to. " I know 'em, Griffin !"

Mr. Fred was of a similar opinion, and even more violent in his denunciation of David, as he had set his heart on turkey, and the appetite died painfully within him.

All the ladies and gentlemen were of various opinions, but all concentrated their rage on the poor, innocent little clerk, and panted for his clerkly death. In the midst of all this commotion the door-bell rang, and intensified it twofold, for nobody could get through to the door but by going around the house. This Superannuated finally did, and brought back with her the identical little clerk,—the poor, agitated, and bowing little clerk who had unconsciously aroused all the indignation and tumult, whom sundry gentlemen at the lower end of the table had threatened with severe punishment if they ever caught sight of him, and who, now catching sight of him, were more than usually silent.

Mr. Griffin looked threateningly at him as, hat in hand, he walked up to him, presented a letter, and, in his faint voice, said,—

"A letter for you, sir, left for me to deliver."

He took it, and David continued tremulously to say,—

"And how can I thank you, sir, and madam," turning to Mrs. Griffin, "for the bounteous gift——"

"Gift?" exclaimed both in a breath; "what gift? Where is the turkey you brought? What gift? What gift?"

"Why, a splendid turkey, with your card kindly——"

This was received by the company with a volley of cries and calls, by a relapse on the part of Mrs. Griffin, and by the descent of Mr. Griffin's hand upon David's coat-collar, and finally by poor, frightened David's ejectment from the kitchen-door, harshly reproached by his employer as a thief and vagabond, and warned never to show his face in his store again.

"Be off, now!" he cried after him, "you ungrateful, deceitful old villain!" and then he slammed the door, and joined the hungry guests, to whom he declaimed at some length on the thanklessness of the lower classes.

Mrs. Griffin was quickly re-restored, this time to a state of injured perfection, and after the united apologies of herself and husband, and more abuse of poor, luckless David Dubbs, the company concluded with pretty bad grace to make the most of what had been prepared in the way of vegetables and side dishes, long ago cold. Mr. Griffin was mad, insulted, and hungry, and the contents of the letter he had received seemed to add very little warmth to the food, but a great deal to his anger, for he tore it up into very small pieces, as if it were David himself he was torturing, and, with a look the company did not consider very sociable, scattered it on the floor.

V.

The sky, as if presaging David Dubbs's misfortune, had grown overcast, and flung down spiteful little sallies of snow as he crossed the river on his way to Mr. Griffin's. The creaking of the bridge's huge timbers and the splitting ice below it made him shiver and pull his threadbare coat close about him and sacrifice his old hands to the wind to save his freezing ears. The same scarf bound them as the night before, but an icy gale like that which swept from the open river would have frozen through arctic furs. Notwithstanding all this, his spirits were lighter than usual. The scene he had left at home floated on before his eyes, and transfused itself with the black, sketchy trees against the sky and blent with the ragged barbs of smoke that depended from cottage chimneys. The wind had been boisterous enough, and would have torn it away on a cantering jaunt not many minutes ago, but, surcharged as it was now with blinding snow, it had its own liberty to look after, and paid little heed to anything else.

The snow came on thicker and thicker, and had begun to whiten the streets by the time David reached Mr. Griffin's house, and now, as he stood shocked and bewildered in the garden again, it lay deep and dreadfully silent as far as the eye could reach. Had he heard truly? Had he, for the first time in a long, and honest, and reputable life, been called a thief? And by the man whom his heart had overflowed in gratitude to but a moment before! David Dubbs a thief! And what of? What had he stolen? Oh, it was cruel to his poor old heart! "And the girls so merry, even now," he thought. How; how could he go to them with these bitter tidings? To be deprived of even the poor means his pen had faithfully and honestly earned for them; to toil so long, so wearily for the meed of a thief, for the name of a thief! and he wept in his utter woe.

His hat was still on his head, his coat was
undone, his scarf had fallen back on his shoulders; his poor old eyes were wide apart again,
now, and the wind tugged at his scanty hair,
and the snow, no whiter than itself, sifted
through it and drifted into the folds of his
clothes. But, stunned, and tortured, and de-
spairing though he was, the old clerk staggered
on insensibly homeward. Back through the
dreary trees; back through the drifted streets;
back to the bridge, where he stopped by some
fatal impulse and leaned near a bleak abut-
ment that overlooked the river—gazing, gazing,
gazing in a blank stare at the driving channel
below. The thought, the lurking purpose was
shadowed dimly on his distraught mind. The
cold, rolling river once passed, the seething
cakes of ice once passed, and it would soon be
over, soon be over. Life had been a worthless
gift to him. His youth had been falsely colored by the visions of childhood; his age had
been falsely colored by the ambitions of youth.
Nothing he had looked to in the distance ever
had grown into reality. Why should he survive his good name! And he clutched the
stones and raised himself up and quivered at
the top of the stone wall.

But now his hand relaxed, and his face,
clouded and suffering before, fell into a calmer

look of attention, almost a smile broke over it, and he gazed out against the sky as if transfixed.

It was the vision that had, like the pillar of cloud by day and of fire by night, preceded and gladdened him on his way; the scene of his happy, unsuspecting girls; of the pale Little Scout—whose simple touch would then have instantly revived and soothed him, whose tender love was his comfort, his sanctuary from pursuing evils; the scene of his old home, far cosier, far more beloved, far more cheerful for all its homeliness, for all its poverty, than the more pretentious one of Emanuel Griffin; the scene of lowly pleasures it had cherished; of the bitter trials it had assuaged; and, finally, of the bright, laughing group he had left there, oh! so little prepared, so little conscious of the blight he would bring among them. This vision, these thoughts had flowed in upon his already disturbed mind, and had driven quite away all consciousness of where he was or how long he had stood in the bitter cold, when a policeman—overcoated, and furred, and frozen-bearded,—came by, and, suspecting things to be not altogether right, caught David by the sleeve, and adjusted his scarf and hat, saying,—

"No loafing on the bridge, old man. Move on; move on, now!" at which David started, looked all around him, and then moved on as commanded. His back, always bent, and his gait, always decrepit and shuffling, were now pitiably so, and he had a long, long journey before him; but, thanks be to Him whose omnipotent care protects and watches over the poor in spirit, he had escaped a far longer one. On and on he went, not cold now, not thinking, not in haste; passing thick-coated travellers who ran, and clapped their hands, and swung their arms for warmth; passing gay companies in cabs that rolled over the snow as softly as footsteps on velvet. But he heeded nothing of all this, and staggered onward to his own poor home.

A light was streaming out from the windows of the old warehouse, crossing the snow piled on the platform above and slanting on the heaps beneath. It was an inviting glimmer, a herald from within to all cold travellers without of the blessedness of home, and, as David approached the corner of the court, his eye was greeted cheerily by its " Welcome home !" and, indeed, it was the first thing he had distinctly seen since leaving the house of Mr. Griffin. But his heart failed him. How could he face his dear girls again and tell them of the destitution of to-morrow ? Of the worse than poverty ? Thus he thought, and lingered, and slunk away

by turns, but the ray of home-born light allured
him, impassively, into its midst, and as he stood
over against the house, a poor, weak, old man,
rambling in his mind, and heroically deciding
rather to leave them in peace to-night, one more
night, and return to them to-morrow, a window
was thrown up, and Jacob Tripple, putting forth
his head, looked up and down the court, and
then directly in front of him, where David
stood immovable in the light.

"Why, there he is, now!" he cried. "What's
gone amiss, David? What's kept you so long?
Here he is! Here he is!" he exclaimed again
and again, and, drawing in his head in much
less time than the words could be said, Jacob
Tripple, followed by the girls, was down-stairs,
was—still followed by the girls—out in the
snow, and had forcibly carried David up with
them.

They laid him on the settee, moaning and
crying aloud against Emanuel Griffin, and
repeating again and again that they were
"Beggars, beggars, beggars!" and exclaiming,
"My poor Little Scout! My poor girls! My
poor——"

"They shall not suffer, father!" said a new
voice, the sound of which raised him up with
wide-opened eyes and palsied hands at his head,
and a long stare at the speaker—"It's Tom,

father. Don't you know me?" repeated the voice.

Know him! How should he know him? tall, and brawny, and whiskered, with pleasant blue eyes, and ruddy cheeks, and good nature streaming from his whole face! Him who, so many years ago,—a beardless youth—had run off to California after gold bubbles, and whom little good had been heard of when anything at all was heard of him. Know him? Of course he did not; but, as he sat down beside him on the settee and shook his old hand, David put his arms about his neck, and hung his head upon his bosom, and saw, in imagination, the thriftless boy of long ago whom he loved for all his waywardness.

Tom's strong arms soon bore him to his old seat near the fire, and, for the first time, David's wandering eye noticed the bower of green holly and red-berried mistletoe that decked the room. General Washington was loaded with it. The old clock, actually striking in a cheerier voice the hour of nine, had its full share. The dresser hid in festoons of it. Even David's chair had its sprig. But what was that on the floor? An opened trunk, like a cloven pomegranate, displaying within rich trinkets that many a lady might covet?

"Wha—what's it all mean, girls? Tell me,

Little Scout," said David, catching her hand.
"What happened to me? I thought I came
home—home to tell you Griffin threw me out in
the snow, and called me a thief, and how all of
them scowled and cried out at me, and I
thought——" then, looking at the tall man, he
cried again,—

"Tom, is it so? Is it so, my dear boy?"

"Yes, father," said Tom, slowly, to calm him,
"it is, happily, all so."

Then his little daughter, who had stood by
his side through it all, kissed him, and said,—

"Come, father, look at the pretty presents
Tom has brought us and you. See here's a
beautiful new coat hanging on your peg for
you, and Molly and Polly are as gay as any
ladies," and she led him, tottering and feeble,
to the loaded table—no longer ashamed of its
defaced back beneath the pile of gifts it bore.

Then Mr. Tripple, hand in hand with the un-
resisting Polly, and Molly, and Tom, an unbroken
circuit, of cheery faces that electrified David
Dubbs into a wrinkled smile in spite of lingering grief, clustered around the table and exclaimed aloud with admiration at the gifts Tom
had brought.

But David, still overshadowed by the events
of the afternoon, said, in a quivering voice,—

"But to-morrow, children, to-morrow! I am

discharged by Griffin; we shall starve to-morrow!"

"Not while I'm about," laughed Tom. "Come, come, be calm, and I'll tell you all about it."

And he did tell of the long years of hope and distress, of despair when unconsciously within reach of fortune; of its final realization and of its golden yield. "So here I am, father, and your old hand shall write no more for Emanuel Griffin."

Then said Dolly, "You don't speak, father; you are surely not sorry?"

Sorry! He was stifled with gratitude; he was transforming into his old self. The familiar tenderness of her voice opened the floodgates of his heart, and he burst into a louder "Hurrah" than over Griffin's turkey, and kissed them all around, Mr. Tripple included, and, indeed, the day had been so successfully employed on the part of that gentleman that his early entrance into the family was far from problematical—so of course David did perfectly right.

Polly here broke in, "And, father, it was Tom who brought the note, and Tom who planned the surprise for you. What did it say, Tom? you can tell us now."

He laughed quietly, and then said, as if he

were reading impressively from the open sheet to Mr. Griffin himself, and making him writhe under his coolness,—

"EMANUEL GRIFFIN,

"SIR: The connection of my father, David Dubbs, Esq., with your counting-house, will cease from this day forth.

"Sir, your obedient servant,

"THOMAS DUBBS."

Told by an English Tourist.

"He seemed to be a kind of con-
necting link between the old
times and the new, and to be,
withal, a little antiquated in the
taste of his accomplishments."
Irving.

A STILL CHRISTMAS.

It was Christmas eve in the year of our Lord 1653. The snow, which had fallen fitfully throughout the day, shrouded in white the sloping roofs and narrow London streets, and lay in little, sparkling heaps on every jutting cornice or narrow window-ledge where it could find a resting-place. But in the west the setting sun shone clearly, firing the steeples into sudden glory and gilding every tiny pane of glass that faced its dying splendor. The thoroughfares were strangely silent and deserted. The roving groups that had been wont at this season to fill them with boisterous merriment, the noise, the bustle, the good cheer of Christmas—all were lacking. No maskers roamed from street to street, jingling their bells, beating their mighty drums, and bidding the delighted crowd to make way for the Lord of Misrule. No shouts of "Noel! Noel!" rang through the frosty air. No children gathered round their neighbors' doors, singing quaint carols and forgotten glees, and bearing off rich guerdon in the shape of

apples, nuts, and substantial Christmas buns.
In place of the old-time gayety a dreary silence
reigned through the deserted highways, and
down the narrow footwalk, with even step and
half-shut eyes, tramped the Puritan herald,
ringing his bell and proclaiming ever and anon
in measured tones, " No Christmas !   No Christmas !"

In sober and sad-hued garments was the herald arrayed, with leathern boots that defied the
snow, and a copious mantle enveloping his
sturdy frame.   Now and then he stopped to
warn a couple of belated idlers that they would
do well to separate and go quietly to their homes.
Now and then a little child peeped at him
timorously from a doorway, and, overawed by
his sombre aspect and heavy frown, retreated
rapidly to hide its fears in the safe shelter of its
mother's gown.   Men shook their heads as he
went by, and muttered something that was not
always complimentary to his presence ; and
women shrugged their shoulders and sighed,
and thought, perchance, of other Christmases
in the past, with Yule-logs burning on the
hearth and stray kisses snatched beneath the
mistletoe.   From a latticed window a girl's face
peered at him with such a light of laughing
malice in the brown eyes that the Puritan,
catching sight of their wicked gleam, paused a

moment, as though to reprove the maiden for
her forwardness, or to inquire what mischief
was afoot under this humble roof. But the
night was growing chill, and he had still far
to go. It might not be worth while to waste
words of counsel on one so evidently godless;
and, with a heavier scowl than usual, he tramped
on, swinging his bell with lusty force. "No
Christmas! No Christmas!" echoed through
the darkening streets, and, as he passed, the
girl contracted her features into a grimace that
would have done credit to the wide-mouthed
gargoyle of a Gothic cathedral.

"Cicely, Cicely!" cried a voice, at this junc-
ture, from within, "close the shutters, do, and
come and help me."

Cicely, who had been inclined to stare out a
little longer, shot the heavy oaken bolt into its
socket, and, opening a door leading to the inner
room, disclosed a scene whose ruddy cheerfulness shone all the brighter in contrast to the
dreary streets outside. A mighty bunch of
fagots blazed and crackled on the hearth, and
above the carved chimney-place hung branches
of holly, their scarlet berries glowing deeply in
the firelight. In one corner, half-veiled by a
tapestry curtain, a waxen Bambino nestled in
its little manger, while before it burned a small
copper lamp. Wreaths of holly and ivy be-

decked the doors, and, standing tip-toed on a
tall wooden chair, a young girl was even now
striving to fasten these securely with the aid of
a very old and wrinkled woman, who seemed
more competent to admire than to assist the
undertaking.

"Some bigger berries, pray, Catherine," she
said, impatiently; "and, Cicely, if you feel you
have loitered enough, hand me those two long
ivy branches. They should droop gracefully—
so! And now stand off a little way and tell
me how it looks."

The younger sister obeyed, and, stationing
herself in the middle of the room, surveyed the
whole effect with much approval. Annis, her
fair face flushed with the exertion, balanced
herself on her lofty perch and gazed complacently upon her handiwork; while even
Mistress Vane, who had been seated quietly on
a deep chair by the fireplace, roused herself as
from a reverie, and looked half-wistfully around
the cheerful room. "What bell was that I
heard just now?" she asked.

"The herald's, proclaiming a still Christmas,"
answered Cicely, promptly; "and he watched
me as sourly as though he knew that we were
plotting treason."

"Cecil, Cecil!" remonstrated her mother, in
alarm. "Surely you did nothing imprudent."

" I ?" returned Cicely, apparently oblivious as
to what she had done. " I cast up the whites
of my eyes, as though repeating psalms for
mine own inward sustainment; and seeing me
so piously disposed, he was fain to pass on to
the correction of greater sinners."

"That were well-nigh impossible," said her
sister, laughing; but Mistress Vane only looked
anxious and disturbed. The sense of insecurity
to which Annis was indifferent, and which
Cicely at fourteen found absolutely amusing,
weighed heavily on the older woman, who had
a better understanding of the danger, and who
had suffered cruelly in the past. Husband and
son had fallen for a lost cause, confiscation had
devoured the larger portion of her once fair
inheritance; and now, with her two young
daughters, she found herself beset by perils,
harassed by stringent laws, and at the mercy
of any ill-wind fate might blow her. Crom-
well's mighty arm held the fretful country in
subjection, making the name of England great
and terrible abroad, and silencing every whisper
of disaffection at home. The Puritans, in their
hour of triumph, stamped upon the land the
impress of their strong and bitter individuality;
and a morose asceticism, part real and part
affected, crushed out of life all the innocent
pleasure of living. With every man determined

I.—*m*

to be better than his neighbor, the competition
in saintliness ran high.   Under its vigorous
stimulus the May-pole and the Yule-log were
alike branded as heathenish observances, the
Christmas-pie became a "pye of abomination,"
and all amusements, from the drama to bear-
baiting, were censured with impartial severity.
Feast-days were abolished, and even to display
the emblems of the Nativity was held to be
sedition.   The Established Church, cowed and
shorn of its splendor, was treated with surly
contempt ; the Catholics were altogether beyond
the pale of charity.   It was not a time calcu-
lated to promote festivity ; yet, while the heralds proclaimed through the frosty streets that
Christmas at last was dead, Annis Vane, with
holly and ivy, with Yule-dough and Babie-cake,
was making all things ready for its mysterious
birth.   And as she worked she sang softly under
breath the refrain of a carol she had learned at
her nurse's knee,—

> " This endris night
> I saw a sight, •
>   A star as bright as day ;
> And ever among
> A maiden sung
>   Lullay, by· by, lullay."

   " Is it not strange, mother," she said, breaking
suddenly off, " that men should deem it a mark

of holiness to cast derision on the birth-night
of their Saviour?"

"Let us be just even to our enemies," replied
Mistress Vane, gently. "They think not to
deride the Nativity, so much as to condemn the
riotous fashion in which Christians were wont
to keep the feast. There have been times,
Annis, when the Lord of Misrule did more dis-
credit to this holy season than does the Puritan
to-day."

Annis opened her blue eyes to their very
utmost. This view of the matter was one she
was hardly prepared to accept "Why, dearest
mother," she protested, "when should we venture to be happy, if not on Christmas-day?
And how can we show ourselves too joyful for
our salvation? And did not his most blessed
majesty King Charles knight with his own
royal hand a Lord of Misrule who held court
in the Middle Temple?"

Mistress Vane smiled at her daughter's vehemence. She knew more about these jovial
monarchs and their courts than Annis did, and
it may even be that his most blessed majesty's
approval carried less weight to her experienced
mind. But in these dark and chilly days a
little enthusiasm was helpful in keeping one's
heart warm, and she was far too wise a mother
to disparage it. "Truly they made a brave

show then upon Christmas-day," she admitted,
" for the lord mayor and his corporation, a
goodly company of gentlemen, rode in procession to the church of St. Thomas Acon, and
thence to dine together with many pleasant
ceremonies. And stoups of wine and huge
venison pasties were despatched to the Temple
for the stay and comfort of the mock-court,
who made merry all day long. And the streets
were crowded, far into the night, with maskers
and revellers; and even the poor might for once
forget their poverty, and were welcome to the
brawn and plum-broth of their richer neighbors."

" And now we have nothing of all this!" cried
Cicely, with passionate regret. " Nothing to
look at and nothing to hear save the cracked
bell of a dingy herald, who does not even ride
a hobby-horse like the merry heralds of old.
In truth, Master Prynne hath made good his
own words when he holds that Christmas should
be rather a day of mourning than one of rejoicing."

" Not so thought my godfather, kind Master Breton," said Annis, thoughtfully. " For he
hath written that it is the duty of Christians to
rejoice for the remembrance of Christ and for
the maintenance of good-fellowship. ' I hold
it,' he hath said, ' a memory of the Heaven's

love and the world's peace, the mirth of the
honest and the meeting of the friendly.'"

Cicely's eyes danced with glee. "That were
well remembered," she said, mockingiy; "if,
now, you can but tell us in turn what your
godfather's nephew, Captain Rupert Breton,
hath thought upon the matter."

Annis flushed scarlet, and the quick tears
welled into her eyes as she turned them re-
proachfully upon her sister. It was not easy
for her to think of her absent lover and maintain the cheerful frame of mind she deemed
appropriate to the season. The shores of France
seemed very far away that night, and the long
months that had elapsed since the defeat at
Wórcester stretched backward like a lifetime,
as she recalled his last hurried farewell. He
had ridden hard and risked much for those few
words, and patiently and bravely she had waited
ever since, hoping, praying, turning her face
steadily to the brighter side, and keeping ever
in mind the happy hour which should reunite
them to each other. Now, in silence, she bound
together the last green boughs and put all in
order for the night. Old Catherine had long
since gone off, yawning and blinking, to bed,
and Cicely, half-asleep, nodded over the dying
fire. Only her mother watched her, with eyes
of loving scrutiny, and Annis smiled brightly as

16

she kissed the careworn face. " I shall not cry myself to sleep to-night," she said, resolutely. " This is a time for gladness; for the star of Bethlehem is shining in the sky, and the birth of the Lord is at hand."

Bright glowed the Christmas-logs on the capacious hearth till every pointed leaf and scarlet holly-berry shone in the generous fire-light.

> " Whosoever against holly doth cry,
> In a rope shall be hung full high."

For, when the oak and ash trees babbled to the wind, and betrayed the Saviour's hiding-place, the holly, the ivy, and the pine kept the secret hidden in their silent hearts; and for this good deed they stand green and living under winter's icy breath, while their companions shiver naked in the blast. Not till the risen sun has danced on Easter morn shall the oak adorn a Christian household and prove itself forgiven. The Christmas-pie—the Christ-cradle, as the Saxons used to call it—had been baked in its oblong dish in memory of the manger at Bethlehem, with the star of the Magi cut deeply in the swelling crust. The Yule-dough, cunningly moulded into the likeness of a little babe, had been carefully laid by as a sovereign protector from the evils of fire, floods, carnage, and—so

say some ancient writers—from the bite of
rabid dogs. Annis Vane, decked out in the
bravest array her altered fortunes would permit,
knelt by the blazing hearth. Her ruff was of
the finest lace, and a row of milk-white pearls
clasped her slender throat. She shaded her
face from the fire, and piled up shining cones
of bright-brown nuts that seemed to tempt the
flames.

"All we lack now is the mistletoe," she said,
half-despondently. "It was no easy task to find
the holly and bring it home unnoticed; but
we cannot gather mistletoe near London, and
there is none for sale throughout the city."

"Of what use is the mistletoe," said the practical Cicely, "when we are but three women
here alone? We can kiss each other as readily
under a sprig of ivy, and we can fire our nuts
without the help of man or lad, provided only
we keep one in our minds. Of whom shall I
think, Annis?" she queried, wrinkling up her
pretty forehead in anxious perplexity over so
disturbing a doubt.

"You are far too young to think of men at
all," answered Annis, reprovingly, and with all
the conscious superiority of age. "Nor do you
know enough as yet to make such pastime
profitable."

Cicely's brows drew together with a frown

which plainly indicated the nature of the retort upon her lips, but a glance from her mother checked her. "The word uttered in vexation is better left unspoken," said Mistress Vane, with gentle authority. "And I am waiting here, not to listen to disputes, which in these stormy times have grown wearisome, but to hear the Christmas carol promised me to-night."

Annis, with flushed cheeks, took down from the wall a little mandolin of Spanish workmanship, and, striking a few chords, began the carol, in which Cicely, after sacrificing some moments to ill-temper, concluded presently to join, her clear flute-notes rising high above her sister's weaker tones,—

"When Christ was born of Mary free,
  In Bethlehem, in that fair citie,
  Angels sungen with mirth and glee,
      In Excelsis Gloria!

"Herdsmen beheld these angels bright
  To them appearèd with great light,
  And said, God's Son is born this night—
      In Excelsis Gloria!

"The King is comen to save kind,
  Even in Scripture as we find;
  Therefore this song have we in mind,
      In Excelsis Gloria!

" Then, dear Lord, for thy great grace,
  Grant us in bliss to see thy face,
  Where we may sing to thee solace,
    In Excelsis Gloria !"

As the sounds died into silence there stood
one in the icy streets and listened. No self-
elected saint was he, scenting out treason to the
Commonwealth, but a cavalier from France,
with his love-locks shorn for sweet prudence's
sake, and a mighty mantle enveloping him from
head to foot. If Annis Vane had waited, and
hoped, and built up her faith in the cheer of
Christmas-night, the joy she coveted was very
near at last. After lingering a few moments,
as though on the chance of hearing more, the
stranger advanced and knocked sharply at the
heavily-barred door. It was opened in due
season and with great caution by old Catherine,
who evidently thought the hour ill-chosen for a
new-comer, and mistrusted sorely the purpose
of his visit. He allowed her scant time, however, to threaten or expostulate, but, putting
her gently on one side, stepped to the inner
room. There, pale with anxiety and terror,
Mistress Vane leaned forward in her chair, while
Cicely, half-frightened, half-defiant, grasped her
mother's skirt. Before the fire stood Annis.
her blue eyes shining like stars, a round, red

16*

spot burning feverishly in each cheek, her lace
ruff rising and falling distressfully with the
heaving bosom within.   The mandolin had fallen
from her hands; the ruddy firelight lit up her
slight figure and fair, disordered curls.   She
stood thus for a moment, swaying breathless
betwixt hope and fear, then, with a low, joyous
cry, sprang forward into her lover's arms.

Welcome now the good cheer of Christmas-
night!   Welcome the Christmas-pie, the pasty
of venison, the pudding. stuffed with plums, and
the flagon of old wine.   Love is a brave ap-
petizer when backed by long fasting and a ten
hours' ride, and Captain Breton brought all the
vigor of youth and happiness and of a noble
hunger to bear upon the viands.   The glow of
the cheerful room was infinitely comforting to
the tired traveller; the sight of Annis's happy
face put fresh hope and courage in his heart.
He had much to tell of the gay court of France,
and of the royal exile, who should one day,
God willing, sit on his father's throne.   Nor
were there lacking adventures and dangers of
his own to give flavor to the narrative, nor
plans for the future, colored with all the happy
confidence of youth.   He had come home to
win his bride, and to carry her away to brighter
scenes until this soured and gloomy England
should be merrie England once more.   "He

who would keep a light heart within London
walls," said he, "must needs be very sure of
heaven, as are Master Prynne and Master Philip
Stubbes, or very much in love, as am I. It
lacks but a covered cart and a bell in every
street to make one feel the Black Death is upon
us. If you can laugh in such an atmosphere
of melancholy, Annis, what will you do in
France ?"

"Mayhap if I laugh enough in sober London
I shall grow too giddy and forward in foolish
France," returned Annis, gayly; "unless——"

"Unless what, dear heart ?"

"Unless while I am safe in Paris you are
fighting the battles of the king in England.
Then tears will come easier than laughter, as in
truth they have done of late."

"Wherever I may be, your prayers will prove
my bulwark," said Captain Breton, confidently.
"It would take more than a silver bullet to find
its way to my heart while you are besieging
heaven's doors in the tumultuous fashion that
only women can attain. I bear a charmed life
as long as you remember your petitions."

Annis answered with a look, and Cicely,
nestling by her mother's chair, watched her
sister with wide, serious eyes. To the child
standing on the threshold of womanhood the
presence of love carries with it an intoxicating

flavor of mystery, It is something that fills
her alike with envy and a vague resentment,
with wonder and an indefinable desire. Its
commonest expression is a perverse antipathy
to one of the lovers, with an irrational increase
of affection for the other; and in this case
Captain Breton came in for his full share of
Cicely's smothered anger and disdain. He,
meanwhile, in happy unconsciousness, chancing
to meet the brown eyes lifted dreamily to his
own, and noting the upward curve of the short,
sweet lip, thought within himself that this
elfish little Cicely was growing almost as pretty
as her sister—a judgment which proves con
clusively the blindness of love; for Annis,
though fair and comely to look upon, came no
nearer to her young sister's beauty than does
the pink-tipped daisy to the half-opened rose-
bud uncurling slowly in the sun. At present,
the girl, seeing that she was watched, turned
away her head pettishly and eyed the leaping
flames.

"Annis said to-night there was but one thing
lacking to her Christmas cheer," she remarked,
after a pause, and with the too evident intention of saying something vexatious.

"And that was I!" interposed the cavalier,
with the ready assurance of a lover.

"It was not you at all," returned Cicely,

"but the mistletoe. We gathered the other greens ourselves, but there was no mistletoe to be found within or without the gates of London."

"By a happy chance we can proceed as though we had it," said Captain Breton, contentedly, while Annis crimsoned like a rose. "It is a welcome little plant, and carries a merry message; but if it be banished in these saintly days, we obstinate sinners must kiss without its sanction."

"But the maid who is not kissed on Christmas-night beneath the mistletoe will never be a wife during the coming year," persisted Cicely, who had laid down her line of attack and was not to be driven therefrom.

"Now, will you wager your ring or your new ear-drop on that, little sister?" said the captain, laughing at the threat. "Or have you a trinket that you value less to risk in such a cause?"

Cicely, deeply affronted, puckered up her brow and drew closer to her mother; but Annis, far too happy to be vexed, leaned over and kissed the pouting lips. With her, joy meant thanksgiving, and her heart was singing—singing the song of the angel of Judea: "In Excelsis Gloria!"

A Norseman's Saga.

> " As he sat there with a sou'wester
> down over his ears, in a long
> pilot coat, his figure appeared to
> assume quite supernatural pro-
> portions, and you might almost
> imagine that you had one of the
> old Vikings before you."
>
> *Asbjörnsen.*

THROND.

THERE was once a man named Alf, who had raised great expectations among his fellow-parishioners because he excelled most of them both in the work he accomplished and in the advice he gave. Now, when this man was thirty years old, he went to live up the mountain, and cleared a piece of land for farming, about fourteen miles from any settlement. Many people wondered how he could endure thus depending on himself for companionship, but they were still more astonished when, a few years later, a young girl from the valley, and one, too, who had been the gayest of the gay at all the social gatherings and dances of the parish, was willing to share his solitude.

This couple were called "the people in the wood," and the man was known by the name of "Alf in the wood." People viewed him with inquisitive eyes when they met him at church or at work, because they did not understand him; but neither did he take the trouble to give them any explanation of his conduct. His wife was only seen in the parish twice, and on one of these occasions it was to present a child for baptism.

This child was a son, and he was called Thrond. When he grew larger his parents often talked about needing help, and, as they could not afford to take a full-grown servant, they hired what they called "a half:" they brought into their house a girl of fourteen, who took care of the boy while the father and mother were busy in the field.

This girl was not the brightest person in the world, and the boy soon observed that his mother's words were easy to comprehend, but that it was hard to get at the meaning of what Ragnhild said. He never talked much with his father, and he was rather afraid of him, for the house had to be kept very quiet when he was home. One Christmas Eve—they were burning two candles on the table, and the father was drinking from a white flask—the father took the boy up in his arms and set him on his lap, looked him sternly in the eyes, and exclaimed,—

"Ugh, boy!" Then he added more gently,— "Why, you are not so much afraid. Would you have the courage to listen to a story?"

The boy made no reply, but he looked full in his father's face. His father then told him about a man from Vaage, whose name was

Blessom. This man was in Copenhagen for
the purpose of getting the king's verdict in a
law-suit he was engaged in, and he was detained
so long that Christmas eve overtook him there.
Blessom was greatly annoyed at this, and, as he
was sauntering about the streets fancying himself at home, he saw a very large man, in a
white, short coat, walking in front of him.

"How fast you are walking!" said Blessom.

"I have a long distance to go in order to get
home this evening," replied the man.

"Where are you going?"

"To Vaage," answered the man, and walked
on.

"Why, that is very nice," said Blessom, "for
that is where I am going, too."

"Well, then, you may ride with me, if you
will stand on the runners of my sledge," answered the man, and turned into a side street
where his horse was standing.

He mounted his seat and looked over his
shoulder at Blessom, who was just getting on
the runners.

"You had better hold fast," said the stranger.

Blessom did as he was told, and it was well
he did, for their journey was evidently not by
land.

"It seems to me that you are driving on the
water," cried Blessom.

"I am," said the man, and the spray whirled about them.

But after a while it seemed to Blessom their course no longer lay on the water.

"It seems to me we are moving through the air," said he.

"Yes, so we are," replied the stranger.

But when they had gone still farther, Blessom thought he recognized the parish they were driving through.

"Is not this Vaage?" cried he.

"Yes, now we are there," replied the stranger, and it seemed to Blessom that they had gone pretty fast.

"Thank you for the good ride," said he.

"Thanks to yourself," replied the man, and added, as he whipped up his horse, "Now you had better not look after me."

"No, indeed," thought Blessom, and started over the hills for home.

But just then so loud and terrible a crash was heard behind him that it seemed as if the whole mountain must be tumbling down, and a bright light was shed over the surrounding landscape; he looked round and beheld the stranger in the white coat driving through the crackling flames into the open mountain, which was yawning wide to receive him, like some huge gate. Blessom felt somewhat strange in regard to his travelling companion; and thought he would look in another direction; but as he had turned his head so it remained, and never more could Blossom get it straight again.

The boy had never heard anything to equal this in all his life. He dared not ask his father for more, but early the next morning he asked his mother if she knew any stories. Yes, of course she did; but hers were chiefly about princesses who were in captivity for seven years, until the right prince came along. The boy believed that everything he heard or read about took place close around him.

He was about eight years old when the first stranger entered their door one winter evening. He had black hair, and this was something Thrond had never seen before. The stranger saluted them with a short "Good-evening!" and came forward. Thrond grew frightened and sat down on a cricket by the hearth. The mother asked the man to take a seat on the bench along the wall, he did so, and then the mother could examine his face more closely.

"Dear me! is not this Knud the fiddler?" cried she.

"Yes, to be sure it is. It has been a long time since I played at your wedding."

"Oh, yes; it is quite a while now. Have you been on a long journey?"

"I have been playing for Christmas on the other side of the mountain. But half-way down the slope I began to feel very badly, and I was obliged to come in here to rest."

The mother brought forward food for him; he sat down to the table, but did not say "in the name of Jesus," as the boy had been accustomed to hear. When he had finished eating, he got up from the table, and said,—

"Now I feel very comfortable; let me rest a little while."

And he was allowed to rest on Thrond's bed.

For Thrond a bed was made on the floor. As the boy lay there, he felt cold on the side that was turned away from the fire, and that was the left side. He discovered that it was because this side was exposed to the chill night air; for he was lying out in the wood. How came he in the wood? He got up and looked about him, and saw that there was fire burning a long distance off, and that he was actually alone in the wood. He longed to go home to the fire; but could not stir from the spot. Then a great fear overcame him; for wild beasts might be roaming about, trolls and ghosts might appear to him; he must get home to the fire; but he could not stir from the spot. Then his terror grew, he strove with all his might to

gain self-control, and was at last able to cry,
" Mother," and then he awoke.

" Dear child, you have had bad dreams," said
she, and took him up.

A shudder ran through him, and he glanced
round. The stranger was gone, and he dared
not inquire after him.

His mother appeared in her black dress, and
started for the parish. She came home with
two new strangers, who also had black hair
and who wore flat caps. They did not say " in
the name of Jesus," when they ate, and they
talked in low tones with the father. Afterwards
the latter and they went into the barn, and came
out again with a large box, which the men carried between them. They placed it on a sled,
and said farewell. Then the mother said,—

" Wait a little, and take with you the smaller
box he brought here with him."

And she went in to get it. But one of the
men said,—

" *He* can have that," and he pointed at
Thrond.

" Use it as well as *he* who is now lying *here*,"
added the other stranger, pointing at the large
box.

Then they both laughed and went on.
Thrond looked at the little box which thus came
into his possession.

"What is there in it?" asked he.

"Carry it in and find out," said the mother.

He did as he was told, but his mother helped him open it. Then a great joy lighted up his face, for he saw something very light and fine lying there.

"Take it up," said his mother.

He put just one finger down on it, but quickly drew it back again in great alarm.

"It cries," said he.

"Have courage," said his mother, and he grasped it with his whole hand and drew it forth from the box.

He weighed it and turned it round, he laughed and felt of it.

"Dear me! what is it?" asked he, for it was as light as a toy.

"It is a fiddle."

This was the way that Thrond Alfson got his first violin.

The father could play a little, and he taught the boy how to handle the instrument; the mother could sing the tunes she remembered from her dancing days, and these the boy learned, but soon began to make new ones for himself. He played all the time he was not at his books; he played until his father once told him he was fading away before his eyes. All the boy had read and heard until that time was put into the fiddle. The tender, delicate string was his mother; the one that lay close beside it, and always accompanied his mother, was Ragnhild. The coarse string, which he seldom ventured to play on, was his father. But of the last solemn string he was half afraid, and he gave no name to it. When he played a wrong note on the E string, it was the cat; but when he took a wrong note on his father's string, it was the ox. The bow was Blessom, who drove from Copenhagen to Vaage in one night. And every tune he played represented something. The one containing the long solemn tones was his mother in her black dress. The one that jerked and skipped was like Moses, who stuttered and smote the rock with his staff. The one that had to be played quietly, with the bow moving lightly over the strings, was the hulder in yonder fog, calling together her cattle, where no one but herself could see.

But the music wafted him onward over the mountains, and a great yearning took possession of his soul. One day, when his father told about a little boy who had been playing at the fair and who had earned a great deal of money, Thrond waited for his mother in the kitchen and asked her softly if he could not go to the fair and play for people.

" Whoever heard of such a thing!" said his

mother; but she immediately spoke to his father about it.

"He will get out into the world soon enough," answered the father; and he spoke in such a way that the mother did not ask again.

Shortly after this, the father and mother were talking at table about some new settlers who had recently moved up on the mountain and were about to be married. They had no fiddler for the wedding, the father said.

"Could not I be the fiddler?" whispered the boy, when he was alone in the kitchen once more with his mother.

"What, a little boy like you?" said she; but she went out to the barn where his father was and told him about it.

"He has never been in the parish," she added; "he has never seen a church."

"I should not think you would ask about such things," said Alf; but neither did he say anything more, and so the mother thought she had permission. Consequently she went over to the new settlers and offered the boy's services.

"The way he plays," said she, "no little boy has ever played before;" and the boy was to be allowed to come.

What joy there was at home! Thrond played from morning until evening and practised new tunes; at night he dreamed about them: they

bore him far over the hills, away to foreign
lands, as though he were afloat on sailing clouds.
His mother made a new suit of clothes for him ;
but his father would not take part in what was
going on.

The last night he did not sleep, but thought
out a new tune about the church which he had
never seen. He was up early in the morning,
and so was his mother, in order to get him his
breakfast, but he could not eat. He put on his
new clothes and took his fiddle in his hand, and
it seemed to him as though a bright light were
glowing before his eyes. His mother accompanied him out on the flag-stone, and stood watching him as he ascended the slopes ; it was the
first time he had left home.

His father got quietly out of bed, and walked
to the window ; he stood there, following the
boy with his eyes until he heard the mother
out on the flag-stone, then he went back to bed
and was lying down when she came in.

She kept stirring about him, as if she wanted
to relieve her mind of something. And finally
it came out,—

" I really think I must walk down to the
church and see how things are going."

He made no reply, and therefore she considered the matter settled, dressed herself, and
started.

It was a glorious, sunny day, the boy walked rapidly onward, he listened to the song of the birds and saw the sun glittering among the foliage, while he proceeded on his way, with his fiddle under his arm. And when he reached the bride's house, he was still so occupied with his own thoughts, that he observed neither the bridal splendor nor the procession; he merely asked if they were about to start, and learned that they were. He walked on in advance with his fiddle, and he played the whole morning into it, and the tones he produced resounded through the trees.

"Will we soon see the church?" he asked over his shoulder.

For a long time he received only "No" for an answer, but at last some one said,—

"As soon as you reach that crag yonder, you will see it."

He threw his newest tune into the fiddle, the bow danced on the strings, and he kept his eyes fixed intently before him. There lay the parish right in front of him!

The first thing he saw was a little light mist, curling, like smoke on the opposite mountain side. His eyes wandered over the green meadow and the large houses, with windows which glistened beneath the scorching rays of the sun, like the glacier on a winter's day. The houses

kept increasing in size, the windows in number,
and here on one side of him lay the enormous
red house, in front of which horses were tied ;
little children were playing on a hill, dogs were
sitting watching them. But everywhere there
penetrated a long, heavy tone, that shook him
from head to foot, and everything he saw seemed
to vibrate with that tone. Then suddenly he
saw a large, straight house, with a tall, glittering
staff reaching up to the skies. And below, a
hundred windows blazed, so that the house
seemed to be enveloped in flames. This must
be the church, the boy thought, and the music
must come from it! Round about stood a vast
multitude of people, and they all looked alike!
He put them forthwith into relations with the
church, and thus acquired a respect mingled
with awe for the smallest child he saw.

"Now I must play," thought Thrond, and
tried to do so.

But what was this? The fiddle had no longer
any sound in it. There must be some defect
in the strings; he examined, but could find
none.

"Then it must be because I do not press on
hard enough," and he drew his bow with a
firmer hand; but the fiddle seemed as if it were
cracked.

He changed the tune that was meant to repre-

18

sent the church into another, but with equally
bad results; no music was produced, only squeak-
ing and wailing. He felt the cold sweat start
out over his face; he thought of all these wise
people who were standing here and perhaps
laughing him to scorn, this boy who at home
could play so beautifully, but who here failed to
bring out a single tone!

"Thank God that mother is not here to see
my shame!" said he softly to himself, as he
played among the people; but lo! there she
stood, in her black dress, and she shrank farther
and farther away.

At that moment he beheld far up on the
spire the black-haired man who had given him
the fiddle. "Give it back to me," he now
shouted, laughing, and stretching out his arms,
and the spire went up and down with him, up
and down. But the boy took the fiddle under
one arm, screaming, "You shall not have it!"
and, turning, ran away from the people, beyond
the houses, onward through meadow and field,
until his strength forsook him, and then sank
to the ground.

There he lay for a long time, with his face
toward the earth, and when finally he looked
round he saw and heard only God's infinite blue
sky that floated above him, with its everlasting
sough. This was so terrible to him that he had

to turn his face to the ground again. When he raised his head once more his eyes fell on his fiddle, which lay at his side.

"This is all your fault!" shouted the boy, and seized the instrument with the intention of dashing it to pieces, but hesitated as he looked at it.

"We have had many a happy hour together," said he, then paused. Presently he said, "The strings must be severed, for they are worthless." And he took out a knife and cut. "Oh!" cried the E string, in a short, pained tone. The boy cut. "Oh!" wailed the next, but the boy cut. "Oh!" said the third, mournfully; and he paused at the fourth. A sharp pain seized him; that fourth string, to which he never dared give a name, he did not cut. Now a feeling came over him that it was not the fault of the strings that he was unable to play, and just then he saw his mother walking slowly up the slope toward where he was lying, that she might take him home with her. A greater fright than ever overcame him; he held the fiddle by the severed strings, sprang to his feet, and shouted down to her,—

"No, mother! I will not go home again until I can play what I have seen to-day."

Contributed by An Oriental Traveller.

" A great, long devil of a Spahi
in his red burnous."

Daudet.

CHRISTMAS IN THE DESERT.

I.

IT seemed all too good to be true: the rest from labor, the swift flight across southern seas, the landing, amid strange, dark faces on a burnished shore, the slow, delicious journey through tamarisk groves and palm forests, and the halt in the Desert that came at last.

I had been doing for the last twelve months what young artists and authors are constantly doing, to their own ruin and the justifiable ill-humor of critics, namely, working against the grain. A sweet, generous, and beautiful Patroness, seeing me on the high road to brain fever or hopeless mediocrity, stepped forward in time, and sent me to the Desert. If ever I achieve anything excellent, it will be owing to that lady, the Vittoria Colonna of her humble Michael Angelo. My little sister Mary came with me, and, when I tell you that she was a teacher in a school, you will easily understand what an intoxicating thing it was for her to see a new world every day, and have nothing to do from

morning till night. The poor child could hardly
believe in an existence without Czerny's scales
being played on three or four pianos at once,
and a barrel-organ and brass band in the street.
" Oh, Tom !" she would say to me, a dozen times
a day, " I've got C scale and ' Wait for the
Wagon' on my brain, and can't get rid of
them ;" so that I verily believe to my beautiful
Vittoria Colonna Mary's present well-being is
due as much as my own.

We halted at a little military station on the
borders of the Great Sahara, about a week before
Christmas-day.   The weather was perfect, and
not too warm.   A delicious, mellow atmosphere
enveloped palm, and plain, and mosque ; the air,
blown across thousands and thousands of acres
of wild thyme and rosemary, refreshed us like
wine : we seemed to have new souls and new
bodies given us, and were as free from care as
the swallows flying overhead.   Travellers never
came to Teschoun, as this little oasis is called ;
but we had placed ourselves under the guidance
of an enterprising Frenchman, who transacted
all sorts of business on the road between Mascara
and Fig-gig, the last French post in the Desert.
IIis name was Dominique, and I shall always
look upon him as the most remarkable man I
ever knew.   He was as witty as Sydney Smith,
as clever at expediences as Robinson Crusoe, as

shrewd a politician as Machiavelli, as apt at
languages as Mezzofanti, and as brave as Gari-
baldi. Being a bachelor, Dominique was none
the less ready to receive us, and, with the help
of an old Corsican named Napoleon, made us
very comfortable. When Dominique was carrying His Imperial Majesty's mails to some remote
stations southward, or had gone to an Arab fair
to buy cattle, Napoleon catered for us and cooked
for us, and did both admirably. Both master
and servant spiced their dishes plentifully with
that mother-wit, never seen in such perfection
as in crude colonies where people without it
would fare so ill.

"What are we to do for society for poor
mademoiselle?" asked Dominique, as he served
our first dinner. "Monsieur can amuse himself
with the officers of the garrison, but there are
no ladies here."

"When my brother is out, I shall stay at home
and talk to Napoleon," Mary said, with a mock
assumption of dignity. "I don't want to be
amused, Monsieur Dominique."

"Mon Dieu, mademoiselle! the officers of the
garrison will fall in love with you, and that
ought to amuse you better than talking to
Napoleon," Dominique answered. "It's a very
dull life they lead here, these poor officers; and
if it weren't for hunting gazelles and hyenas,

and playing the deuce with the Arabs, they'd die of ennui; but a pretty young lady like you will turn their heads soon enough."

Mary blushed, and tried to turn the conversation.

"What do they do with themselves all day long?" she asked.

"I'll tell you that quickly enough, mademoiselle. M. le Commandant has to see that the Cadi gets what he can out of the Sheiks, and the Sheiks get what they can out of the tribes, and that the tribes hold their tongue. That is what the Commandant has to do, young lady, and he does it pretty well. M. le Capitaine has an easier time of it, except when there is an insurrection, and then he makes a raid against the Arabs, and, after keeping his men out of their way very cleverly, sticks up the French flag somewhere in the Desert and comes home. M. le Lieutenant does odd jobs for the Commandant and the Capitaine, and plays the flute; but we have got M. le Général down here for a few days, and he is setting everybody to work. I dare say the end of it will be an expedition into the Desert. You may look, monsieur. I'm not talking at random, I assure you; generals love war as umbrella-makers love bad weather; and it is easier to make people fight than it is to make it rain "

" I think French officers must be a wicked
set; I hope none of them will come near us,"
Mary said. "The poor Arabs! how my heart
bleeds for them."

"Tiens! mademoiselle, there is no reason for
your heart to bleed. Big flies live on little ones
all the world over; and if the French eat up
the Arabs, the Arabs eat up each other. The
officers are very nice, harmless gentlemen, I
assure you; and as to the Commandant, though
he thinks fighting the best fun in the world, he
wouldn't hurt a fly. To see him pet his little
gazelle would make you cry. She's the only
lady in the place, and I believe, if she died, it
would break his heart. But people must have
something to be fond of. My old Napoleon,
yonder, has taken a fancy to a cat, and when
the cat dies, Napoleon will be as lost as his
namesake the Emperor was at St. Helena.
Listen a moment; that's the Lieutenant practising on his flute: he has a little lodging next
door."

The Lieutenant played very prettily, and
Mary seemed to like his playing much better
than Dominique's stories. As her room adjoined
the Lieutenant's, she seemed likely to have the
full benefit of his musical capacities; but I do
not think she lay awake to be serenaded that
night. We were fairly intoxicated with the

sweet air of the Desert we had been breathing all day, and went to bed at eight o'clock, too tired and happy to dream.

Next morning Dominique informed us that he had himself delivered our letter of introduction to M. le Commandant, who promised to wait upon us in the course of the day. Not knowing at what hour we might expect him, we set to work immediately after breakfast to prepare my room for the reception of so distinguished a visitor. I helped Mary as well as I was able, and, when nothing remained to do but the dusting, retired into a recess to trim my beard.

An Englishwoman is never so well dressed as when she emerges from her bedroom at early morning; and I must say that Mary looked the daintiest little housewife possible to conceive as she went about dusting and polishing in a pink cambric dress and tiny black apron. But, neat as she was, and neat as my beard and the room were in a fair way of becoming, we were overwhelmed with surprise and confusion at what followed, for quite suddenly the door was thrown open; there was a military tramp and a rattling of a sword outside, and Dominique exclaimed, in a voice of thunder, " M. le Commandant !"

Impassible self-possession is a beautiful quality,

and while Mary and I stood blushing and aghast, like school children caught at stealing cherries, M. le Commandant had made a courteous speech, welcoming us to Teschoun. Then we all sat down, and M. le Commandant talked to us. He was a sunburnt, soldierly man about fifty-five, with a rough manner but a kind smile, and we felt at home with him in a moment.

" I presume that monsieur wishes to see as much of the country as possible," he said ; " and I shall be enchanted to place at monsieur's disposal horses, and my servant and a spahi as guides. But what will mademoiselle do while her brother is away ? I must send her my little gazelle to play with her."

" My sister will like to go with me where it is practicable," I said.

The Commandant opened his eyes, and looked at Mary much as one looks upon a pretty little duckling or a year-old baby.

" Monsieur is evidently jesting," he answered. " Mademoiselle would be too fatigued to undertake such journeys."

" I don't think so," Mary said. " I have no fear, monsieur, and I like to be with my brother."

" Ah, what courage you English ladies have ! Well, mademoiselle, we will find you a quiet horse, and make everything as pleasant as pos-

sible." And after inviting us to dine with him
one evening, and bidding us to make use of him
in every possible way, he took leave of us.

" How nice he is !" cried Mary, as soon as the
door was closed; "if all French officers were
like this one, Tom, I think we shall not care
how long we stay in the Desert——"

" Your heart has very quickly ceased to bleed
for the poor Arabs, I see."

" But how can we be sure that Dominique's
stories are all true ? No, Tom; I won't believe
any harm of this kind-looking Commandant. I
only wish he had not come till the room was
tidied and I had got on a muslin frock, but, as
we are sure of having no more visitors, I'll finish
your room and then unpack."

We were fairly at our work again, when
another military step sounded, and another
sword rattled in the passage outside. This time
Dominique's arm swung back the door with less
pomposity, and Dominique's voice was a trifle
less emphatic as he ushered in " M. le Capitaine."

Again Mary and I scuttled about like young
rabbits, and then stood still, staring shyly, and
again our embarrassment was met by the calm-
est nonchalance. The second figure was a man
of much more presence than the Commandant.
He had the polished, graceful ease of a man of

the world, and, though quite as good-natured as
the Commandant, his good-nature pleased us less,
because it was less spontaneous.

"I hope you will stay some time at Teschoun," he said, looking at Mary. "The ennui
of our lives here is terrible. Think of it, mademoiselle; we have no theatre, no music, no
society, and no domestic life. To find a lady
here is like the miraculous advent of an angel."
Mary blushed, and had no courage to make the
sprightly answers she had made the Commandant.

The fine air and grand compliments of the
Capitaine overcame the little thing, but she
looked distractingly pretty as she sat opposite
to him, smiling and blushing when he addressed
her, and only saying, " Oui, monsieur," or " Non,
monsieur," or at most, " Vraiment, monsieur."

" Does mademoiselle ride ?" asked the gallant
Capitaine.

" Oui, monsieur."

" Then mademoiselle shall ride my little barb ;
there is hardly such a horse anywhere, mademoiselle, so docile, so sweet-tempered, and so
sure-footed. It is not every lady I would trust
with my little horse ; but I know how an Englishwoman can sit in the saddle, and I am proud to
offer it to mademoiselle."

" Je vous remercie bien, monsieur."

Then the Capitaine talked of Christmas-day.

" We will have a little fête-champêtre in mademoiselle's honor," he said ; " we will go to the great waterfalls of Boisel-Kebir and breakfast there. I will invite my Commandant and all the officers of the garrison. Monsieur can make a sketch and mademoiselle can gather flowers."

We expressed ourselves delighted at the proposal, and, after promising to send Mary ostrich eggs and jackal skins to take to England, the Capitaine left us.

" I don't like the Capitaine as well as the Commandant," Mary said ; " but how kind they all are to us! It is as if we were princes on a journey of triumph. Oh, Tom! what days to remember are these !"

" I think your head will be fairly turned, what with the Commandant's dinners and the Capitaine's fêtes-champêtres," I said ; " and if the Lieutenant——"

" M. le Lieutenant!" announced Dominique, opening the door calmly, as if nothing was the matter.

We had been twice so shocked and surprised that we had no more embarrassment to expend on the Lieutenant. Indeed, he was rather shy himself, which was the very thing to reassure a warm-hearted, sympathetic little creature like my sister, and they began to talk together without any effort.

He was young and handsome, with a very frank, pleasant expression.

"I am afraid that it is useless for me to offer my poor services," he said, very modestly, "my superior officers having forestalled me; but it will make me very happy to do anything for you. If mademoiselle would like any stuffed birds, or dried flowers and plants, it will give me pleasure to procure them for her; and perhaps monsieur would like me to show him some wonderful things to paint. I draw a little myself, and know where the finest points of view are to be found."

We thanked him heartily, and accepted all that he offered us. As it was now time for our second breakfast, or, more properly speaking, lunch, we pressed him to partake of it with us, which he did. We should not have ventured upon inviting the Commandant, much less the Capitaine, so unceremoniously, but the Lieutenant's diffident manner had set us quite at our ease.

"I have a very humble apartment," he said; "but if monsieur and mademoiselle will visit me, I will do the honors of it with pride and pleasure. I can at least offer them a little music."

"Yes, I know that you play," Mary said, smiling; "our rooms join, and I heard you playing before I went to sleep last night."

"Oh, mademoiselle! I shall never forgive myself if I disturbed you."

"No, indeed, you did not, monsieur. Much as I liked the music, I was too tired to listen to it, and went to sleep all the same."

Then they both laughed gleefully, like children, and the Lieutenant promised to play to her and send her to sleep every night.

After breakfast he accompanied us on a tour of inspection. We soon saw all that there was to see of Teschoun, namely, a little line of bazaars kept by Jews and negroes, a little boulevard of a year's growth, two imposing-looking gates,— one looking towards Morocco, one towards the Sahara,—a straggling camp, and a wall of circumvallation. There were gardens in embryo here and there, but no trees of any size, and not till you had got fairly away from Teschoun could you perceive that its aspect was striking or imposing. Then, looking back from the craggy heights that surrounded it, the white line of the camp and the belt of verdure encircling it like a ribbon, struck the eye as a pleasant contrast to the warm, yellow atmosphere of earth and sky. The warmth and the yellowness were delicious. A fresh, sweet breeze blew across our faces from the Desert. We sat down and drew it in with long, devouring breaths.

A hundred yards behind us, his bright-brown body sharply outlined against the pale, amber-colored sky, stood a little Bedouin smiling down upon us. It was a perfect personification of Eastern life, and I made a sketch, while the Lieutenant told Mary of his hard campaign southward, and his joy at catching the first glimpse of Teschoun from the distance.

When we returned home we found that the Commandant's servant had left a bunch of roses for Mary, with his master's compliments; that the Capitaine's servant had been sent round with his master's horse for her to try, and that the Général had sent word by his aide-de-camp that he would himself have the pleasure of calling upon us that evening.

Mary and I felt utterly overwhelmed by such goodness and condescension. A real starred, laced Général was about to call on us! We could hardly believe that we were our identical, insignificant selves, who, but for you, oh! most sweet and honored Patroness, would have sunk under the burden of toil imposed upon us. But how all was changed! The poor, un-known artist was treated as if he had been Sir Peter Paul Rubens; the humble little school teacher was fêted and flattered like the wife of a conquering commander-in-chief.

We had invited the young Lieutenant to drink tea with us at eight o'clock, and were enjoying a little music after a very sociable fashion, when a noisy excitement seemed to shake the house like a shock of an earthquake, and M. le Général was announced in Dominique's most impressive manner.

M. le Général was by no means an awful-looking person ; and, indeed, we had so expended our surprise already, that we had no more at command.

He was an excessively stout, merry person, middle-aged, of a beautiful complexion, and a capacity to wink that would have vulgarized any one else but a general. He made himself very pleasant, accepted a cup of tea, praised Mary's French, said that he intended to dine with us at the Commandant's to-morrow, and told us some laughable stories about the Arabs. I noticed that the Lieutenant seemed quite over-awed by the presence of the Général, and sat, flute in hand, like a statue. Mary tried to put him at his ease, but to no purpose. It did not mend matters when the Général began first to twit him about his musical accomplishments, and then to catechise him on military matters.

"You were in that affair of '59, in Kabylia, weren't you?" he asked, in that quick, positive, military tone to which we with difficulty get accustomed.

"Oui, mon Général."

"It was a badly managed thing, I believe. The Kabyles got the better of you more than once, didn't they?"

"I believe so, mon Général."

"Bah!" cried the Général, turning to me. "You see what these young officers know of their trade. I have no doubt that Monsieur le Lieutenant's musical education is much more advanced, and to screnade mademoiselle suits him much better than to make war against the enemies of his country."

And, at the mention of the enemies of his country, the Général indulged in a wink. When he was ready to go, he sent the Lieutenant to order his horse, much as if he had been a little boy of ten years old; and on taking leave added half a dozen commissions in the same peremptory tone. The poor Lieutenant listened very submissively, but no sooner had the Général dashed down the street, followed by his servant, equally well mounted, than he grew gay and easy again.

As soon as we were alone, Mary brought out her slender supply of gala dresses, and we dis-

I.—*p*

cussed the important subject of her toilet of the
next evening.

"It seems to me," I said, "that if you dress
for the Lieutenant, you will displease the Capitaine; if you dress for the Capitaine, you will
displease the Commandant; and if you dress
for the Commandant, you will displease the
Général."

Mary gathered up her fineries in alarm.
"Don't you think I had better stay away from
the dinner altogether, Tom?"

"By no means," I said; "settle the matter
by dressing to please me."

Which she accordingly did, and the result
was a semi-moresque, dainty, and glowing bit
of costume quite in keeping with the time and
place.

II.

Precisely at seven o'clock we presented ourselves at the Commandant's, Mary looking very
pretty in her transparent white dress, brilliant
sack of Tunis silk, and necklets and bracelets
of coral and palm-seeds. The little thing had
such loving, dark eyes, such a soft bloom on her
cheeks, and such a sweet mouth, that I could
hardly blame the Général for wishing to have
her sit beside him at dinner. The Commandant,
being a little shy, would have given up all his
privileges as host, but the Général insisted upon

the Commandant leading her in, and she sat between the two. It was very mortifying for the Capitaine and the Lieutenant; the former made an effort to be complimentary and entertaining across the table, but the latter looked quite crestfallen, and hardly raised his eyes from his plate. When we retired to the drawing-room, matters went a little better. The tame gazelle was brought in for Mademoiselle Marie to see; and while the Général and the Commandant had a long discussion on military affairs, the rest of us sported with the pretty creature and made pleasant plans for the morrow. Then an amusing game of cards was set on foot, over which we were growing very merry, when up came the Général and the Commandant.

"Eh, bien!" said the Général, slyly nudging the Capitaine. "We have not been so engrossed, but we heard one or two pleasant things talked of. Upon my word, Capitaine, I am half disposed not to go to Mascara till after your picnic to the water-falls."

"You will do my poor little fête great honor, mon Général," answered the Capitaine, adding, naïvely, "but I think that the wild geese flying northwards means rain."

"Not a bit of it. We shall have no rain until a fortnight after Christmas. Mademoi-

selle Marie, I shall do myself the honor of offering you one of my horses to ride."

"Mademoiselle has already condescended to
accept mine," the Capitaine put in, with stiff-
ness.

"Mademoiselle Marie, this gentleman has no
horse fit to carry a lady. The brute he offers
you has no more mouth than an elephant.
Keep on the safe side and ride mine, which is a
lamb, I assure you, mademoiselle,—a lamb."

The Général spoke in jest, but the Capitaine
was very near losing his temper. Mary being
thus appealed to, thought to extricate herself
from the difficulty by declaring herself half
afraid to ride either horse, being an inexperi-
enced horsewoman. But both the gentlemen
had mules, and both the gentlemen's mules were
the best. Poor Mary colored, and looked at me
in despair.

"I think," I said, "the safest plan will be for
my sister to try the horses, and see which suits
her the best."

Then the different routes to the water-falls
were discussed, and the different Douars or
Arab villages where it would be best to have a
Diffa, or feast, provided,—Mary's judgment being
asked in every instance. All this time the Lieutenant had turned over the leaves of a newspaper
very meekly, and the Commandant had caressed

his tame gazelle. As soon as she could politely free herself, Mary went up to him.

"How pretty, and playful, and fond it is!" she said, stooping down to stroke the little creature. The grave face of the Commandant brightened.

"Yes; it would be very *triste* here without the little thing."

"Do you never go to France, monsieur?"

"I shall perhaps go in two years' time; but you see, mademoiselle, that is a long time to look forward to; and if my mother should not be living, I might as well stay here."

"Do you like fighting the Arabs in the Desert, then, monsieur?"

"Mademoiselle, when one takes up the profession of arms, fighting and exile are *choses entendues*. I often sigh for a settled, domestic life; but I might have been worse off. I might have gone to Mexico, for instance."

The Commandant's manner was so simple, so manly, and so tinged with sadness, that I think any woman would have sympathized with him as much as my little sister Mary did. She, poor child, having lived all her life in a school-room, was quite ready to make a hero of any man that smiled kindly upon her; and here were four heroes, in handsome uniforms, all smiling upon her at once! There was the sweet sense

20

of youth drawing her to the Lieutenant; but I think the Commandant stood next in her favor, and she could not for a moment forget the courteous kindness of the other two.

"It must all be a dream, Tom," she said, as she gave me her good-night kiss; "but, oh! if it is a dream, don't let me wake yet."

We dreamed some wonderful things in the next few days. Dominique made us get up, one morning, very early, and drove us in his little wooden gig to an Arab encampment miles away in the Desert. It was dawn when we started, and large, pale stars were shining in a violet sky; then, like a gorgeous butterfly emerging from a dusky chrysalis, came the Eastern day, and we felt as if living in a world warmed by a hundred suns. The warm, intoxicating light took possession of our senses, and so sweet, so rarefied, so indescribably delicious was the air, that it seemed to give wings to our dull bodies. Every now and then we were overtaken by clouds of locusts, their little wings glistening like diamonds against the soft sky, or flocks of starlings darkened the air, or a serried line of wild geese passed majestically overhead. Then we came to the tents, and at our approach a dozen dogs rushed out to snap and snarl, and a hundred little naked children scampered and scuttled across the way. A stately Bedouin

made us welcome, and, while Dominique transacted business with him, his women gathered
around us, chattering and grinning like children.
Then we were feasted upon cous-cous sou and
figs, and took leave, after many " salamaleks."

Another day we went out hunting gazelles,
bivouacking along a riverside, and feasting,
Arab fashion, off a sheep roasted whole. Dominique had found a pretty little French girl,
daughter of a travelling farrier, to act as Mary's
handmaid ; and she now felt less isolated among
so many men, and less shy, too. The poor child
stood a fair chance of being spoiled, what with
suddenly finding herself transformed from a
school-room Cinderella to a fairy-tale princess,
and having four lovers, all heroes, at once. For
it was impossible to deny that the Général, the
Commandant, the Capitaine, and the Lieutenant
all behaved like lovers, presenting her with jackal
skins, ostrich plumes and eggs, rare birds, and
other treasures of the Sahara. The Général
went so far as to give her a little negro boy
about ten, years old, though this gift we had
accepted only temporarily, not quite knowing
what to do with him when we left Teschoun.

Christmas-day came at last. Mary had art-
fully evaded the delicate point about horses by
declaring herself afraid of every one's beast but
Dominique's ; accordingly, mounted on Domi-

nique's ugly hack, she led the way with the
Général, her long, bright hair flowing in curls
over her shoulders, her cheeks glowing with
excitement. The pleasure and picturesqueness
of the last few days—for Mary had an artistic
perception of beauty—had brought out a new
side to her character; and she quite surprised
me, from time to time, with her saucy humor
and quick repartee.

We made a brilliant cavalcade, what with the
uniforms of the officers, and the richly embroidered saddles and bright-red burnouses of our
attendant spahis. After riding some miles across
a monotonous tract of stony desert, we came to
a majestic sierra of crag, down which fell a dozen
water-falls, narrow and bright as sword-blades.
A thin little stream threaded the ravine, and
on its banks grew clumps of the tamarisk, the
oleander, and the thuya, making an oasis grateful to the eyes.   Here we sat down and ate our
Christmas breakfast, with stray thoughts of
village bells chiming at home, and school children lustily singing their Christmas hymns.

. Our host, the Capitaine, had provided a sumptuous feast of Desert fare,—roast quails and
plovers, cous-cous-sou, figs, dates, and bananas,
with the addition of champagne ; and we were
very merry.

" Mademoiselle," said the Capitaine, " think

what our next Christmas will be if you are not here. Persuade monsieur, your brother, to purchase some land between Mascara and Teschoun, so that we shall not lose you altogether."

The Général nudged the Commandant.

" You see what our friend the Capitaine is dreaming of! Mon Capitaine, your escadron is sure to be sent into the interior this spring; put all romances out of your head, my dear fellow, and do not entice monsieur into the committal of follies."

" I am not the only one to entertain romances," said the Capitaine, coolly. " You, mon Général, did us all the honor to spend Christmas at Teschoun. We can but attribute such a condescension to the gracious influence of mademoiselle."

" Look well after the Commandant when I am gone, gentlemen," continued the Général, looking round with a smile. " Matters are gone so far already that he loses his temper if a fellow-officer but jests with him. What a terrible slur it would be upon the glorious annals of French-African conquest, if such a brave officer should show himself fonder of stuffing birds for an English demoiselle than running swords through ungrateful Arabs!" and the Général looked round with a very comical expression of mock horror.

" Mademoiselle has indiscriminately accepted

20*

our tokens of homage," the Commandant said, maliciously.

" But it yet remains to be seen whose offering has been most acceptable to her," went on the Général, adding, *au grand sérieux*, " we won't resort to duels unless absolutely necessary."

This sort of banter lasted so long that poor Mary's cheeks burned with mixed vanity and mortification, and she made an excuse to leave us.

" And what does our Lieutenant advise monsieur to do ?" asked the Général,—" to settle here, or to follow his escadron to the Desert ?" Whereupon the poor Lieutenant colored, and said nothing.

What an experience it was, that Christmas-day in the Desert ! The noonday sun seemed to dissolve in the warm atmosphere, and, instead of a single orb shining overhead, large and golden, we had melted suns innumerable about us, and almost lost the sense of corporeity in their charmed medium.

When the short bright day waned, and the large stars were coming out one by one, we found ourselves near home ; and when the heavens had turned to bluish-black, and the stars to splendid silvery moons, we passed under the gate of Teschoun, and saw our shadows, darker and deeper than real things, fall across the white walls of mosque and fortress. For shadow and substance lost their identity in the Desert and one is always on the point of mistaking the one for the other: if anything, shadow is the more real of the two.

So absorbed was I in the suggestions of this mysterious beauty, that I had forgotten all about my sister's lovers till we were fairly in our little sitting-room. Then Mary began to sigh and blush, and to hint that she thought we had better leave Teschoun very soon.

" You see, Tom, dear," she said, with tears in her eyes, " the Général says he adores me, and the Commandant says he never loved any one in the world until he saw me, and the Capitaine says that if I go away he will blow his brains out, and what am I to do?"

" And the Lieutenant,—what did he say?"

" He says nothing," said Mary, looking down; " and,"—here came a sob,—" and I like him best of all!"

" But, if he does not declare the same liking for you, we must leave him out of the question, and choose between the other three, I suppose."

" He does not speak because he is too modest: I'm sure he likes me," Mary added, still ready to cry.

" His state of feeling does not help us much, unless expressed," I replied. " Meantime, what

am I to say to the Général, the Commandant,
and the Capitaine, if they ask to marry you?"

The little thing plucked at the folds of her
riding-skirt in the greatest perplexity.

"I like the Général and I like the Commandant, and I ought not to dislike the Capitaine;
but I cannot marry one without offending the
others; and, if I were to marry out here in the
Desert, Tom, would you stay, too?"

We had been living in such utter fairy-land
lately, that I felt as if it were quite possible
for me to marry some brown-skinned, soft-eyed
Rebecca, and turn Mahometan. But, in any
case, could I desire for my sister a happier fate
than to marry one of these brave gentlemen, and
live in the sunny South all the rest of her days?
She would be rescued from a life of toil and
friendlessness, and have another protector besides her Bohemian of a brother.

"My dear child," I said, "it would be impossible for me to say that our lives should be
spent together; but you may be quite sure that
nothing would utterly divide them. The chief
point is, of all your lovers, whom do you love?"

To this question I could elicit no positive
reply. Mary, in fact, was half in love with the
Général and the Commandant, and wholly in
love with the Lieutenant, and was quite in-
capable of deciding her own fate.

" You must not laugh at me," she said, simply, as we bade each other good-night; " it is so new to me to have lovers, and so delightful, that I wish I could go on forever being happy, and making them happy, without marrying either." Then she blushed and ran off to bed.

The next morning we were taking our early coffee, when we heard the clatter of horses' feet, and, looking out, saw one of the Général's splendid, brown-skinned, red-cloaked spahis dashing into the town at a furious rate. He pulled up at Dominique's door, and, letting his little barb prance and rear at will, looked towards us, showing his white teeth and waving a letter in one hand.

I left my breakfast and ran down to him. We exchanged " salamaleks," and then he put the letter in my hand, adding, in broken French, " Le Général,—envoyer cela,—va faire le guerre, —la-bas." Then he put spurs to his horse's flanks, and dashed away as fast as he had come.

I broke the seal of the Général's letter, which ran as follows :

" MONSIEUR,—This morning at daybreak I received telegraphic information that a serious rising has taken place among the tribes southward of Fig-gig, and I have resolved to march upon them without delay. Judge, monsieur,

how more than sorry I am to be forced to quit
the society of your charming sister and yourself without making my adieux ; but a soldier's
duty forces him from the consummation of his
fondest desires, when such a consummation
seems close at hand, and I go, if not with joy,
at least without soldierly reluctance.   I shall
never forget, monsieur, this episode, an oasis in
the desert of my military life ; and, while wishing
for mademoiselle and yourself all possible prosperity, I hope you will remember Teschoun and
the poor exiled officers there, who will never
think of you both without regret.

"I feel it right, under the grave circumstances
of the revolt, to advise your speedy return to
Mascara, and will order a trusty escort to be in
readiness for you when you shall require it.

"Meantime, receive, monsieur, the expression
of my utmost esteem.

"DE MARION."

We were both of us talking over the astound-
ing contents of the Général's letter, when Napoleon came in, full of news.   The insurgents
numbered thousands, and there were skirmishing
parties close to Teschoun.   Teschoun would be
most likely besieged, as it had been more than
once, etc., etc.   As the day wore on, the excitement increased.   Little groups of French or

Jewish shopkeepers collected together and talked gravely, Arabs walked about in stately fashion, smiling superciliously. In the French camp it was the old story on a lesser scale :

> " And there was mounting in hot haste ; the steed,
> The mustering squadron, and the clattering car
> Went pouring forward with impetuous speed."

And so great was the need for hurry that we doubted whether we should see either of our gallant hosts again. Late in the afternoon, however, the Capitaine paid us a formal, sentimental visit, and after him came the Commandant, who stood up before us, square and stiff, and stammered out a word or two with tears in his kind eyes. Mary held out her little hand ; but he seemed overcome with shyness or sadness, or both, and rushed away without having taken it.

Last of all, when we had quite given him up, came the poor Lieutenant : he had been busy on a hundred errands for his superior officers, and had only five minutes to spare. We can never do anything with a few last moments, and Mary and the Lieutenant ·had not a word to say to each other, though I could see well enough what both would fain have said.

So I quietly left them under the pretext of fetching a cigar, and when I returned, at the close of the fifth minute, all that was necessary

had been said. We then embraced each other
after the hearty French fashion. Mary and the
Lieutenant exchanged rings, and he went off to
fight the disaffected Arabs as happy as a king!

It was a fine sight to see the troops march
out of Teschoun. Color is really color in the
South, and the lines of blue zouaves and crimson
spahis against the mellow afternoon sky were
vivid and picturesque beyond description.

On they went, arms flashing, drums beating,
colors flying, till the last column had turned the
hill, and then evening came on all at once, and
we felt a dreary sense of disenchantment creeping over us. It was as if we had been dreaming
during the last few weeks, and now we were
waked, indeed! Dominique recalled us to ourselves with a cynical smile.

" Bah !" he cries, " it's all play ; let 'em pretend
to put down insurrection as often as they please.
It is good for trade and promotion, and the
Arabs know how to defend themselves."

But events falsified this sarcasm of Monsieur
Dominique's, for the insurrection proved serious,
and it was months before we heard of our Lieutenant. When we did hear, the news was good ;
and the news of him and of his English wife—
dowered by our Vittoria Colonna—has been good
ever since.

END OF BOOK I.

IN THE
YULE-LOG GLOW

CHRISTMAS TALES FROM
'ROUND THE WORLD

" Sic as folk tell ower at a winter ingle"

Scott

EDITED BY

HARRISON S. MORRIS

THREE VOLUMES IN ONE.

Book II.

PHILADELPHIA

J. B. LIPPINCOTT COMPANY

1900.

Copyright, 1891, by J. B. LIPPINCOTT COMPANY.

PRINTED BY J. B. LIPPINCOTT COMPANY, PHILADELPHIA.

CONTENTS OF BOOK II.

	PAGE
CHRISTMAS WITH THE BARON	7
By Angelo J. Lewis.	
A CHRISTMAS MIRACLE	45
By Harrison S. Morris.	
SALVETTE AND BERNADOU	63
From the French of Alphonse Daudet.	
By Harrison S. Morris.	
THE WOLF TOWER	78
THE PEACE EGG	129
By Juliana Horatia Ewing.	
A STORY OF NUREMBERG	167
By Agnes Repplier.	
A PICTURE OF THE NATIVITY BY FRA FILIPPO LIPPI	195
By Vernon Lee.	
MELCHIOR'S DREAM	205
By Juliana Horatia Ewing.	
MR. GRAPEWINE'S CHRISTMAS DINNER	243
By Harrison S. Morris.	

3

ILLUSTRATIONS, BOOK II.

THE DAUGHTER OF THE BARON . . . . Page   8

THE HOSPITAL . . . .   "   68

MUMMERS . . . .   " 148

"A HILLY COUNTRY" . . . .   " 196

.

A Droll Chapter by a Swiss Gossip.

> "I here beheld an agreeable old
> fellow, forgetting age, and show-
> ing the way to be young at sixty-
> five."
>
> *Goldsmith.*

1*

CHRISTMAS WITH THE BARON.

I.

ONCE upon a time—fairy tales always begin
with once upon a time—once upon a time there
lived in a fine old castle on the Rhine a certain
Baron von Schrochslofsleschshoffinger. You
will not find it an easy name to pronounce; in
fact, the baron never tried it himself but once,
and then he was laid up for two days afterwards;
so in future we will merely call him "the baron,"
for shortness, particularly as he was rather a
dumpy man.

After having heard his name, you will not be
surprised when I tell you that he was an exceedingly bad character. For a baron, he was
considered enormously rich; a hundred and fifty
pounds a year would not be thought much in
this country; but still it will buy a good deal of
sausage, which, with wine grown on the estate,
formed the chief sustenance of the baron and
his family.

Now, you will hardly believe that, notwithstanding he was the possessor of this princely
revenue, the baron was not satisfied, but op-

7

pressed and ground down his unfortunate tenants to the very last penny he could possibly
squeeze out of them.   In all his exactions he
was seconded and encouraged by his steward,
Klootz, an old rascal who took a malicious
pleasure in his master's cruelty, and who
chuckled and rubbed his hands with the great
est apparent enjoyment when any of the poor
landholders could not pay their rent, or afforded
him any opportunity for oppression.

Not content with making the poor tenants
pay double value for the land they rented, the
baron was in the habit of going round every
now and then to their houses and ordering anything he took a fancy to, from a fat pig to a
pretty daughter, to be sent up to the castle.
The pretty daughter was made parlor-maid, but
as she had nothing a year, and to find herself,
it wasn't what would be considered by careful
mothers an eligible situation.   The fat pig became sausage, of course.

Things went on from bad to worse, till, at
the time of our story, between the alternate
squeezings of the baron and his steward, the
poor tenants had very little left to squeeze out
of them.   The fat pigs and pretty daughters
had nearly all found their way up to the castle,
and there was little left to take.

The only help the poor fellows had was the

baron's only daughter, Lady Bertha, who always had a kind word, and frequently something more substantial, for them when her father was not in the way.

Now, I'm not going to describe Bertha, for the simple reason that if I did you would imagine that she was the fairy I'm going to tell you about, and she isn't. However, I don't mind giving you a few outlines.

In the first place, she was exceedingly tiny, —the nicest girls, the real lovable little pets, always are tiny,—and she had long silken black hair, and a dear, dimpled little face full of love and mischief. Now, then, fill up the outline with the details of the nicest and prettiest girl you know, and you will have a slight idea of her. On second thoughts, I don't believe you will, for your portrait wouldn't be half good enough; however, it will be near enough for you.

Well, the baron's daughter, being all your fancy painted her and a trifle more, was naturally much distressed at the goings-on of her unamiable parent, and tried her best to make amends for her father's harshness. She generally managed that a good many pounds of the sausage should find their way back to the owners of the original pig; and when the baron tried to squeeze the hand of the pretty parlor-maid, which he occasionally did after dinner,

Bertha had only to say, in a tone of mild remonstrance, "Pa!" and he dropped the hand
instantly and stared very hard the other way.

Bad as this disreputable old baron was, he
had a respect for the goodness and purity of his
child. Like the lion tamed by the charm of
Una's innocence, the rough old rascal seemed
to lose in her presence half his rudeness, and,
though he used awful language to her sometimes (I dare say even Una's lion roared occasionally), he was more tractable with her
than with any other living being. Her presence
operated as a moral restraint upon him, which,
possibly, was the reason that he never stayed
down-stairs after dinner, but always retired to
a favorite turret, which, I regret to say, he had
got so in the way of doing every afternoon that
I believe he would have felt unwell without it.

The hour of the baron's afternoon sympo-
sium was the time selected by Bertha for her
errands of charity. Once he was fairly settled
down to his second bottle, off went Bertha, with
her maid beside her carrying a basket, to bestow
a meal on some of the poor tenants, among whom
she was always received with blessings.

At first these excursions had been undertaken
principally from charitable motives, and Bertha
thought herself plentifully repaid in the love
and thanks of her grateful pensioners.

Of late, however, another cause had led her to take even stronger interest in her walks, and occasionally to come in with brighter eyes and a rosier cheek than the gratitude of the poor tenants had been wont to produce.

The fact is, some months before the time of our story, Bertha had noticed in her walks a young artist, who seemed to be fated to be invariably sketching points of interest in the road she had to take. There was one particular tree, exactly in the path which led from the castle-gate, which he had sketched from at least four points of view, and Bertha began to wonder what there could be so very particular about it.

At last, just as Carl von Sempach had begun to consider where on earth he could sketch the tree from next, and to ponder seriously upon the feasibility of climbing up into it and taking it from *that* point of view, a trifling accident occurred which gave him the opportunity of making Bertha's acquaintance,—which, I don't mind stating confidentially, was the very thing he had been waiting for.

It so chanced that, on one particular afternoon, the maid, either through awkwardness, or possibly through looking more at the handsome painter than the ground she was walking on, stumbled and fell.

Of course, the basket fell, too, and equally of

course, Carl, as a gentleman, could not do less than offer his assistance in picking up the damsel and the dinner.

The acquaintance thus commenced was not suffered to drop; and handsome Carl and our good little Bertha were fairly over head and ears in love, and had begun to have serious thoughts of a cottage in a wood, *et cætera*, when their felicity was disturbed by their being accidentally met, in one of their walks, by the baron.

Of course the baron, being himself so thorough an aristocrat, had higher views for his daughter than marrying her to a "beggarly artist," and accordingly he stamped, and swore, and threatened Carl with summary punishment with all sorts of weapons, from heavy boots to blunderbusses, if ever he ventured near the premises again.

This was unpleasant; but I fear it did not *quite* put a stop to the young people's interviews, though it made them less frequent and more secret than before.

Now, I am quite aware this was not at all proper, and that no properly regulated young lady would ever have had meetings with a young man her papa didn't approve of.

But then it is just possible Bertha might not have been a properly regulated young lady.   1 only know she was a dear little pet, worth twenty model young ladies, and that she loved Carl very dearly.

And then consider what a dreadful old tyrant of a papa she had! My dear girl, it's not the slightest use your looking so provokingly correct; it's my deliberate belief that if you had been in her shoes (they'd have been at least three sizes too small for you, but that doesn't matter) you would have done precisely the same.

Such was the state of things on Christmas eve in the year—— Stay! fairy tales never have a year to them, so, on second thoughts, I wouldn't tell the date if I knew,—but I don't.

Such was the state of things, however, on the particular 24th of December to which our story refers—only, if anything, rather more so.

The baron had got up in the morning in an exceedingly bad temper; and those about him had felt its effects all through the day.

His two favorite wolf-hounds, Lutzow and Teufel, had received so many kicks from the baron's heavy boots that they hardly knew at which end their tails were; and even Klootz himself scarcely dared to approach his master.

In the middle of the day two of the principal tenants came to say that they were unprepared with their rent, and to beg for a little delay.

The poor fellows represented that their families were starving, and entreated for mercy; but the baron was only too glad that he had at last found so fair an excuse for venting .his ill-humor.

He loaded the unhappy defaulters with every abusive epithet he could devise (and being called names in German is no joke, I can tell you); and, lastly, he swore by everything he could think of that, if their rent was not paid on the morrow, themselves and their families should be turned out of doors to sleep on the snow, which was then many inches deep on the ground. They still continued to beg for mercy, till the baron became so exasperated that he determined to put them out of the castle himself. He pursued them for that purpose as far as the outer door, when fresh fuel was added to his anger.

Carl, who, as I have hinted, still managed, notwithstanding the paternal prohibition, to see Bertha occasionally, and had come to wish her a merry Christmas, chanced at this identical moment to be saying good-by at the door, above which, in accordance with immemorial usage, a huge bush of mistletoe was suspended. What they were doing under it at the moment of the baron's appearance, I never knew exactly; but his wrath was tremendous!

I regret to say that his language was unparliamentary in the extreme. He swore until he was mauve in the face; and if he had not providentially been seized with a fit of coughing, and sat down in the coal-scuttle,—mistaking it for a three-legged stool,—it is impossible to say to what lengths his feelings might have carried him.

Carl and Bertha picked him up, rather black behind, but otherwise not much the worse for his accident.

In fact, the diversion of his thoughts seemed to have done him good; for, having sworn a little more, and Carl having left the castle, he appeared rather better.

II.

After enduring so many and various emotions, it is hardly to be wondered at that the baron required some consolation; so, after having changed his trousers, he took himself off to his favorite turret to allay, by copious potations, the irritations of his mind.

Bottle after bottle was emptied, and pipe after pipe was filled and smoked. The fine old Burgundy was gradually getting into the baron's head; and, altogether, he was beginning to feel more comfortable.

The shades of the winter afternoon had deepened into the evening twilight, made dimmer still by the aromatic clouds that came, with dignified deliberation, from the baron's lips, and curled and floated up to the carved ceiling of the turret, where they spread themselves into a dim canopy, which every successive cloud brought lower and lower.

The fire, which had been piled up mountain-high earlier in the afternoon, and had flamed and roared to its heart's content ever since, had now got to that state—the perfection of a fire to a lazy man—when it requires no poking or attention of any kind, but just burns itself hollow, and then tumbles in, and blazes jovially for a little time, and then settles down to a genial glow, and gets hollow, and tumbles in again.

The baron's fire was just in this delightful *da capo* condition, most favorable of all to the enjoyment of the *dolce far niente.*

For a little while it would glow and kindle quietly, making strange faces to itself, and building fantastic castles in the depths of its red recesses, and then the castles would come down with a crash, and the faces disappear, and a bright flame spring up and lick lovingly the sides of the old chimney ; and the carved heads of improbable men and impossible women, hewn so deftly round the panels of the old oak wardrobe opposite, in which the baron's choicest vintages were deposited, were lit up by the flickering light, and seemed to nod and wink at the fire in return, with the familiarity of old acquaintances.

Some such fancy as this was disporting itself in the baron's brain; and he was gazing at the old oak carving accordingly, and emitting huge volumes of smoke with reflective slowness, when a clatter among the bottles on the table caused him to turn his head to ascertain the cause.

The baron was by no means a nervous man; however, the sight that met his eyes when he turned round did take away his presence of mind a little; and he was obliged to take four distinct puffs before he had sufficiently regained his equilibrium to inquire, "Who the—Pickwick —are you?" (The baron said "Dickens," but, as that is a naughty word, we will substitute "Pickwick," which is equally expressive, and not so wrong.) Let me see; where was I? Oh, yes! "Who the Pickwick are you?"

Now, before I allow the baron's visitor to answer the question, perhaps I had better give a slight description of his personal appearance.

If this was not a true story, I should have liked to have made him a model of manly beauty; but a regard for veracity compels me to confess that he was not what would be generally considered handsome; that is, not in figure, for his face was by no means unpleasing.

II.—*b*   2*

His body was, in size and shape, not very unlike a huge plum-pudding, and was clothed in a bright-green, tightly-fitting doublet, with red holly-berries for buttons.

His limbs were long and slender in proportion to his stature, which was not more than three feet or so.

His head was encircled by a crown of holly and mistletoe.

The round red berries sparkled amid his hair, which was silver-white, and shone out in cheerful harmony with his rosy, jovial face. And that face! it would have done one good to look at it.

In spite of the silver hair, and an occasional wrinkle beneath the merry, laughing eyes, it seemed brimming over with perpetual youth. The mouth, well garnished with teeth, white and sound, which seemed as if they could do ample justice to holiday cheer, was ever open with a beaming, genial smile, expanding now and then into hearty laughter. Fun and good-fellowship were in every feature.

The owner of the face was, at the moment when the baron first perceived him, comfortably seated upon the top of the large tobacco-jar on the table, nursing his left leg.

The baron's somewhat abrupt inquiry did not appear to irritate him; on the contrary, he seemed rather amused than otherwise.

" You don't ask prettily, old gentleman," he replied; " but I don't mind telling you, for all that. I'm King Christmas." .

" Eh ?" said the baron.

" Ah !" said the goblin. Of course, you have guessed he was a goblin ?

" And pray what's your business here ?" said the baron.

" Don't be crusty with a fellow," replied the goblin. " I merely looked in to wish you the compliments of the season. Talking of crust, by the way, what sort of a tap is it you're drinking ?" So saying, he took up a flask of the baron's very best and poured out about half a glass. Having held the glass first on one side and then on the other, winked at it twice, sniffed it, and gone through the remainder of the pantomime in which connoisseurs indulge, he drank it with great deliberation, and smacked his lips scientifically. " Hum ! Johannisberg ! and not so *very* bad—for you. But I tell you what it is, baron, you'll have to bring out better stuff than this when *I* put my legs on your mahogany."

" Well, you are a cool fish," said the baron. " However, you're rather a joke, so, now you're here, we may as well enjoy ourselves. Smoke ?"

" Not anything you're likely to offer me !"

" Confound your impudence !" roared the

baron, with a horribly complicated oath. "That tobacco is as good as any in all Rhineland."

"That's a nasty cough you've got, baron. Don't excite yourself, my dear boy; I dare say you speak according to your lights. I don't mean Vesuvians, you know, but your opportunities for knowing anything about it. Try a weed out of my case, and I expect you'll alter your opinion."

The baron took the proffered case and selected a cigar. Not a word was spoken till it was half consumed, when the baron took it, for the first time, from his lips, and said, gently, with the air of a man communicating an important discovery in the strictest confidence, "Das ist gut!"

"Thought you'd say so," said the visitor. "And now, as you like the cigar, I should like you to try a thimbleful of what *I* call wine. I must warn you, though, that it is rather potent, and may produce effects you are not accustomed to."

"Bother that, if it is as good as the weed," said the baron; "I haven't taken my usual quantity by four bottles yet."

"Well, don't say I didn't warn you, that's all. I don't think you'll find it unpleasant, though it is rather strong when you're not accustomed to it." So saying, the goblin produced from some mysterious pocket a black, big-bellied bottle, crusted, apparently, with the dust of ages.

It did strike the baron as peculiar, that the bottle, when once produced, appeared nearly as big round as the goblin himself; but he was not the sort of man to stick at trifles, and he pushed forward his glass to be filled just as composedly as if the potion had been shipped and paid duty, in the most commonplace way.

The glass was filled and emptied, but the baron uttered not his opinion. Not in words, at least, but he pushed forward his glass to be filled again in a manner that sufficiently bespoke his approval.

"Aha! you smile!" said the goblin. And it was a positive fact; the baron was smiling; a thing he had not been known to do in the memory of the oldest inhabitant. "That's the stuff to make your hair curl, isn't it?"

"I believe you, my b-o-o-oy!" The baron brought out this earnest expression of implicit confidence with true unction. "It warms one *here!*"

Knowing the character of the man, one would have expected him to put his hand upon his stomach. But he didn't; he laid it upon his *heart.*

"The spell begins to operate, I see," said the goblin. "Have another glass?"

The baron had another glass, and another after that.

The smile on his face expanded into an expression of such geniality that the whole character of his countenance was changed, and his own mother wouldn't have known him. I doubt myself—inasmuch as she died when he was exactly a year and three months old— whether she would have recognized him under any circumstances; but I merely wish to express that he was changed almost beyond recognition.

"Upon my word," said the baron, at length, "I feel so light I almost think I could dance a hornpipe. I used to, once, I know. Shall I try?"

"Well, if you ask my advice," replied the goblin, "I should say, decidedly, don't. 'Barkis is willing,' I dare say, but trousers are weak, and you might split 'em."

"Hang it all," said the baron, "so I might. I didn't think of that. But still I feel as if I must do something juvenile!"

"Ah! that's the effect of your change of nature," said the goblin. "Never mind, I'll give you plenty to do presently."

"Change of nature! What do you mean, you old conundrum?" said the baron.

"You're another," said the goblin. "But

never mind. What I mean is just this. What
you are now feeling is the natural consequence
of my magic wine, which has changed you into
a fairy. That's what's the matter, sir."

" A fairy! me!" exclaimed the baron. " Get
out. I'm too fat."

" Fat! Oh! that's nothing. We shall put you
in regular training, and you'll soon be slim
enough to creep into a lady's stocking. Not
that you'll be called upon to do anything of the
sort; but I'm merely giving you an idea of
your future figure."

" No, no," said the baron; " me thin! that's
too ridiculous. Why, that's worse than being a
fairy. You don't mean it, though, do you? I
do feel rather peculiar."

" I do, indeed," said the visitor. " You don't
dislike it, do you?"

" Well, no, I can't say I do, entirely. It's
queer, though, I feel so uncommon friendly. I
feel as if I should like to shake hands or pat
somebody on the back."

" Ah!" said the goblin, " I know how it is.
Rum feeling, when you're not accustomed to it.
But come; finish that glass, for we must be off.
We've got a precious deal to do before morning,
I can tell you. Are you ready?"

" All right," said the baron. " I'm just in the
humor to make a night of it."

" Come along, then," said the goblin.

They proceeded for a short time in silence along the corridors of the old castle. They carried no candle, but the baron noticed that everything seemed perfectly light wherever they stood, but relapsed into darkness as soon as they had passed by. The goblin spoke first.

" I say, baron, you've been an uncommon old brute in your time, now, haven't you ?"

" H'm," said the baron, reflectively ; " I don't know. Well, yes, I rather think I have."

" How jolly miserable you've been making those two young people, you old sinner ! You know who I mean."

" Eh, what ? You know that, too ?" said the baron.

" Know it ; of course I do. Why, bless your heart, I know everything, my dear boy. But you *have* made yourself an old tyrant in that quarter, considerably. Ar'n't you blushing, you hard-hearted old monster ?"

" Don't know, I'm sure," said the baron, scratching his nose, as if that was where he expected to feel it. " I believe I have treated them badly, though, now I come to think of it."

At this moment they reached the door of Bertha's chamber   The door opened of itself at their approach.

" Come along," said the goblin ; " you won't wake her. Now, old flinty-heart, look there."

The sight that met the baron's view was one that few fathers could have beheld without affectionate emotion. Under ordinary circumstances, however, the baron would not have felt at all sentimental on the subject, but to-night something made him view things in quite a different light.

I shouldn't like to make affidavit of the fact, but it's my positive impression that he sighed.

Now, my dear reader, don't imagine I'm going to indulge your impertinent curiosity with an elaborate description of the sacred details of a lady's sleeping apartment. *You're* not a fairy, you know, and I don't see that it can possibly matter to you whether fair Bertha's dainty little bottines were tidily placed on a chair by her bedside, or thrown carelessly, as they had been taken off, upon the hearth-rug, where her favorite spaniel reposed, warming his nose in his sleep before the last smouldering embers of the decaying fire ; or whether her crinoline—but if she did wear a crinoline, what can that possibly matter to you ?

All I shall tell you is, that everything looked snug and comfortable ; but, somehow, any place got that look when Bertha was in it.

And now a word about the jewel in the

casket—pet Bertha herself. Really, I'm at a
loss to describe her. How do you look when
you're asleep ?—Well, it wasn't like *that;* not a
bit ! Fancy a sweet girl's face, the cheek faintly
flushed with a soft, warm tint, like the blush in
the heart of the opening rose, and made brighter
by the contrast of the snowy pillow on which it
rested ; dark silken hair, curling and clustering
lovingly over the tiniest of tiny ears, and the
softest, whitest neck that ever mortal maiden
was blessed with ; long silken eyelashes, fring-
ing lids only less beautiful than the dear earnest
eyes they cover. Fancy all this, and fancy, too,
if you can, the expression of perfect goodness
and purity that lit up the sweet features of the
slumbering maiden with a beauty almost angelic, and you will see what the baron saw that
night. Not quite all, however, for the baron's
vision paused not at the bedside before him, but
had passed on from the face of the sleeping
maiden to another face as lovely, that of the
young wife, Bertha's mother, who had, years
before, taken her angel beauty to the angels.

The goblin spoke to the baron's thought.
" Wonderfully like her, is she not, baron ?"
The baron slowly inclined his head.

" You made her very happy, didn't you ?"

The tone in which the goblin spoke was harsh
and mocking.

" A faithful husband, tender and true ! She must have been a happy wife, eh, baron ?"

The baron's head had sunk upon his bosom. Old recollections were thronging into his awakened memory. Solemn vows to love and cherish somewhat strangely kept. Memories of bitter words and savage oaths showered at a quiet and uncomplaining figure, without one word in reply. And, last, the memory of a fit of drunken passion, and a hasty blow struck with a heavy hand. And then of three months of fading away; and last, of her last prayer—for her baby and him.

" A good husband makes a good father, baron. No wonder you are somewhat chary of rashly intrusting to a suitor the happiness of a sweet flower like this. Poor child ! it is hard, though, that she must think no more of him she loves so dearly. See ! she is weeping even in her dreams. But you have good reasons, no doubt. Young Carl is wild, perhaps, or drinks, or gambles, eh ? What ! none of these ? Perhaps he is wayward and uncertain ; and you fear that the honeyed words of courtship might turn to bitter sayings in matrimony. They do, sometimes, eh, baron ? By all means guard her from such a fate as that. Poor, tender flower ! Or who knows, worse than that, baron ! Hard words break no bones, they say, but angry men are quick, and a blow is soon struck, eh?"

The goblin had drawn nearer and nearer, and laid his hand upon the baron's arm, and the last words were literally hissed into his ears.

The baron's frame swayed to and fro under the violence of his emotion. At last, with a cry of agony, he dashed his hands upon his forehead. The veins were swollen up like thick cords, and his voice was almost inarticulate in its unnatural hoarseness.

"Tortures! release me! Let me go, let me go and do something to forget the past, or I shall go mad and die!"

He rushed out of the room and paced wildly down the corridor, the goblin following him. At last, as they came near the outer door of the castle, which opened of itself as they reached it, the spirit spoke:

"This way, baron, this way. I told you there was work for us to do before morning, you know."

"Work!" exclaimed the baron, absently, passing his fingers through his tangled hair; "oh! yes, work! the harder the better; anything to make me forget."

The two stepped out into the courtyard, and the baron shivered, though, as it seemed, unconsciously, at the breath of the frosty midnight air. The snow lay deep on the ground, and the baron's heavy boots sank into it with a crisp, crushing sound at every tread.

He was bareheaded, but seemed unconscious of the fact, and tramped on, as if utterly indifferent to anything but his own thoughts. At last, as a blast of the night wind, keener than ordinary, swept over him, he seemed for the first time to feel the chill. His teeth chattered, and he muttered, " Cold, very cold."

" Ay, baron," said the goblin, " it is cold even to us, who are healthy and strong, and warmed with wine. Colder still, though, to those who are hungry and half-naked, and have to sleep on the snow."

" Sleep? snow?" said the baron. " Who sleeps on the snow? Why, I wouldn't let my dogs be out on such a night as this."

" Your dogs, no !" said the goblin ; " I spoke of meaner animals—your wretched tenants. Did you not order, yesterday, that Wilhelm and Friedrich, if they did not pay their rent to-morrow, should be turned out to sleep on the snow? A snug bed for the little ones, and a nice white coverlet, eh? Ha! ha! twenty florins or so is no great matter, is it? I'm afraid their chance is small ; nevertheless, come and see."

The baron hung his head. A few minutes

brought him to the first of the poor dwellings, which they entered noiselessly. The fireless grate, the carpetless floor, the broken window-panes, all gave sufficient testimony to the want and misery of the occupants. In one corner lay sleeping a man, a woman, and three children, and nestling to each other for the warmth which their ragged coverlet could afford. In the man, the baron recognized his tenant Wilhelm, one of those who had been with him to beg for indulgence on the previous day.

The keen features, and bones almost starting through the pallid skin, showed how heavily the hand of hunger had been laid upon all.

The cold night wind moaned and whistled through the many flaws in the ill-glazed, ill-thatched tenement, and rustled over the sleepers, wno shivered even in their sleep.

" Ha, baron !" said the goblin, " death is breathing in their faces even now, you see ; it is hardly worth while to lay them to sleep in the snow, is it ? They would sleep a little sounder, that's all."

The baron shuddered, and then, hastily pulling the warm coat from his own shoulders, he spread it over the sleepers.

"Oho !" said the goblin; " bravely done, baron ! By all means keep them warm to-night ; they'll enjoy the snow more to-morrow, you know."

Strange to say, the baron, instead of feeling chilled when he had removed his coat, felt a strange glow of warmth spread from the region of the heart over his entire frame. The goblin's continual allusions to his former intention, which he had by this time totally relinquished, hurt him, and he said, rather pathetically,—

" Don't talk of that again, good goblin. I'd rather sleep on the snow myself."

" Eh ! what ?" said the goblin; " you don't mean to say you're sorry ? Then what do you say to making these poor people comfortable ?"

" With all my heart," said the baron, " if we had only anything to do it with."

" You leave that to me," said the goblin. " Your brother fairies are not far off, you may be sure."

As he spoke he clapped his hands thrice, and before the third clap had died away the poor cottage was swarming with tiny figures, whom the baron rightly conjectured to be the fairies themselves.

Now, you may not be aware (the baron was not, until that night) that there are among the fairies trades and professions, just as with ordinary mortals.

However, there they were, each with the accompaniments of his or her particular business, and to it they went manfully. A fairy

glazier put in new panes to the shattered windows, fairy carpenters replaced the doors upon
their hinges, and fairy painters, with incon-
ceivable celerity, made cupboards and closets as
fresh as paint could make them; one fairy
housemaid laid and lit a roaring fire, while
another dusted and rubbed chairs and tables to
a miraculous degree of brightness; a fairy
butler uncorked bottles of fairy wine, and a
fairy cook laid out a repast of most tempting
appearance.

The baron, hearing a tapping above him,
cast his eyes upward, and beheld a fairy slater
rapidly repairing a hole in the roof; and when
he bent them down again they fell on a fairy
doctor mixing a cordial for the sleepers. Nay,
there was even a fairy parson, who, not having
any present employment, contented himself
with rubbing his hands and looking pleasant,
probably waiting till somebody might want to be
christened or married.

Every trade, every profession or occupation
appeared, without exception, to be represented;
nay, we beg pardon, with one exception only,
for the baron used to say, when afterwards
relating his experiences to bachelor friends,—

"You may believe me or not, sir, there was
every mortal business under the sun, *but deil a
bit of a lawyer.*"

The baron could not long remain inactive. He was rapidly seized with a violent desire to do something to help, which manifested itself in insane attempts to assist everybody at once. At last, after having taken all the skin off his knuckles in attempting to hammer in nails in aid of the carpenter, and then nearly tumbling over a fairy housemaid, whose broom he was offering to carry, he gave it up as a bad job, and stood aside with his friend the goblin.

He was just about to inquire how it was that the poor occupants of the house were not awakened by so much din, when a fairy Sam Slick, who had been examining the cottager's old clock with a view to a thorough repair, touched some spring within it, and it made the usual purr preparatory to striking. When, lo! and behold, at the very first stroke, cottage, goblin, fairies, and all disappeared into utter darkness, and the baron found himself in his turret-chamber, rubbing his toe, which he had just hit with considerable force against the fender. As he was only in his slippers, the concussion was unpleasant, and the baron rubbed his toe for a good while.

After he had finished with his toe he rubbed his nose, and, finally, with a countenance of deep reflection, scratched the bump of something or other at the top of his head.

II.—*c*

The old clock on the stairs was striking three, and the fire had gone out.

The baron reflected for a short time longer, and finally decided that he had better go to bed, which he did accordingly.

III.

The morning dawned upon the very ideal, as far as weather was concerned, of a Christmas-day. A bright winter sun shone out just vividly enough to make everything look genial and pleasant, and yet not with sufficient warmth to mar the pure, unbroken surface of the crisp, white snow, which lay like a never-ending white lawn upon the ground, and glittered in myriad silver flakes upon the leaves of the sturdy ever-greens.

I am afraid the baron had not had a very good night; at any rate, I know that he was wide-awake at an hour long before his usual time of rising.

He lay first on one side, and then on the other, and then, by way of variety, turned on his back, with his magenta nose pointing per-pendicularly towards the ceiling; but it was all of no use. Do what he would, he couldn't get to sleep, and at last, not long after daybreak, he tumbled out of bed and proceeded to dress.

Even after he was out of bed his fidgetiness continued. It did not strike him, until after he had got one boot on, that it would be a more natural proceeding to put his stockings on first; after which he caught himself in the act of trying to put his trousers on over his head.

In a word, the baron's mind was evidently preoccupied; his whole air was that of a man who felt a strong impulse to do something or other, but could not quite make up his mind to it.

At last, however, the good impulse conquered, and this wicked old baron, in the stillness of the calm, bright Christmas morning, went down upon his knees and prayed.

Stiff were his knees and slow his tongue, for neither had done such work for many a long day past; but I have read in the Book of the joy of angels over a repenting sinner.

There needs not much eloquence to pray the publican's prayer, and who shall say but there was gladness in heaven that Christmas morning?

The baron's appearance down-stairs at such an early hour occasioned quite a commotion. Nor were the domestics reassured when the baron ordered a bullock to be killed and jointed instantly, and all the available provisions in the larder, including sausage, to be packed up in baskets, with a good store of his own peculiar wine.

One ancient retainer was heard to declare, with much pathos, that he feared master had gone insane.

However, insane or not, they knew the baron must be obeyed, and in an exceedingly short space of time he sallied forth, accompanied by three servants carrying the baskets, and wondering what in the name of fortune their master would do next.

He stopped at the cottage of Wilhelm, which he had visited with the goblin on the previous night. The labors of the fairies did not seem to have produced much lasting benefit, for the appearance of everything around was as wretched as could be.

The poor family thought that the baron had come himself to turn them out of house and home; and the children huddled up timidly to their mother for protection, while the father attempted some words of entreaty for mercy.

The pale, pinched features of the group, and their looks of dread and wretchedness, were too much for the baron.

"Eh! what! what do you mean, confound you? Turn you out? Of course not: I've brought you some breakfast. Here! Fritz— Carl; where are the knaves? Now, then, unpack, and don't be a week about it. Can't you see the people are hungry, ye villains ? Here, lend me the corkscrew."

This last being a tool the baron was tolerably accustomed to, he had better success than with those of the fairy carpenters ; and it was not long before the poor tenants were seated before a roaring fire, and doing justice, with the appetite of starvation, to a substantial breakfast.

The baron felt a queer sensation in his throat at the sight of the poor people's enjoyment, and had passed the back of his hand twice across his eyes when he thought no one was looking; but his emotion fairly rose to boiling when the poor father, Wilhelm, with tears in his eyes, and about a quarter of a pound of beef in his mouth, sprang up from the table and flung himself at the baron's knees, invoking blessings on him for his goodness.

"Get up, you audacious scoundrel!" roared the baron. "What the deuce do you mean by such conduct, eh? confound you!"

At this moment the door opened, and in walked Mynheer Klootz, who had heard nothing of the baron's change of intentions, and who, seeing Wilhelm at the baron's feet, and hearing the latter speaking, as he thought, in an angry tone, at once jumped to the conclusion that Wilhelm was entreating for longer indul-

4

gence. He rushed at the unfortunate man and collared him. "Not if *we* know it," exclaimed he ; "you'll have the wolves for bedfellows to-night, I reckon. Come along, my fine fellow." As he spoke he turned his back towards the baron, with the intention of dragging his victim to the door.

The baron's little gray eyes twinkled, and his whole frame quivered with suppressed emotion, which, after the lapse of a moment, vented itself in a kick, and such a kick! Not one of your *Varsovianna* flourishes, but a kick that employed every muscle from hip to toe, and drove the worthy steward up against the door like a ball from a catapult.

Misfortunes never come singly, and so Mynheer Klootz found with regard to the kick, for it was followed, without loss of time, by several dozen others, as like it as possible, from the baron's heavy boots.

Wounded lions proverbially come badly off, and Fritz and Carl, who had suffered from many an act of petty tyranny on the part of the steward, thought they could not do better than follow their master's example, which they did to such good purpose, that when the unfortunate Klootz did escape from the cottage at last, I don't believe he could have had any *os sacrum* left.

After having executed this little act of poetical justice, the baron and his servants visited the other cottages, in all of which they were received with dread and dismissed with blessings.

Having completed his tour of charity, the baron returned home to breakfast, feeling more really contented than he had done for many a long year. He found Bertha, who had not risen when he started, in a considerable state of anxiety as to what he could possibly have been doing. In answer to her inquiries, he told her, with a roughness he was far from feeling, to "mind her own affairs."

The gentle eyes filled with tears at the harshness of the reply; perceiving which, the baron was beyond measure distressed, and chucked her under the chin in what was meant to be a very conciliatory manner.

"Eh! what, my pretty, tears? No, surely. Bertha must forgive her old father. I didn't mean it, you know, my pet; and yet, on second thoughts, yes, I did, too." Bertha's face was overcast again. "My little girl thinks she has no business anywhere, eh! Is that it? Well, then, my pet, suppose you make it your business to write a note to young Carl von Sempach, and say I'm afraid I was rather rude to him yesterday, but if he'll overlook it, and come take a snug family dinner and a slice of the pudding with us to-day——"

" Why, pa, you don't mean—yes, I do really believe you do——"

The baron's eyes were winking nineteen to the dozen.

" Why, you dear, dear, dear old pa !" and at the imminent risk of upsetting the breakfast table, Bertha rushed at the baron, and flinging two soft white arms about his neck, kissed him—oh ! how she *did* kiss him ! I shouldn't have thought, myself, she could possibly have had any left for Carl; but I dare say Bertha attended to his interests in that respect somehow.

IV.

Well, Carl came to dinner, and the baron was, not very many years after, promoted to the dignity of a grandpapa, and a very jolly old grandpapa he made.

Is that all you wanted to know ? About Klootz ? Well, Klootz got over the kicking, but he was dismissed from the baron's service ; and on examination of his accounts it was discovered that he had been in the habit of robbing the baron of nearly a third of his yearly income, which he had to refund ; and with the money he was thus compelled to disgorge, the baron built new cottages for his tenants, and new-stocked their farms. Nor was he poorer in the end, for his tenants worked with the energy of gratitude, and he was soon many times richer than when the goblin visited him on that Christmas eve.

And was the goblin ever explained? Certainly not. How dare you have the impertinence to suppose such a thing?

An empty bottle, covered with cobwebs, was found the next morning in the turret-chamber, which the baron at first imagined must be the bottle from which the goblin produced his magic wine; but as it was found, on examination, to be labelled " Old Jamaica Rum," of course that could not have had anything to do with it. However it was, the baron never thoroughly enjoyed any other wine after it, and as he did not thenceforth get intoxicated, on an average, more than two nights a week, or swear more than eight oaths a day, I think King Christmas may be considered to have thoroughly reformed him.

And he always maintained, to the day of his death, that he was changed into a fairy, and became exceedingly angry if contradicted.

Who doesn't believe in fairies after this? I only hope King Christmas may make a few more good fairies this year, to brighten the

4*

homes of the poor with the light of Christmas charity.

Truly, we need not look far for alms-men. Cold and hunger, disease and death, are around us at all times; but at no time do they press more heavily on the poor than at this jovial Christmas season.

Shall we shut out, in our mirth and jollity, the cry of the hungry poor? or shall we not rather remember, in the midst of our happy family circles, round our well-filled tables and before our blazing fires, that our brothers are starving out in the cold, and that the Christmas song of the angels was " Good-will to men" ?

The Spaniard's Episode.

"He was a pleasant-looking fellow, with huge black whiskers and a roguish eye. He touched the guitar with masterly skill, and sang little amorous ditties with an expressive leer."

Irving.

A CHRISTMAS MIRACLE.

You have never heard of Alcala? Well, it is a little village nestling between the Spanish hills, a league from great Madrid. There is a ring of stone houses, each with its white-walled patio and grated windows; each with its balcony, whence now and then a laughing face looks down upon the traveller. There is an ancient inn by the roadside, a time-worn church, and above, on the hill-top, against the still blue sky, the castle, dusky with age, but still keeping a feudal dignity, though half its yellow walls have crumbled away.

This is the Alcala into which I jogged one winter evening in search of rest and entertainment after a long day's journey on mule-back.

The inn was in a doze when my footsteps broke the silence of its stone court-yard; but presently a woman came through an inner door to answer my summons, and I was speedily cast under the quiet spell of the place by finding myself behind a screen of leaves, with a straw-covered bottle at my elbow and a cold fowl within comfortable reach.

The bower where I sat was unlighted save by the waning sun, and I could see but little of its long vista, without neglecting a very imperious appetite. The lattice was covered, I thought, with vine-leaves, and I felt sure, too, that some orange boughs, reaching across the patio wall, mingled with the foliage above my head. But all I was certain of was the relish of the fowl and the delicious refreshment of the cool wine. Having finished these, I lay back in my chair, luxuriating in the sense of healthy fatigue, and going over again, in fancy, the rolling roads of my journey.

I believe I, also, fell into the prevailing slumber of the place, lulled by the soft atmosphere and gentle wine, and might have slept there till morning had a furious sneeze not awakened me with a start. I looked confusedly about in the dusk, but could see nothing save, at last, the tip of a lighted cigarette in the remote depths of the bower. I called out,—

"Who's there?" and was answered, courteously, by a deep, gruff voice in Spanish,—

"It is I, señor, Jose Rosado."

"Are you a guest of ' La Fonda' ?" said I, for I had learned that this was the name of the inn, and was a little doubtful whether I had fallen into the hands of friend or foe.

"Ha! ha! ha!" with a long explosion of guttural sounds, was my only answer. Then, after a brightening of the cigarette-fire, to denote that the smoker was puffing it into life, he said,—

"I, señor, am the host."

At this I drew my chair closer, and found, in the thin reflection of the cigarette, a round, bronzed face beaming with smiles and picturing easy good health.

It was winter in Spain, but the scent of flowers was abroad, and the soft, far-off stars twinkled through the moving leaves. What wonder, then, that we fell into talk,—I, the inquiring traveller, he, the arch-gossip of Alcala, —and talked till the moon rose high into the night?

"And who lives in the castle on the hill?" I asked, after hearing the private history of half the town.

"Ah," said mine host, as if preparing to swallow a savory morsel, "there's a bit of gossip; there's a story, indeed!" He puffed away for a minute in mute satisfaction, and then began.

"That is a noble family, the Aranjuez. None can remember in Alcala when there was not a

noble Aranjuez living in its castle, and they have
led our people bravely in all the wars of Spain.
I remember as a boy——"

But, having become acquainted with mine
host's loquacity, I broke in with a question
more to the point,—

"Who, Señor Jose, lives in the castle now?"

He would have answered without a suspicion
of my ruse, had not a bell just then rung solemnly forth, awakening the still night, and
arousing Jose Rosado from his comfortable
bench, promptly to his feet.

"Come," he said; "that is for the Christmas
Mass. I will tell you as we go."

The little inn was lively enough as we emerged
from the bower and crossed the court-yard
towards the road. The woman who had prepared my supper came forth arrayed in a
capulet of white and scarlet, and two younger
girls who accompanied her wore veils and long,
black robes which fell about their forms like
Oriental garments. Two or three men, attendants and hostlers of the place, were also about
to start, trigged out in queer little capes and
high-crowned hats. All this fine apparel, mine
host informed me, was peculiar to Christmas,
and I soon found the highway full of peasants
in similar garb.

As we got off, Jose Rosado resumed his story,

which was brief enough to beguile us just to the church-door.

"You ask me, señor, who lives in the castle now? The Donna Isabella is alone there, now, the only survivor of the noble race, except—except señor," (he laid a peculiar emphasis on the word,) "except a wilful son, whom she has disowned and driven from her house. He is a handsome lad, and married, here in Alcala, the beauty of the town, in spite of his mother's wounded pride. It was a love-match of stolen wooing and secret wedding,—but, ha! ha! *we* saw it all, knew it all, before even they did themselves. Many an evening have I met them on these roads, billing and cooing like the doves on La Fonda's eaves. They were made by nature for each other, though, and even the rage of the proud Donna Isabella could never part them."

"And do they still live in the town?" I asked.

"Oh, yes," said Jose; "over there in the white house where the olive trees are, at the bottom of the long hill."

I looked in the direction whither he pointed, but I could see little in the dim moonlight save a white wall amid dense shadows.

"And is Donna Isabella a very old lady?" I asked, because very old ladies are often charged with peculiar severity to very young ones.

" No, no, no," said Jose Rosado, with a quick turn of the head to each no. " She's a widow lady of middle age ; very proud and very handsome. You shall see her presently, for she has consented to take part in the Christmas play at the church."

As I had come a long journey to see this same Christmas play, my expectation was doubly aroused as we approached the old edifice, whose open belfry and rows of cloisters stood before us at the top of the hill we were ascending.

As we entered, the bells stopped ringing, for it was precisely midnight, and the priest at the altar began to say the Christmas Masses. When he had reached the Gospel, he was interrupted by the appearance of a matron, dressed all in white, who stood at the end of the nave. She was clad like the Madonna, and was accompanied by Joseph, who wore the garb of a mountaineer, with a hatchet in his hand. An officious little officer with a halberd opened the way through the crowd before these personages, and they came solemnly up the aisle towards the chancel, which had been arrayed to represent Bethlehem, the Madonna reciting, as she moved forward, a plaintive song about her homelessness. Joseph replied cheeringly, and led her under a roof of leaves in the sanctuary, formed in the manner of a stable, in

which we could see the manger against the wall.
Here she took rest from her journey, while a
little crib, wherein lay the Bambino—or waxen
image of the Babe—all adorned with ribbons
and laces, was brought from the sacristy and
placed in the straw at her feet.

As the Madonna passed us, Jose Rosado
nudged me, and whispered audibly enough to
make the crowd about us turn and stare,—

"Hist! here's the Donna Isabella, señor!
She looks like a saint to-night!"

I watched her closely as she went by me, and
marked, under the meek expression assumed by
the Virgin, a more characteristic one of severe
resolution. She was, however, a queenly woman,
in the ripest stage of maturity, but she bore
herself, in the part she had taken, with a
matronly grace something too conscious for the
lowly Mary.

As she seated herself on the heap of straw, a
little boy in a surplice, representing an angel,
with wings of crimped lawn at his shoulders,
was raised in a chair, by a cord and pulley, to
the very top of the sanctuary arch, where he
sang a carol to the shepherds,—

> "Shepherds, hasten all
> With flying feet from your retreat;
> On rustic pipes now play
> Your sweetest, sweetest lay;

for"—so ran the song—" Mary and the King of
Heaven are in yonder cave."

At this, an orchestra, concealed behind the
high altar, set up a tooting from bagpipes, and
flute, and violin, which served as a prelude to
the appearance of the shepherds, who were concealed in the gallery.

Up they got, with long cloaks and crooked
staffs, murmuring their surprise and incredulity
at what the angel had said; some pretending to
grumble at being awakened from sleep, others
anxious to prove the truth of the strange
tidings.

Then the angel sang a more appealing ditty
still, whereat they were all about ready to advance, when one of their number, of a sceptical
turn, urged them to avoid such fanciful matters
and give heed to their sheep, who would otherwise become the prey of the wolf.

Hereupon, an old shepherd appeared, who
gave three loud knocks with his crook, and denounced those who should disobey the heavenly
messenger. The practical man was thus silenced,
and they expressed their willingness to go to
the manger,—and at the same moment an angel
appeared to guide them thither.

They descended from the gallery to the outer
porch of the church and knocked loudly at the
door, saying, as if to the innkeeper at Bethlehem:

" Pray, good master of the inn,
Open the door and let us in."

But Joseph became alarmed at the approach
of such a number of rustics, and inquired who
they were. They held a songful colloquy with
him; but he continued to refuse them admittance, until an angel again intervened, this time
in the form of a tall acolyte from the sanctuary,
accompanied by two little angelic choristers.
He reassured Joseph, and invited the shepherds
to enter and worship the Babe. They came up
the aisle flourishing their be-ribboned crooks
and singing in praise of the Child, but they
were sorely vexed, when they saw the stable,
that so humble a place had been found for His
shelter. Joseph explained, in several couplets,
that no other house would receive them, and
the shepherds replied in several others, mingling
sympathy and good advice, intended not for
Joseph, but for the throng, who listened in religious awe.

After paying due homage to the child and
Mary, the shepherds exchanged some more
verses with Joseph, and then retired to the
other end of the church, singing in chorus as
they went.

All these ceremonies had so claimed my attention that I had given scarcely any heed to

5*

the Virgin. She was seated humbly in the
straw beside the little crib, in which still nestled
the Bambino, and, with eyes cast down in maternal thoughtfulness, she was a lovely object
there beneath the roof of the leafy stable. She
did not appear to notice the actors in the
drama; and now, when three young girls, in
gayest holiday attire, came forward with dis-
taffs that streamed with bright ribbons, and
knelt before her, she reached forth a hand as if
to bless them, but kept her eyes turned meekly
upon the ground.

As these three girls retired from the manger,
another and larger band appeared beneath the
gallery opposite the shepherds, singing in sweet
voices a salutation to the three who had just
left the chancel. These made answer that they
had come from the stable where the Saviour
was born; and so, in alternate questions and
answers, they described all that they had seen.
The two groups, having advanced a step or
two at each stanza, now met, and went back to
the manger together, singing the same air the
shepherds had previously sung.

When they arrived at the stable they made
their offering, setting up a tent the while, ornamented with plenteous ribbons and flowers,
among which blackbirds, thrushes, turtle-doves
and partridges fluttered about at the ends of

cords to which they were fastened. They
brought with them, also, bunches of purple
grapes and strings of yellow apples, chaplets
of dried prunes and heaps of walnuts and chestnuts. After arranging these rustic offerings,
the shepherdesses returned, singing in chorus as
they went :

> "In Bethlehem, at midnight,
> The Virgin mother bore her child.
> This world contains no fairer sight
> Than this fair Babe and Mary mild.
> Well may we sing at sight like this,
> *Gloria in Excelsis.*"

I now had another unobstructed view of
Donna Isabella, and Jose Rosado's gossip, intensified by her romantic appearance as the
Virgin, had given me a deep interest in her every
movement.

She reached down into the little crib to lift
out the Bambino, and I could plainly see a look
of astonishment rise to her face as she started
back, both hands held wide apart, as if having
encountered something they were unprepared
to touch. Then she turned hurriedly to Joseph
and whispered a word in his ear, whereupon he
too bent with surprise over the little crib. After
gazing at it a moment, he reached down and
lifted out, not the waxen Bambino, but a sweet

young baby that smiled and reached its tiny arms from Joseph towards the white Virgin.

Donna Isabella was visibly affected at this, and took the tender infant into her arms, caressing and soothing it, while it fondled her face and white head-dress.

The audience had now become aware that, instead of the waxen image in the crib, there had been found a living baby, and the impetuous and susceptible minds of the Spanish peasants had jumped at the conclusion that they had witnessed a new miracle. They crowded up to the manger, telling their beads and murmuring prayers, while they pushed and jostled each other madly for a glimpse of the holy infant.

One of the acolytes reached his arms forth to take it from Donna Isabella and bring it to the chancel rail for the crowd to see, but she held it more closely to her bosom, and refused to let it go from her. As she stood there, a tall and stately figure, folded in the white gown of the Virgin and wearing the close head-dress which concealed all save her splendid face, she seemed the creation of some old painter, and the curious crowd of peasants was hushed into admiration by her beauty and her tenderness for the child. She, too, became a part of the strange miracle. The infant Christ had been born anew among them, and lay there in his very mother's arms, an object of mystery and worship. As the silence of wonder ensued, Donna Isabella seemed to collect her startled senses, and looked around her as if expecting the mother of the child to come and claim it. A woman of her resolution was not to be hurried into superstitious follies by some pretty trick or accident. But the little one lay so softly in her arms and reached with such tiny, appealing fingers at her throat, that she began to feel a motherly fondness for it. And, moreover, had it not been sent her, who was alone now in the great castle on the hill, as a mysterious gift of Providence? Ought she not to feel it a sacred charge, coming as it did, from the very manger, to her arms?

Thus thinking, the Donna Isabella came slowly to the chancel rail, and, holding forth the infant at arms' length, she said:

" Good people of Alcala, my part in the Christmas play is done. The good Lord has sent me this little one to take care of; and here, before you all, I accept the charge and promise to cherish and love it. If any of you know its mother, say that the Donna Isabella has carried it to the castle of Aranjuez, and tell her to follow it there, for where her child is, there the mother should be also." This broke the spell. The silent crowd fell into murmurs

and gestures, and each one asked his neighbor
where the child belonged. There was no longer
any doubt. It was merely a human child ; but
the mystery of the manger surrounded it with
a hallowed interest, and everybody was eager to
discover its parents and bear them the good
news of its adoption by the great lady.

Now, Jose Rosado was too old a hand, too
jolly a host, to be long deceived. He whispered
me his views as we stood near the leafy stable,
and they were to the effect that the wayward
son of the Aranjuez knew more about the child
in the manger than any one else thereabouts.

And Jose was right; for, before the bustle
of inquiry had quite died away, from out the
sacristy door came a young girl wearing a veil
and dressed in the long black gown of the
Christmas ceremonies. She walked demurely
through the crowd, which parted for her with
inquiring looks, and, going straight up to the
chancel, dropped on her knees before the Donna
Isabella. She held down her head and made no
motion ; but all knew instinctively that she was
the mother of the child.

The noble Virgin stooped and raised her head
with a loving compassion. She put aside her
veil and moved as if to kiss her, but one look at
the mother's face turned her kindness into rage.
She cried, " What, you ?" and overwhelmed at

the discovery sank down on the straw of the
stable, clasping the child with a firmer hold, as
if to shield it from a foe.

It was a sore conflict for an unyielding will
like that of the Donna Isabella; but the part
she had played in the sacred ceremonies and the
surrounding emblems of peace and good-will
were softening influences. More potent even
than these was the persuasive contact of the
little hands which opened and shut in playful
touches at her throat. I could see from the
varying expressions of her .face that she questioned herself. Should she yield? The pride
of birth, the disobedience of a youthful son to
a mother of her indulgent nature, the stigma of
a low connection upon a noble family name—all
these things pleaded urgently, No. She looked up
vindictively at the gaping congregation, which
seemed spellbound in wanton curiosity, wherewith was mingled not a little religious dread.
And then, again, she turned her eyes down upon
the innocent face beside her bosom, so guileless,
to be the cause of such varying passions in the
throng about it. No, she could not give it up.
All the old maternal instincts were aroused in
her, and the firmness of her will was redoubled
by the sentiment of love for her grandchild.
Was it not her son's child, then, as well as this
woman's? Surely, she had a right to keep it,

and, glancing up with this last plea for possession on her lips, she saw beside the kneeling
wife a new figure, whose presence made her
pause and falter.

Only for an instant, however, for a kindlier
light came into her clear eyes, and reaching forth
the one arm which was free she threw it around
her son's neck and kissed him fondly, while the
little child which had wrought the change,—
a latter-day miracle of broken affections made
whole, of bitter wounds healed by the touch
of innocence,—lay there between them, striving,
with its playful hands, to catch at its mother's
bowing head.

As Jose Rosado and I walked homeward
through the pale-blue moonlight, we did not say
much. I was deeply moved by the touching
scene I had beheld ; and he was exceedingly reflective.

At last, as we neared La Fonda's vine-run
walls, he said :

"Señor, do you think the miracles are all
over nowadays ?"

" I know not, Señor Jose," I answered ; "but
there are certainly strange potencies lurking in
the depths of a mother's love."

From a Cuirassier's Note-Book.

"He was a handsome fellow, the son of a peasant; but he carried his blue dolman very well, this young soldier."

De Maupassant.

SALVETTE AND BERNADOU.

1.

It is the eve of Christmas in a large village of Bavaria. Along the snow-whitened streets, amid the confusion of the fog and noise of carriages and bells, the crowd presses joyously about cook-shops, wine-booths, and busy stores. Rustling with a light sweep of sound against the flower-twined and be-ribboned stalls, branches of green holly, or whole saplings, graced with pendants and shading the heads below like boughs of the Thuringian forest, go by in happy arms : a remembrance of nature in the torpid life of winter.

Day dies out. Far away, behind the gardens of the Résidence, linge ∶ a glimmer of the departing sun, red in the fog ; and in the town is such gaiety, such hurry of preparation for the holiday, that each jet of light which springs up in the many windows seems to hang from some vast Christmas-tree.

This is, in truth, no ordinary Christmas. It is the year of grace eighteen hundred and seventy, and the holy day is only a pretext the more to drink to the illustrious Von der Than and celebrate the triumph of the Bavarian troops.

"Noël, Noël!" The very Jews of the old town join in the mirth. Behold the aged Augustus Cahn who turns the corner by the "Blue Grapes!" Truly, his eyes have never shined before as they do to-night; nor has his little wicker satchel ever jingled so lightly. Across his sleeve, worn by the cords of sacks, is passed an honest little hamper, full to the top and covered with a cold napkin, from under which stick out the neck of a bottle and a twig of holly.

What on earth can the old miser want with all this? Can it be possible that he means to celebrate Christmas himself? Does he mean to have a family reunion and drink to the German fatherland? Impossible! Everybody knows old Cahn has no country. His fatherland is his strong box. And, moreover, he has neither family nor friends,—nothing but debtors. His sons and his associates are gone away long ago with the army. They traffic in the rear among the wagons, vending the water of life, buying watches, and, on nights of battle, emptying the pockets of the dead, or rifling the baggage tumbled in the ditches of the route.

Too old to follow his children, Father Cahn has remained in Bavaria, where he has made magnificent profits from the French prisoners of war. He is always prowling about the barracks to buy watches, shoulder-knots, medals, post-orders. You may see him glide through the hospitals, beside the ambulances. He approaches the beds of the wounded and demands, in a low, hideous growl,—

" Haf you anyting to sell?"

And, hold! At this same moment, the reason he trots so gayly with his basket under his arm, is solely that the military hospital closes at five o'clock, and that there are two Frenchmen who await him high up in that tall black building with straight, iron-barred windows, where Christmas finds nothing to welcome her approach save the pale lights which guard the pillows of the dying.

II.

These two Frenchmen are named Salvette and Bernadou. They are infantrymen from the same village of Provençe, enrolled in the same battalion, and wounded by the same shell. But Salvette had the stronger frame, and already he begins to grow convalescent, to take a few steps from his bed towards the window.

Bernadou, though, will never be cured. Through the pale curtains of the hospital bed,

II.—*e*   6*

his figure looks more meagre, more languished
day by day; and when he speaks of his home,
of return thither, it is with that sad smile of
the sick wherein there is more of resignation
than of hope.

To-day, now, he is a little animated by the
thought of the cheerful Christmas time, which,
in our country of Provençe, is like a grand bon-
fire of joy lighted in the midst of winter; by
remembrance of the departure for Mass at midnight; the church bedecked and luminous; the
dark streets of the village full of people; then
the long watch around the table; the three
traditional flambeaux; the ceremony of the
Yule-log; then the grand promenade around
the house, and the sparkle of the burning wine.

" Ah, my poor Salvette, what a sad Christmas
we are going to have this year! If only we
had money to buy a little loaf of white bread
and a flask of claret wine! What a pleasure it
would be before passing away forever to sprinkle
once again the Yule-log, with thee!"

And, in speaking of white bread and claret
wine, the eyes of the sick youth glistened with
pleasure.

But what to do? They had nothing, neither
money nor watches. Salvette still held hidden
in the seam of his mantle a post-order for forty
francs. But that was for the day when they

should be free and the first halt they should
make in a cabaret of France. That was sacred;
not to be touched!

But poor Bernadou is so sick. Who knows
whether he will ever be able to return? And,
then, it is Christmas, and they are together,
perhaps, for the last time. Would it not be
better to use it, after all?

Then, without a word to his comrade, Salvette
loosens his tunic to take out the post-order, and
when old Cahn comes, as he does every morning
to make his tour of the aisles, after long debates
and discussions under the breath, he thrusts into
the Jew's hands the slip of paper, worn and
yellow, smelling of powder and dashed with
blood.

From that moment Salvette assumed an air
of mystery. He rubbed his hands and laughed
all to himself when he looked at Bernadou.
And, as night fell, he was on the watch, his
forehead pressed eagerly against the window-
pane, until he saw, through the fog of the
deserted court below, old Augustus Cahn, who
came panting with his exertions, and carrying a
little basket on his arm.

III.

This solemn midnight, which sounds from all
the bells of the town, falls sadly into the pale

night of the sick. The hospital is silent, lit
only by the night-lamps suspended from the
ceiling. Great running shadows flit over the
beds and bare walls in a perpetual balancing,
which seems to image the heavy respiration of
all the sufferers lying there.

At times, dreamers talk high in their feverish
sleep, or groan in the clutches of nightmares;
while from the street there mounts up a vague
rumor of feet and voices, mingled in the cold
and sonorous night like sounds made under a
cathedral porch.

Salvette feels the gathering haste, the mystery
of a religious feast crossing the hours of sleep,
the hanging forth in the dark village of the blind
light of lanterns and the illumination of the windows of the church.

" Are you asleep, Bernadou ?"

Softly, on the little table next his comrade's
bed, Salvette has placed a bottle of *vin de Lunel*
and a loaf of bread, a pretty Christmas loaf,
where the twig of holly is planted straight in
the centre.

Bernadou opens his eyes encircled with fever.
By the indistinct glow of the night-lamps and
under the white reflection of the great roofs
where the moonlight lies dazzlingly on the
snow, this improvised Christmas feast seems but
a fantastic dream.

"Come, arouse thee, comrade! It shall not be said that two sons of Provençe have let this midnight pass without sprinkling a drop of claret!" And Salvette lifts him up with the tenderness of a mother. He fills the goblets, cuts the bread, and then they drink and talk of Provençe.

Little by little Bernadou grows animated and moved by the occasion,—the white wine, the remembrances! With that child-like manner which the sick find in the depths of their feebleness he asks Salvette to sing a Provençal Noël. His comrade asks which: "The Host," or "The Three Kings," or "St. Joseph Has Told Me"?

"No; I like the 'Shepherds' best. We chant that always at home."

"Then, here's for the 'Shepherds.'"

And in a low voice, his head between the curtains, Salvette began to sing.

All at once, at the last couplet, when the shepherds, coming to see Jesus in His stable, have placed in the manger their offerings of fresh eggs and cheeses, and when, bowing with an affable air,

> "Joseph says, 'Go! be very sage:
> Return, and make you good voyage,
> Shepherds,
> Take your leave!'"

—all at once poor Bernadou slipped and fell
heavily on the pillow. His comrade thought
he had fallen asleep, and called him, shook him.
But the wounded boy rested immovable, and
the little twig of holly lying across the rigid
cloth, seemed already the green palm they place
upon the pillows of the dead.

Salvette.understood at last. Then, in tears,
a little weakened by the feast and by his grief,
he raised in full voice, through the silence of
the room, the joyous refrain of Provençe,—

> " Shepherds,
> Take your leave !"

A Breton Peasant's Romance.

> "Eyes dark; face thin, long, and
> sallow; nose aquiline, but not
> straight, having a peculiar in-
> clination towards the left cheek;
> expression, therefore, sinister."
>
> *Dickens.*

THE WOLF TOWER.

I.

LONG ago, in Brittany, under the government of St. Gildas the Wise, seventh abbot of Ruiz, there lived a young tenant of the abbey who was blind in the right eye and lame in the left leg. His name was Sylvestre Ker, and his mother, Josserande Ker, was the widow of Martin Ker, in his lifetime the keeper of the great door of the Convent of Ruiz.

The mother and the son lived in a tower, the ruins of which are seen at the foot of Mont Saint Michel de la Trinité, in the grove of chestnut-trees that belongs to Jean Maréchal, the mayor's nephew. These ruins are now called the Wolf Tower, and the Breton peasants shudder as they pass through the chestnut-grove; for at midnight, around the Wolf Tower, and close to the first circle of great stones erected by the Druids at Carnac, are seen the phantoms of a young man and a young girl— Pol Bihan and Matheline du Coat-Dor.

The young girl is of graceful figure, with

long, floating hair, but without a face; and the young man is tall and robust, but the sleeves of his coat hang limp and empty, for he is without arms.

Round and round the circle they pass in opposite directions, and, strange to tell, they never meet, nor do they ever speak to each other.

Once a year, on Christmas night, instead of walking they run; and all the Christians who cross the heath to go to the midnight Mass hear from afar the young girl cry,—

"Wolf Sylvestre Ker, give me back my beauty!" and the deep voice of the young man adds, "Wolf Sylvestre Ker, give me back my strength!"

II.

And this has lasted for thirteen hundred years; therefore you may well think there is a story connected with it.

When Martin Ker, the husband of Dame Josserande, died, their son Sylvestre was only seven years old. The widow was obliged to give up the guardianship of the great door to a man-at-arms, and retire to the tower, which was her inheritance; but little Sylvestre Ker had permission to follow the studies in the convent school.

The boy showed natural ability, but he studied little except in the class of chemistry, taught by an old monk named Thaèl, who was said to have discovered the secret of making gold out of lead by adding to it a certain substance which no one but himself knew; for certainly, if the fact had been communicated, all the lead in the country would have been quickly turned into gold.

As for Thaël himself, he had been careful not to profit by his secret, for Gildas the Wise had once said to him,—

"Thaèl, Thaél, God does not wish you to change the work of His hands. Lead is lead, and gold is gold. There is enough gold, and not too much lead. Leave God's works alone; if not, Satan will be your master."

Most assuredly such precepts would not be well received by modern industry; but St. Gildas knew what he said, and Thaël died of extreme old age before he had changed the least particle of lead into gold. This, however, was not from want of will, which was proved after his death, as the rumor spread about that Thaël did not altogether desert his laboratory, but at times returned to his beloved labors. Many a time, in the lonely hours of the night, the fishermen, in their barks, watched the glimmer of the light in his former cell; and Gildas the Wise, having

been warned of the fact, arose one night before
Lauds, and with quiet steps crossed the corridors, thinking to surprise his late brother, and
perhaps ask of him some details of the other
side of the dreaded door which separates life
from death.

When he reached the cell he listened, and
heard Thaël's great bellows puffing and blowing,
although no one had yet been appointed to succeed him. Gildas suddenly opened the door
with his master-key, and saw before him little
Sylvestre Ker actively employed in relighting
Thaël's furnaces.

St. Gildas was not a man to give way to sudden wrath; he took the child by the ear, drew
him outside, and said to him, gently,—

"Ker, my little Ker, I know what you are
attempting and what tempts you to make the
effort; but God does not wish it, nor I either,
my little Ker."

"I do it," replied the boy, "because my dear
mother is so poor."

"Your mother is what she is; she has what
God gives her. Lead is lead and gold is gold.
If you go against the will of God, Satan will
be your master."

Little Ker returned to the tower crestfallen,
and never again slipped into the cell of the
dead Thaël; but when he was eighteen years

old a modest inheritance was left him, and he
bought materials for dissolving metals and dis-
tilling the juice of plants. He gave out that
his aim was to learn the art of healing; for
that great purpose he read great books which
treated of medical science and many other things
besides.

He was then a youth of fine appearance, with
a noble, frank face, neither one-eyed nor lame,
and led a retired life with his mother, who
ardently loved her only son.

No one visited them in the tower except the
laughing Matheline, the heiress of the tenant
of Coat-Dor and god-daughter of Josserande;
and Pol Bihan, son of the successor of Martin
Ker as armed keeper of the great door.

Both Pol and Matheline often conversed together, and upon what subject do you think?
Always of Sylvestre Ker. Was it because they
loved him? No. What Matheline loved most
was her own fair self, and Pol Bihan's best
friend was named Pol Bihan.

Matheline passed long hours before her little
mirror of polished steel, which faithfully reflected her laughing mouth full of pearls; and
Pol was proud of his great strength, for he was
the best wrestler in the Carnac country. When
they spoke of Sylvestre Ker, it was to say,
" What if some fine morning, he should find the

secret of the fairy-stone that is the' mother of gold !"

And each one mentally added,—

" I must continue to be friendly with him, for if he becomes wealthy he will enrich me."

Josserande also knew that her beloved son sought after the fairy-stone, and even had mentioned it to Gildas the Wise, who shook his venerable head and said,—

" What God wills will be. Be careful that your son wears a mask over his face when he seeks the cursed thing; for what escapes from the crucible is Satan's breath, and the breath of Satan causes blindness."

Josserande, meditating upon these words, went to kneel before the cross of St. Cado, which is in front of the seventh stone of Cæsar's camp,—the one that a little child can move by touching it with his finger, but that twelve horses harnessed to twelve oxen cannot stir from its solid foundation. Thus prostrate, she prayed : " O Lord Jesus ! Thou who hast mercy for mothers on account of the Holy Virgin, Thy mother, watch well over my little Sylvestre, and take from his head this thought of making gold. Nevertheless, if it is Thy will that he should be rich, Thou art the Master of all things, my sweet Saviour !"

And as she rose she murmured : " What a

beautiful boy he would be with a cloak of fine cloth and a hood bordered with fur, if he only had means to buy them."

III.

It came to pass that as all these young people, Pol Bihan, Matheline, and Sylvestre Ker, gained a year each time that twelve months rolled by, they reached the age to think of marriage ; and Josserande, one morning, proceeded to the dwelling of the farmer of Coat-Dor to ask the hand of Matheline for her son, Sylvestre Ker; at which proposal Matheline opened her rosy mouth so wide, to laugh the louder, that far back she showed two pearls which had never before been seen.

When her father asked her if the offer suited her, she replied, " Yes, father and godmother, provided that Sylvestre Ker gives me a gown of cloth of silver embroidered with rubies, like that of the Lady of Lannelar, and that Pol Bihan may be our groomsman."

Pol, who was there, also laughed, and said, " I will assuredly be groomsman to my friend Sylvestre Ker, if he consents to give me a velvet mantle striped with gold, like that of the Castellan of Gâvre, the Lord of Carnac."

Whereupon Josserande returned to the tower, and said to her son, " Ker, my darling, I advise

you to choose another friend and another
bride; for those two are not worthy of your
love."

But the young man began to sigh and groan,
and answered, "No friendship or love will I
ever know except for Pol, my dear comrade,
and Matheline, your god-daughter, my beautiful
playfellow."

And Josserande having told him of the two
new pearls that Matheline had shown in the
back of her mouth, nothing would do but he
must hurry to Coat-Dor to try and see them,
also.

On the road from the tower to the farm of
Coat-Dor is the Point of Hinnic, where the
grass is salt, which makes the cows and rams
very fierce while they are grazing.

As Sylvestre Ker walked down the path at
the end of which is the Cross of St. Cado, he
saw, on the summit of the promontory, Pol and
Matheline strolling along, talking and laughing;
so he thought,—

"I need not go far to see Matheline's two
pearls."

And, in fact, the girl's merry laughter could
be heard below, for it always burst forth if Pol
did but open his lips. When, lo, and behold! a
huge old ram, which had been browsing on the
salt grass, tossed back his two horns, and, fuming

at the nostrils, bleated as loud as the stags cry when chased, and rushed in the direction of Matheline's voice; for, as every one knows, the rams become furious if laughter is heard in their meadow.

He ran quickly, but Sylvestre Ker ran still faster, and arrived the first by the girl, so that he received the shock of the ram's butting while protecting her with his body. The injury was not very great, only his right eye was touched by the curved end of one of the horns when the ram raised his head, and thus Sylvestre Ker became one-eyed.

The ram, prevented from slaughtering Matheline, dashed after Pol Bihan, who fled; reached him just at the end of the cliff, and pushed him into the ŝea, that beat against the rocks fifty feet below.

Well content with his work, the ram walked off, and the legend says he laughed behind his woolly beard.

But Matheline wept bitterly, and cried,—

"Ker, my handsome Ker, save Bihan, your sweet friend, from death, and I pledge my faith I will be your wife without any condition."

At the same time, amid the roaring of the waves, was heard the imploring voice of Pol Bihan crying,—

"Sylvestre, O Sylvestre Ker! my only friend,

II.—*f*

I cannot swim. Come quickly and save me from dying without confession, and all you may ask of me you shall have, were it the dearest treasure of my heart."

Sylvestre Ker asked,—

"Will you be my groomsman?" And Bihan replied,—

"Yes, yes; and I will give you a hundred crowns. And all that your mother may ask of me she shall have. But hasten, hasten, dear friend, or the waves will carry me off."

Sylvestre Ker's blood was pouring from the wound in his eye, and his sight was dimmed; but he was generous of heart, and boldly leaped from the top of the promontory. As he fell, his left leg was jammed against a jutting rock and broke, so there he was, lame as well as one-eyed; nevertheless, he dragged Bihan to the shore and asked,—

"When shall the wedding be?"

As Matheline hesitated in her answer—for Sylvestre's brave deeds· were too recent to be forgotten—Pol Bihan came to her assistance and gayly cried,—

"You must wait, Sylvestre, my saviour, until your leg and eye are healed."

"Still longer," added Matheline (and now Sylvestre Ker saw the two new pearls, for in her laughter she opened her mouth from ear to

ear); " still longer, as limping, one-eyed men
are not to my taste—no, no!"

"But," cried Sylvestre Ker, "it is for your
sakes that I am one-eyed and lame."

"That is true," said Bihan.

"That is true," also repeated Matheline, for
she always spoke as he did.

"Ker, my friend Ker," resumed Bihan, "wait
until to-morrow, and we will make you happy."

And off they went, Matheline and he, arm-in-
arm, leaving Sylvestre to go hobbling along to
the tower, alone with his sad thoughts.

Would you believe it? Trudging wearily
home, he consoled himself by thinking he had
seen two new pearls behind the smile. You
may, perhaps, think you have never met such
a fool. Undeceive yourself; it is the same with
all the men, who only look for laughing girls
with teeth like pearls. But the sorrowful one
was Josserande, the widow, when she saw her
son with only one eye and one sound leg.

"Where did all this happen," she asked, with
tears.

And as Sylvestre Ker gently answered, "I
have seen them, mother; they are very beautiful," Josserande divined that he spoke of her
god-daughter's two pearls, and cried,—

"By all that is holy, he has also lost his mind!"

Then seizing her staff, she went to the Abbey

of Ruiz to consult St. Gildas as to what could
be done in this unfortunate case. And the wise
man replied,—

"You should not have spoken of the two
pearls; your son would have remained at home.
But, now that the evil is done, nothing will happen to him contrary to God's holy will. At
high tide the sea comes foaming over the sands,
yet see how quietly it retires. What is Sylvestre Ker doing now?"

"He is lighting his furnaces," replied Josserande.

The wise man paused to reflect, and after a
little while said,—

"In the first place, you must pray devoutly
to the Lord our God, and afterwards look well
before you to know where to put your feet.
The weak buy the strong, the unhappy the
happy; did you know that, my good woman?
Your son will persevere in search of the fairy-
stone that changes lead into gold, to pay for
Pol's wicked friendship and for the pearls behind the dangerous smiles of that Matheline.
Since God permits it, all is right. Yet see that
your son is well protected against the smoke of
his crucible, for it is the very breath of Satan;
and make him promise to go to the midnight
Mass."

For it was near the glorious Feast of Christmas.

IV.

Josserande had no difficulty in making Sylvestre Ker promise to go to the midnight Mass, for he was a good Christian; and she bought for him an iron armor to put on when he worked around his crucibles, so as to preserve him from Satan's breath.

And it happened that, late and early, Pol Bihan now came to the tower, bringing with him the laughing Matheline; for it was rumored that at last Sylvestre Ker would soon find the fairy-stone and become a wealthy man.

It was not only two new pearls that Matheline showed at the corners of her rosy mouth, but a brilliant row that shone, and chattered, and laughed, from her lips down to her throat; for Pol Bihan had said to her: "Laugh as much as you can; for smiles attract fools, as the turning mirror catches larks."

We have spoken of Matheline's lips, of her throat, and of her smile, but not of her heart; of that we can only say the place where it should have been was nearly empty; so she replied to Bihan,—

"As much as you will. I can afford to laugh to be rich; and when the fool shall have given me all the gold of the earth, all the pleasures of the world, I will be happy, happy. . . . I will

8

have them all for myself, for myself alone, and
I will enjoy them."

Pol Bihan clasped his hands in admiration,
so lovely and wise was she for her age; but
he thought: "I am wiser still than you, my
beauty; we will share between us what the fool
will give—one-half for me, and the other also;
the rest for you. Let the water run under the
bridge."

The day before Christmas they came together
to the tower,—Matheline carrying a basket of
chestnuts, Pol a large jug, full of sweet cider,—
to make merry with the godmother.

They roasted the chestnuts in the ashes, heated
the cider before the fire, adding to it fermented
honey, wine, sprigs of rosemary, and marjoram
leaves; and so delicious was the perfume of the
beverage that even Dame Josserande longed for
a taste.

On the way thither, Pol had advised Matheline adroitly to question Sylvestre Ker, to know
when he would at last find the fairy-stone.

Sylvestre Ker neither ate chestnuts nor drank
wine, so absorbed was he in the contemplation
of Matheline's bewitching smiles; and she said
to him,—

"Tell me, my handsome, lame, and one-eyed
bridegroom, will I soon be the wife of a wealthy
man?"

Sylvestre Ker, whose eye shot forth lurid flame, replied,—

" You would have been as rich as you are beautiful to-morrow, without fail, if I had not promised my dear mother to accompany her to the midnight Mass to-night. The favorable hour falls just at the first stroke of Matins."

" To-day ?"

" Between to-day and to-morrow."

" And can it not be put off?"

" Yes, it can be put off for seven years."

Dame Josserande heard nothing, as Pol was relating an interesting story, so as to distract her attention ; but, while talking, he listened with all his ears.

Matheline laughed no longer, and thought,—

" Seven years ! Can I wait seven years ?" Then she continued :

" Beautiful bridegroom, how do you know that the propitious moment falls precisely at the hour of Matins ? Who told you so ?"

" The stars," replied Sylvestre Ker. " At midnight Mars and Saturn will arrive in diametrical opposition; Venus will seek Vesta ; Mercury will disappear in the sun ; and the planet without a name, that the deceased Thaél divined by calculation, I saw last night, steering its unknown route through space to come in conjunction with Jupiter. Ah ! if I only dared

disobey my dear mother." He was interrupted
by a distant vibration of the bells of Plouharnel, which rang out the first signal of the midnight Mass.

Josserande instantly left her wheel.

"It would be a sin to spin one thread more,"
said she. "Come, my son Sylvestre, put on
your Sunday clothes, and let us be off for the
parish church, if you please."

Sylvestre wished to rise, for never yet had he
disobeyed his mother; but Matheline, seated at
his side, detained him and murmured in silvery
tones,—

"My handsome friend, you have plenty of
time."

Pol, on his side, said to Dame Josserande,—

"Get your staff, neighbor, and start at once,
so as to take your time. Your god-daughter
Matheline will accompany you; and I will
follow with friend Sylvestre, for fear some accident might happen to him with his lame leg
and sightless eye." As he proposed, so it was
done; for Josserande suspected nothing, knowing that her son had promised, and that he
would not break his word.

As they were leaving, Pol whispered to
Matheline,—

"Amuse the good woman well, for the fool
must remain here."

And the girl replied,—

"Try and see the caldron in which our fortune is cooking. You will tell me how it is done."

Off the two women started; a large, kind mother's heart full of tender love, and a sparrow's little gizzard, narrow and dry, without enough room in it for one pure tear. For a moment Sylvestre Ker stood on the threshold of the open door to watch them depart. On the gleaming white snow their two shadows fell—the one bent and already tottering, the other erect, flexible, and each step seemed a bound. The young lover sighed. Behind him, in a low voice, Pol Bihan said,—

"Ker, my comrade, I know what you are thinking about, and you are right to think so; this must come to an end. She is as impatient as you are, for her love equals yours; for both of you it is too long to wait."

Sylvestre Ker turned pale with joy.

" Do you speak truth ?" he stammered. " Am I fortunate enough to be loved by her ?"

" Yes, on my faith !" replied Pol Bihan ; " she loves you too well for her own peace. When a girl laughs too much, it is to keep from weeping, —that's the real truth."

8*

V.

Well might they call him "the fool," poor
Sylvestre Ker! Not that he had less brains
than another man,—on the contrary, he was
now very learned—but love crazes him who
places his affections on an unworthy object.

Sylvestre Ker's little finger was worth two
dozen Pol Bihan's and fifty Matheline's; in
spite of which Matheline and Pol Bihan were
perfectly just in their contempt, for he who
ascends the highest falls lowest.

When Sylvestre had re-entered the tower, Pol
commenced to sigh heavily, and said,—

"What a pity! What a great, great pity!"

"What is a pity?" asked Sylvestre Ker.

"It is a pity to miss such a rare opportunity."

Sylvestre Ker exclaimed, "What opportunity? So you were listening to my conversation
with Matheline?"

"Why, yes," replied Pol. "I always have an
ear open to hear what concerns you, my true
friend. Seven years! Shall I tell you what I
think? You would only have twelve months
to wait to go with your mother to another
Christmas Mass."

"I have promised," said Sylvestre.

"That is nothing: if your mother loves you
truly, she will forgive you."

"If she loves me!" cried Sylvestre Ker. "Oh, yes, she loves me with her whole heart."

Some chestnuts still remained, and Bihan shelled one while he said,—

"Certainly, certainly, mothers always love their children; but Matheline is not your mother. You are one-eyed, you are lame, and you have sold your little patrimony to buy your furnaces. Nothing remains of it. Where is the girl that can wait seven years? Nearly the half of her age! . . . If I were in your place, I would not throw away my luck as you are about to do, but at the hour of Matins I would work for my happiness."

Sylvestre Ker was standing before the fireplace. He listened, his eyes bent down, with a frown upon his brow.

"You have spoken well," at last he said; "my dear mother will forgive me. I shall remain, and will work at the hour of Matins."

"You have decided for the best!" cried Bihan. "Rest easy; I will be with you in case of danger. Open the door of your laboratory. We will work together; I will cling to you like your shadow!"

Sylvestre Ker did not move, but looked fixedly upon the floor, and then, as if thinking aloud, murmured,—

" It will be the first time I have ever caused
my dear mother sorrow !"

He opened a door, but not that of the laboratory, pushed Pol Bihan outside, and said,—

" The danger is for myself alone; the gold
will be for all. Go to the Christmas Mass in
my place; say to Matheline that she will be
rich, and to my dear mother that she will have
a happy old age, since she will live and die with
her fortunate son."

VI.

When Sylvestre Ker was alone, he listened to
the noise of the waves dashing upon the beach
and the sighing of the wind among the great
oaks,—two mournful sounds. And he looked
with conflicting feelings at the empty seats of
Matheline and of his dear mother Josserande.
Little by little had he seen the black hair of
the widow become gray, then white, around her
sunken temples. That night memory carried
him back even to his cradle, over which had
bent the sweet, noble face of her who had
always spoken to him of God.

But whence came those golden ringlets that
mingled with Josserande's black hair, and which
shone in the sunlight above his mother's snowy
locks? And that laugh, oh! that silvery laugh
of youth, which prevented Sylvestre Ker from

hearing, in his pious recollections, the calm, grave voice of his mother. Whence did it come?

Seven years! Pol had said. "Where is the girl who can wait seven years?" and these words floated in the air. Never had the son of Martin Ker heard such strange voices amid the roaring of the ocean, nor in the rushing winds of the forest of the Druids.

Suddenly the tower also commenced to speak, not only through the cracks of the old windows where the mournful wind sighed, but with a confusion of sounds that resembled the busy whispering of a crowd, that penetrated through the closed doors of the laboratory, under which a bright light streamed. Sylvestre Ker opened the door, fearing to see all in a blaze, but there was no fire; the light that streamed under the door came from the round, red eye of his furnace, and happened to strike the stone of the threshold. No one was in the laboratory; still, the noises, similar to the chattering of an audience awaiting a promised spectacle, did not cease. The air was full of speaking things; the spirits could be felt swarming around, as closely packed as the wheat in the barn or the sand on the seashore. And, although not seen, they spoke all kinds of phantom-words, which were heard right and left, before and behind, above and below, and which penetrated through the pores of the skin like quicksilver passing through a cloth.

They said,—

"The Magi has started, my friend."

"My friend, the Star shines in the East."

"My friend, my friend, the little King Jesus is born in the manger, upon the straw."

"Sylvestre Ker will surely go with the shepherds."

"Not at all; Sylvestre Ker will not go."

"Good Christian he was."

"Good Christian he is no longer."

"He has forgotten the name of Joseph."

"And the name of Mary."

"No, no, no!"

"Yes, yes, yes!"

"He will go!"

"He will not go!"

"He will go, since he promised Dame Josserande."

"He will not go, since Matheline told him to stay."

"My friend, my friend, to-night Sylvestre Ker will find the golden secret."

"To-night, my friend, my friend, he will win the heart of the one he loves."

And the invisible spirits, thus disputing, sported through the air, mounting, descending, whirling around like atoms of dust in a sunbeam, from the flag-stones of the floor to the rafters of the roof.

Inside the furnace, in the crucible, some other thing responded, but it could not be well heard, as the crucible had been hermetically sealed.

" Go out from here, you wicked crowd," cried Sylvestre Ker, sweeping around with a broom of holly branches. " What are you doing here? Go outside, cursed spirits, damned souls—go, go!"

From all the corners of the room came laughter; Matheline seemed everywhere. Suddenly there was profound silence, and the wind from the sea brought the sound of the bells of Plouharnel, ringing the second peal for the midnight Mass.

" My friend, what are they saying?"

" They say Christmas, my friend—Christmas, Christmas, Christmas!"

" Not at all! They say, Gold, gold, gold!"

" You lie, my friend!"

" My friend, you lie!"

And the other voices, those that were grumbling in the interior of the furnace, swelled and puffed.

The fire, that no person was blowing, kept up by itself, hot as the soul of a forge should be. The crucible became red, and the stones of the furnace were dyed a deep scarlet.

In vain did Sylvestre Ker sweep with his
holly broom; between the branches, covered
with sharp leaves, the spirits passed,—nothing
could catch them; and the heat was so great
the boy was bathed in perspiration.

After the bells had finished their second peal,
he said,—

"I am stifling. I will open the window to
let out the heat as well as this herd of evil
spirits."

But as soon as he opened the window, the
whole country commenced to laugh under its
white mantle of snow—barren heath, ploughed
land, Druid stones, even to the enormous oaks
of the forest, with their glistening summits,
that shook their frosty branches, saying,—

"Sylvestre Ker will go! Sylvestre Ker will
not go!"

Not a spirit from within flew out, while all
the outside spirits entered, muttering, chattering,
laughing,—

"Yes, yes, yes, yes! No, no, no, no!" And
I believe they fought.

At the same time the sound of a cavalcade
advancing was heard on the flinty road that
passed before the tower; and Sylvestre Ker
recognized the long procession of the monks of
Ruiz, led by the grand abbot, Gildas the Wise,
arrayed in cope and mitre, with his crozier in

his hand, going to the Mass of Plouharnel, as the convent chapel was being rebuilt.

When the head of the cavalcade approached the tower, the grand abbot cried out,—

" My armed guards, sound your horns to awaken Dame Josserande's son !"

And instantly there was a blast from the horns, which rang out until Gildas the Wise exclaimed,—

" Be silent, for there is my tenant wide awake at his window."

When all was still, the grand abbot raised his crozier and said,—

" My tenant, the first hour of Christmas approaches, the glorious Feast of the Nativity. Extinguish your furnaces and hasten to Mass, for you have barely time." And on he passed, while those in the procession, as they saluted Ker, repeated,—

" Sylvestre Ker, you have barely time ; make haste !"

The voices of the air kept gibbering: " He will go ! He will not go !" and the wind whistled in bitter sarcasm.

Sylvestre Ker closed his window. He sat down, his head clasped by his trembling hands. His heart was rent by two forces that dragged him, one to the right, the other to the left,—his mother's prayer and Matheline's laughter.

He was no miser; he did not covet gold for the sake of gold, but that he might buy the row of pearls and smiles that hung from the lips of Matheline. . . .

" Christmas !" cried a voice in the air.

" Christmas, Christmas, Christmas !" repeated all the other voices.

Sylvestre Ker suddenly opened his eyes, and saw that the furnace was fiery red from top to bottom, and that the crucible was surrounded with rays so dazzling he could not even look at it.   Something was boiling inside that sounded like the roaring of a tempest.

" Mother !   Oh, my dear mother !" cried the terrified man, " I am coming.   I'll run . . . "

But thousands of little voices stung his ears with the words,—

" Too late, too late, too late !   It is too late !"

Alas ! alas ! the wind from the sea brought the third peal of the bells of Plouharnel, and they also said to him : " Too late !"

VII.

As the sound of the bells died away, the last drop of water fell from the clepsydra and marked the hour of midnight.   Then the furnace opened and showed the glowing crucible, which burst with a terrible noise, and threw out a gigantic flame that reached the sky through the torn roof. Sylvestre Ker, enveloped by the fire, fell prostrate on the ground, suffocated in the burning smoke.

The silence of death followed. Suddenly an awful voice said to him: "Arise." And he arose.

On the spot where had stood the furnace, of which not a vestige remained, was standing a man, or rather a colossus; and Sylvestre Ker needed but a glance to recognize in him the demon. His body appeared to be of iron, red-hot and transparent; for in his veins could be seen the liquid gold, flowing into, and then re-treating from, his heart, black as an extinguished coal.

The creature, who was both fearful and beautiful to behold, extended his hand towards the side of the tower nearest the sea, and in the thick wall a large breach was made.

" Look !" said Satan.

Sylvestre Ker obeyed. He saw, as though distance were annihilated, the interior of the humble church of Plouharnel where the faithful were assembled. The officiating priest had just ascended the altar, brilliant with the Christmas candles, and there was great pomp and splendor; for the many monks of Gildas the Wise were assisting the poor clergy of the parish.

In a corner, under the shadow of a column, knelt Dame Josserande in fervent prayer, but often did the dear woman turn towards the door to watch for the coming of her son.

Not far from her was Matheline du Coat-Dor, bravely attired and very beautiful, but lavishing the pearls of her smiles upon all who sought them, forgetting no one but God; and, close to Matheline, Pol Bihan squared his broad shoulders. Then, even as Satan had given to Sylvestre Ker's sight the power of piercing the walls, so did he permit him to look into the depth of hearts. In his mother's heart he saw himself as in a mirror. It was full of him. Good Josserande prayed for him; she prayed to Jesus, whose feast is Christmas, in the pious prayer which fell from her lips; and ever and ever said her heart to God: "My son, my son, my son!"

In the heart of Pol, Sylvestre Ker saw pride of strength and gross cupidity; in the spot where should have been the heart of Matheline, he saw Matheline, and nothing but Matheline, in adoration before Matheline.

"I have seen enough," said Sylvestre Ker.

"Then," replied Satan, "listen!" And immediately the sacred music resounded in the ears of the young tenant of the tower as plainly as though he was in the church of Plouharnel.

They were singing the Sanctus: "Holy, holy, holy, Lord God of Hosts! The heavens and the earth are full of Thy glory. Hosanna in the highest! Blessed is He that cometh in the name of the Lord. Hosanna in the highest!"

Dame Josserande repeated the words with the others, but the refrain of her heart continued: "O Jesus, Infinite Goodness! may he be happy. Deliver him from all evil, from all sin. I have only him to love. . . . Holy, holy, holy, give me all the suffering and keep for him all the happiness!"

Can you believe it? Even while piously inhaling the perfume of this celestial hymn, the young tenant wished to know what Matheline was saying to God. Everything speaks to God, —the wild beasts in the forest, the birds in the air, even the plants, whose roots are in the ground.

But miserable girls who sell the pearls of their smiles are lower than the animals and vegetables. Nothing is beneath them,—Pol Bihan excepted. Instead of speaking to God, Pol Bihan and Matheline whispered together, and Sylvestre Ker heard them as distinctly as if he had been between them.

"How much will the fool give?" asked Matheline.

"The idiot will give you all," replied Pol.

"And must I really squint with that one-eyed creature, and limp with the lame wretch?"

Sylvestre Ker felt his heart die away within him.

Meanwhile, Josserande prayed earnestly for Sylvestre Ker.

"Never mind," continued Bihan; "it is worth while limping and squinting for a time to win all the money in the world."

"That is true; but for how long?"

Sylvestre Ker held his breath to hear the better.

"As long as you please," answered Pol Bihan.

There was a pause, after which the gay Matheline resumed in a lower tone,—

"But. . . . they say after a murder one can never laugh, and I wish to laugh always. . . ."

"Will I not be there?" replied Bihan. "Some time or other the idiot will certainly seek a quarrel with me, and I will crack his bones by only squeezing him in my arms; you can count upon my strength."

"I have heard enough," said Sylvestre Ker to Satan.

"And do you still love this Bihan?"

"No: I despise him."

"And Matheline,—do you love her yet?"

" Yes, oh ! yes ! . . . but . . . I hate her !"

" I see," said Satan, " that you are a coward, and wicked like all men. Since you have heard and seen enough at a distance, listen, and look at your feet. . . ."

The wall closed with a loud crash of the stones as they came together, and Sylvestre Ker saw that he was surrounded by an enormous heap of gold-pieces, as high as his waist, which gently floated, singing the symphony of riches. All around him was gold, and through the gap in the roof the shower of gold fell, and fell, and fell.

" Am I the master of all this ?" asked Sylvestre Ker.

" Yes," replied Satan ; " you have compelled me, who am gold, to come forth from my caverns ; you are therefore the master of gold, provided you purchase it at the price of your soul. You cannot have both God and gold. You must choose one or the other."

" I have chosen," said Sylvestre Ker. " I keep my soul."

" You have firmly decided ?"

" Irrevocably."

" Once, twice, . . . reflect ! You have just acknowledged that you still love the laughing Matheline."

" And that I hate her. . . . Yes, . . . it is so.

. . . But in eternity I wish to be with my dear mother, Josserande."

"Were there no mothers," growled Satan, "I could play my game much better in the world!"

And he added,—

"For the third time, . . . adjudged!"

The heap of gold became as turbulent as the water of a cascade, and leaped and sang; the millions of little sonorous coins clashed against each other, and then all was silent and they vanished.

The room appeared as black as a place where there had been a fire; nothing could be seen but the lurid gleam of Satan's iron body. Then said Sylvestre Ker,—

"Since all is ended, retire!"

VIII.

But the demon did not stir.

"Do you think, then," he asked, "that you have brought me hither for nothing? There is the law. You are not altogether my slave, since you have kept your soul; but as you have freely called me, and I have come, you are my vassal. I have a half claim over you. The little children know that; I am astonished at your ignorance. . . . From midnight to three o'clock in the morning you belong to me, in the form of an animal, restless, roving, complaining, without help from God. This is what you owe to your strong friend and beautiful bride. Let us settle the affair before I depart. What animal do you wish to be,—roaring lion, bellowing ox, bleating sheep, crowing cock? If you become a dog, you can crouch at Matheline's feet, and Bihan can lead you by a leash to hunt in the woods. . . ."

" I wish," cried Sylvestre Ker, whose anger burst forth at these words, " I wish to be a wolf, to devour them both !"

" So be it," said Satan; " wolf you shall be three hours of the night during your mortal life. . . . Leap, wolf!"

And the wolf, Sylvestre Ker, leaped, and with one dash shattered the casement of the window as he cleared it with a bound. Through the aperture in the roof Satan escaped, and, spreading a pair of immense wings, rapidly disappeared in an opposite direction from the steeple of Plouharnel, whose chimes were ringing across the snow.

IX.

I do not know if you have ever seen a Breton village come forth after the midnight Mass. It is a joyous sight, but a brief one, as all are in a hurry to return home, where the midnight meal awaits them,—a frugal feast, but eaten with such cheerful hearts. The people, for a moment massed in the cemetery, exchange hospitable invitations, kind wishes, and friendly jokes; then divide into little caravans, which hurry along the roads, laughing, talking, singing. If it is a clear, cold night, the clicking of their wooden shoes may be heard for some time; but if it is damp weather, the sound is stifled, and after a few moments the faint echo of an "adieu" or Christmas greeting is all that can be heard around the church as the beadle closes it.

In the midst of all this cheerfulness Josserande alone returned with a sad heart; for through the whole Mass she had in vain watched for her beloved son. She walked fifty paces behind the cavalcade of the monks of Ruiz, and dared not approach the Grand Abbot Gildas, for fear of being questioned about her boy. On her right was Matheline du Coat-Dor, on her left Bihan, —both eager to console her; for they thought that by that time Sylvestre Ker must have learned the wonderful secret which would secure him untold wealth, and to possess the son they should cling to the mother; therefore there were promises and caresses, and " will you have this, or will you have that?"

" Dear godmother, I shall always be with

you," said Matheline, "to comfort and rejoice your old age; for your son is my heart."

Pol Bihan continued,—

" I will never marry, but always remain with my friend, Sylvestre Ker, whom I love more than myself. And nothing must worry you; if he is weak, I am strong, and I will work for two."

To pretend that Dame Josserande paid much attention to all these words would be false; for her son possessed her whole soul, and she thought,—

" This is the first time he has ever disobeyed and deceived me. The demon of avarice has entered into him. Why does he want so much money? Can all the riches in the world pay for one of the tears that the ingratitude of a beloved son draws from his mother's eyes?"

Suddenly her thoughts were arrested, for the sound of a trumpet was heard in the still night.

" It is the convent horn," said Matheline.

" And it sounds the wolf-alarm," added Pol.

" What harm can the wolf do," asked Josserande, " to a well-mounted troop like the cavalry of Gildas the Wise? And, besides, cannot the holy abbot with a single word put to flight a hundred wolves?"

They arrived at the heath of Carnac, where

are the two thousand seven hundred and twenty-
nine Druid stones, and the monks had already
passed the round point where nothing grows,
neither grass nor heath, and which resembles an
enormous caldron,—a caldron wherein to make
oaten-porridge,—or rather a race-course, to exercise horses.

On one side might be seen the town, dark
and gloomy; on the other, as far as the eye
could reach, rows of rugged obelisks, half-black,
half-white, owing to the snow, which threw
into bold relief each jagged outline. Josserande, Matheline, and Pol Bihan had just turned
from the sunken road which branches towards
Plouharnel; and the moon played hide-and-go-
seek behind a flock of little clouds that flitted
over the sky like lambs.

Then a strange thing happened. The cavalcade of monks was seen to retreat from the
entrance of the avenues to the middle of the
circle, while the horn sounded the signal of distress, and loud cries were heard of "Wolf!
wolf! wolf!" At the same time could be distinguished the clashing of arms, the stamping
of horses, and all the noise of a ferocious
struggle, above which rose the majestic tones
of Gildas the Wise, as he said, with calm-
ness,—

"Wolf, wicked wolf, I forbid you to touch

God's servants!" But it seemed that the wicked wolf was in no hurry to obey, for the cavalcade plunged hither and thither as though shaken by convulsion; and the moon having come forth from the clouds, there was seen an enormous beast struggling with the staffs of the monks, the halberds of the armed guard, the pitchforks and spears of the peasants, who had hastened from all directions at the trumpet-call from Ruiz.

The animal received many wounds, but it was fated not to die. Again and again it charged upon the crowd, rushed up and down, round and round, biting, tearing with its great teeth so fearfully that a large circle was made around the grand abbot, who was finally left alone in face of the wolf. For a wolf it was. And the grand abbot having touched it with his crosier, the wolf crouched at his feet, panting, trembling, and bloody.

Gildas the Wise bent over it, looked at it attentively, then said,—

" Nothing happens contrary to God's will. Where is Dame Josserande ?"

" I am here," replied a mournful voice full of tears, " and I dread a great misfortune."

She also was alone; for Matheline and Pol Bihan, seized with terror, had rushed across the fields at the first alarm and abandoned their

precious charge.   The grand abbot called Josserande and said,—

"Woman, do not despair.   Above you is the
Infinite Goodness, who holds in His hands the
heavens and the whole earth.   Meanwhile, protect your wolf; we must return to the monas-
tery to gain from sleep strength to serve the
Lord our God!"

And he resumed his course, followed by his
escort.

The wolf did not move; his tongue lay on
the snow, which was reddened by his blood.
Josserande knelt beside him and prayed fervently.   For whom?   For her beloved son.
Did she already know that the wolf was Sylvestre Ker?   Certainly; such a thing could
scarcely be divined; but under what form cannot a mother discover her darling child?

She defended the wolf against the peasants,
who had returned to strike him with their pitchforks and pikes, as they believed him dead.
The two last who came were Pol Bihan and
Matheline.   Pol Bihan kicked him on the head,
and said, "Take that, you fool!" and Matheline
threw stones at him, and cried: "Idiot, take
that, and that, and that!"

They had hoped for all the gold in the world,
and this dead beast could give them nothing
more.

After a while two ragged beggars passed by
and assisted Josserande in carrying the wolf
into the tower. Where is charity most often
found? Among the poor, who are the figures
of Jesus Christ.

X.

Day dawned. A man slept in the bed of
Sylvestre Ker, where widow Josserande had
laid a wolf. The room still bore the marks of a
fire, and snow fell through the hole in the roof.
The young tenant's face was disfigured with
blows, and his hair, stiffened with blood, hung
in heavy locks. In his feverish sleep he talked,
and the name that escaped his lips was Matheline's. At his bedside the mother watched and
prayed.

When Sylvestre Ker awoke he wept, for the
thought of his condemnation returned; but the
remembrance of Pol and Matheline dried the
tears in his burning eyes.

"It was for those two," said he, "that I
forgot God and my mother. I still feel my
friend's heel upon my forehead, and even to the
bottom of my heart the shock of the stones
thrown at me by my betrothed!"

"Dearest," murmured Josserande, "dearer to
me than ever, I know nothing; tell me all."

Sylvestre Ker obeyed, and when he had finished, Josserande kissed him, took up her staff, and proceeded towards the convent of Ruiz to ask, according to her custom, aid and counsel from Gildas the Wise. On the way, men, women, and children looked curiously at her, for throughout the country it was already known that she was the mother of a wolf. Even behind the hedge which enclosed the abbey orchard Matheline and Pol were hidden to see her pass; and she heard Pol say,—

"Will you come to-night to see the wolf run around?"

"Without fail," replied Matheline; and the sting of her laughter pierced Josserande like a poisonous thorn.

The grand abbot received her, surrounded by great books and dusty manuscripts. When she wished to explain her son's case, he stopped her, and said,—

"Widow of Martin Ker, poor, good woman, since the beginning of the world, Satan, the demon of gold and pride, has worked many such wickednesses. Do you remember the deceased brother, Thaël, who is a saint for having resisted the desire of making gold,—he who had the power to do it?"

"Yes," answered Josserande; "and would to heaven my Sylvestre had imitated him!"

"Very well," replied Gildas the Wise. "Instead of sleeping, I passed the rest of the night with St. Thaël, seeking a means to save your son, Sylvestre Ker."

"And have you found it, father?"

The grand abbot neither answered yes nor no, but he began to turn over a very thick manuscript filled with pictures; and, while turning the leaves, he said,—

"Life springs from death, according to the divine word; death seizes the living, according to the pagan law of Rome; and it is nearly the same thing in the order of miserable temporal ambition, whose inheritance is a strength, a life, shot forth from a coffin. This is a book of the defunct Thaël's, which treats of the question of maladies caused by the breath of gold,—a deadly poison. . . . Woman, would you have the courage to strike your wolf a blow on his head powerful enough to break the skull?"

At these words Josserande fell her full length upon the tiles, as if she had been stabbed to the heart; but in the very depth of her agony—for she thought herself dying—she replied,—

"If you should order me to do it, I would."

"You have this great confidence in me, poor woman?" cried Gildas, much moved.

"You are a man of God," answered Josserande, "and I have faith in God."

Gildas the Wise prostrated himself on the

II.—*h*   10*

ground and struck his breast, knowing that he had felt a movement of pride. Then, standing up, he raised Josserande, and kissed the hem of her robe, saying,—

"Woman, I adore you in the most holy faith. Prepare your axe, and sharpen it!"

XI.

In the days of Gildas the Wise, intense silence always reigned at night through the dense oak forest of the Armorican country. One of the most lonely places was Cæsar's camp, the name was given to the huge masses of stone that encumbered the barren heath; and it was the common opinion that the pagan giants, supposed to be buried under them, rose from their graves at midnight and roamed up and down the long avenues, watching for the late passers-by, to twist their necks.

This night, however,—the night after Christmas,—many persons could be seen, about eleven o'clock, on the heath before the stones of Carnac, all around the Great Basin or circle, whose irregular outline was clearly visible by moonlight. The enclosure was entirely empty. Outside no one was seen, it is true; but many could be heard gabbling in the shadow of the high rocks, under the shelter of the stumps of oaks,

even in the tufts of thorny brambles; and all
this assemblage watched for something, and
that something was the wolf, Sylvestre Ker.
They had come from Plouharnel, and also from
Lannelar, from Carnac, from Kercado, even from
the old town of Crach, beyond La Trinité.

Who had brought together all these people,
young and old, men and women? The legend
does not say; but very probably Matheline had
strewn around the cruel pearls of her laughter,
and Pol Bihan had not been slow to relate what
he had seen after the midnight Mass.

By some means or other, the entire country
around for five or six leagues knew that the
son of Martin Ker, the tenant of the abbey,
had become a man-wolf, and that he was doomed
to expiate his crime in the spot haunted by the
phantoms,—the Great Basin of the Pagans, between the tower and the Druid stones.

Many of the watchers had never seen a man-
wolf, and there reigned in the crowd, scattered
in invisible groups, a fever of curiosity, terror, and impatience; the minutes lengthened as
they passed, and it seemed as though midnight,
stopped on the way, would never come.

There were at that time no clocks in the
neighborhood to mark the hour, but the matin-
bell of the convent of Ruiz gave notice that
the wished-for moment had arrived.

While waiting there was busy conversation : they spoke of the man-wolf, of phantoms, and also of betrothals, for the rumor was spread that the bans of Matheline du Coat-Dor, the promised bride of Sylvestre Ker, with the strong Pol Bihan, who had never found a rival in the wrestling-field, would be published on the following Sunday; and I leave you to imagine how Matheline's laughter ran in pearly cascades when congratulated on her approaching marriage.

By the road which led up to the tower a shadow slowly descended; it was not the wolf, but a poor woman in mourning, whose head was bent upon her breast, and who held in her hand an object that shone like a mirror, and the brilliant surface of which reflected the moonbeams.

" It is Josserande Ker !" was whispered around the circle, behind the rocks, in the brambles, and under the stumps of the oaks.

" 'Tis the widow of the armed keeper of the great door !"

" 'Tis the mother of the wolf, Sylvestre Ker !"

" She also has come to see. . . ."

" But what has she in her hand ?"

Twenty voices asked the question. Matheline, who had good eyes, and such beautiful ones, replied,—

" It looks like an axe. . . . Happy am I to be
rid of those two, the mother and son! With
them I could never laugh."

But there were two or three good souls who
said in low tones,—

" Poor widow! her heart must be full of
sorrow."

" But what does she want with that axe ?"

" It is to defend her wolf," again replied
Matheline, who carried a pitchfork.

Pol Bihan held an enormous hollow stick
which resembled a club. Every one was armed
either with threshing-flails or rakes or hoes;
some even bore scythes, carried upright; for
they had not only come to look on, but to make
an end of the man-wolf.

Again was heard the chime of the matin-
bells of the convent of Ruiz, and immediately a
smothered cry ran from group to group,—

" Wolf! wolf! wolf!"

Josserande heard it, for she paused in her descent and cast an anxious look around; but, seeing no one, she raised her eyes to heaven and
clasped her hands over the handle of her axe.

The wolf, in the meantime, with fuming nostrils and eyes which looked like burning coals,
leaped over the stones of the enclosure and
began to run around the circle.

" See, see !" said Pol Bihan; " he no longer

limps." And Matheline, dazzled by the red light from his eyes, added : " It seems he is no longer one-eyed !"

Pol brandished his club, and continued,—

" What are we waiting for? Why not attack him ?"

" Go you first," said the men.

" I caught cold the other day, and my leg is stiff, which keeps me from running," answered Pol.

" Then I will go first!" cried Matheline, raising her pitchfork. " I will soon show how I hate the wretch !"

Dame Josserande heard her, and sighed,—

" Girl, whom I blessed in baptism, may God keep me from cursing you now !"

This Matheline, whose pearls were worth nothing, was no coward ; for she carried out her words, and marched straight up to the wolf, while Bihan stayed behind and cried,—

" Go, go, my friends ; don't be afraid! Ah! but for my stiff leg, I would soon finish the wolf, for I am the strongest and bravest."

Round and round the circle galloped the wolf as quickly as a hunted stag ; his eyes darted fire, his tongue was hanging from his mouth. Josserande, seeing the danger that threatened him, wept and cried out,—

" O Bretons ! is there among you all not one

kind soul to defend the widow's son in the hour
when he bitterly expiates his sin ?"

" Let us alone, godmother," boldly replied
Matheline.

And from afar Pol Bihan added : " Don't
listen to the old woman ; go !"

But another voice was heard in answer to
Dame Josserande's appeal, and it said,—

" As last night, we are here !"

Standing in front of Matheline and barring the
passage were two ragged beggars, with their
wallets, leaning upon their staffs. Josserande
recognized the two poor men who had so
charitably aided her the night before ; and one
of them, who had snow-white hair and beard,
said,—

" My brethren, why do you interfere in this ?
God rewards and punishes. This poor man-
wolf is not a damned soul, but one expiating a
great crime. Leave justice to God, if you do
not wish some great misfortune to happen to
you."

And Josserande, who was kneeling down, said
imploringly,—

" Listen, listen to the saint !"

But from behind, Pol Bihan cried out,—

" Since when have beggars been allowed to
preach sermons ? Ah ! if it were not for my stiff
leg. . . . Kill him, kill him ! . . . wolf ! wolf !"

" Wolf! wolf!" repeated Matheline, who tried to drive off the old beggar with her pitchfork. But the fork broke like glass in her hands as it touched the poor man's tatters, and at the same time twenty voices cried,—

"The wolf! the wolf! Where has the wolf gone?"

Soon it was seen where the wolf had gone. A black mass dashed through the crowd, and Pol Bihan uttered a horrible cry,—

"Help! help! Matheline!"

You have often heard the noise made by a dog when crunching a bone. This was the noise they heard, but louder, as though there were many dogs crunching many bones. And a strange voice, like the growling of a wolf, said,—

"The strength of a man is a dainty morsel for a wolf to eat. Bihan, traitor, I eat your strength!"

The black mass again bounded through the terrified crowd, his bloody tongue hanging from his mouth, his eyes darting fire.

This time it was from Matheline that a scream still more horrible than that of Pol's was heard; and again there was the noise of another terrible feast, and the voice of the wild beast, which had already spoken, growled,—

" The pearls of a smile make a dainty morsel

for a wolf to eat. Matheline, serpent that
stung my heart, seek for your beauty. I have
eaten it!"

XII.

The white-haired beggar had endeavored to
protect Matheline against the wolf, but he was
very old, and his limbs would not move as
quickly as his heart. He only succeeded in
throwing down the wolf. It fell at Josserande's
feet and licked her knees, uttering doleful
moans. But the people, who had come thither
for entertainment, were not well pleased with
what had happened. There was now abundance of light, as men with torches had arrived
from the abbey in search of Gildas the Wise,
whose cell had been found empty at the hour
of Compline.

The glare from the torches shone upon two
hideous wounds made by the wolf, who had devoured Matheline's beauty and Pol's strength,—
that is to say, the face of the one and the arms
of the other—flesh and bones. It was frightful
to behold. The women wept while looking at
the repulsive, bleeding mass which had been
Matheline's smiling face; the men sought in
the double bloody gaps some traces of Pol's
arms, for the powerful muscles, the glory of the
athletic games; and every heart was filled with
wrath.

And the legend says that the tenant of Coat-Dor, Matheline's poor father, knelt beside his daughter and felt around in the blood for the scattered pearls, which were now as red as holly-berries.

"Alas!" said he, "of these dead, stained things, which when living were so beautiful, which were admired and envied and loved, I was so proud and happy."

Alas! indeed, alas! Perhaps it was not the girl's fault that her heart was no larger than a little bird's; and yet for this defect was not Matheline cruelly punished?

"Death to the wolf! death to the wolf! death to the wolf!"

From all sides was this cry heard, and brandishing pitchforks, cudgels, ploughshares, and mallets, came rushing the people towards the wolf, who still lay panting, with open jaws and pendent tongue, at the feet of Dame Josserande.

Around them the torch-bearers formed a circle: not to throw light upon the wolf and Dame Josserande, but to render homage to the white-haired beggar, in whom, as though the scales had suddenly fallen from their eyes, every one recognized the Grand Abbot of Ruiz, Gildas the Wise.

The grand abbot raised his hand, and the armed crowd's eager advance was checked, as if their feet had been nailed to the ground. Calmly he surveyed them, blessed them, and said,—

" Christians, the wolf did wrong to punish, for chastisement belongs to God alone ; therefore the wolf's fault should not be punished by you. In whom resides the power of God ? In the holy authority of fathers and mothers. So here is my penitent Josserande, who will rightfully judge the wolf and punish him ; she is his mother."

When Gildas the Wise ceased speaking, you could have heard a mouse run across the heath. Each one thought to himself: " So the wolf is really Sylvestre Ker." But not a word was uttered, and all looked at Dame Josserande's axe, which glistened in the moonlight.

Josserande's heart sank within her, and she murmured,—

" My beloved one, my beloved one, whom I have borne in my arms and nourished with my milk,—ah ! me, can the Lord God inflict this cruel martyrdom upon me ?"

No one replied, not even Gildas the Wise, who silently adjured the All-Powerful, and recalled to Him the sacrifice of Abraham.

Josserande raised her axe, but she had the misfortune to look at the wolf, who fixed his eyes, full of tears, upon her, and the axe fell from her hands.

It was the wolf who picked it up, and when he gave it back to her, he said,—

"I weep for you, my mother."

"Strike!" cried the crowd; for what remained of Pol and Matheline uttered terrible groans. "Strike! strike!"

While Josserande again seized her axe, the grand abbot had time to say,—

"Do not complain, you two unhappy ones; for your suffering here below changes your hell into heaven."

Three times Josserande raised the axe, three times she let it fall without striking; but at last she said, in a hoarse tone that sounded like a death-rattle, "I have great faith in the good God!" and then she struck boldly, for the wolf's head split in two halves.

XIII.

A sudden wind extinguished the torches, and some one prevented Dame Josserande from falling, as she sank fainting to the ground, by supporting her in his arms.

By the light of the halo which shone around the blessed head of Gildas the Wise, the good people saw that this somebody was the young tenant, Sylvestre Ker, no longer lame and one-eyed, but with two straight legs and two perfect eyes.

At the same time there were heard voices in the clouds chanting. And why? Because heaven and earth quivered with emotion at witnessing this supreme act of faith soaring from the depth of anguish in a mother's heart.

XIV.

This is the legend that for many centuries has been related at Christmas-time on the shores of the Petite-Mer, which, in the Breton tongue, is called Armor bihan, the Celtic name of Brittany.

If you ask what moral these good people draw from this strange story, I will answer that it contains a basketful. Pol and Matheline, condemned to walk around the Basin of the Pagans until the end of time,—one without arms, the other without a face,—offer a severe lesson to those who are too proud of their broad shoulders and brute force, and gossiping flirts of girls with smiling faces and wicked hearts; the case of Sylvestre Ker teaches young men not to listen to the demon of money; the blow of Josserande's axe shows the miraculous power of faith.

Still further, that you may bind together these diverse morals in one, here is a proverb which is current in the province: " Never stoop

to pick up the pearls of a smile." After this,
ask me no more.

As to the authenticity of the story, I have
already said that the chestnut-grove belongs to
the mayor's nephew, which is one guarantee;
and I will add that the spot is called Sylvestre-
ker, and that the ruins hung with moss have
no other name than "The Wolf Tower."

An Indian Officer's Idyll.

"An officer and a gentleman—
which is an enviable thing."
Kipling.

THE PEACE EGG.

I.

EVERY one ought to be happy at Christmas. But there are many things which ought to be, and yet are not; and people are sometimes sad even in the Christmas holidays.

The Captain and his wife were sad, though it was Christmas Eve. Sad, though they were in the prime of life, blessed with good health, devoted to each other and to their children, with competent means, a comfortable house on a little freehold property of their own, and, one might say, everything that heart could desire. Sad, though they were good people, whose peace of mind had a firmer foundation than their earthly goods alone; contented people, too, with plenty of occupation for mind and body. Sad—and in the nursery this was held to be past all reason— though the children were performing that ancient and most entertaining play or Christmas Mystery of Good St. George of England, known as "The Peace Egg," for their benefit and behoof alone.

II.—*i*   129

The play was none the worse that most of the
actors were too young to learn parts, so that
there was very little of the rather tedious dialogue, only plenty of dress and ribbons, and of
fighting with wooden swords. But though St.
George looked bonny enough to warm any
father's heart, as he marched up and down with
an air learned by watching many a parade in
barrack-square and drill-ground, and though the
Valiant Slasher did not cry in spite of falling
hard and the Doctor treading accidentally on
his little finger in picking him up, still the Captain and his wife sighed nearly as often as they
smiled, and the mother dropped tears as well as
pennies into the cap which the King of Egypt
brought round after the performance.

II.

Many, many years back the Captain's wife
had been a child herself, and had laughed to see
the village mummers act " The Peace Egg," and
had been quite happy on Christmas Eve. Happy,
though she had no mother. Happy, though her
father was a stern man, very fond of his only
child, but with an obstinate will that not even
she dared thwart. She had lived to thwart it,
and he had never forgiven her. It was when
she married the Captain. The old man had
a prejudice against soldiers, which was quite

reason enough, in his opinion, for his daughter to sacrifice the happiness of her future life by giving up the soldier she loved. At last he gave her her choice between the Captain and his own favor and money, She chose the Captain, and was disowned and disinherited.

The Captain bore a high character, and was a good and clever officer, but that went for nothing against the old man's whim. He made a very good husband, too ; but even this did not move his father-in-law, who had never held any intercourse with him or his wife since the day of their marriage, and who had never seen his own grandchildren. Though not so bitterly prejudiced as the old father, the Captain's wife's friends had their doubts about the marriage. The place was not a military station, and they were quiet country folk who knew very little about soldiers, while what they imagined was not altogether favorable to " red-coats," as they called them.

Soldiers are well-looking generally, it is true, and the Captain was more than well-looking— he was handsome ; brave, of course it is their business, and the Captain had V. C. after his name and several bits of ribbon on his patrol jacket. But then, thought the good people, they are here to-day and gone to-morrow, you " never know where you have them ;" they are probably in debt, possibly married to several women in several foreign countries, and, though they are very courteous in society, who knows how they treat their wives when they drag them off from their natural friends and protectors to distant lands, where no one can call them to account?

"Ah, poor thing!" said Mrs. John Bull, junior, as she took off her husband's coat on his return from business, a week after the Captain's wedding, "I wonder how she feels? There's no doubt the old man behaved disgracefully; but it's a great risk marrying a soldier. It stands to reason, military men aren't domestic; and I wish—Lucy Jane, fetch your papa's slippers, quick!—she'd had the sense to settle down comfortably among her friends with a man who would have taken care of her."

"Officers are a wild set, I expect," said Mr. Bull, complacently, as he stretched his limbs in his own particular arm-chair, into which no member of his family ever intruded. But the red-coats carry the day with plenty of girls who ought to know better. You women are always caught by a bit of finery. However, there's no use our bothering our heads about it. As she has brewed she must bake."

The Captain's wife's baking was lighter and more palatable than her friends believed. The

Captain, who took off his own coat when he came home, and never wore slippers but in his dressing-room, was domestic enough.

A selfish companion must, doubtless, be a great trial amid the hardships of military life, but when a soldier is kind-hearted, he is often a much more helpful and thoughtful and handy husband than any equally well-meaning civilian. Amid the ups and downs of their wanderings, the discomforts of shipboard and of stations in the colonies, bad servants, and unwonted sicknesses, the Captain's tenderness never failed. If the life was rough, the Captain was ready. He had been, by turns, in one strait or another, sick-nurse, doctor, carpenter, nursemaid, and cook to his family, and had, moreover, an idea that nobody filled these offices quite so well as himself. Withal, his very profession kept him neat, well-dressed, and active. In the roughest of their ever-changing quarters he was a smarter man, more like the lover of his wife's young days, than Mr. Bull amid his stationary comforts.

Then if the Captain's wife was—as her friends said—"never settled," she was also forever entertained by new scenes; and domestic mischances do not weigh very heavily on people whose possessions are few and their intellectual interests many.

12

It is true that there were ladies in the Captain's regiment who passed by sea and land from one quarter of the globe to another, amid strange climates and customs, strange trees and flowers, beasts and birds, from the glittering snow of North America to the orchids of the Cape, from beautiful Pera to the lily-covered hills of Japan, and who in no place rose above the fret of domestic worries, and had little to tell on their return but of the universal misconduct of servants, from Irish "helps" in the colonies to *compradors* and China-boys at Shanghai. But it was not so with the Captain's wife. Moreover, one becomes accustomed to one's fate, and she moved her whole establishment from the Curragh to Corfu with less anxiety than that felt by Mrs. Bull over a port-wine stain on the best table-cloth.

And yet, as years went and children came, the Captain and his wife grew tired of travelling. New scenes were small comfort when they heard of the death of old friends. One foot of murky English sky was dearer, after all, than miles of the unclouded heavens of the South. The gray hills and overgrown lanes of her old home haunted the Captain's wife by night and day, and homesickness, that weariest of all sicknesses, began to take the light out of her eyes before their time. It preyed upon the

Captain, too. Now and then he would say, fretfully, "I should like an English resting-place, however small, before everybody is dead! But the children's prospects have to be considered." The continued estrangement from the old man was an abiding sorrow also, and they had hopes that, if only they could get to England, he might be persuaded to peace and charity this time.

At last they were sent home. But the hard old father still would not relent. He returned their letters unopened. This bitter disappointment made the Captain's wife so ill that she almost died, and in one month the Captain's hair became iron gray. He reproached himself for having ever taken the daughter from her father, "to kill her at last," as he said. And, thinking of his own children, he even reproached himself for having robbed the old widower of his only child. After two years at home his regiment was ordered to India. He failed to effect an exchange, and they prepared to move once more, —from Chatham to Calcutta. Never before had the packing, to which she was so well accustomed, been so bitter a task to the Captain's wife.

It was at the darkest hour of this gloomy time that the Captain came in, waving above his head a letter which changed all their plans.

Now close by the old home of the Captain's wife there had lived a man, much older than herself, who yet had loved her with a devotion as great as that of the young Captain. She never knew it, for, when he saw that she had given her heart to his young rival, he kept silence, and he never asked for what he knew he might have had—the old man's authority in his favor. So generous was the affection which he could never conquer, that he constantly tried to reconcile the father to his children while he lived, and, when he died, he bequeathed his house and small estate to the woman he had loved.

"It will be a legacy of peace," he thought, on his death-bed. "The old man cannot hold out when she and her children are constantly in sight. And it may please God that I shall know of the reunion I have not been permitted to see with my eyes."

And thus it came about that the Captain's regiment went to India without him, and that the Captain's wife and her father lived on opposite sides of the same road.

III.

The eldest of the Captain's children was a boy. He was named Robert, after his grandfather, and seemed to have inherited a good deal of the old gentleman's character, mixed with gentler traits. He was a fair, fine boy, tall and stout for his age, with the Captain's regular features, and, he flattered himself, the Captain's firm step and martial bearing. He was apt—like his grandfather—to hold his own will to be other people's law, and happily for the peace of the nursery this opinion was devoutly shared by his brother Nicholas. Though the Captain had sold his commission, Robert continued to command an irregular force of volunteers in the nursery, and never was a colonel more despotic. His brothers and sisters were by turn infantry, cavalry, engineers, and artillery, according to his whim, and when his affections finally settled upon the Highlanders of "The Black Watch," no female power could compel him to keep his stockings above his knees, or his knickerbockers below them.

The Captain alone was a match for his strong-willed son.

"If you please, sir," said Sarah, one morning, flouncing in upon the Captain, just as he was about to start for the neighboring town, "if you please, sir, I wish you'd speak to Master Robert. He's past my powers."

"I've no doubt of it," thought the Captain; but he only said, "Well, what's the matter?"

"Night after night do I put him to bed," said Sarah, "and night after night does he get up as

soon as l'm out of the room, and says he's orderly
officer for the evening, and goes about in his
night-shirt and his feet as bare as boards."

The Captain fingered his heavy moustache to
hide a smile, but he listened patiently to Sarah's
complaints.

"It ain't so much him I should mind, sir,"
she continued, " but he goes round the beds and
wakes up the other young gentlemen and Miss
Dora, one after another, and when I speak to
him he gives me all the sauce he can lay his
tongue to, and says he's going round the guards.
The other night I tried to put him back in his
bed, but he got away and ran all over the house,
me hunting him everywhere, and not a sign of
him, till he jumps out on me from the garret-
stairs and nearly knocks me down.   ' I've visited
the outposts, Sarah,' says he; ' all's well,' and
off he goes to bed as bold as brass."

"Have you spoken to your mistress?" asked
the Captain.

"Yes, sir," said Sarah.   "And misses spoke
to him, and he promised not to go round the
guards again."

"Has he broken his promise?" asked the
Captain, with a look of anger and also surprise.

"When I opened the door last night, sir,"
continued Sarah, in her shrill treble, "what
should I see in the dark but Master Robert

a-walking up and down with the carpet-brush stuck in his arm. 'Who goes there?' says he. 'You owdacious boy!' says I. 'Didn't you promise your ma you'd leave off them tricks?' 'I'm not going round the guards,' says he; 'I promised not. But I'm for sentry-duty to-night.' And say what I would to him, all he had for me was. 'You mustn't speak to a sentry on duty.' So I says, 'As sure as I live till morning, I'll go to your pa,' for he pays no more attention to his ma than me, nor to any one else."

"Please to see that the chair-bed in my dressing-room is moved into your mistress's bed-room," said the Captain. "I will attend to Master Robert."

With this Sarah had to content herself, and she went back to the nursery. Robert was nowhere to be seen, and made no reply to her summons. On this the unwary nursemaid flounced into the bedroom to look for him, when Robert, who was hidden beneath a table, darted forth and promptly locked her in.

"You're under arrest," he shouted through the keyhole.

"Let me out!" shrieked Sarah.

"I'll send a file of the guard to fetch you to the orderly-room by-and-by," said Robert, "for 'preferring frivolous complaints,'" and he departed to the farmyard to look at the ducks.

That night, when Robert went up to bed, the Captain quietly locked him into his dressing-room, from which the bed had been removed.

" You're for sentry-duty to-night," said the captain. " The carpet-brush is in the corner. Good-evening."

As his father anticipated, Robert was soon tired of the sentry game in these new circumstances, and long before the night had half worn away he wished himself safely undressed and in his own comfortable bed. At half-past twelve o'clock he felt as if he could bear it no longer, and knocked at the Captain's door.

" Who goes there?" said the Captain.

" Mayn't I go to bed, please?" whined poor Robert.

" Certainly not," said the Captain. " You're on duty."

And on duty poor Robert had to remain, for the Captain had a will as well as his son. So he rolled himself up in his father's railway rug and slept on the floor.

The next night he was glad to go quietly to bed, and remain there.

IV.

The Captain's children sat at breakfast in a large, bright nursery. It was the room where the old bachelor had died, and now *her* children made it merry. This is just what he would have wished.

They all sat round the table, for it was breakfast-time. There were five of them, and five bowls of boiled bread-and-milk smoked before them. Sarah, a foolish, gossiping girl, who acted as nurse till better could be found, was waiting on them, and by the table sat Darkie, the black retriever, his long, curly back swaying slightly from the difficulty of holding himself up, and his solemn hazel eyes fixed very intently on each and all of the breakfast bowls. He was as silent and sagacious as Sarah was talkative and empty-headed. The expression of his face was that of King Charles I. as painted by Vandyke. Though large, he was unassuming. Pax, the pug, on the contrary, who came up to the first joint of Darkie's leg, stood defiantly on his dignity and his short stumps. He always placed himself in front of the bigger dog, and made a point of hustling him in door-ways and of going first down stairs. He strutted like a beadle, and carried his tail more tightly curled than a bishop's crook. He looked as one may imagine the frog in the fable would have looked had he been able to swell himself rather nearer to the size of the ox. This was partly due to his very prominent eyes, and partly to an obesity favored by habits of lying inside the fender, and of eating meals proportioned more to his consequence than to his hunger. They were both favorites of two years' standing, and had very nearly been given away, when the good news came of an English home for the family, dogs and all.

Robert's tongue was seldom idle, even at meals. "Are you a Yorkshire woman, Sarah?" he asked, pausing, with his spoon full in his hand.

"No, Master Robert," said Sarah.

"But you understand Yorkshire, don't you? I can't, very often; but mamma can, and can speak it, too. Papa says mamma always talks Yorkshire to servants and poor people. She used to talk Yorkshire to Themistocles, papa said, and he said it was no good; for, though Themistocles knew a lot of languages, he didn't know that. And mamma laughed, and said she didn't know she did. Themistocles was our man-servant in Corfu," Robin added, in explanation. "He stole lots of things, Themistocles did; but papa found him out."

Robin now made a rapid attack on his bread-and-milk, after which he broke out again,—

"Sarah, who is that tall gentleman at church, in the seat near the pulpit? He wears a cloak like what the Blues wear, only all blue, and is tall enough for a Life-guardsman. He stood when we were kneeling down, and said, 'Almighty and most merciful Father,' louder than anybody."

Sarah knew who the old gentleman was, and knew also that the children did not know, and that their parents did not see fit to tell them as yet. But she had a passion for telling and hearing news, and would rather gossip with a child than not gossip at all. "Never you mind, Master Robin," she said, nodding sagaciously. "Little boys aren't to know everything."

"Ah, then, I know you don't know," replied Robert; "if you did, you'd tell. Nicholas, give some of your bread to Darkie and Pax. I've done mine. For what we have received, the Lord make us truly thankful. Say your grace, and put your chair away, and come along. I want to hold a court-martial." And, seizing his own chair by the seat, Robin carried it swiftly to its corner. As he passed Sarah, he observed, tauntingly, "You pretend to know, but you don't."

"I do," said Sarah.

"You don't," said Robin.

"Your ma's forbid you to contradict, Master Robin," said Sarah; "and if you do, I shall tell her. I know well enough who the old gentleman is, and perhaps I might tell you, only you'd go straight off and tell again."

"No, no, I wouldn't!" shouted Robin. "I can keep a secret; indeed, I can! Pinch my little finger, and try. Do, do tell me, Sarah; there's a dear Sarah, and then I shall know you know." And he danced round her, catching at her skirts.

To keep a secret was beyond Sarah's powers.

"Do let my dress be, Master Robin," she said; "you're ripping out all the gathers, and listen while I whisper. As sure as you're a living boy, that gentleman's your own grandpapa."

Robin lost his hold on Sarah's dress; his arm fell by his side, and he stood with his brows knit, for some minutes, thinking. Then he said, emphatically,—

"What lies you do tell, Sarah!"

"Oh, Robin!" cried Nicholas, who had drawn near, his thick curls standing stark with curiosity; "mamma said 'lies' wasn't a proper word, and you promised not to say it again."

"I forgot," said Robin. "I didn't mean to break my promise. But she does tell—ahem! —you know what."

"You wicked boy!" cried the enraged Sarah; "how dare you say such a thing, and everybody in the place knows he's your ma's own pa."

"I'll go and ask her," said Robin, and he was at the door in a moment; but Sarah, alarmed by the thought of getting into a scrape herself, caught him by the arm.

" Don't you go, love; it'll only make your ma angry. There; it was all my nonsense."

" Then it's not true ?" said Robin, indignantly. " What did you tell me so for ?"

" It was all my jokes and nonsense," said the unscrupulous Sarah. " But your ma wouldn't like to know I've said such a thing. And Master Robert wouldn't be so mean as to tell tales, would he, love ?"

" I'm not mean," said Robin, stoutly; " and I don't tell tales; but you do, and you tell—you know what—besides. However, I won't go this time; but I'll tell you what,—if you tell tales of me to papa any more, I'll tell him what you said about the old gentleman in the blue cloak." With which parting threat Robin strode off to join his brothers and sister.

Sarah's tale had put the court-martial out of his head, and he leaned against the tall fender, gazing at his little sister, who was tenderly nursing a well-worn doll. Robin sighed.

" What a long time that doll takes to wear out, Dora !" said he. " When will it be done ?"

" Oh, not yet, not yet !" cried Dora, clasping the doll to her, and turning away. " She's quite good, yet."

" How miserly you are," said her brother;

II.—G   *k*   13

"and selfish, too; for you know I can't have a
military funeral till you'll let me bury that old
thing."

Dora began to cry.

"There you go, crying!" said Robin, impatiently. "Look here: I won't take it till
you get the new one on your birthday. You
can't be so mean as not to let me have it
then!"

But Dora's tears still fell. "I love this one
so much," she sobbed. "I love her better than
the new one." ·

"You want both; that's it," said Robin,
angrily. "Dora, you're the meanest girl I ever
knew!"

At which unjust and painful accusation Dora
threw herself and her doll upon their faces, and
wept bitterly. The eyes of the soft-hearted
Nicholas began to fill with tears, and he squatted
down before her, looking most dismal. He had
a fellow-feeling for her attachment to an old
toy, and yet Robin's will was law to him.

"Couldn't we make a coffin, and pretend the
body was inside?" he suggested.

"No, we couldn't," said Robin. "I wouldn't
play the 'Dead March' after an empty candle-
box. It's a great shame,—and I promised she
should be chaplain in one of my night-gowns,
too."

" Perhaps you'll get just as fond of the new
one," said Nicholas, turning to Dora.

But Dora only cried, " No, no ! He shall have
the new one to bury, and I'll keep my poor,
dear, darling Betsey." And she clasped Betsey
tighter than before.

" That's the meanest thing you've said yet,"
retorted Robin ; " for you know mamma wouldn't
let me bury the new one." And, with an air of
great disgust, he quitted the nursery.

V.

Nicholas had sore work to console his little
sister, and Betsey's prospects were in a very
unfavorable state, when a diversion was caused
in her favor by a new whim which put the
military funeral out of Robin's head.

After he left the nursery he strolled out of
doors, and, peeping through the gate at the end
of the drive, he saw a party of boys going
through what looked like a military exercise
with sticks and a good deal of stamping ; but
instead of mere words of command, they all
spoke by turns, as in a play. In spite of their
strong Yorkshire accent, Robin overheard a
good deal, and it sounded very fine.

Not being at all shy, he joined them, and
asked so many questions that he soon got to
know all about it. They were practising a

Christmas mumming-play, called "The Peace
Egg." Why it was called that they could not
tell him, as there was nothing whatever about
eggs in it, and, so far as its being a play of
peace, it was made up of a series of battles
between certain valiant knights and princes, of
whom St. George of England was chief and
conqueror. The rehearsal being over, Robin
went with the boys to the sexton's house, (he
was father to the " King of Egypt,") where they
showed him the dresses they were to wear.
These were made of gay-colored materials, and
covered with ribbons, except that of the " Black
Prince of Paradine," which was black, as became his title. The boys also showed him the
book from which they learned their parts, and
which was to be bought for one penny at the
post-office shop.

" Then are you the mummers who come round
at Christmas, and act in people's kitchens, and
people give them money, that mamma used to
tell us about?" said Robin.

St. George of England looked at his companions as if for counsel as to how far they might
commit themselves, and then replied, with
Yorkshire caution, " Well, I suppose we are."

" And do you go out in the snow from one
house to another at night; and, oh, don't you
enjoy it ?" cried Robin.

"We like it well enough," St. George admitted.

Robin bought a copy of "The Peace Egg." He was resolved to have a nursery performance, and to act the part of St. George himself. The others were willing for what he wished, but there were difficulties.

In the first place, there are eight characters in the play, and there were only five children. They decided among themselves to leave out the "Fool," and mamma said that another character was not to be acted by any of them, or, indeed, mentioned; "the little one who comes in at the end," Robin explained. Mamma had her reasons, and these were always good. She had not been altogether pleased that Robin had bought the play. It was a very old thing, she said, and very queer; not adapted for a child's play.

If mamma thought the parts not quite fit for the children to learn, they found them much too long; so, in the end, she picked out some bits for each, which they learned easily, and which, with a good deal of fighting, made quite as good a story of it as if they had done the whole. What may have been wanting otherwise was made up for by the dresses, which were charming.

Robin was St. George. Nicholas the Valiant Slasher, Dora the Doctor, and the other two

13*

Hector and the King of Egypt. "And now we've no Black Prince!" cried Robin, in dismay.

"Let Darkie be the Black Prince," said Nicholas. "When you have your stick he'll jump for it, and then you can pretend to fight with him."

"It's not a stick, it's a sword," said Robin. "However, Darkie may be the Black Prince."

"And what's Pax to be?" asked Dora; "for you know he will come if Darkie does, and he'll run in before everybody else, too."

"Then he must be the Fool," said Robin; "and it will do very well, for the Fool comes in before the rest, and Pax can have his red coat on, and the collar with the little bells."

VI.

Robin thought that Christmas would never come. To the Captain and his wife it seemed to come too fast. They had hoped it might bring reconciliation with the old man, but it seemed they had hoped in vain.

There were times, now, when the Captain almost regretted the old bachelor's bequest. The familiar scenes of her old home sharpened his wife's grief. To see her father every Sunday in church, with marks of age and infirmity upon him, but with not a look of tenderness for his only child, this tried her sorely.

"She felt it less abroad," thought the Captain.

"An English home, in which she frets herself to death, is, after all, no great boon."

Christmas Eve came.

"I'm sure it's quite Christmas enough, now," said Robin. "We'll have 'The Peace Egg' to-night."

So, as the Captain and his wife sat sadly over their fire, the door opened, and Pax ran in, shaking his bells, and followed by the nursery mummers. The performance was most success-ful. It was by no means pathetic, and yet, as has been said, the Captain's wife shed tears.

"What is the matter, mamma?" said St. George, abruptly dropping his sword and run-ning up to her.

"Don't tease mamma with questions," said the Captain; "she is not very well, and rather sad. We must all be very kind and good to poor, dear mamma;" and the Captain raised his wife's hand to his lips as he spoke. Robin seized the other hand and kissed it tenderly. He was very fond of his mother. At this moment Pax took a little run and jumped on to mamma's lap, where, sitting facing the company, he opened his black mouth and yawned with a ludicrous inappropriateness worthy of any clown. It made everybody laugh.

"And now we'll go and act in the kitchen," said Nicholas.

"Supper at nine o'clock, remember," shouted the Captain. "And we are going to have real frumenty and Yule-cakes, such as mamma used to tell us of when we were abroad."

"Hurray!" shouted the mummers, and they ran off, Pax leaping from his seat just in time to hustle the Black Prince in the doorway.

When the dining-room door was shut, St. George raised his hand, and said, "Hush!"

The mummers pricked their ears, but there was only a distant harsh and scraping sound, as of stones rubbed together.

"They're cleaning the passages," St. George went on; "and Sarah told me they meant to finish the mistletoe, and have everything cleaned up by supper-time. They don't want us, I know. Look here; we will go real mumming, instead. That will be fun!"

The Valiant Slasher grinned with delight.

"But will mamma let us?" he inquired.

"Oh, it will be all right if we are back by supper-time," said St. George, hastily. · "Only, of course, we must take care not to catch cold. Come and help me to get some wraps."

The old oak chest in which spare shawls, rugs, and coats were kept was soon ransacked, and the mummers' gay dresses hidden by motley wrappers. But no sooner did Darkie and Pax behold the coats, etc., than they at once began to leap and bark, as it was their custom to do when they saw any one dressing to go out.

Robin was sorely afraid that this would betray them; but, though the Captain and his wife heard the barking, they did not guess the cause. So, the front door being very gently opened and closed, the nursery mummers stole away.

VII.

It was a very fine night. The snow was well trodden on the drive, so that it did not wet their feet, but on the trees and shrubs it hung soft and white.

" It's much jollier being out at night than in the daytime," said Robin.

" Much," responded Nicholas, with intense feeling.

" We'll go a wassailing next week," said Robin. " I know all about it; and perhaps we shall get a good lot of money, and then we'll buy tin swords with scabbards for next year. I don't like these sticks. Oh, dear, I wish it wasn't so long between one Christmas and another."

" Where shall we go first?" asked Nicholas, as they turned into the high-road. But before Robin could reply, Dora clung to Nicholas, crying, " Oh, look at those men!"

The boys looked up the road, down which three men were coming in a very unsteady fashion, and shouting as they rolled from side to side.

"They're drunk," said Nicholas; "and they're shouting at us."

"Oh, run, run!" cried Dora; and down the road they ran, the men shouting and following them. They had not run far, when Hector caught his foot in the Captain's great-coat, which he was wearing, and came down headlong in the road. They were close by a gate, and when Nicholas had set Hector on his legs, St. George hastily opened it.

"This is the first house," he said. "We'll act here;" and all, even the Valiant Slasher, pressed in as quickly as possible. Once safe within the grounds, they shouldered their sticks and resumed their composure.

"You're going to the front door," said Nicholas. "Mummers ought to go to the back."

"We don't know where it is," said Robin, and he rang the front-door bell. There was a pause. Then lights shone, steps were heard, and at last a sound of much unbarring, unbolting, and unlocking. It might have been a prison. Then the door was opened by an elderly, timid-looking woman, who held a tallow candle above her head.

"Who's there," she said, "at this time of night?"

"We're Christmas mummers," said Robin, stoutly; "we didn't know the way to the back door, but——"

"And don't you know better than to come here?" said the woman. "Be off with you, as fast as you can!"

"You're only the servant," said Robin. "Go and ask your master and mistress if they wouldn't like to see us act. We do it very well."

"You impudent boy, be off with you!" repeated the woman. "Master'd no more let you nor any other such rubbish set foot in this house——"

"Woman!" shouted a voice close behind her, which made her start as if she had been shot, "who authorizes you to say what your master will or will not do, before you ask him? The boy is right. You are the servant, and it is not your business to choose for me whom I shall or shall not see."

"I meant no harm, sir, I'm sure," said the house-keeper; "but I thought you'd never——"

"My good woman," said her master, "if I had wanted somebody to think for me, you're the last person I should have employed. I hire you to obey orders, not to think."

"I'm sure, sir," said the house-keeper, whose only form of argument was reiteration, "I never thought you would have seen them——"

"Then you were wrong," shouted her master. "I will see them. Bring them in."

He was a tall, gaunt old man, and Robin stared at him for some minutes, wondering where he could have seen somebody very like him. At last he remembered. It was the old gentleman of the blue cloak.

The children threw off their wraps, the house-keeper helping them, and chatting ceaselessly, from sheer nervousness.

"Well, to be sure," said she, "their dresses are pretty, too, and they seem quite a better sort of children; they talk quite genteel. I might ha' knowed they weren't like common mummers, but I was so flustered hearing the bell go so late, and——"

"Are they ready?" said the old man, who had stood like a ghost in the dim light of the flaring tallow candle, grimly watching the proceedings.

"Yes, sir. Shall I take them to the kitchen, sir——"

"For you and the other idle hussies to gape and grin at? No. Bring them to the library," he snapped, and then he stalked off, leading the way.

The house-keeper accordingly led them to the

library, and then withdrew, nearly falling on
her face as she left the room by stumbling over
Darkie, who clipped in last like a black shadow.

The old man was seated in a carved oak chair
by the fire.

" I never said the dogs were to come in," he
said.

" But we can't do without them, please," said
Robin, boldly. " You see, there are eight people
in ' The Peace Egg,' and there are only five of us ;
and so Darkie has to be the Black Prince, and
Pax has to be the Fool, and so we have to have
them."

" Five and two make seven," said the old
man, with a grim smile ; " what do you do for the
eighth ?"

" Oh, that's the little one at the end," said
Robin, confidentially. " Mamma said we weren't
to mention him, but I think that's because we're
children. You're grown up, you know, so I'll
show you the book, and you can see for yourself," he went on, drawing "The Peace Egg"
from his pocket. " There, that's the picture of
him on the last page ; black, with horns and a
tail."

The old man's stern face relaxed into a broad
smile as he examined the grotesque wood-cut ;
but, when he turned to the first page, the smile
vanished in a deep frown, and his eyes shone

14

like hot coals, with anger.   He had seen Robin's name.

" Who sent you here ?" he asked, in a hoarse voice.   " Speak, and speak the truth ! Did your mother send you here ?"

Robin thought the old man was angry with them for playing truant. He said slowly, " N—no. She didn't exactly send us ; but I don't think she'll mind our having come if we get back in time for supper.   Mamma never forbid our going mumming, you know.''

" I don't suppose she ever thought of it,'' Nicholas said, candidly, wagging his curly head from side to side.

" She knows we're mummers," said Robin, " for she helped us. When we were abroad, you know, she used to tell us about the mummers acting at Christmas when she was a little girl. And so we acted to papa and mamma, and so we thought we'd act to the maids, but they were cleaning the passages, and so we thought we'd really go mumming ; and we've got several other houses to go to before supper-time. We'd better begin, I think,'' said Robin, and without more ado he began to march round and round, raising his sword and shouting,—

" I am St. George, who from Old England sprung,
  My famous name throughout the world hath rung.''

And the performance went off quite as credit-
ably as before.

As the children acted, the old man's anger
wore off. He watched them with an interest
he could not repress. When Nicholas took
some hard thwacks from St. George without
flinching, the old man clapped his hands; and,
after the encounter between St. George and the
Black Prince, he said he would not have the
dogs excluded on any consideration. It was
just at the end, when they were all marching
round and round, holding on by each other's
swords " over the shoulder," and singing " A
mumming we will go, etc.," that Nicholas suddenly brought the circle to a stand-still by stopping dead short and staring up at the wall
before him.

" What are you stopping for ?" said St. George,
turning indignantly round.

" Look there !" cried Nicholas, pointing to a
little painting which hung above the old man's
head.

Robin looked, and said, abruptly, " It's Dora."

" Which is Dora ?" asked the old man, in a
strange, sharp tone.

" Here she is," said Robin and Nicholas in
one breath, as they dragged her forward.

" She's the Doctor," said Robin ; " and you
can't see her face for her things. Dor, take off

your cap and pull back that hood.   There! Oh,
it is like her!"

It was a portrait of her mother as a child ;
but ƀf this the nursery mummers knew nothing.

The old man looked as the peaked cap and
hood fell away from Dora's face and fair curls,
and then he uttered a sharp cry and buried
his head upon his hands.   The boys stood stupe-
fied, but Dora ran up to him and, putting her
little hands on his arms, said, in childish, pitying
tones, "Oh, I am so sorry! Have you got a
headache? May Robin put the shovel in the
fire for you? Mamma has hot shovels for her
headaches."   And, though the old man did not
speak or move, she went on coaxing him and
stroking his head, on which the hair was white.
At this moment Pax took one of his unexpected
runs and jumped on the old man's knee, in his
own particular fashion, and then yawned at the
company.   The old man was startled, and lifted
his face suddenly.

It was wet with tears.

"Why, you're crying!" exclaimed the children, with one breath.

"It's very odd," said Robin, fretfully. "I
can't think what's the matter to-night. Mamma
was crying, too, when we were acting ; and
papa said we weren't to tease her with questions ; and he kissed her hand, and I kissed her

hand, too. And papa said we must all be very kind to poor, dear mamma; and so I mean to be, she's so good. And I think we'd better go home, or perhaps she'll be frightened," Robin added.

"She's so good, is she?" asked the old man. He had put Pax off his knee and taken Dora on to it.

"Oh, isn't she!" said Nicholas, swaying his curly head from side to side as usual.

"She's always good," said Robin, emphatically; "and so's papa. But I'm always doing something I oughtn't to," he added, slowly. "But then you know I don't pretend to obey Sarah. I don't care a fig for Sarah; and I won't obey any woman but mamma."

"Who's Sarah?" asked the grandfather.

"She's our nurse," said Robin; "and she tells —I mustn't say what she tells,—but it's not the truth. She told one about you the other day," he added.

"About me?" said the old man.

"She said you were our grandpapa. So then I knew she was telling 'you know what.'"

"How did you know it wasn't true?" the old man asked.

"Why, of course," said Robin, "if you were our mamma's father, you'd know her, and be fond of her, and come and see her. And then you'd be our grandfather, too, and you'd have

us to see you, and perhaps give us Christmas-
boxes. I wish you were," Robin added, with a
sigh; "it would be very nice."

" Would you like it?" asked the old man of
Dora.

And Dora, who was half asleep and very
comfortable, put her little arms about his neck
as she was wont to put them round the Captain's, and said, " Very much."

He put her down at last, very tenderly,
almost unwillingly, and left the children alone.
By-and-by he returned, dressed in the blue cloak,
and took Dora up again.

" I will see you home," he said.

The children had not been missed. The clock
had only just struck nine when there came a
knock on the door of the dining-room, where
the Captain and his wife sat still by the Yule-
log. She said " Come in," wearily, thinking it
was the frumenty and the Christmas cakes.

But it was her father, with her child in his
arms!

VIII.

Lucy Jane Bull and her sisters were quite
old enough to understand a good deal of grown-
up conversation when they overheard it. Thus,
when a friend of Mrs. Bull's observed, during
an afternoon call, that she believed that " offi-

cers wives were very dressy," the young ladies were at once resolved to keep a sharp lookout for the Captain's wife's bonnet in church on Christmas day.

The Bulls had just taken their seats when the Captain's wife came in. They really would have hid their faces, and looked at the bonnet afterwards, but for the startling sight that met the gaze of the congregation. The old grand-father walked into the church abreast of the Captain.

"They've met in the porch," whispered Mr. Bull, under the shelter of his hat.

"They can't quarrel publicly in a place of worship," said Mrs. Bull, turning pale.

"She's gone into his seat," cried Lucy Jane, in a shrill whisper.　•

"And the children after her," added the other sister, incautiously aloud.

There was no doubt about the matter. The old man, in his blue cloak, stood for a few moments politely disputing the question of pre-cedence with his handsome son-in-law. Then the Captain bowed and passed in, and the old man followed him.

By the time that the service was ended every-body knew of the happy peace-making, and was glad. One old friend after another came up with blessings and good wishes. This was a

proper Christmas, indeed, they said.   There was
a general rejoicing.

But only the grandfather and his children
knew that it was hatched from " The Peace
Egg."

By a Bavarian Comrade.

"Over his tumbler of Gukguk he
sat reading journals, sometimes
contemplatively looking   into
the clouds of his tobacco-pipe:
an   agreeable   phenomenon,—
more especially when he opened
his lips for speech."

Carlyle.

A STORY OF NUREMBERG.

IT was a Christmas eve in the beginning of the sixteenth century, and through the streets of Nuremberg came drifting a feathery snow that heaped itself in fantastic patterns on the projecting windows and fretted stone balconies of the quaint and crowded houses. It was not an honest and single-minded snow-storm, such as would seek to shroud the whole city in its delicate white mantle, but rather a tricksy and capricious sprite, that neglected one spot to hurl itself with wanton violence on another. Borne on the breath of a keen and shifting wind, it came tossing gleefully full in the face of a solitary artisan who, wrapped in a heavy cloak, was making the best of his way homeward. Truly it was not a pleasant night to be abroad, with the snow-drifts dancing in your eyes like a million of tiny arrow-points, and the sharp wind cutting like a knife; and the way-farer was consoling himself for his present discomfort by picturing the warm fireside and the hot supper that awaited him at home, when his

cheerful dreams were broken by a sharp cry
that seemed to come from under his very feet.

Startled, and not a little alarmed, he checked
his rapid walk and listened. There was no mistaking the sound : it was neither imp nor fairy,
but a real child, from whose little lungs came
forth that wail at once pitiful and querulous.
As he heard it, Peter Burkgmäier's kindly heart
flew with one rapid bound to the cradle at
home where slumbered his own infant daughter,
and, hastily lowering his lantern, he searched
under the dark archway whence the cry
had come. There, sheltered by the wall and
wrapped in a ragged cloak, was a baby boy,
perhaps between two and three years old, but
so tiny and emaciated as to seem hardly half
that age. When the lantern flickered in his
face he gave a frightened sob, and then lay
quiet and exhausted in the strong arms that
held him.

" Poor little wretch !" said the man. " Abandoned on Christmas eve to die in the snow !"
And wrapping the child more closely in his own
mantle, he hurried on until he reached his home,
from whose latticed panes shone forth a cheerful stream of light. His wife, with her baby on
her breast, met him at the door, and stared with
a not unnatural amazement as her husband un-
rolled his cloak and showed her the boy, who,

blinking painfully at the sudden light, tried to struggle down from his arms.

" See, Lisbeth !" he said, " I have found you a Christmas present where I least expected one— an unhappy baby left in the streets to die of cold and hunger."

His wife laid her own infant in the cradle and gazed alternately at her husband and at the child he carried. She was at all times slow to receive impressions, and slower yet to put her thoughts into words. When she spoke, it was without apparent emotion of any kind. " What are you going to do with him, Peter ?" she said.

" What am I going to do with him ?" was the reply. " I am going to feed and clothe and shelter him, and make an honest man out of him, please God. It cannot be that you would refuse the poor child a home ?"

Lisbeth made no answer. She was a large, fair, sleepy-eyed woman, who had been ac- counted a beauty in her day. A model wife, too, people said ; neat in dress, quiet of tongue, her conduct staid, her whole thoughts centred in her household. She now took the boy, noting with a woman's eye his coarse and ragged cloth- ing, and stood him on his unsteady little feet. A faint expression of disgust rippled over her smooth, unthinking face.

H   15

" He is a humpback," she said, slowly.

Her husband started to his feet. In all ages
physical deformity has been a thing repulsive
to our eyes ; but at this early day it was regarded with unmixed horror and aversion, and
was too often considered as the index of a
crooked mind within. Peter Burkgmäier, tall
and erect, with a frame of iron and sinews of
steel, as became a master stone-mason, stood
gazing at the poor little atom of misshappen
humanity who tottered over the polished
wooden floor. The spinal column was sadly
bent, and from between the humped shoulders
the pale face peered with an old, uncanny look.
Yet the boy was not otherwise ugly. His forehead was broad and smooth, and his dark blue
eyes were well and deeply set. The artisan
watched him for a minute in painful silence,
then turned to his wife and took her passive
hand in his.

" Lisbeth," he said, with grave kindness, " I
know that I am asking a great deal of you
when I beg you to take this child under our
roof. He will be to you much care and trouble,
and may never find his way into your heart.
At any other time, believe me, I would not
put this burden on your shoulders. But it is
Christmas eve, and were I to refuse a shelter to
this helpless baby I would feel like one of those

who had no room within their inns for the Holy Child. Dear wife, will you not receive him for love of me and of God, and let him share with little Kala in your care?"

Lisbeth's only reply was one characteristic of the woman. She was moved by her husband's appeal, against what she considered her better judgment; and without a single word she picked up the boy from the floor and laid him in the cradle by the side of her own little daughter. Then, with a smile—and her smiles came but rarely—she proceeded to carry off Peter's wet cloak and to bring in his supper. So with this mute assent the matter was settled, and the deformed child was received into the stone-mason's family.

And in a different way he became the source of much gratification to both husband and wife. The first regarded him with real kindness and an almost fatherly affection, for the boy soon began to manifest a quick intelligence and a winning gentleness that might readily have found their way into a harder heart. Lisbeth, too, had her reward; for it was sweet to her soul to hear her neighbors say, as they stopped to watch the two children playing in the doorway: " Ah! Lisbeth, it is not many a woman who would take the care you do of a wretched little humpback like that;" or, " It was a lucky

chance for the poor child that threw him into
such hands as yours, Mistress Burkgmáier ;" or,
" Did ever little Kala look so fair and straight
as when she had that crooked boy by her
side ?"

And did not the good pastor from the Frauenkirche say to her, with tears starting in his
gentle eyes : " God will surely reward you for
your kindness to this helpless little one ?" Nay,
better yet, did not the Stadtholder's lady lean
out from her beautiful carriage, and say before
three of the neighbors, who were standing by
and heard every word : " You are a good
woman, Mistress Burkgmaier, to take the same
care of this miserable child as of your own
pretty little daughter" ?—which was something
to be really proud of; for, whereas it was the
obvious duty of a priest to admire a virtuous
act, it was not often that a noble lady deigned
thus to express her approbation.

Yes, Lisbeth felt, as she listened serenely to
all this praise—surely so well merited—that
there was some compensation in 'the world for
such charitable deeds as hers, even when they
involved a fair amount of sacrifice. And little
Gabriel, before whom many of these remarks
were uttered, pondered over them in secret, and
gradually evolved three facts from the curious
puzzle of his life—first, that he did not really

belong to what seemed to be his home; second, that he was not loved in it as was Kala; third, that Kala was pretty and he was ugly. So with these three melancholy scraps of knowledge the poor child began his earthly education.

And Kala was very pretty. Tall and strong-limbed, with her mother's beautiful hair and skin, and with her mother's clear, meaningless blue eyes, the little girl attracted attention wherever she was seen. No better foil to her vigorous young beauty could have been found than the pale, misshapen boy whom all the world called ugly. The children played together under Lisbeth's watchful eye, and Gabriel in all things yielded to his companion's imperious will, so that peace reigned ever over their sports. But when Sigmund Wahnschaffe, the son of the bronze-worker in the neighboring street, joined them, then Kala would have no more of Gabriel's company. For Sigmund was strong as a young Hercules and surpassed all the other lads in their boyish games. When he would play with her, Kala turned her back ungratefully upon the patient companion of her idler moments, who was fain to watch in silence the pleasures he might not share.

Yet from Sigmund she met no easy compliance with her wishes. His will was a law not to be disputed, and once, when she had ventured to assert herself in rebellious fashion, he promptly maintained his precedence by pushing her into the mud. Kala began to cry, and, like a flash, Gabriel, in a storm of rage, flung himself upon the older boy, only to be shaken off as a feather into the same muddy gutter. It was over in a minute, nor would Sigmund deign to further punish the little humpback who had been ridiculous enough to attack him. Serenely unmoved he strolled away, while Kala and Gabriel went sadly home together, to be both well scolded for the ruin of their clothes and sent supperless to bed ; Lisbeth priding herself, above all things, on the strictly impartial character of her retributive justice.

But Gabriel had at least one pastime which could be shared with none, and which bade fair to recompense him for all the childish sports he was denied. With a small block of wood and a few simple tools his skilful fingers wrought such wonders that Kala and Sigmund, and the very children who hooted at him in the street, could not withhold their admiration,—sometimes a brooding dove with pretty, ruffled plumage ; sometimes the head and curving horns of a mountain chamois, instinct with graceful life ; sometimes a group of snails, each tiny spiral reproduced with loving accuracy in the hard grained wood. To Peter Burkgmäier these ovi-

dences of a talent then in such high repute gave
most unbounded satisfaction. His own trade
was far too severe for the boy's frail strength,
but wood-carving was fully as profitable, and
might lead to wealth and fame. Had not Veit
Stoss, of whose genius Nuremberg felt justly
proud, already finished his wonderful group of
angels saluting the Virgin, which hung from
the roof of St. Lorenz? With such an example
before him, what might not the boy hope to
achieve through talent and persevering labor?
And Gabriel felt his own heart burn as he
looked with wistful eyes upon that masterpiece
of rare and delicate carving.

Nuremberg was then alive with the spirit of
art, and everywhere he turned there was something beautiful to quicken his pulse and feed
the flame within his soul, that was half rapture
and half bitterness. No idle boast was the old
rhyme,—

> " Nuremberg's hand
> Goes through every land."

For the city's renown had spread far and wide,
and in its many branches of industry, as well
as in the higher walks of art, it had reached
the zenith of its fame. Already, indeed, the
canker-worm was gnawing at the root, and un-
erring retribution was creeping on a blinded

people ; but no sign of the future was manifested
in the universal prosperity of the day. Every
street furnished its food for the artist's soul :
the Frauenkirche, enriched with the loving gifts
of devout generations ; St. Sebald's, with its
carved portal, its stained windows, its treasures
of bronze, and, above all, the shrine where
Peter Vischer and his sons labored for thirteen
years. Gabriel loved St. Sebald's dearly, but
closer still to his heart was the majestic church
of St. Lorenz, where, in sharp relief against the
dull red pillars, rose that dream in stone, the
Sacrament House of Adam Krafft, its slender,
fretted spire springing to the very roof, clasped
in the embrace of the curling vine tendrils
carved around it.

Here the boy would linger for hours, never
weary of studying every detail of this faultless
shrine. With envious eyes he gazed upon the
kneeling figures of Adam Krafft and his two
fellow-laborers, who, carved in stone, now supported the treasure their hands had wrought.
Surely this was the crowning summit of human
ambition—to live thus forever in the house of
God, and before the eyes of men, a part of the
very work which had ennobled the artist's life.
Ah! if he, the despised humpback, could but
descend to posterity immortalized by the labor
of his hands. What to the dreaming lad was

the picture of Adam Krafft dying in a hospital, poor, unfriended, and alone, in the midst of a city his genius had enriched ? What was it to him that Nuremberg, which now heaped honors on the dead, had denied bread to the living? Such bitter truths come not to the young. They are the heritage of age, and Gabriel was but·a boy, with all a boy's fond hopes and aspirations. Often as he studied the graceful beauty of the Sacrament House, where, cut in the pure white stone, he saw the Last Supper and Christ blessing little children, he wondered whether among those Jewish boys and girls was one who, deformed and repulsive to the eye, yet felt the Saviour's loving touch and was comforted.

A few more years rolled by, and each succeed-ing spring saw Kala taller and prettier, and Gabriel working harder still at his laborious art. Not so engrossed, however, but that he knew that Kala was fair, and that when her soft fin-gers touched his a swift and sudden fire leaped through his heart. Kala's beauty lurked in his dreams by night and in his long, solitary days of toil, and became the motive power of all his best endeavors. If he should gain wealth, it would be but to lay it at her feet. If he, the desolate waif, should win fame and distinction, it would be but to gild her name with his.

II.—*m*

Surely these things must be some recompense in a woman's eyes for a pale face and a stunted form ; and Gabriel, lost in foolish dreams, worked on.

Sigmund Wahnschaffe, too, had grown into early manhood and had adopted his father's calling. Strong arms were as useful in their way as a creative brain, and if Sigmund could never be an artist like Peter Vischer, he promised at least to make an excellent workman. People said he was the handsomest young artisan in Nuremberg, with his dark skin bronzed by the fires among which he labored, and his black eyes sparkling with a keen and merry light. Times had changed since the day he pushed little Kala into the mud, and he looked upon her now as some frail and delicate blossom, that to handle would be desecration. Yet Kala was no rare flower, but a common plant, with nothing remarkable about her except her beauty ; and, once married, Sigmund would be prompt enough to recognize this fact. Gabriel, with a chivalrous and imaginative soul, might perhaps retain his ideal unbroken till his death ; but in the young bronze-worker's practical mind ideals had no place, and his bride would slip naturally into the post of housewife, from whom nothing more exalted would be demanded than thrifty habits and a cheerful temper.

And Kala knew perfectly that both these young men loved her, and that one day she would be called upon to choose between them, between Sigmund, strong, handsome, and resolute, with a laugh and a gay word for all who met him ; and Gabriel, dwarfed and silent, who had caught the trick of melancholy in his unloved childhood and could not shake it off. But it was not merely the sense of physical deformity that saddened Gabriel's soul. The air he breathed was filled with a subtle spirit of discord ; for upon Nuremberg, with her many churches and monuments of mediæval art, the Reformation had laid its chilling hand. Its influence was felt on every side—in art, where the joyous simplicity of Wohlgemuth had given place to the fantastic melancholy of Albrecht Dürer, fit imprint of a troubled and storm-tossed mind ; as well as in literature, where the bitter raillery and coarse jests of Hans Sachs, the cobbler-poet, now passed with swift approval from mouth to mouth.

The day had not yet come when Nuremberg, in her blind arrogance, was to close her gates upon those who had given her life and fame ; but already were heard the first faint murmurs of the approaching storm. What wonder that Gabriel shrank from the darkening future, and that men like Peter Burkgmäier, pondering

with set mouths and frowning brows, were
slowly making up their minds that the city
which had been their birthplace should never
shelter their old age. But Lisbeth went stolidly
about the daily routine of her life; Kala's smiles
were as bright and as frequent as ever; and
Sigmund troubled himself not at all with matters beyond his ken.

Winter had set in early, and already Novem-
ber had brought in its train snow and biting
winds, and the promise of severe cold to come.
It was a busy season for the bronze-workers,
and Sigmund toiled unceasingly, his cheerful
thoughts giving zest to his labors and new
strength to his mighty arm. For did not each
evening see him by Kala's side, and had she not,
after months of vain coquetting, at last fairly
yielded up her heart?

"Kala will make a good wife," said Lisbeth,
proudly. "And she goes not empty-handed to
her husband's house."

"They are a well-matched pair," said Peter,
meditatively. "Health and beauty and dulness
are no mean heritage in these troubled times."

And though the neighbors hesitated to call
the young couple dull, they one and all agreed
that the marriage was a suitable one, and that
they had long foreseen it. "Why, they were
little lovers in childhood, even!" said Theresa,

the wife of Johann Dyne, the toy-vender in the next street; and Kala, who had perhaps forgotten the time when her child-lover had knocked her into the gutter, smiled, and showed her beautiful white teeth, and suffered the remark to pass uncontradicted.

But even the most stolid of women have always some lurking tenderness for those who they know have loved them vainly, and Kala, though she had without a demur accepted Sigmund for her husband, yet broke the news to Gabriel with much gentleness, and was greatly comforted by the apparent composure with which it was received. He grew perhaps a trifle paler and quieter than before, if such a thing were possible, and shut himself up more resolutely with his work; but that was all. No one would have dreamed that life with its fair promises had suddenly grown worthless in his hands, and that the rich gifts which still were left him seemed as nothing compared with the valueless treasure he had lost. Even his art had become hateful, freighted as it was with dead hopes; and often, when all believed him to be toiling in his little den, he was wandering aimlessly through the streets of Nuremberg, seeking comfort in those haunts which had once been to him as dear friends and companions. For hours he would linger in the church of St.

16

Lorenz, and then slowly make his way to the Thiergarten Gate, where, along the Seilersgasse to the churchyard, rise at regular intervals the seven stone pillars on which Adam Krafft has carved, in beautiful bas-reliefs, scenes from the Passion of the Lord. Years before the simple piety of a Nuremberg citizen had erected these monuments of holy art, and their founder, Martin Ketzel, had even travelled into Palestine, that he might measure the exact distances of that most sorrowful journey from the house of Pontius Pilate to the hill of Calvary. Heedless of the severe weather, Gabriel visited daily these primitive stations, striving to forget his own bitterness in the presence of a divine grief; and, laying his troubled heart at his Saviour's feet, would return, strengthened and comforted, into the busy city.

Christmas now was drawing near, and with its approach a new resolve took possession of his soul. A fresh light had dawned upon him, and, shaking off his apathy, he started to work in earnest. All day long he toiled with a steady purpose, though none were permitted to see the fruit of his labors. Kala, indeed, unaccustomed to be thwarted in her curiosity, presented herself at his work-shop door and implored admittance; but not even to her was the secret revealed.

"It is very unkind of you!" she pouted, hardly doubting that she would gain her point. "You never kept anything from me in your life before."

Gabriel took her hand and looked with strange, wistful eyes into her pretty face. "I am keeping nothing from you now," he said. "It is your wedding-gift that I am fashioning; but you must be content to wait its completion before you see it. By Christmas it shall be your own."

So Kala, comforted with the thought of future possession, bided her time, and Gabriel was left in undisputed enjoyment of his solitude. At first he worked languidly and with little zest; but from interest grew ambition, and from ambition a passionate love for the labor of his hands, which threw all other hopes and fears into the background. Kala was forgotten, and Gabriel, absorbed in the contemplation of his art and striving as he had never striven before, felt as though some power not his own were working in him, and that the supreme effort of his life had come. Yet ever in the midst of his feverish activity a strange weakness seized and held him powerless in its grasp; and like a keen and sudden pain came the bitter thought that he might die before his work was done. Instinctively he felt that his hopes of future

fame rested on these few weeks that were flying
pitilessly by, each one carrying with it some
portion of his wasted strength; and that if
death should overtake him with his labor un-
completed his name and memory must perish
from the world. So, like one who flies across
a Russian steppe pursued by starving wolves,
Gabriel sped on his task, seeking to out-distance
the grim and noiseless wolf that followed close
upon his track.

It was Christmas eve, the anniversary of that
snowy night when Peter Burkgmäier had carried home the deformed child, and now all was
bustle and glad preparation in the stone-mason's
household. Within three days Kala was to be
married, and Lisbeth, who felt that her reputation as cook and housewife was at stake,
spared neither time nor trouble in her hospitable
labors. Since early morning the great fires had
roared in her spacious kitchen, and all the poor
who came to beg a Christmas bounty tasted
freely of her good cheer. With light heart and
busy fingers Kala assisted her mother, and
doled out the bread and cakes—not too lavishly
—to the ragged children who clamored around
the door; wondering much in the meanwhile
what trinket Sigmund would bring her with
which to deck herself on Christmas morning.

And in his little room Gabriel stood looking
at his finished work, and asking himself if his
heart spoke truly when it whispered: " You,
too, are great." It was sweet to realize that
his task was done and that he might rest at
last; it was sweeter still to see in the bit of
carved wood before him the fulfilment of all his
dearest dreams. So, while daylight faded into
dusk and evening into night, he sat lost in a
maze of tangled thoughts that crowded wearily
through his listless brain. It was now too dark
for him to discern the image by his side, but
from time to time he laid his hand upon it with
a gentle touch, as a mother might caress a
sleeping child, and was happy in its dumb companionship.

How long he had been sitting thus he never
knew, when suddenly out into the frosty air
rang the great bells of St. Lorenz, calling the
faithful to midnight Mass.

Clearly and joyfully they pealed, as if their
brazen tongues were striving to utter in words
their messages of good-will to men. Gabriel's
heart leaped at the sound, and a great yearning
seized him to kneel once more within those beloved walls, and amid their solemn beauty to
adore the new-born Babe. Jubilantly rang the
bells, and their glad voices seemed to speak to
him as old friends, and with one accord to

16*

urge him on. Weak and dizzy, he crept down
the narrow stairs and out into the bitter night.
The sharp wind struck him in the face, and
worried him as it had worried years before the
baby abandoned to its cruel embraces. Yet
with the appealing music of the bells ringing
in his ears he never thought of turning back,
but struggled bravely onward until the frowning walls of St. Lorenz rose up before him.
Through the open doors poured a little crowd
of devotees, and Gabriel, entering, stole softly
up to the Sacrament House, where so often the
carved Christ had looked with gentle eyes upon
his lonely childhood.

Mass had begun, and the great church was
hardly a third full, for Nuremberg's weakening
faith exempted her children from such untimely
services. But in the faces of the scattered
worshippers there was something never seen
before—a grave severity, a solemn purpose, as
when men are banded together to resist in
silence an advancing foe. Gabriel, dimly conscious of this, strove to restrain his wandering
thoughts, and fixed his eyes upon the gleaming
altar. But no prayer rose to his lips, though
into his heart came that deep sense of rest and
contentment which found an utterance long ago
in the words of an apostle: " Lord, it is good
for us to be here." Like a child he had come

to his Father's feet, and, laying there his rejected human love, his ungratified human ambition, he gained in their place the peace which
passeth all understanding. The two shadows
which had mocked him during life vanished into
nothingness at the hour of death, and with clear
eyes he saw the value of an immortal soul.

Mass was over, and the congregation moved
slowly through the shadowy aisles out into the
starlit night. But Gabriel sat still, his head
resting against the stone pillar, his dead eyes
fixed upon the Sacrament House, and upon the
sculptured Christ rising triumphant from the
grave.

Four weeks had gone by since the body of
the humpback had been carried sorrowfully past
the stations of the Seilersgasse into the quiet
churchyard beyond. The dusk of a winter
evening shrouded the empty streets when a
stranger, of grave demeanor and in the prime
of life, knocked at the stone-mason's door.
Kala opened it, and her father, recognizing the
visitor, rose with wondering respect to greet
him. It was Veit Stoss, the wood-carver, then
at the zenith of his fame. With quick, keen
eyes he glanced around the homely room, taking
in every detail of the scene before him—Lisbeth
weaving placidly by the fire; Kala fair and

blushing in the lamp-light ; and Sigmund playing idly with the crooked little turnspit at his
feet. Then he turned to Peter, and for a minute
the two men stood looking furtively at one
another, as though each were trying to read his
companion's thoughts. Finally, the wood-carver
spoke.

"I grieve, Master Burkgmaier," he said, with
courteous sympathy, "that you should have
lost your foster-son, to whom report says you
were much attached. And I hear also that the
young man promised highly in his calling."

"Then you heard not all," answered the stone-
mason, slowly. "Gabriel did more, for he ful-
filled his promise."

A sudden light came into the artist's eyes.
"It is true, then," he said, eagerly, "that the
boy left behind him a rare piece of work, which
has not yet been seen outside these walls. I
heard the rumor, but thought it idle folly."

Peter Burkgmäier crossed the room and
opened a deep cupboard. "You shall see it,"
he said simply, "and answer for yourself. No
one in Nuremberg is more fit to judge." Then,
lifting out something wrapped in a heavy cloth,
he carried it to the table, unveiled it with a
reverent hand, and, stepping back, waited in
silence for a verdict.

There was a long, breathless pause, broken

only by the low whir of Lisbeth's busy wheel.
Veit Stoss stood motionless, while Peter's eyes
never stirred from the table before them.
There, carved in the fair white wood, rested the
divine Babe, as on that blessed Christmas night
when his Mother " wrapped him up in swaddling-clothes and laid him in a manger." The
lovely little head nestled on its rough pillow as
though on Mary's bosom; the tiny limbs were
relaxed in sleep; the whole figure breathed at
once the dignity of the Godhead and the pathetic helplessness of babyhood. Instinctively
one loved, and pitied, and adored. Nor was this
all. Every broken bit of straw that thrust its
graceful, fuzzy head from between the rough
bars of the manger, every twisted knot of grass,
every gnarl and break in the wood itself, had
been wrought with the tender accuracy of the
true artist, who finds nothing too simple for his
utmost care and skill.

Veit Stoss drew a heavy breath and turned to
his companion. " It is a masterpiece," he said,
gravely, " which I should be proud to call my
own. I congratulate you on the possession of
so great a treasure."

" It is not mine," returned the artisan, " but
my daughter's. Gabriel wrought it for her
wedding-gift."

The wood-carver's keen blue eyes scanned

Kala's pretty, stolid face, and then wandered to
Sigmund's broad shoulders and mighty bulk. A
faint, derisive smile curled his well-cut lips.
" Your daughter's beauty merits, indeed, the
rarest of all rare tokens," he said, slowly. " But
perhaps there are other things more needful to
a young housewife than even this precious bit
of carving. If she will part with it I will pay
her seventy thalers, and it shall lie in St. Sebald's
Church near my own Virgin, that all may see its
loveliness and remember the hand that fashioned
it."

Seventy thalers ! Sigmund dropped the dog
and lifted his handsome head with a look of
blank bewilderment. Seventy thalers for a bit
of wood like that, when his own strong arms
could not earn as much in months ! He stared
at the little image in wondering perplexity, as
though striving to see by what mysterious process it had arrived at such a value ; while into
his heart crept a thought strictly in keeping
with his practical nature. If the humpback
could have produced work worth so much, what
a thousand pities he should die with only one
piece finished !

On Lisbeth, too, a revelation seemed to have
fallen. Her wheel had stopped, and in her mind
she was rapidly running over a list of household goods valued at seventy thalers. It was a

mental calculation quickly and cleverly accomplished; for Lisbeth was not slow in all things, and years of thrift had taught her the full worth of money. Instinctively she glanced at her husband and marvelled at his unmoved face.

"Your offer is a liberal one, Master Stoss," said Peter, gravely. "And I rejoice to think that the poor lad's genius will be recognized. In him Nuremberg would have had another famous son."

"In him Nuremberg has now a famous son," corrected Veit Stoss, laying his hand upon the statue. "No other proof of greatness can be needed." With gentle care he replaced the cloth and lifted the precious burden in his arms, when suddenly Kala sprang forward, her cheeks ablaze, her blue eyes dark with anger. Transfigured for one instant into a new and passionate beauty, she snatched the image from his hands.

"It is mine!" she cried, fiercely; "mine! Gabriel loved me, and carved it for me when he knew that he was dying. It was for me he did it, and you shall not take it from me."

She gathered it to her bosom with a low, broken cry, and darted from the room. God only knows what late love, and pity, and remorse were working in her breast. Veit Stoss turned softly to her father. "It is enough," he said. " Your daughter has the prior right, and I came not here to wrong her."

And so the hand which had robbed Gabriel of love and life robbed him of fame. For the statue which should have given joy to generations remained unknown in the artisan's family. At first many came to see and wonder at its beauty; but with the advent of a colder creed men wanted not such tokens of a vanished fervor, and the little Christ-Child was soon forgotten by the world. Perhaps Kala's sturdy grandchildren destroyed it as a useless toy; perhaps it perished by fire, or flood, or evil accident. No memory of it lingers in the streets of Nuremberg; and Gabriel, lifted beyond the everlasting hills, knoweth the vanity of all human wishes.

The Italian Guest's Selection.

"He is a Tuscan born, of an old
noble race in that part of Italy."
Hawthorne.

A PICTURE OF THE NATIVITY
BY FRA FILIPPO LIPPI

AS EXPLAINED BY A PIOUS FLORENTINE GOSSIP OF HIS DAY.

" Now, I cannot affirm that things did really take place in this manner, but it greatly pleases me to think that they did."—FRA DOMENICO CAVALCA : *Life of the Magdalen.*

THE silly folks do not at all understand about the birth of our Lord. They say that our Lord was born at Bethlehem, and because the inns were all full, owing to certain feasts kept by those Jews, in a stable. But I tell you this is an error, and due to little sense, for our Lord was indeed placed in a manger, because none of the hostleries would receive Joseph and the Blessed Virgin ; but it took place differently.

For you must know that beyond Bethlehem, which is a big village walled and moated, of those parts, lies a hilly country, exceeding wild, and covered with dense woods of firs, pines, larches, beeches, and similar trees, which the people of Bethlehem cut down at times, going in bands, and burn to charcoal, packing it on mules, to sell in the valley; or tie together whole trunks such as serve for beams, rafters, and masts, and float them down the rivers, which are many and very rapid.

In these mountains, then, in the thickest part of the woods, a certain man, of the wood-cutting trade, bethought him to build a house wherein to store the timber and live, himself and his family, when so it pleased him, and keep his beasts; and for this purpose he employed certain pillars and pieces of masonry that stood in the forest, being remains of a temple of the heathen, the which had long ceased to exist. And he cleared the wood round about, leaving only tree stumps and bushes; and close by in a ravine, between high fir-trees, ran a river, always full to the brim even in midsummer, owing to the melting snows, and of greenish waters, cold and rapid exceedingly; and around, up hill and down dale, stretched the wood of firs, larches, pines, and other noble and useful trees, emitting a very pleasant and virtuous fragrance. The man thought to enjoy his house, and came with his family, and servants, and horses, and mules, and oxen, which he had employed to carry down the timber and charcoal.

But scarcely were they settled than an earth-

quake rent the place, tearing wall from wall
and pillar from pillar, and a voice was heard
in the air, crying, " Ecce domus domini dei."
Whereupon they fled, astonished and in terror,
and returned into the town.

And no one of that man's family ventured
henceforth to return to that wood, or to that
house, save one called Hilarion, a poor lad and
a servant, but of upright heart and faith in the
Lord, which offered to go back and take his
abode there, and cut down the trees and burn
the charcoal for his master.

So he went, being a poor lad and poorly clad
in leathern tunic and coarse serge hood And
Hilarion took with him an ox and an ass to
load with charcoal and drive down to Bethlehem
to his master.

And the first night that Hilarion slept in that
house, which was fallen to ruin, only a piece of
roof remaining, which he thatched with pine-
branches, he heard voices singing in the air, as
of children, both boys and maidens. But he
closed his eyes and repeated a Paternoster, and
turned over and slept. And again, another
night, he heard voices, and knew the house to
be haunted, and trembled. But, being clear of
heart, he said two Aves and went to sleep.
And once more did he hear voices, and they
were passing sweet; and with them came a

fragrance as of crushed herbs, and many kinds
of flowers, and frankincense, and orris-root;
and Hilarion shook, for he feared lest it be the
heathen gods, Mercury, or Macomet, or Apol-
linis. But he said his prayer and slept.

But at length, one night, as Hilarion heard
those songs as usual, he opened his eyes. And,
behold! the place was light, and a great staircase of light, like golden cobwebs, stretched up
to heaven, and there were angels going about in
numbers, coming and going, with locks like
honeycomb, and dresses pink, and green, and
sky-blue, and white, thickly embroidered with
purest pearls, and wings as of butterflies and
peacock's tails, with glories of solid gold about
their head. And they went to and fro, carrying garlands and strewing flowers, so that,
although mid-winter, it was like a garden in
June, so sweet of roses, and lilies, and gilly-
flowers. And the angels sang; and when they
had finished their work, they said, "It is well,"
and departed, holding hands and flying into the
sky above the fir-trees.

And Hilarion wondered greatly, and said five
Paters and six Aves. And the next day, as he
was cutting a fir-tree in the wood, there met
him, among the rocks, a man old, venerable,
with a long gray beard and a solemn air. And
he was clad in crimson, and under his arm he

carried written books and a scourge. And
Hilarion said,—

"Who art thou? for this forest is haunted by
spirits, and I would know whether thou be of
them or of men."

And the ancient made answer: "My name
is Hieronymus. I am a wise man and a king.
I have spent all my days learning the secrets
of things. I know how the trees grow and
waters run, and where treasure lies; and I can
teach thee what the stars sing, and in what
manner the ruby and emerald are smelted in the
bowels of the earth; and I can chain the winds
and stop the sun, for I am wise above all men.
But I seek one wiser than myself, and go through
the woods in search of him, my master."

And Hilarion said: "Tarry thou here, and
thou shalt see, if I mistake not, him whom thou
seekest."

So the old man, whose name was Hieronymus,
tarried in the forest and built himself a hut of
stones.

And the day after that, as Hilarion went
forth to catch fish in the river, he met on the
bank a lady, beautiful beyond compare, the
which for all clothing wore only her own hair,
golden and exceeding long. And Hilarion
asked,—

"Who art thou? for this forest is haunted by

spirits, and I would know whether thou art one of such, and of evil intent, as the demon Venus, or a woman like the mother who bore me."

And the lady answered: "My name is Magdalen. I am a princess and a courtesan, and the fairest woman that ever be. All day the princes and kings of the earth have brought gifts to my house, and hung wreaths on my roof, and strewed flowers in my yard; and the poets all day have sung to their lutes, and all have lain groaning at my gates at night; for I am beautiful beyond all creatures. But I seek one more beautiful than myself, and go searching my master by the lakes and the rivers."

And Hilarion made answer: "Tarry thou here, and thou shalt see, if I mistake not, him whom thou seekest?"

And the lady, whose name was Magdalen, tarried by the river and built herself a cabin of reeds and leaves. And that night was the longest and coldest of the winter.

And Hilarion made for himself a bed of fern and hay in the stable of the ox and the ass, and lay close to them for warmth. And, lo! in the middle of the night the ass brayed and the ox bellowed, and Hilarion started up.

And he saw the heavens open with a great brightness as of beaten and fretted gold, and angels coming and going, and holding each

other by the hand, and wreathed in roses, and
singing "Gloria in Excelsis Deo, et in terra
pax hominibus bonæ voluntatis."

And Hilarion wondered and said ten Paters
and ten Aves.

And that day, towards noon, there came
through the wood one bearing a staff, and leading a mule, on which was seated a woman, that
was near unto her hour and moaning piteously.
And they were poor folk and travel-stained.

And the man said to Hilarion: "My name is
Joseph. I am a carpenter from the city of
Nazareth, and my wife is called Mary, and she
is in travail. Suffer thou us to rest, and my
wife to lie on the straw of the stable."

And Hilarion said: "You are welcome. Bene-
dictus qui venit in nomine domini;" and Hilarion
laid down more fern and hay, and gave provender
to the mule. And the woman's hour came, and
she was delivered of a male child. And Hilarion
took it and laid it in the manger. And he went
forth into the woods and found the ancient
wizard Hieronymus, and the lady Magdalen,
and said,—

"Come with me to the ruined house, for truly
there is He whom you be seeking."

And they followed him to the ruined house
where the fir-trees were cleared above the
river; and they saw the babe lying in the

manger, and Hieronymus and Magdalen kneeled down, saying, " Surely this is He that is our Master, for He is wiser and more fair than either."

And the skies opened, and there came forth angels, such as Hilarion had seen, with glories of solid gold round their heads, and garlands of roses about their necks, and they took hands and danced, and sang, flying up, " Gloria in Excelsis Deo."

By The Stay-At-Home Traveller.

"He prepares to read by wiping
his spectacles, carefully adjust-
ing them on his eyes, and drawing the candle close to him—is
very particular in having his
slippers ready for him at the
fire."

Hunt.

MELCHIOR'S DREAM.

"WELL, father, I don't believe the Browns are
a bit better off than we are; and yet, when I
spent the day with young Brown, we cooked
all sorts of messes in the afternoon; and he
wasted twice as much rum and brandy and
lemons in his trash as I should want to make
good punch of. He was quite surprised, too,
when I told him that our mince-pies were kept
shut up in the larder, and only brought out at
meal-times, and then just one apiece; he said
they had mince-pies always going, and he got
one whenever he liked. Old Brown never blows
up about that sort of thing; he likes Adolphus
to enjoy himself in the holidays, particularly at
Christmas."

The speaker was a boy—if I may be allowed
to use the word in speaking of an individual
whose jackets had for some time past been re-
signed to a younger member of his family, and
who daily, in the privacy of his own apartment,
examined his soft cheeks by the aid of his
sisters' "back-hair glass." He was a handsome

boy, too; tall, and like David—"ruddy, and of a
fair countenance;" and his face, though clouded
then, bore the expression of general amiability.
He was the eldest son in a large young family,
and was being educated at one of the best public
schools. He did not, it must be confessed, think
either small beer or small beans of himself; and
as to the beer and beans that his family thought
of him, I think it was pale ale and kidney-beans
at least.

When the lords of the creation of all ages
can find nothing else to do, they generally take
to eating and drinking; and so it came to pass
that our hero had set his mind upon brewing a
jorum of punch, and sipping it with an accompaniment of mince-pies; and Paterfamilias
had not been quietly settled to his writing for
half an hour, when he was disturbed by an application for the necessary ingredients. These
he had refused, quietly explaining that he could
not afford to waste his French brandy, etc., in
school-boy cookery, and ending with, " You see
the reason, my dear boy?"

To which the dear boy replied as above, and
concluded with the disrespectful (not to say
ungrateful) hint, " Old Brown never blows up
about that sort of thing; he likes Adolphus to
enjoy himself in the holidays."

Whereupon Paterfamilias made answer, in the

mildly deprecating tone in which the elder sometimes do answer the younger in these topsy-
turvy days :—

"That's quite a different case. Don't you see,
my boy, that Adolphus Brown is an only son,
and you have nine brothers and sisters ? If you
have punch and mince-meat to play with, there
is no reason why Tom should not have it, and
James, and Edward, and William, and Benjamin,
and Jack. And then there are your sisters.
Twice the amount of the Browns' mince-meat
would not serve you. The Christmas bills, too,
are very heavy, and I have a great many calls
on my purse ; and you must be reasonable.
Don't you see ?"

"Well, father——" began the boy ; but his
father interrupted him. He knew the unvary-
ing beginning of a long grumble, and dreading
the argument, cut it short.

"I have decided. You must amuse yourself
some other way. And just remember that young
Brown's is quite another case. He is an only
son."

Whereupon Paterfamilias went off to his
study and his sermon ; and his son, like the
Princess in Andersen's story of the swineherd,
was left outside to sing,—

> "O dearest Augustine,
> All's clean gone away !"

Not that he did say that—that was the princess's song—what he said was,—

"*I wish I were an only son!*"

This was rather a vain wish, for round the dining-room fire (where he soon joined them) were gathered his nine brothers and sisters, who, to say the truth, were not looking much more lively and cheerful than he. And yet (of all days in the year on which to be doleful and dissatisfied!) this was Christmas Eve.

Now I know that the idea of dulness or discomfort at Christmas is a very improper one, particularly in a story. We all know how every little boy in a story-book spends the Christmas holidays. First, there is the large hamper of good things sent by grandpapa, which is as inexhaustible as Fortunatus's purse, and contains everything, from a Norfolk turkey to grapes from the grandpaternal vinery. There is the friend who gives a guinea to each member of the family, and sees who will spend it best. There are the godpapas and godmammas, who might almost be fairy sponsors from the number of expensive gifts that they bring upon the scene. The uncles and aunts are also liberal.

One night is devoted to a magic-lantern (which has a perfect focus), another to the pantomime, a third to a celebrated conjurer, a fourth to a Christmas tree and juvenile ball.

The happy youth makes himself sufficiently ill with plum-pudding, to testify to the reader how good it was, and how much there was of it; but recovers in time to fall a victim to the negus and trifle at supper for the same reason. He is neither fatigued with late hours, nor surfeited with sweets; or if he is, we do not hear of it.

But as this is a strictly candid history, I will at once confess the truth, on behalf of my hero and his brothers and sisters. They had spent the morning in decorating the old church, in pricking holly about the house, and in making a mistletoe bush. Then in the afternoon they had tasted the Christmas soup, and seen it given out; they had put a finishing touch to the snow-man by crowning him with holly, and had dragged the yule-logs home from the carpenter's. And now, the early tea being over, Paterfamilias had gone to finish his sermon for to-morrow; his friend was shut up in his room; and Mater-familias was in hers, with one of those painful headaches which even Christmas will not always keep away. So the ten children were left to amuse themselves, and they found it rather a difficult matter.

"Here's a nice Christmas!" said our hero. He had turned his youngest brother out of the arm-chair, and was now lying in it with his legs

II.—o   18*

over the side. " Here's a nice Christmas ! A
fellow might just as well be at school. I wonder
what Adolphus Brown would think of being
cooped up with a lot of children like this ! It's
his party to-night, and he's to have champagne
and ices. I wish I were an only son."

" Thank you," said a chorus of voices from
the floor. They were all sprawling about on
the hearth-rug, pushing and struggling like so
many kittens in a sack, and every now and then
with a grumbled remonstrance :—

" Don't, Jack ! you're treading on me."

" You needn't take all the fire, Tom."

" Keep your legs to yourself, Benjamin."

" It wasn't I," etc., with occasionally the feebler cry of a small sister,—

" Oh ! you boys are so rough."

" And what are you girls, I wonder ?" inquired
the proprietor of the arm-chair, with cutting
irony. " Whiney piney, whiney piney. I wish
there were no such things as brothers and
sisters !"

" *You wish* WHAT ?" said a voice from the
shadow by the door, as deep and impressive as
that of the ghost in Hamlet.

The ten sprang up ; but when the figure came
into the firelight, they saw that it was no ghost,
but Paterfamilias's old college friend, who spent
most of his time abroad, and who, having no

home or relatives of his own, had come to spend
Christmas at his friend's vicarage. " You wish
what ?" he repeated.

" Well, brothers and sisters are a bore," was
the reply. " One or two would be all very well ;
but just look, here are ten of us ; and it just
spoils everything. Whatever one does, the rest
must do ; whatever there is, the rest must share ;
whereas, if a fellow was an only son, he would
have the whole—and by all the rules of arith-
metic, one is better than a tenth."

" And by the same rules, ten is better than
one," said the friend.

" Sold again !" sang out Master Jack from the
floor, and went head over heels against the
fender.

His brother boxed his ears with great prompti-
tude ; and went on—" Well, I don't care ; confess, sir ; isn't it rather a nuisance ?"

Paterfamilias's friend looked very grave, and
said quietly, " I don't think I am able to judge.
I never had brother or sister but one, and he
was drowned at sea. Whatever I have had, I
have had the whole of, and would have given it
away willingly for some one to give it to. I
remember that I got a lot of sticks at last, and
cut heads and faces to all of them, and carved
names on their sides, and called them my
brothers and sisters. If you want to know

what I thought a nice number for a fellow to have, I can only say that I remember carving twenty-five. I used to stick them in the ground and talk to them. I have been only, and lonely, and alone, all my life, and have never felt the nuisance you speak of."

" I know what would be very nice," insinuated one of the sisters.

" What ?"

" If you wouldn't mind telling us a very short story till supper-time."

" Well, what sort of a story is it to be ?"

" Any sort," said Richard ; " only not too true, if you please. I don't like stories like tracts. There was an usher at a school I was at, and he used to read tracts about good boys and bad boys to the fellows on Sunday afternoon. He always took out the real names, and put in the names of the fellows instead. Those who had done well in the week, he put in as good ones, and those who hadn't as the bad. He didn't like me, and I was always put in as a bad boy, and I came to so many untimely ends, I got sick of it. I was hanged twice, and transported once for sheep stealing ; I committed suicide one week, and broke into the bank the next ; I ruined three families, became a hopeless drunkard, and broke the hearts of my twelve distinct parents. I used to beg him to let me

be reformed next week ; but he said he never
would till I did my Cæsar better. So, if you
please, we'll have a story that can't be true."

" Very well," said the friend, laughing ; " but
if it isn't true, may I put you in ? All the best
writers, you know, draw their characters from
their friends, nowadays, May I put you in ?"

" Oh, certainly !" said Richard, placing himself in front of the fire, putting his feet on the
hob, and stroking his curls with an air which
seemed to imply that whatever he was put into
would be highly favored.

The rest struggled, and pushed, and squeezed
themselves into more modest but equally comfortable quarters ; and after a few moments of
thought, Paterfamilias's friend commenced the
story of

MELCHIOR'S DREAM.

" Melchior is my hero. He was—well, he
considered himself a young man, so we will
consider him so too. He was not perfect ; but
in these days the taste in heroes is for a good
deal of imperfection, not to say wickedness.
He was not an only son. On the contrary, he
had a great many brothers and sisters, and
found them quite as objectionable as my friend
Richard does."

" I smell a moral," murmured the said Richard.

" Your scent must be keen," said the story-teller, "for it is a long way off. Well, he had never felt them so objectionable as on one particular night, when the house being full of company, it was decided that the boys should sleep in 'barracks,' as they called it; that is, all in one large room."

"'Thank goodness we have not come to that!'" said the incorrigible Richard; but he was reduced to order by threats of being turned out, and contented himself with burning the soles of his boots against the bars of the grate in silence : and the friend continued :

"But this was not the worst Not only was he, Melchior, to sleep in the same room with his brothers, but his bed being the longest and largest, his youngest brother was to sleep at the other end of it—foot to foot. True, by this means he got another pillow, for of course that little Hop-o'-my-thumb could do without one, and so he took his ; but in spite of this, he determined that, sooner than submit to such an indignity, he would sit up all night. Accordingly, when all the rest were fast asleep, Melchior, with his boots off and his waistcoat easily unbuttoned, sat over the fire in the long lumber-room, which served that night as 'barracks.' He had refused to eat any supper down-stairs to mark his displeasure, and now repaid himself by a stolen meal according to his own taste. He had got a pork-pie, a little bread and cheese, some large onions to roast, a couple of raw apples, an orange, and papers of soda and tartaric acid to compound effervescing draughts. When these dainties were finished, he proceeded to warm some beer in a pan, with ginger, spice, and sugar, and then lay back in his chair and sipped it slowly, gazing before him, and thinking over his misfortunes.

"The night wore on, the fire got lower and lower; and still Melchior sat, with his eyes fixed on a dirty old print, that had hung above the mantel-piece for years, sipping his 'brew,' which was fast getting cold. The print represented an old man in a light costume, with a scythe in one hand, and an hour-glass in the other; and underneath the picture in flourishing capitals was the word TIME.

"'You're a nice old beggar,' said Melchior, dreamily. 'You look like an old haymaker, who has come to work in his shirt-sleeves, and forgotten the rest of his clothes. Time! time you went to the tailor's, I think.'

"This was very irreverent: but Melchior was not in a respectful mood; and as for the old man, he was as calm as any philosopher.

"The night wore on, and the fire got lower and lower, and at last went out altogether.

"'How stupid of me not to have mended it!

said Melchior; but he had not mended it, and so there was nothing for it but to go to bed; and to bed he went accordingly.

"'But I won't go to sleep,' he said; · no, no; I shall keep awake, and to-morrow they shall know that I have had a bad night.'

"So he lay in bed with his eyes wide open, and staring still at the old print, which he could see from his bed by the light of the candle, which he had left alight on the mantel-piece to keep him awake. The flame waved up and down, for the room was draughty; and, as the lights and shadows passed over the old man's face, Melchior almost fancied that it nodded to him, so he nodded back again; and as that tired him he shut his eyes for a few seconds. When he opened them again there was no longer any doubt—the old man's head was moving; and not only his head, but his legs, and his whole body. Finally, he put his feet out of the frame, and prepared to step right over the mantel-piece, candle, and all.

"'Take care,' Melchior tried to say, 'you'll set fire to your shirt.' But he could not utter a sound; and the old man arrived safely on the floor, where he seemed to grow larger and larger, till he was fully the size of a man, but still with the same scythe and hour-glass, and the same airy costume. Then he came across the room, and sat down by Melchior's bedside.

" ' Who are you ?' said Melchior, feeling rather creepy.

" ' TIME,' said his visitor, in a deep voice, which sounded as if it came from a distance.

" ' Oh, to be sure, yes ! In copper plate capitals.'

" ' What's in copper-plate capitals ?' inquired Time.

" ' Your name, under the print.'

" ' Very likely,' said Time.

" Melchior felt more and more uneasy. ' You must be very cold,' he said. ' Perhaps you would feel warmer if you went back into the picture.'

" ' Not at all,' said Time ; ' I have come on purpose to see you.'

" ' I have not the pleasure of knowing you,' said Melchior, trying to keep his teeth from chattering.

" ' There are not many people who have a personal acquaintance with me,' said his visitor. ' You have an advantage, — I am your god-father.'

" ' Indeed,' said Melchior ; ' I never heard of it.'

" ' Yes,' said his visitor ; ' and you will find it a great advantage.'

" ' Would you like to put on my coat ?' said Melchior, trying to be civil.

K   19

" ' No, thank you,' was the answer. ' You will want it yourself. We must be driving soon.'

" ' Driving !' said Melchoir.

" ' Yes,' was the answer; ' all the world is driving; and you must drive; and here come your brothers and sisters.'

" Melchoir sat up; and there they were, sure enough, all dressed, and climbing one after the other on to the bed—*his* bed!

" There was that little minx of a sister with her curls. There was that clever brother, with his untidy hair and bent shoulders, who was just as bad the other way, and was forever moping and reading. There was that little Hop-o'-my-thumb, as lively as any of them, a young monkey, the worst of all; who was always in mischief, and consorting with the low boys in the village. There was the second brother, who was Melchior's chief companion, and against whom he had no particular quarrel. And there was the little pale lame sister, whom he dearly loved; but whom, odd to say, he never tried to improve at all. There were others who were all tiresome in their respective ways; and one after the other they climbed up.

" ' What are you doing, getting on to my bed ?' inquired the indignant brother, as soon as he could speak.

" ' Don't you know the difference between a bed and a coach, godson ?' said Time, sharply.

" Melchior was about to retort, but, on looking round, he saw that they were really in a large sort of coach with very wide windows. ' I thought I was in bed,' he muttered. ' What can I have been dreaming of ?'

" ' What, indeed !' said the godfather. ' But be quick, and sit close, for you have all to get in ; you are all brothers and sisters.'

" ' Must families be together ?' inquired Melchior, dolefully.

" ' Yes, at first,' was the answer ; ' they get separated in time. In fact, every one has to cease driving sooner or later. I drop them on the road at different stages, according to my orders,' and he showed a bundle of papers in his hands ; ' but as I favor you, I will tell you in confidence that I have to drop all your brothers and sisters before you. There, you four oldest sit on this side, you five others there, and the little one must stand or be nursed.'

" ' Ugh !' said Melchior, ' the coach would be well enough if one was alone ; but what a squeeze with all these brats ! I say, go pretty quick, will you ?'

" ' I will,' said Time, ' if you wish it. But beware that you cannot change your mind. If I go quicker for your sake, I shall never go slow

again; if slower, I shall not again go quick;
and I only favor you so far, because you are
my godson. Here, take the check-string; when
you want me, pull it, and speak through the
tube. Now we're off.'

"Whereupon the old man mounted the box,
and took the reins. He had no whip; but when
he wanted to start, he shook the hour-glass, and
off they went. Then Melchior saw that the
road where they were driving was very broad,
and so filled with vehicles of all kinds that he
could not see the hedges. The noise and crowd
and dust were very great; and to Melchior all
seemed delightfully exciting. There was every
sort of conveyance, from the grandest coach to
the humblest donkey-cart; and they seemed to
have enough to do to escape being run over.
Among all the gay people there were many
whom he knew; and a very nice thing it seemed
to be to drive among all the grandees, and to
show his handsome face at the window, and bow
and smile to his acquaintance. Then it appeared
to be the fashion to wrap one's self in a tiger-skin
rug, and to look at life through an opera-glass,
and old Time had kindly put one of each into
the coach.

"But here again Melchior was much troubled
by his brothers and sisters. Just at the moment
when he was wishing to look most fashionable

and elegant, one or other of them would pull
away the rug, or drop the glass, or quarrel, or
romp, or do something that spoiled the effect. In
fact, one and all, they 'just spoilt everything;'
and the more he scolded, the worse they became. The 'minx' shook her curls, and flirted
through the window with a handsome but ill-
tempered looking man on a fine horse, who
praised her 'golden locks,' as he called them;
and oddly enough, when Melchior said that the
man was a lout, and that the locks in question
were corkscrewy carrot shavings, she only
seem'ed to like the man and his compliments
the more. Meanwhile, the untidy brother pored
over his book, or if he came to the window, it
was only to ridicule the fine ladies and gentlemen, so Melchior sent him to Coventry. Then
Hop-o'-my-thumb had taken to make signs and
exchange jokes with some disreputable-looking
youths in a dog-cart; and when his brother
would have put him to 'sit still like a gentleman' at the bottom of the coach, he seemed
positively to prefer his low companions; and the
rest were little better.

" Poor Melchior! Surely there never was a
clearer case of a young gentleman's comfort destroyed solely by other people's perverse deter-
mination to be happy in their own way instead
of in his.

At last he lost patience, and pulling the check-string, bade Godfather Time drive as fast as she could.

" Godfather Time frowned, but shook his glass all the same, and away they went at a famous pace. All at once they came to a stop.

" ' Now for it,' said Melchior; ' here goes one at any rate.'

" Time called out the name of the second brother over his shoulder; and the boy stood up, and bade his brothers and sisters good-bye.

" ' It is time that I began to push my way in the world,' said he, and passed out of the coach and in among the crowd.

" ' You have taken the only quiet boy,' said Melchior to the godfather, angrily. ' Drive fast, now, for pity's sake; and let us get rid of the tiresome ones.'

" And fast enough they drove, and dropped first one and then the other; but the sisters, and the reading boy, and the youngest still remained.

" ' What are you looking at ?' said Melchior to the lame sister.

" ' At a strange figure in the crowd,' she answered.

" ' I see nothing,' said Melchior. But on looking again after a while, he did see a figure wrapped in a cloak, gliding in and out among the people, unnoticed, if not unseen.

" ' Who is it ?' Melchior asked of the god-father.

" ' A friend of mine,' Time answered. ' His name is Death.'

" Melchior shuddered, more especially as the figure had now come up to the coach, and put its hand in through the window, on which, to his horror, the lame sister laid hers and smiled. At this moment the coach stopped.

" ' What are you doing ?' shrieked Melchior. ' Drive on ! drive on !'

" But even while he sprang up to seize the check-string the door had opened, the pale sister's face had dropped upon the shoulder of the figure in the cloak, and he had carried her away ; and Melchior stormed and raved in vain.

" ' To take her, and to leave the rest ! Cruel ! cruel !'

" In his rage and grief, he hardly knew it when the untidy brother was called, and putting his book under his arm, slipped out of the coach without looking to the right or left. Presently the coach stopped again ; and when Melchior looked up the door was open, and at it was the fine man on the fine horse, who was lifting the sister on to the saddle before him. ' What fool's game are you playing ?' said Melchior, angrily.

' I know that man.   He is both ill-tempered and
a bad character.'

" ' You never told her so before,' muttered
young Hop-o'-my-thumb.

" ' Hold your tongue,' said Melchior.   ' I for-
bade her to talk to him, which was enough.'

" ' I don't want to leave you; but he cares for
me, and you don't,' sobbed the sister; and she
was carried away.

" When she had gone, the youngest brother
slid down from his corner and came up to
Melchior.

" ' We are alone now, brother,' he said; ' let
us be good friends.   May I sit on the front seat
with you, and have half the rug?   I will be
very good and polite, and will have nothing
more to do with those fellows, if you will talk
to me.'

" Now Melchior really rather liked the idea;
out as his brother seemed to be in a submissive
mood, he thought he would take the opportunity
of giving him a good lecture, and would then
graciously relent and forgive.   So he began by
asking him if he thought that he was fit company for him (Melchior), what he thought that
gentlefolks would say to a boy who had been
playing with such youths as young Hop-o'-my-
thumb had, and whether the said youths were
not scoundrels?   And when the boy refused to

say that they were, (for they had been kind to
him,) Melchior said that his tastes were evidently as bad as ever, and even hinted at the old
transportation threat. This was too much ; the
boy went angrily back to his window corner,
and Melchior—like too many of us!—lost the
opportunity of making peace for the sake of
wagging his own tongue.

" ' But he will come round in a few minutes,
he thought. A few minutes passed, however,
and there was no sign. A few minutes more,
and there was a noise, a shout ; Melchoir looked
up, and saw that the boy had jumped through
the open window into the road, and had been
picked up by the men in the dog-cart, and was
gone.

" And so at last my hero was alone. At first
he enjoyed it very much. But though every
one allowed him to be the finest young fellow
on the road, yet nobody seemed to care for the
fact as much as he did ; they talked, and compli-
mented, and stared at him, but he got tired of it.
Sometimes he saw the youngest brother, looking each time more wild and reckless ; and
sometimes the sister, looking more and more
miserable ; but he saw no one else.

" At last there was a stir among the people,
and all heads were turned towards the distance,
as if looking for something. Melchior asked

II.—*p*

what it was, and was told that the people were
looking for a man, the hero of many battles,
who had won honor for himself and for his
country in foreign lands, and who was coming
home. Everybody stood up and gazed, Melchior with them. Then the crowd parted, and
the hero came on. No one asked whether he
were handsome or genteel, whether he kept
good company, or wore a tiger-skin rug, or
looked through an opera-glass? They knew
what he had *done*, and it was enough.

"He was a bronzed, hairy man, with one
sleeve empty, and a breast covered with stars;
but in his face, brown with sun and wind, overgrown with hair, and scarred with wounds,
Melchior saw his second brother! There was
no doubt of it. And the brother himself, though
he bowed kindly in answer to the greetings
showered on him, was gazing anxiously for the
old coach, where he used to ride and be so un-
comfortable, in that time to which he now
looked back as the happiest of his life.

"'I thank you, gentlemen. I am indebted to
you, gentlemen. I have been away long. I am
going home.'

"'Of course he is!' shouted Melchior, waving
his arms widely with pride and joy. 'He is
coming home; to this coach, where he was—oh,
it seems but an hour ago; Time goes so fast.

We were great friends when we were young together. My brother and I, ladies and gentlemen, the hero and I—my brother—the hero with the stars upon his breast—he is coming home!'

"Alas! what avail stars and ribbons on a breast where the life-blood is trickling slowly from a little wound? The crowd looked anxious; the hero came on, but more slowly, with his dim eyes straining for the old coach; and Melchior stood with his arms held out in silent agony. But just when he was beginning to hope, and the brothers seemed about to meet, a figure passed between—a figure in a cloak.

"'I have seen you many times, friend, face to face,' said the hero; 'but now I would fain have waited for a little while.'

"'To enjoy his well-earned honors,' murmured the crowd.

"'Nay,' he said, 'not that; but to see my home, and my brothers and sisters But if it may not be, friend Death, I am ready, and tired, too.' With that he held out his hand, and Death lifted up the hero of many battles like a child, and carried him away, stars, and ribbons, and all.

"'Cruel Death!' cried Melchior; 'was there no one else in all this crowd, that you must take him?'

"His friends condoled with him; but they

soon went on their own ways; and the hero seemed to be forgotten; and Melchior, who had lost all pleasure in the old bowings and chattings, sat idly gazing out of the window, to see if he could see any one for whom he cared. At last, in a grave dark man, who was sitting on a horse, and making a speech to the crowd, he recognized his clever untidy brother.

" ' What is that man talking about?' he asked of some one near him.

" ' That man!' was the answer. ' Don't you know? He is *the* man of the time. He is a philosopher. Everybody goes to hear him. He has found out that—well—that everything is a mistake.'

" ' Has he corrected it?' said Melchior.

" ' You had better hear for yourself,' said the man. ' Listen.'

" Melchior listened, and a cold, clear voice rang upon his ear, saying,—

" ' The world of fools will go on as they have ever done; but to the wise few, to whom I address myself, I would say, Shake off at once and forever the fancies and feelings, the creeds and customs that shackle you, and be true. We have come to a time when wise men will not be led blindfold in the footsteps of their predecessors, but will tear away the bandage, and see for themselves. I have torn away mine, and looked. There is no Faith—it is shaken to its rotten foundation; there is no Hope—it is disappointed every day; there is no Love at all. There is nothing for any man or for each, but his fate; and he is happiest and wisest who can meet it most unmoved.'

" ' It is a lie !' shouted Melchior. ' I feel it to be so in my heart. A wicked, foolish lie ! Oh ! was it to teach such evil folly as this that you left home and us, my brother ? Oh, come back ! come back !'

" The philosopher turned his head coldly, and smiled. ' I thank the gentleman who spoke,' he said, still in the same cold voice, ' for his bad opinion, and for his good wishes. I think the gentleman spoke of home and kindred. My experience of life has led me to find that home is most valued when it is left, and kindred most dear when they are parted. I have happily freed myself from such inconsistencies. I am glad to know that fate can tear me from no place that I care for more than the next where it shall deposit me, nor take away any friends that I value more than those it leaves. I recommend a similar self-emancipation to the gentleman who did me the honor of speaking.'

" With this the philosopher went his way, and the crowd followed him.

20

" ' There is a separation more bitter than death,' said Melchior.

" At last he pulled the check-string, and called to Godfather Time in an humble, entreating voice.

" ' It is not your fault,' he began; 'it is not your fault, godfather; but this drive has been altogether wrong. Let us turn back and begin again. Let us all get in afresh and begin again.'

" ' But what a squeeze with all the brats!' said Godfather Time, ironically.

" ' We should be so happy,' murmured Melchior, humbly; 'and it is very cold and chilly; we should keep each other warm.'

" ' You have the tiger-skin rug and the opera-glass, you know,' said Time.

" ' Ah, do not speak of me!" cried Melchior, earnestly. 'I am thinking of them. There is plenty of room; the little one can sit on my knee; and we shall be so happy. The truth is, godfather, that I have been wrong. I have gone the wrong way to work. A little more love, and kindness, and forbearance might have kept my sisters with us, might have led the little one to better tastes and pleasures, and have taught the other by experience the truth of the faith and hope and love which he now reviles. Oh, I have sinned! I have sinned! Let us turn back, Godfather Time, and begin again. And oh! drive very slowly, for partings come only too soon.'

" ' I am sorry,' said the old man in the same bitter tone as before, ' to disappoint your rather unreasonable wishes. What you say is admirably true, with this misfortune, that your good intentions are too late. Like the rest of the world, you are ready to seize the opportunity when it is past. You should have been kind *then*. You should have advised *then*. You should have yielded *then*. You should have loved your brothers and sisters while you had them. It is too late now.'

" With this he drove on, and spoke no more, and poor Melchior stared sadly out of the window. As he was gazing at the crowd, he suddenly saw the dog-cart, in which were his brother and his wretched companions. Oh, how old and worn he looked! and how ragged his clothes were! The men seemed to be trying to persuade him to do something that he did not like, and they began to quarrel; but in the midst of the dispute he turned his head, and caught sight of the old coach; and Melchior, seeing this, waved his hands, and beckoned with all his might. The brother seemed doubtful; but Melchior waved harder, and (was it fancy?) Time seemed to go slower. The brother made up his mind; he turned and jumped from the dog-cart as he had jumped from the old coach long ago, and, ducking in and out among the horses and carriages, ran for his life. The men came after him ; but he ran like the wind—pant, pant, nearer, nearer ; at last the coach was reached, and Melchior seized the prodigal by his rags and dragged him in.

" ' Oh, thank God, I have got you safe, my brother !'

" But what a brother ! with wasted body and sunken eyes ; with the old curly hair turned to matted locks, that clung faster to his face than the rags did to his trembling limbs ; what a sight for the opera-glasses of the crowd ! Yet poor Hop-o'-my-thumb was on the front seat at last, with Melchior kneeling at his feet, and fondly stroking the head that rested against him

" ' Has powder come into fashion, brother ?' he said. ' Your hair is streaked with white.'

" ' If it has,' said the other, laughing, ' your barber is better than mine, Melchior, for your head is as white as snow.'

" Is it possible ? are we so old ? has Time gone so very fast ? But what are you staring at through the window ? I shall be jealous of that crowd, brother.'

" ' I am not looking at the crowd,' said the prodigal in a low voice ; ' but I see——'

" ' You see what ?' said Melchior.

" ' A figure in a cloak, gliding in and out——'

" Melchior sprang up in horror. ' No ! no !' he cried, hoarsely. ' No ! surely no !'

" Surely yes ! Too surely the well-known figure came on ; and the prodigal's sunken eyes looked more sunken still as he gazed. As for Melchior, he neither spoke nor moved, but stood in a silent agony, terrible to see. All at once a thought seemed to strike him ; he seized his brother, and pushed him to the farthest corner of the seat, and then planted himself firmly at the door, just as Death came up and put his hand into the coach. Then he spoke in a low, steady voice, more piteous than cries or tears.

" ' I humbly beseech you, good Death, if you must take one of us, to take me. I have had a long drive, and many comforts and blessings, and am willing, if unworthy, to go. He has suffered much, and had no pleasure ; leave him for a little to enjoy the drive in peace, just for a very little ; he has suffered so much, and I have been so much to blame ; let me go instead of him.'

" Poor Melchior ! In vain he laid both his hands in Death's outstretched palm ; they fell to him again as if they had passed through air ; he was pushed aside—Death passed into the coach —' one was taken and the other left.'

" As the cloaked figure glided in and out
20*

among the crowd, many turned to look at his
sad burden, though few heeded him.   Much was
said; but the general voice of the crowd was
this: 'Ah! he is gone, is he? Well! a born
rascal! It must be a great relief to his
brother!' A conclusion which was about as
wise, and about as near the truth, as the
world's conclusions generally are.   As for
Melchior, he neither saw the figure nor heard
the crowd, for he had fallen senseless among the
cushions.

" When he came to his senses, he found himself lying still upon his face; and so bitter was
his loneliness and grief, that he lay still and did
not move.   He was astonished, however, by the
(as it seemed to him) unusual silence.   The
noise of the carriage had been deafening, and
now there was not a sound.   Was he deaf? or
had the crowd gone?   He opened his eyes.   Was
he blind? or had the night come?   He sat right
up, and shook himself, and looked again.   The
crowd *was* gone; so, for matter of that, was the
coach; and so was Godfather Time.   He had
not been lying among cushions, but among pillows; he was not in any vehicle of any kind,
but in bed.   The room was dark, and very still;
but through the ' barracks' window, which had
no blind, he saw the winter sun pushing through
the mist, like a red-hot cannon-ball hanging in

the frosty trees; and in the yard outside, the cocks were crowing.

"There was no longer any doubt that he was safe in his old home; but where were his brothers and sisters? With a beating heart he crept to the other end of the bed; and there lay the prodigal, with no haggard cheeks or sunken eyes, no gray locks or miserable rags, but a rosy, yellow-haired urchin fast asleep, with his head upon his arm. 'I took his pillow,' muttered Melchior, self-reproachfully.

"A few minutes later, young Hop-o'-my-thumb, (whom Melchior dared not lose sight of for fear he should melt away,) seated comfortably on his brother's back, and wrapped up in a blanket, was making a tour of the 'barracks.'

"'It's an awful lark,' said he, shivering with a mixture of cold and delight.

"If not exactly a *lark*, it was a very happy tour to Melchior, as, hope gradually changing into certainty, he recognized his brothers in one shapeless lump after the other in the little beds. There they all were, sleeping peacefully in a happy home, from the embryo hero to the embryo philosopher, who lay with the invariable book upon his pillow, and his hair looking (as it always did) as if he lived in a high wind.

"'I say,' whispered Melchior, pointing to him,

'what did he say the other day about being a parson ?'

" ' He said he should like to be one,' returned Hop-o'-my-thumb; 'but you said he would frighten away the congregation with his looks.'

" ' He will make a capital parson,' said Melchior, hastily, ' and I shall tell him so to-morrow. And when I'm the squire here, he shall be vicar, and I'll subscribe to all his dodges without a grumble. I'm the eldest son. And I say, don't you think we could brush his hair for him in a morning, till he learns to do it himself ?'

" ' Oh, I will !' was the lively answer; ' I'm an awful dab at brushing. Look how I brush your best hat !'

" ' True,' said Melchior. ' Where are the girls to-night ?'

" ' In the little room at the end of the long passage,' said Hop o'-my-thumb, trembling with increased chilliness and enjoyment. ' But you're never going there ! we shall wake the company, and they will all come out to see what's the matter.'

" ' I shouldn't care if they did,' said Melchior, ' it would make it feel more real.'

" As he did not understand this sentiment, Hop-o'-my-thumb said nothing, but held on very tightly; and they crept softly down the cold gray passage in the dawn. The girls' door was open; for the girls were afraid of robbers, and left their bed-room door wide open at night, as a natural and obvious means of self-defence. The girls slept together; and the frill of the pale sister's prim little night-cap was buried in the other one's uncovered curls.

" 'How you do tremble!' whispered Hop-o'-my-thumb; 'are you cold?' This inquiry received no answer; and after some minutes he spoke again. 'I say, how very pretty they look! don't they?'

" But for some reason or other, Melchior seemed to have lost his voice; but he stooped down and kissed both the girls very gently, and then the two brothers crept back along the passage to the 'barracks.'

" 'One thing more,' said Melchior; and they went up to the mantel-piece. 'I will lend you my bow and arrow to-morrow, on one condition——'

" 'Anything!' was the reply, in an enthusiastic whisper.

" 'That you take that old picture for a target, and never let me see it again.'

" It was very ungrateful! but perfection is not in man; and there was something in Melchior's muttered excuse,—

" 'I couldn't stand another night of it.'

" Hop-o'-my-thumb was speedily put to bed

again, to get warm, this time with both the pillows; but Melchior was too restless to sleep, so he resolved to have a shower-bath and to dress. After which he knelt down by the window, and covered his face with his hands.

" 'He's saying very long prayers,' thought Hop-o'-my-thumb, glancing at him from his warm nest; 'and what a jolly humor he is in this morning!'

" Still, the young head was bent and the handsome face hidden; and Melchior was finding his life every moment more real and more happy. For there was hardly a thing, from the well-filled 'barracks' to the brother bedfellow, that had been a hardship last night, which this morning did not seem a blessing. He rose at last, and stood in the sunshine, which was now pouring in; a smile was on his lips, and on his face were two drops, which, if they were water, had not come from the shower-bath, or from any bath at all."

" Is that the end?" inquired the young lady on his knee, as the story-teller paused here.

" Yes, that is the end."

" It's a beautiful story," she murmured, thoughtfully; " but what an extraordinary one! I don't think I could have dreamt such a wonderful dream."

" Do you think you could have eaten such a wonderful supper ?" said the friend, twisting his moustaches.

After this point, the evening's amusements were thoroughly successful. Richard took his smoking boots from the fireplace, and was called upon for various entertainments for which he was famous.

The door opened at last, and Paterfamilias entered with Materfamilias (whose headache was better), and followed by the candles. A fresh log was then thrown upon the fire, the yule cakes and furmety were put upon the table, and everybody drew round to supper; and Paterfamilias announced that, although he could not give the materials to play with, he had no objection now to a bowl of moderate punch for all, and that Richard might compound it. This was delightful; and as he sat by his father ladling away to the rest, Adolphus Brown could hardly have felt more jovial, even with the champagne and ices.

The rest sat with radiant faces and shining heads in goodly order; and at the bottom of the table, by Materfamilias, was the friend, as happy in his unselfish sympathy as if his twenty-five sticks had come to life, and were supping with him. As happy—nearly—as if a certain woman's grave had never been dug under the southern sun that could not save her, and as if the children gathered round him were those of whose faces he had often dreamt, but might never see.

His health had been drunk, and everybody else's too, when, just as supper was coming to a close, Richard (who had been sitting in thoughtful silence for some minutes) got up with sudden resolution, and said,—

" I want to propose Mr. What's-his-name's health on my own account. I want to thank him for his story, which had only one mistake in it. Melchior should have kept the effervescing papers to put into the beer; it's a splendid drink! Otherwise it was first-rate; though it hit me rather hard. I want to say that though I didn't mean all I said about being an only son, (when a fellow gets put out he doesn't know what he means,) yet I know I was quite wrong, and the story is quite right. I want particularly to say that I'm very glad there are so many of us, for the more, you know, the merrier. I wouldn't change father or mother, brothers or sisters, with any one in the world. It couldn't be better, we couldn't be happier. We are all together, and to-morrow is Christmas-Day. Thank God."

Read by the Landlord.

> " A jolly negation, who took upon
> him the ordering of the bills of
> fare."
>
> *Lamb.*

MR. GRAPEWINE'S CHRISTMAS DINNER.

" My dear," said Mr. Grapewine, over the din-
ner-table, about a fortnight before Christmas,—
" how many days to Christmas?"

Mrs. Grapewine counted on her fingers; looked
a little uncertain up towards the ceiling, and at
last applied to the calendar on the wall behind
her, exclaiming, when she had mentally calcu-
lated the time,—

" Week and six days; comes on Thursday."

" True," said Mr. Grapewine, and he fell to
devouring the residuum of his meal, a very
savory mixture, which he swallowed with an
amazing relish.

" There !" said he, after the last sip of coffee,
" I believe I don't want another thing to eat
till Christmas-day. Mrs. G., you have the art
of concocting the most appetizing meals. I
never seem to get enough of them."

" Two a day !" suggested Mrs. Grapewine, in
her sharp manner.

" No, no, no ! Mrs. G., you *are* an experienced

cateress, that I confess. But there is a delicacy
in the thing which two such meals a day would
utterly destroy. You misunderstand me? It is
the expectancy, the snuffing up of the fumes
beforehand, the very consciousness of your in-
ability to cope with it, which makes such a
meal delicious. Now two a day would leave a
man no chance to get properly hungry. That's
the point. It is the preparation, the deferred
hope, which render a good dinner one of the
completest luxuries of life. The hungrier one
is, the more prolonged the satisfaction of the
palate. I don't think I have ever been hungry
to the fullest extent of my capacity in my life."

" Trip across Sahara !" interpolated Mrs.
Grapewine.

" Yes, that would do, my dear ; but I think we
could accomplish it at home by artificial means.
I *think* we could. Fasting would not do, because
the appetite would at last grow unable to dis-
criminate. Drugs would enfeeble it. (I'll thank
you for another cup of coffee, my dear. Ah,
delicious cup of coffee !)—Drugs would enfeeble
it. There is really no direct stimulant that I
know of; but I *think* we could intensify the
appetite by a little course of diplomacy. Let us
eat frugally—sandwiches, crackers and cheese,
potted meats—for the next two weeks ; and,
if you 'please, cook us at each luncheon-time,

as a sort of stimulating accompaniment, some
odorous dish,—roast-beef, stuffed leg of lamb,
roast turkey, codfish, anything with an odor,
—which we shall smell, but not taste of.   Don't
you see, madam?"

" No!"

" Don't you see that our stomachs will yearn
for these strong delicacies, and, going unsatisfied,
will relish them the more when we at last attack
them?"

" No!"

" You have something to propose then, my
dear.   What is it?   What have you to propose?"

" Turkish bath!'

" What a woman you are.   A Turkish bath!
How, Mrs. Grapewine, can a Turkish bath tickle
a man's appetite?   How can a Turkish——"

" Empty stomach."

" Ah, now I begin to see: a Turkish bath on
an empty stomach.   Yes, yes; very good.   But,
perhaps, if we tried my plan and yours together,
we should arrive at the ideal appetite.   I think
a Christmas feast composed of guests each with
such an appetite would be nearly the greatest
pleasure we can know.   Well, well, madam, let
us think of it (The bell?   Yes, quite through),"
and, saying this last to the tinkling of the little
silver bell, Mr. Grapewine got up from the table.

21*

undid the napkin from his neck, and yawned
both his arms quite over his fat, rosy head as
he trode towards the door. Mrs. Grapewine's
step was like her conversation,—sharp and de-
cisive. She took her husband's arm in an angu-
lar manner and led him, still yawning, to the
sofa in the library, where she set herself over
against him, ready to hear his plans.

" Let us have a Christmas banquet, my dear."
Mr. Grapewine steadily rubbed his eyes and
yawned.

" Who ?" said Mrs. Grapewine.

" Why, Totty and his wife, and Colonel
Killiam, and—and Dr. Tuggle and lady, and
old Mrs. Gildenfenny and—and——" Mr. Grapewine snored.

" Who ?" said Mrs. Grapewine, somewhat
loudly.

—" And—and—Pill."

" Who's Pill ?" said she.

" Why—oh, I mean your poor cousin Pillet.
It would be a kindness to him, you know."

" Yes," said she.

"Will that be enough ? Let me see, that is
seven—nine with us two."

" Quite enough," said she. And so Mr. Grapewine, arousing himself. rose from the sofa, put
on his hat and coat, and went out to his busi-
.ness.

He was full of the idea. He talked about it to his clerks at the store. He looked into restaurant windows, humming a tune in the excess of his delight. He looked into bakers' windows and confectionery shops, and a whiff of frying bacon from a little blind court he passed almost set him dancing. Indeed, Mr. Grapewine was a man of juvenile impulse. In figure as well as character he seemed rather to have expanded into a larger sort of babyhood than to have left that stage of his life behind. His face was broad and rosy and whiskerless, his hands were round and well-dimpled, and his body chubby to a degree. Once an idea got possession of him, he was its bondsman until another conquered it and enslaved him anew. But, really loving good cheer above everything else, his latest whim tickled him into laughter whenever it entered his mind. It was the happiest idea of his life.

" Why, sir," he said to his book-keeper, " I think if a man would practise my system he could easily eat a whole turkey—not to speak of other dishes—at a meal. Magnificent idea ! William. I wonder no one ever thought of it before. Wonderful !"

" A little bilious, sir," said William.

" Bilious ! bilious ! Why, my man, how can anything produce biliousness in an empty stomach? No; it may bring inertia,—the Lotos does that,—but never biliousness."

In the evening, Mr. Grapewine visited the Turkish baths and learned all about them before he went home. He encountered another idea on his way thither, and was taken captive by it without resistance. He could not—it would never do—it would not be courteous to eat so plentifully in the presence of guests whose appetites were merely natural. Nor could he well ask them to take the stimulating course he proposed for himself. But they *could* take a Turkish bath, and it would be quite a neat little social device to enclose a ticket for a bath with each invitation.

"There, madam!" he said to Mrs. Grapewine, "I think that's perfect. We shall have the heartiest, merriest dinner on Christmas-day that man ever devoured. Bring pen and paper, and I'll write to all the guests immediately, ma'am."

After a moment's scratching of the pen, Mr. Grapewine leaned back in his chair and held off the wet sheet at arm's length, reading with strong emphasis as follows,—

"DEAR CAPTAIN KILLIAM,—Mrs. Grapewine and myself would be most happy to have you join a small company of friends at our house on Christmas-day, for dinner, at one P.M. The affair will be quite informal, and, to add to the thorough enjoyment of it, I enclose a coupon for a Turkish bath, which please use on Christmas morning before the hour named.

> " Yours, sincerely,
>> " GEORGE GRAPEWINE."

By the next morning Mr. Grapewine's invitations had found their way to the breakfast-tables of all his expected guests.

Mr. Pillet's breakfast-table was composed of the top of a flat trunk, and to find its way there the invitation went up three pairs of stairs. Mr. Pillet was a writer, and his income was by no means as great as his ability. He had often to point out a similar disparity in the lives of other writers, because this was his one way of accounting for his want of success. He did not write books, to be sure. He only wrote poetical advertisements. But they were printed and paid for, and this gave him a sort of prestige among his less lucky friends. He was seedy; only moderately clean, and wholly unshaven, thus avoiding, by one happy invention, both soap and the barber. Fierce he was to look at, with his rugged beard and eyebrows, and fierce in his resentment of the world's indifference.

A Christmas invitation to the Grapewine's made his eyes glisten with delight: a good dinner, guests to tell his tale to, and women, lovely women, who would sympathize with his unrequited hopes. He read on:

"I enclose a ticket for a Turkish bath——"

"Great heavens!" he cried, "what can this mean?"

He read the words again, and then read the coupon.

"Insulted! Insulted by a man I have ever befriended. He must apologize. I'll shake the words from his throat. I'll—I'll not eat another mouthful till I have his apology! Turkish bath! Why——" and Mr. Pillet walked violently—gesticulating, with the open note in his hand—up and down the creaking floor of his apartment. He did not finish his breakfast, but put on his hat—perhaps forgetting an overcoat —and hurried down-stairs.

Colonel Killiam took breakfast at the "Furlough Club." He perused Mr. Grapewine's note with a majestic condescension, and decided to go to the dinner, where, of course, those present would recognize his superior rank. Each sentence he read was sandwiched between two sips of chocolate, and he reached the latter clause only by slow degrees. When he got that far, the colonel started to his feet and sternly summoned the waiter.

"Ask Major Fobbs to call at my table as soon as he can."

The waiter obeyed, and Major Fobbs followed him back to the colonel's table.

"Major," said the colonel, "will you please spell those words?"

"T-u-r-k-i-s-h b-a-t-h, Turkish bath," read the major.

"Thank heaven, I am still rational!" said the colonel. "I feared reason was dethroned. Thank you, major. Good-day," and Colonel Killiam strode out of the room, rigid with indignation.

Old Mrs. Gildenfenny received her invitation over a breakfast-table that stood against her bedside. The note was handed in by an aged servant, who thereupon leaned over her mistress's shoulder and helped her to read it. Mrs. Gildenfenny was an energetic old lady; but she loved, most of all things in the world, her idle hour in bed of a morning with a smoking meal of hot-cakes and coffee at her elbow. She disliked, most of all things in the world, to be robbed of this comfort, and she hated the being who committed such an offence with a vehemence which was her chief characteristic. The two old women read Mrs. Gildenfenny's note aloud en duet, with now and then a pleased comment. Mrs. Gildenfenny said she would wear her green silk, and gave directions, as she read on, about her shoes, her hair, her linen, and twenty articles of her toilet that came into her mind at mention of dining out.

"Lord a-mercy!" says Mrs. Gildenfenny, when she had read a little further; "Lord a-mercy! if I'm not decent, why does he ask me? Why don't he say, at once, 'Please wash yourself before you come; and if you can't afford soap and water, here's a ticket'? Susan, get me up! Dress me right away! I must have this explained."

"But your breakfast, ma'am," says Susan.

"Eat? eat? with such a thing on my mind? No! I'll go at once to his house!" and in a few moments Mrs. Gildenfenny also went out.

Mr. and Mrs. Totty were served with their invitation over a breakfast-table where meekness and humility were administered with the rolls and poured out with the weak cambric tea of the little ones. The meal was an impressive ceremony, where discourses on duty and against excess of the palate were often the only relishes present.

Mr. Totty would paint the miseries of the epicure, and Mrs. Totty those of the dyspeptic, in words of eloquence which made milk-and-sugar-and-water a liquid of priceless moral value, though they never succeeded in strengthening its nutritive effects. While the eldest Totty had answered the postman's summons, Mr. Totty was exhorting his youngest son to avoid butter to his bread as a pitfall through which he must eventually come to a state of depravity too dreadful to be put in words. He opened the envelope very deliberately, supposing it to contain a bill, but with a smile on his benevolent face which betokened a reverent spirit under suffering. As he read the opening lines and went onward, the smile passed through the stages of surprise, gratification, appetite, eagerness, and then passed into a look of doubt. He laughed in a gently acid way, and said,—

"My dear, Mr. Grapewine invites us to a Christmas dinner, which, of course, we could not attend——"

"Why not?" exclaims Mrs. Totty, eagerly.

"Which it would do gross injury to our principles to attend," continued Mr. Totty; "and I will call on him, with our refusal, this morning, myself."

Mrs. Totty resignedly helped him on with his overcoat, and submitted to the mildly spoken

22

decree which was law in the house of the Tottys.

In a short time her husband went out with the invitation in his pocket and a look of unusual benevolence in his eyes.

Dr. Tuggle and lady read the invitation together over their breakfast-table, and fell to quarrelling so dreadfully about the purport of Mr. Grapewine's singular request, that the doctor rushed from the house, threatening to pull Mr. Grapewine's nose, and to divorce himself forever from his hateful spouse.

On this same morning Mr. Grapewine's bell was rung five times, at very short intervals, in the most tremendously violent manner, and five loud altercations took place in the hall between the servant and the five callers.

" Where is he ?"

" Bring him down, or I'll go up after him !"

" What does he mean by it?"

" Insult a respectable lady !"

" Let me catch him, that's all !"

" Where has he gone ?"

" I'll send him a challenge by Fobbs !"

" Where's his wife ?"

This was what Mr. Grapewine, listening at the top of the stairs, heard in a confused tumult

in his parlor. He could not understand it. He
was extremely agitated; but the servant insisted on his going down, and he did so, clad
in a loose morning dress and slippers. As he
entered the parlor-door he was met by four
furious gentlemen and an elderly lady, flourishing his invitations in their hands and crying
hotly for explanations.

"What do you mean, sir? What do you
mean by alluding to my—my toilet in this impertinent manner?" said Colonel Killiam.

The light began to flow in upon Mr. Grapewine's puzzled understanding. He confessed
his mistake, and would have urged them to
forget it and come to the dinner as if nothing
had happened, but before he could do so he
found himself alone in the room, with five notes
of invitation on the floor at his feet, and nothing
but the remembrance of one of the best ideas
he had ever had in his life.

END OF BOOK II.

IN THE
YULE-LOG GLOW

CHRISTMAS POEMS FROM
'ROUND THE WORLD

"Sic as folk tell ower at a winter ingle"

Scott

EDITED BY

HARRISON S. MORRIS

THREE VOLUMES IN ONE.

Book III.

PHILADELPHIA
J. B. LIPPINCOTT COMPANY
1900.

Copyright, 1891, by J. B. LIPPINCOTT COMPANY.

PRINTED BY J. B. LIPPINCOTT COMPANY, PHILADELPHIA.

BETWEEN THE TALE-TELLING.

FANCY, if you will, Gentle Reader, that, between the intervals of tale-telling,—the Yule-log still ruddy upon the visages of your fellow-guests from many lands,—fancy that a quiet traveller draws out of his side-pocket a little, well-worn pair of books from which he reads some scrap of verse or some melodious Christmas poem. Fancy, too, that, beneath the inn windows, in the snow outside, an occasional band of the Waits strikes up an ancient carol with voice and horn, begging, when the music is done, admittance to the glowing warmth within doors and a share in the plenteous cakes and ale.

Imagine this, if you will, and choose, from the pages to come, whatever of old or new will fit well into the conceit; for not a few carols or legends lie there which have done service under the snow-covered gables or by the crackling wood, and which will help, with their quaint heartiness or simple beauty, to realize the charm of Christmas the world around,—that charm which flows from hearty and generous good-will towards men; which has for its inner light the kindly desire for peace on earth.

3

ILLUSTRATIONS, BOOK III.

THE BARON'S HALL . . . . " 66

A SHEPHERD . . . . " 142

A VISION . . . . " 200

CONTENTS OF BOOK III.

Legends in Song.   PAGE

 The Hallowed Time 11

 On the Morning of Christ's Nativity 12

 The First Roman Christmas 23

 The Three Damsels 25

 King Olaf's Christmas* 29

 Halbert and Hob 33

 Good King Wenceslas 39

 The Wise Men of the East 41

 Christmas at Sea 46

 " Last Christmas was a Year ago"† 50

As It Fell Upon A Day.

 A Christmas " Now" 59

 Christmas Eve Customs 63

 Merry Souls 64

 Christmas in the Olden Time 66

 Ceremonies for Christmas 68

* By the courtesy of Messrs. Houghton, Mifflin & Co.
† By the courtesy of The Century Company.

PAGE

Bringing in the Boar's Head 69

The Boar's Head Carol 70

To be Eaten with Mustard 71

Christmas-Day in the Morning 72

Praise of Christmas 73

Winter's Delights 78

A Christmas Catch 79

The Epic 80

The Country Life 89

Christmas Omnipresent 90

An Old English Christmas-Tide 94

Signs of Christmas 97

The Mistletoe 99

Christmas of Old 101

A Plea for a Present 112

A New-Year's Gift Sent to Sir Simeon Steward 114

The New-Year's Gift 116

An Invitation to the Revel 117

A Christmas Ditty 120

At the End of the Feast 121

Twelfth Night; or, King and Queen 123

Ceremonies for Candlemas Eve 125

Another Ceremony 126

The Ceremonies for Candlemas Day 127

Another Ceremony 127

Saint Distaff's Day, the Morrow after Twelfth

  Day 128

THE SHEPHERDS.

	PAGE
On Oaten Pipes	131
Pipe-Playing	132
The First Carol	134
In Bethlehem	137
A Carol in the Pastures	139
The Shepherds	141
On Shepherds' Pipes	144
Angel Tidings	145
The News-Bearers	146
Hymn for Christmas-Day	149
A Hymn of the Nativity	150
Sung by the Shepherd	155
From "The Light of the World"*	158

IT BRINGS GOOD CHEER.

Old Christmas Returned	179
The Trencherman	184
Ban and Blessing	186
Thrice Welcome!	187
Christmas Provender	188
Glee and Solace	189
On Saint John's Day	191
Christmas Alms	193
Christmas at the Round-Table	195

LULLABY.

A Carol at the Manger	199

---

* By the courtesy of Messrs Funk & Wagnalls.

8   *Contents of Book III.*

	PAGE
A Dream Carol	200
The King in the Cradle	202
Madonna and Child . . . . : .	205
A Rocking Hymn	209
A Cradle-Song of the Virgin	212
Whispering Palms	214
A Christmas Lullaby	215
The Virgin's Cradle-Hymn	216
The Sovereign	217
By the Cradle-Side	219
The Virgin Mary to the Child Jesus	221
A Bedside Ditty	230
Given Back on Christmas Morn	231
A Lulling Song	237
Good-Night	239

Legends in Song.

"Tell sweet old tales,
Sing songs as we sit bending o'er
  the hearth,
Till the lamp flickers and the
  memory fails."
                    Frederick Tennyson.

THE HALLOWED TIME.

Some say that ever 'gainst that season comes
Wherein our Saviour's birth is celebrated,
The bird of dawning singeth all night long;
And then, they say, no spirit dares stir abroad;
The nights are wholesome, then no planets
    strike,
No fairy takes, nor witch hath power to charm,
So hallowed and so gracious is the time.

                        Shakespeare.

ON THE MORNING OF CHRIST'S NATIVITY.

This is the month, and this the happy morn,
  Wherein the Son of Heaven's eternal King,
Of wedded maid and virgin mother born,
  Our great redemption from above did bring;
  For so the holy sages once did sing,
That he our deadly forfeit should release,
And with his Father work us a perpetual peace.

That glorious form, that light insufferable,
  And that far-beaming blaze of majesty,
Wherewith he wont at heaven's high council-
    table
  To sit the midst of Trinal Unity,
  He laid aside; and, here with us to be,
Forsook the courts of everlasting day,
And chose with us a darksome house of mortal
    clay.

Say, heavenly Muse, shall not thy sacred vein
  Afford a present to the Infant-God?
Hast thou no verse, no hymn, or solemn strain
  To welcome him to this his new abode,
  Now while the heaven, by the sun's team
    untrod,

Hath took no print of the approaching light,
And all the spangled host kept watch in squad-
    ron bright ?

See, how from far, upon the eastern road,
    The star-led wizards haste with odors sweet;
O run, prevent them with thy humble ode,
    And lay it lowly at his blessed feet;
    Have thou the honor first thy Lord to greet,
And join thy voice unto the angel-quire,
From out his secret altar touch'd with hallow'd
    fire.

THE HYMN.

It was the winter wild,
While the heaven-born Child
    All meanly wrapt in the rude manger lies;
Nature in awe to him,
Had doff'd her gaudy trim,
    With her great Master so to sympathize:
It was no season then for her
To wanton with the sun, her lusty paramour.

Only with speeches fair
She woos the gentle air
    To hide her guilty front with innocent snow;
And on her naked shame,
Pollute with sinful blame,
    The saintly veil of maiden-white to throw;

Confounded, that her Maker's eyes
Should look so near upon her foul deformities.

But he, her fears to cease,
Sent down the meek-eyed Peace ;
   She, crown'd with olive green, came softly
      sliding
Down through the turning sphere,
His ready Harbinger,
   With turtle wing the amorous clouds di-
      viding ; •
And, waving wide her myrtle wand,
She strikes an universal peace through sea and
      land.

No war, or battle's sound
Was heard the world around ;
   The idle spear and shield were high up-
      hung ;
The hooked chariot stood
Unstain'd with hostile blood ;
   The trumpet spake not to the armed throng ;
And kings sat still with awful eye,
As if they surely knew their sovereign Lord
      was by.

But peaceful was the night
Wherein the Prince of Light
   His reign of peace upon the earth began :

The winds, with wonder whist,
Smoothly the waters kist,
　Whispering new joys to the mild ocean,
Who now hath quite forgot to rave,
While birds of calm sit brooding on the
　　charmed wave.

The stars, with deep amaze,
Stand fix'd in steadfast gaze,
　Bending one way their precious influence ;
And will not take their flight,
For all the morning light,
　Or Lucifer that often warn'd them thence ;
But in their glimmering orbs did glow,
Until their Lord himself bespake, and bid
　　them go.

And, though the shady gloom
Had given day her room,
　The sun himself withheld his wonted speed,
And hid his head for shame,
As his inferior flame
　The new-enlighten'd world no more should
　　need.
He saw a greater Sun appear
Than his bright throne, or burning axletree,
　　could bear.

The shepherds on the lawn,
Or e'er the point of dawn,
  Sat simply chatting in a rustic row ;
Full little thought they then
That the mighty Pan
  Was kindly come to live with them below ;
Perhaps their loves, or else their sheep,
Was all that did their silly thoughts so busy
      keep.

When such music sweet
Their hearts and ears did greet,
  As never was by mortal fingers strook ;
Divinely-warbled voice
Answering the stringed noise,
  As all their souls in blissful rapture took ;
The air, such pleasure loth to lose,
With thousand echoes still prolongs each heav-
      enly close.

Nature that heard such sound,
Beneath the hollow round
  Of Cynthia's seat, the airy region thrilling,
Now was almost won
To think her part was done,
  And that her reign had here its last fulfilling ;
She knew such harmony alone
Could hold all heaven and earth in happier union.

At last surrounds their sight
A globe of circular light,
    That with long beams the shame-faced night
        array'd;
The helmed cherubim,
And sworded seraphim,
    Are seen in glittering ranks with wings dis-
        play'd,
Harping in loud and solemn quire,
With unexpressive notes, to Heaven's new-born
        Heir.

Such music as, 'tis said,
Before was never made,
    But when of old the sons of morning sung,
While the Creator great
His constellations set,
    And the well-balanced world on hinges hung,
And cast the dark foundations deep,
And bid the weltering waves their oozy channel
        keep.

Ring out, ye crystal spheres,
Once bless our human ears,
    If ye have power to touch our senses so;
And let your silver chime
Move in melodious time,
    And let the base of Heaven's deep organ
        blow,
    III.—*b*   2*

And, with your ninefold harmony,
Make up full concert to the angelic symphony.

For, if such holy song
Enwrap our fancy long,
   Time will run back and fetch the age of gold,
And speckled Vanity
Will sicken soon and die,
   And leprous Sin will melt from earthly mould,
And Hell itself will pass away,
And leave her dolorous mansions to the peering
      day.

Yea, Truth and Justice then
Will down return to men,
   Orb'd in a rainbow; and, like glories wearing,
Mercy will sit between,
Throned in celestial sheen,
    With radiant feet the tissued clouds down
      steering;
And Heaven, as at some festival,
Will open wide the gates of her high palace-hall.

But wisest Fate says No,
This must not yet be so;
   The Babe lies yet in smiling infancy,
That on the bitter cross
Must redeem our loss,
   So both himself and us to glorify:

Yet first, to those ychain'd in sleep,
The wakeful trump of doom must thunder
    through the deep ;

With such a horrid clang
As on Mount Sinai rang,
  While the red fire and smouldering clouds
    outbreak :
The aged earth aghast
With terror of that blast,
  Shall from the surface to the centre shake ;
When at the world's last session,
The dreadful Judge in middle air shall spread
    his throne.

And then at last our bliss
Full and perfect is,
  But now begins ; for, from this happy day,
The Old Dragon, under ground
In straighter limits bound,
  Not half so far casts his usurped sway ;
And, wroth to see his kingdom fail,
Swinges the scaly horror of his folded tail.

The oracles are dumb,
No voice or hideous hum
  Runs through the arched roof in words de-
    ceiving.

Apollo from his shrine
Can no more divine,
  With hollow shriek the steep of Delphos leaving.
No nightly trance, or breathed spell,
Inspires the pale-eyed priest from the prophetic
    cell.

The lonely mountains o'er,
And the resounding shore,
  A voice of weeping heard and loud lament;
From haunted spring and dale,
Edged with poplar pale,
  The parting Genius is with sighing sent;
With flower-inwoven tresses torn,
The Nymphs in twilight shade of tangled thick-
    ets, mourn.

In consecrated earth,
And on the holy hearth,
  The Lars and Lemures moan with midnight
    plaint;
In urns, and altars round,
A drear and dying sound
  Affrights the Flamens at their service quaint;
And the chill marble seems to sweat,
While each peculiar power foregoes his wonted
    seat.

Peor and Baälim
Forsake their temples dim,

With that twice-batter'd god of Palestine ;
And mooned Ashtaroth,
Heaven's queen and mother both,
  Now sits not girt with tapers' holy shine ;
The Lybic Hammon shrinks his horn,
In vain the Tyrian maids their wounded Tham-
    muz mourn.

And sullen Moloch, fled,
Hath left in shadows dread
  His burning idol all of blackest hue ;
In vain with cymbals' ring
They call the grisly king,
  In dismal dance about the furnace blue ;
The brutish gods of Nile as fast,
Isis, and Orus, and the dog Anubis, haste.

Nor is Osiris seen
In Memphian grove or green,
  Trampling the unshower'd grass with lowings
    loud :
Nor can he be at rest
Within his sacred chest ;
  Naught but profoundest hell can be his
    shroud ;
In vain, with timbrell'd anthems dark,
The sable-stoled sorcerers bear his worshipt ark.

He feels from Judah's land
The dreaded Infant's hand,

The rays of Bethlehem blind his dusky eyn;
Nor all the gods beside
Longer dare abide,
  Nor Typhon huge ending in snaky twine;
Our Babe, to show his Godhead true,
Can in his swaddling-bands control the damned
    crew.

So, when the sun in bed,
Curtain'd with cloudy red,
  Pillows his chin upon an orient wave,
The flocking shadows pale
Troop to the infernal jail,
  Each fetter'd ghost slips to his several grave;
And the yellow-skirted fays
Fly after the night-steeds, leaving their moon-
    loved maze.

But see, the Virgin blest
Hath laid her Babe to rest;
  Time is our tedious song should here have
    ending:
Heaven's youngest teemed star
Hath fix'd her polished car,
  Her sleeping Lord, with handmaid lamp at-
    tending:
And all about the courtly stable
Bright-harnessed angels sit in order serviceable.
                      John Milton.

THE FIRST ROMAN CHRISTMAS.

It was the calm and silent night!
  Seven hundred years and fifty-three
Had Rome been growing up to might,
  And now was queen of land and sea.
No sound was heard of clashing wars,
  Peace brooded o'er the hushed domain;
Apollo, Pallas, Jove, and Mars
  Held undisturbed their ancient reign,
    In the solemn midnight
      Centuries ago.

'Twas in the calm and silent night!
  The senator of haughty Rome
Impatient urged his chariot's flight,
  From lonely revel rolling home.
Triumphal arches, gleaming, swell
  His breast with thoughts of boundless sway;
What recked the Roman what befell
  A paltry province far away
    In the solemn midnight
      Centuries ago?

Within that province far away
  Went plodding home a weary boor;
A streak of light before him lay,
  Fallen through a half-shut stable-door,

Across his path.   He passed; for naught
  Told what was going on within.
How keen the stars! his only thought;
  The air how calm, and cold, and thin!
    In the solemn midnight
      Centuries ago.

O strange indifference!   Low and high
  Drowsed over common joys and cares;
The earth was still, but knew not why;
  The world was listening unawares.
How calm a moment may precede
  One that shall thrill the world forever!
To that still moment none would heed,
  Man's doom was linked, no more to sever,
    In the solemn midnight
      Centuries ago.

It is the calm and solemn night!
  A thousand bells ring out and throw
Their joyous peals abroad, and smite
  The darkness, charmed, and holy now!
The night that erst no name had worn,
  To it a happy name is given;
For in that stable lay, new-born,
  The peaceful Prince of earth and heaven,
    In the solemn midnight
      Centuries ago.

                              Alfred H. Domett.

THE THREE DAMSELS.

(SUGGESTED BY A DRAWING OF DANTE GABRIEL
ROSSETTI'S.)

Three damsels in the queen's chamber,
  The queen's mouth was most fair;
She spake a word of God's mother
  As the combs went in her hair.
      Mary that is of might,
      Bring us to thy Son's sight.

They held the gold combs out from her
  A span's length off her head;
She sang this song of God's mother
  And of her bearing-bed.
      Mary most full of grace,
      Bring us to thy Son's face.

When she sat at Joseph's hand,
  She looked against her side;
And either way from the short silk band
  Her girdle was all wried.
      Mary that all good may,
      Bring us to thy Son's way.

Mary had three women for her bed,
  The twain were maidens clean;

The first of them had white and red,
  The third had riven green.
    Mary that is so sweet,
    Bring us to thy Son's feet.

She had three women for her hair,
  Two were gloved soft and shod;
The third had feet and fingers bare,
  She was the likest God.
    Mary that wieldeth land,
    Bring us to thy Son's hand.

She had three women for her ease,
  The twain were good women;
The first two were the two Maries,
  The third was Magdalen.
    Mary that perfect is,
    Bring us to thy Son's kiss.

Joseph had three workmen in his stall,
  To serve him well upon;
The first of them were Peter and Paul,
  The third of them was John.
    Mary, God's handmaiden,
    Bring us to thy Son's ken.

"If your child be none other man's,
  But if it be very mine,

The bedstead shall be gold two spans,
    The bed-foot silver fine."
        Mary that made God mirth,
        Bring us to thy Son's birth.

"If the child be some other man's,
    And if it be none of mine,
The manger shall be straw two spans,
    Betwixen kine and kine."
        Mary that made sin cease,
        Bring us to thy Son's peace.

Christ was born upon this wise:
    It fell on such a night,
Neither with sounds of psalteries,
    Nor with fire for light.
        Mary that is God's spouse,
        Bring us to thy Son's house.

The star came out upon the east
    With a great sound and sweet:
Kings gave gold to make him feast
    And myrrh for him to eat.
        Mary of thy sweet mood,
        Bring us to thy Son's good.

He had two handmaids at his head,
    One handmaid at his feet;

The twain of them were fair and red,
The third one was right sweet.
Mary that is most wise,
Bring us to thy Son's eyes.

Amen.

Algernon Charles Swinburne.

KING OLAF'S CHRISTMAS.

At Drontheim, Olaf the King
Heard the bells of Yule-tide ring,
　　As he sat in his banquet hall,
Drinking the nut-brown ale,
With his bearded Berserks hale
　　And tall.

Three days his Yule-tide feasts
He held with Bishops and Priests,
　　And his horn filled up to the brim;
But the ale was never too strong,
Nor the Sagaman's tale too long,
　　For him.

O'er his drinking-horn, the sign
He made of the cross divine
　　As he drank, and muttered his prayers;
But the Berserks evermore
Made the sign of the Hammer of Thor
　　Over theirs.

The gleams of the fire-light dance
Upon helmet and hauberk and lance
　　And laugh in the eyes of the king;
3*

And he cries to Halfred the Scald,
Gray-bearded, wrinkled, and bald :
  " Sing !

" Sing me a song divine,
With a sword in every line,
  And this shall be thy reward ;"
And he loosened the belt at his waist,
And in front of the singer placed
  His sword.

" Quern-biter of Hakon the Good,
Wherewith at a stroke he hewed
  The millstone through and through,
And Foot-breadth of Thoralf the Strong
Were neither so broad nor so long
  Nor so true."

Then the Scald took his harp and sang,
And loud through the music rang
  The sound of that shining word ;
And the harp-strings a clangor made
As if they were struck with the blade
  Of a sword.

And the Berserks round about
Broke forth into a shout
  That made the rafters ring ;

They smote with their fists on the board,
And shouted, " Long live the sword
  And the King !"

But the king said, " O my son,
I miss the bright word in one
  Of thy measures and thy rhymes."
And Halfred the Scald replied,
" In another 'twas multiplied
  Three times."

Then King Olaf raised the hilt
Of iron, cross-shaped and gilt,
  And said, " Do not refuse ;
Count well the gain and the loss,
Thor's hammer or Christ's cross :
  Choose !"

And Halfred the Scald said, " This,
In the name of the Lord, I kiss,
  Who on it was crucified !"
And a shout went round the board,
" In the name of Christ the Lord
  Who died !"

Then over the waste of snows
The noonday sun uprose
  Through the driving mists revealed,

Like the lifting of the Host,
By incense-clouds almost
   Concealed.

On the shining wall a vast
And shadowy cross was cast
   From the hilt of the lifted sword,
And in foaming cups of ale
The Berserks drank " Was-hael!
   To the Lord!"

          Henry Wadsworth Longfellow.

HALBERT AND HOB.

Here is a thing that happened. Like wild
 beasts whelped, for den,
In a wild part of North England, there lived
 once two wild men,
Inhabiting one homestead, neither a hovel nor
 hut,
Time out of mind their birthright: father and
 son, these,—but,—
Such a son, such a father! Most wildness by
 degrees
Softens away: yet, last of their line, the wild-
 est and worst were these.

Criminals, then? Why, no: they did not murder and rob;
But give them a word, they returned a blow,—
 old Halbert as young Hob:
Harsh and fierce of word, rough and savage of
 deed,
Hated or feared the more—who knows?—the
 genuine wild-beast breed.

Thus were they found by the few sparse folk
 of the country-side;
III.—*c*

But how fared each with other? E'en beasts
    couch, hide by hide.
In a growling, grudged agreement: so father
    son lay curled
The closelier up in their den because the last of
    their kind in the world.

Still, beast irks beast on occasion. One Christ-
    mas night of snow,
Came father and son to words—such words!
    more cruel because the blow
To crown each word was wanting, while taunt
    matched gibe, and curse
Competed with oath in wager, like pastime in
    hell,—nay, worse:
For pastime turned to earnest, as up there
    sprang at last
The son at the throat of the father, seized him,
    and held him fast.

" Out of this house you go !"—there followed a
    hideous oath—
" This oven where now we bake, too hot to hold
    us both !
If there's snow outside, there's coolness: out
    with you, bide a spell
In the drift, and save the sexton the charge of
    a parish shell !"

Now, the old trunk was tough, was solid as
    stump of oak
Untouched at the core by a thousand years:
    much less had its seventy broke
One whipcord nerve in the muscly mass from
    neck to shoulder-blade
Of the mountainous man, whereon his child's
    rash hand like a feather weighed.

Nevertheless at once did the mammoth shut
    his eyes,
Drop chin to breast, drop hands to sides, stand
    stiffened,—arms and thighs
All of a piece—struck mute, much as a sentry
    stands,
Patient to take the enemy's fire: his captain so
    commands.

Whereat the son's wrath flew to fury at such
    sheer scorn
Of his puny strength by the giant eld thus
    acting the babe new-born:
And "Neither will this turn serve!" yelled he.
    "Out with you! Trundle, log!
If you cannot tramp and trudge like a man,
    try all-fours like a dog!"

Still the old man stood mute. So, logwise,—
    down to floor

Pulled from his fireside place, dragged on from
    hearth to door,—
Was he pushed, a very log, staircase along,
    until
A certain turn in the steps was reached, a yard
    from the house-door sill.

Then the father opened his eyes,—each spark
    of their rage extinct,—
Temples, late black, dead-blanched, right-hand
    with left-hand linked,—
He faced his son submissive; when slow the
    accents came,
They were strangely mild though his son's rash
    hand on his neck lay all the same.

" Halbert, on such a night of a Christmas long
    ago,
For such a cause, with such a gesture, did I
    drag—so—
My father down thus far: but, softening here,
    I heard
A voice in my heart, and stopped: you wait for
    an outer word.

" For your own sake, not mine, soften you too!
    Untrod
Leave this last step we reach, nor brave the
    finger of God!

I dared not pass its lifting : I did well. I nor
blame

Nor praise you. I stopped here : Halbert, do
you the same !"

Straightway the son relaxed his hold of the
father's throat.

They mounted, side by side, to the room again :
no note

Took either of each, no sign made each to
either : last

As first, in absolute silence, their Christmas-
night they passed.

At dawn, the father sate on, dead, in the selfsame place,

With an outburst blackening still the old bad
fighting-face :

But the son crouched all a-tremble like any
lamb new-yeaned.

When he went to the burial, some one's staff he
borrowed,—tottered and leaned.

But his lips were loose, not locked,—kept muttering, mumbling. "There !

At his cursing and swearing !" the youngsters
cried ; but the elders thought, " In
prayer."

4

A boy threw stones ; he picked them up and
    stored them in his vest ;
So tottered, muttered, mumbled he, till he died,
    perhaps found rest.
" Is there a reason in nature for these hard
    hearts ?" O Lear,
That a reason out of nature must turn them
    soft, seems clear !

               Robert Browning.

GOOD KING WENCESLAS.

Good King Wenceslas looked out,
  On the feast of Stephen,
When the snow lay round about,
  Deep, and crisp, and even;
Brightly shone the moon that night,
  Tho' the frost was cruel,
When a poor man came in sight,
  Gathering winter fuel.

" Hither, page, and stand by me,
  If thou know'st it, telling,
Yonder peasant, who is he?
  Where and what his dwelling?"
" Sire, he lives a good league hence,
  Underneath the mountain;
Right against the forest fence,
  By Saint Agnes' fountain."

" Bring me flesh, and bring me wine,
  Bring me pine-logs hither:
Thou and I will see him dine,
  When we bear them thither."
Page and monarch forth they went,
  Forth they went together
Thro' the rude wind's wild lament
  And the bitter weather.

" Sire, the night is darker now,
  And the wind blows stronger;
Fails my heart, I know not how,
  I can go no longer."
" Mark my footsteps, good my page;
  Tread thou in them boldly:
Thou shalt find the winter's rage
  Freeze thy blood less coldly."

In his master's steps he trod,
  Where the snow lay dinted;
Heat was in the very sod
  Which the saint had printed.
Therefore, Christian men, be sure,
  Wealth or rank possessing,
Ye who now will bless the poor,
  Shall yourselves find blessing.

Translated from the Latin, by J. M. Neale.

THE WISE MEN OF THE EAST.

Three kings went riding from the East
　Through fine weather and wet;
" And whither shall we ride," they said,
　" Where we ha' not ridden yet?"

" And whither shall we ride," they said,
　" To find the hidden thing
That times the course of all our stars
　And all our auguring?"

They were the Wise Men of the East,
　And none so wise as they;
" Alas!" the King of Persia cried,
　" And must ye ride away?

" Yet since ye go a-riding, sirs,
　I pray ye, ride for me,
And carry me my golden gifts
　To the King o' Galilee.

" Go riding into Palestine,
　A long ride and a fair!"
" 'Tis well!" the Mages answered him,
　" As well as anywhere!"

4*

They rode by day, they rode by night,
　　The stars came out on high,—
" And, oh !" said King Balthazar,
　　As he gazed into the sky,

" We ride by day, we ride by night,
　　To a King in Galilee ;
We leave a king in Persia,
　　And kings no less are we.

" Yet often in the deep blue night,
　　When stars burn far and dim,
I wish I knew a greater King,
　　To fall and worship him.

" A king who should not care to reign,
　　But wonderful and fair ;
A king—a king that were a star
　　Aloft in miles of air !"

" A star is good," said Melchior,
　　" A high, unworldly thing ;
But I would choose a soul alive
　　To be my Lord and King.

" Not Herod, nay, nor Cyrus, nay,
　　Not any king at all ;
For I would choose a new-born child
　　Laid in a manger-stall."

" 'Tis well," the black King Casper cried,
  " For mighty men are ye ;
But no such humble king were meet
  For my simplicity.

" A star is small and very far,
  A babe's a simple thing ;
The very Son of God himself
  Shall be my Lord and King !"

Then smiled the King Balthazar ;
  " A good youth !" Melchior cried ;
And young and old, without a word,
  Along the hills they ride,

Till, lo ! among the western skies
  There grows a shining thing—
" The star ! Behold the star," they shout ;
  " Behold Balthazar's King !"

And, lo ! within the western skies
  The star begins to flit ;
The three kings spur their horses on,
  And follow after it.

And when they reach the king's palace,
  They cry, " Behold the place !"
But, like a shining bird, the star
  Flits on in heaven apace.

Oh they rode on, and on they rode,
　Till they reached a lonely wold,
Where shepherds keep their flocks by night,
　And the night was chill and cold.

Oh they rode on, and on they rode,
　Till they reach a little town,
And there the star in heaven stands still
　Above a stable brown.

The town is hardly a village,
　The stable's old and poor,
But there the star in heaven stands still
　Above the stable door.

And through the open door, the straw
　And the tired beasts they see ;
And the Babe, laid in a manger,
　That sleepeth peacefully.

" All hail, the King of Melchior !"
　The three Wise Men begin ;
King Melchior swings from off his horse,
　And he would have entered in.

But why do the horses whinny and neigh ?
　And what thing fills the night
With wheeling spires of angels,
　And streams of heavenly light ?

Above the stable roof they turn
   And hover in a ring,
And " Glory be to God on high
   And peace on earth," they sing.

King Melchior kneels upon the grass
   And falls a-praying there ;
Balthazar lets the bridle drop,
   And gazes in the air.

But Casper gives a happy shout,
   And hastens to the stall ;
" Now, hail !" he cries, " thou Son of God,
   And Saviour of us all."
A. Mary F. Robinson.

CHRISTMAS AT SEA.

The sheets were frozen hard, and they cut the
    naked hand ;
The decks were like a slide, where a seaman
    scarce could stand ;
The wind was a nor'wester, blowing squally off
    the sea ;
And cliffs and spouting breakers were the only
    things a-lee.

They heard the surf a-roaring before the break
    of day ;
But 'twas only with the peep of light we saw
    how ill we lay.
We tumbled every hand on deck instanter, with
    a shout,
And we gave her the maintops'l, and stood by
    to go about.

All day we tacked and tacked between the
    South Head and the North ;
All day we hauled the frozen sheets, and got
    no further forth ;
All day as cold as charity, in bitter pain and
    dread,
For very life and nature, we tacked from head
    to head.

We gave the South a wider berth, for there the
tide-race roared ;
But every tack we made we brought the North
Head close aboard ;
So's we saw the cliffs and houses, and the
breakers running high,
And the coast-guard in his garden, with his
glass against his eye.

The frost was on the village roofs as white as
ocean foam ;
The good red fires were burning bright in every
'longshore home ;
The windows sparkled clear, and the chimneys
volleyed out ;
And I vow we sniffed the victuals as the vessel
went about.

The bells upon the church were rung with a
mighty jovial cheer ;
For it's just that I should tell you how (of all
days in the year)
This day of our adversity was blessed Christmas morn,
And the house above the coast-guard's was the
house where I was born.

Oh, well I saw the pleasant room, the pleasant
faces there,

My mother's silver spectacles, my father's silver
    hair;
And well I saw the firelight, like a flight of
    homely elves,
Go dancing round the china plates that stand
    upon the shelves.

And well I knew the talk they had, the talk
    that was of me,
Of the shadow on the household, and the son
    that went to sea;
And, oh, the wicked fool I seemed, in every
    kind of way,
To be here and hauling frozen ropes on blessed
    Christmas Day.

They lit the high sea-light, and the dark began
    to fall.
" All hands to loose topgallant sails!" I heard
    the captain call.
" By the Lord, she'll never stand it," our first
    mate, Jackson, cried.
· · · "It's the one way or the other, Mr. Jack-
    son," he replied.

She staggered to her bearings, but the sails were
    new and good,
And the ship smelt up to windward just as
    though she understood.

As the winter's day was ending, in the entry
    of the night,
We cleared the weary headland, and passed
    below the light.

And they heaved a mighty breath, every soul
    on board but me,
As they saw her nose again pointing handsome
    out to sea;
But all that I could think of, in the darkness
    and the cold,
Was just that I was leaving home and my
    folks were growing old.

Robert Louis Stevenson.

III.—c   *d*   5

"LAST CHRISTMAS WAS A YEAR AGO."

(THE OLD LADY SPEAKS.)

Last Christmas was a year ago
Says I to David, I-says-I,
" We're goin' to mornin' service, so
You hitch up right away : I'll try
To tell the girls jes what to do
Fer dinner.   We'll be back by two."
I didn't wait to hear what he
Would more'n like say back to me,
But banged the stable-door and flew
Back to the house, jes plumb chilled through.

Cold !   *Wooh !* how cold it was !   My-oh !
Frost flyin', and the air, you know—
" Jes sharp enough," heerd David swear,
" To shave a man and cut his hair !"
And blow *and* blow ! and *snow* and snow,
Where it had drifted 'long the fence
And 'crost the road,—some places, though,
Jes swep' clean to the gravel, so
The goin' was as bad for sleighs
As 't was fer wagons,—and *both* ways,
'Twixt snow-drifts and the bare ground, I've
Jes wondered we got through alive ;
I hain't saw nothin' 'fore er sence

'At beat it *anywheres* I know—
Last Christmas was a year ago.

And David said, as we set out,
'At Christmas services was 'bout
As cold and wuthless kind o' love
To offer up as *he* knowed of;
And, as fer *him*, he railly thought
'At the Good Bein' up above
Would think more of us—as he ought—
A-stayin' home on sich a day
And thankin' of him thataway.
And jawed on in an undertone,
'Bout leavin' Lide and Jane alone
There on the place, and me not there
To oversee 'em, and p'pare
The stuffin' for the turkey, and
The sass and all, you understand.

I've always managed David by
Jes sayin' nothin.'   That was why
He'd chased Lide's beau away—'cause Lide
She'd allus take up Perry's side
When David tackled him ; and so,
Last Christmas was a year ago,—
Er ruther 'bout a week *afore*,—
David and Perry'd quarr'l'd about
Some tom-fool argyment, you know,
And pap told him to " Jes git out

O' there, and not to come no more,
And, when he went, to *shet the door !*"
And as he passed the winder, we
Saw Perry, white as white could be,
March past, onhitch his hoss, and light
A *see*-gyar, and lope out o' sight.
Then Lide she come to me and cried.
And I said nothin'—was no need.
And yit, you know, that man jes got
Right out o' there's ef he'd be'n shot—
P'tendin' he must go and feed
The stock er somepin'. Then I tried
To git the pore girl pacified.

But gittin' back to—where was we ?—
Oh, yes—where David lectered me
All way to meetin', high and low,
Last Christmas was a year ago.
Fer all the awful cold, they was
A fair attendunce ; mostly, though,
The crowd was 'round the stoves, you see,
Thawin' their heels and scrougin' us.
Ef't 'adn't be'n fer the old Squire
Givin' his seat to us, as in
We stomped, a-fairly perishin',
And David could 'a' got no fire,
He'd jes 'a' drapped there in his tracks.
And Squire, as I was tryin' to yit

Make room fer him, says, " No ; the facks
Is I got to git up and git
'Ithout no preachin'.   Jes got word—
Trial fer life—can't be deferred !"
And out he put.   And all way through
The sermont—and a long one, too—
I couldn't he'p but think o' Squire
And us changed round so, and admire
His gintle ways—to give his warm
Bench up, and have to face the storm.
And when I noticed David he
Was needin' jabbin', I thought best
To kind o' sort o' let him rest—
'Peared like he slep' so peacefully !
And then I thought o' home, and how
And what the girls was doin' now,
And kind o' prayed, 'way in my breast,
And breshed away a tear er.two
As David waked, and church was through.

By time we'd " howdyed" round, and shuck
Hands with the neighbors, must 'a' tuck
A half-hour longer : ever' one
A-sayin' " Christmas-gift !" afore
David er me—so we got none.
But David warmed up, more and more,
And got so jokey-like, and had
His sperits up, and 'peared so glad,

I whispered to him, " S'pose you ast
A passel of 'em come and eat
Their dinners with us.—Girls 's got
A full-and-plenty fer the lot
And all their kin." So David passed
The invite round. And ever' seat
In ever' wagon-bed and sleigh
Was jes *packed*, as we rode away—
The young folks, mild er so along,
A-strikin' up a sleighin' song.
Tel David laughed and yelled, you know,
And jes whirped up and sent the snow
And gravel flyin' thick and fast—
Last Christmas was a year ago.
W'y, that-air seven-mild ja'nt we come—
Jes seven mild scant from church to home—
It didn't 'pear, that day, to be
Much furder railly 'n 'bout three.

But I was purty squeamish by
The time home hove in sight and I
See two *vehickles* standin' there
Already. So says I, " Prepare !"
All to myse'f. And presently
David he sobered ; and says he,
" Hain't that-air Squire Hanch's old
Buggy," he says, " and claybank mare ?"
Says I, " Le's git in out the cold—

Your company's nigh 'bout froze." He says,
" Whose sleigh's that-air a-standin' there ?"
Says I, " It's no odds whose— you jes
Drive to the house and let us out,
'Cause we're jes freezin', nigh about."
Well, David swung up to the door
And out we piled. At first I heerd
Jane's voice ; then *Lide's*—I thought afore
I reached that girl I'd jes die, shore ;
And *when* I reached her, wouldn't keered
Much ef I had, I was so glad,
A-kissin' her through my green veil,
And jes excitin' her so bad
'At *she* broke down, *herse'f*—and Jane
She cried—and we all hugged again.
And David—David jes turned pale !—
Looked at the girls and then at me,
Then at the open door—and then
" Is old Squire Hanch in there ?" says he.
The old Squire suddenly stood in
The doorway, with a sneakin' grin.
" Is Perry Anders in there, too ?"
Says David, limberin' all through,
As Lide and me both grabbed him, and
Perry stepped out and waved his hand
And says, " Yes, pap." And David jes
Stooped and kissed Lide, and says, " I guess
Your mother's much to blame as you.
Ef *she* kin resk him, *I kin* too."

The dinner we had then hain't no
Bit better'n the one to-day
'At we'll have fer 'em. Hear some sleigh
A-jinglin' now.—David, fer *me*,
I wish you'd jes go out and see
Ef they're in sight yit. It jes does
Me good to think, in times like these,
Lide's done so well. And David he's
More tractabler 'n what he was
Last Christmas was a year ago.

James Whitcomb Riley.

As It Fell Upon A Day.

"A handsome hostess, merry host,
A pot of ale and now a toast,
Tobacco, and a good coal-fire,
Are things this season doth re-
quire."

Poor Robin.

A CHRISTMAS "NOW."

So, now is come our joyfulst feast,
  Let every man be jolly;
Each room with ivy-leaves is drest,
  And every post with holly.
Though some churls at our mirth repine,
Round your foreheads garlands twine;
Drown sorrow in a cup of wine,
  And let us all be merry.

Now all our neighbors' chimneys smoke,
  And Christmas logs are burning;
Their ovens they with baked meats choke,
  And all their spits are turning.
Without the door let sorrow lie;
And if for cold it hap to die,
We'll bury 't in a Christmas-pie,
  And evermore be merry.

Now every lad is wondrous trim,
  And no man minds his labor;
Our lasses have provided them
  A bagpipe and a tabor;
Young men and maids, and girls and boys,
Give life to one another's joys;

And you anon shall by their noise
    Perceive that they are merry.

Rank misers now do sparing shun;
    Their hall of music soundeth;
And dogs thence with whole shoulders run,
    So all things there aboundeth.
The country folks themselves advance
For crowdy-mutton's come out of France;
And Jack shall pipe, and Jill shall dance,
    And all the town be merry.

Ned Squash has fetched his bands from pawn,
    And all his best apparel;
Brisk Ned hath bought a ruff of lawn
    With droppings of the barrel;
And those that hardly all the year
Had bread to eat or rags to wear
Will have both clothes and dainty fare,
    And all the day be merry.

Now poor men to the justices
    With capons make their arrants;
And if they hap to fail of these,
    They plague them with their warrants:
But now they feed them with good cheer,
And what they want they take in beer;
For Christmas comes but once a year,
    And then they shall be merry.

Good farmers in the country nurse
  The poor that else were undone;
Some landlords spend their money worse
  On lust and pride at London.
There the roysters they do play,
Drab and dice their lands away,
Which may be ours another day;
  And therefore let's be merry.

The client now his suit forbears,
  The prisoner's heart is eased;
The debtor drinks away his cares,
  And for the time is pleased.
Though other purses be more fat,
Why should we pine or grieve at that?
Hang sorrow! care will kill a cat,
  And therefore let's be merry.

Hark! how the wags abroad do call
  Each other forth to rambling:
Anon you'll see them in the hall
  For nuts and apples scrambling.
Hark! how the roofs with laughter sound!
Anon they'll think the house goes round:
For they the cellar's depth have found,
  And there they will be merry.

The wenches with their wassail bowls,
  About the streets are singing;

The boys are come to catch the owls,
　　The wild mare in is bringing.
Our kitchen-boy hath broke his box,
And to the dealing of the ox
Our honest neighbors come by flocks,
　　And here they will be merry.

Now kings and queens poor sheep-cotes have,
　　And mate with everybody;
The honest now may play the knave,
　　And wise men play at noddy.
Some youths will now a mumming go,
Some others play at Rowland-ho,
And twenty other gameboys mo,
　　Because they will be merry.

Then wherefore in these merry days,
　　Should we, I pray, be duller?
No, let us sing some roundelays
　　To make our mirth the fuller.
And, whilst thus inspired, we sing,
Let all the streets with echoes ring,
Woods, and hills, and everything
　　Bear witness we are merry.

George Wither.

CHRISTMAS EVE CUSTOMS.

I.

Come, guard this night the Christmas-pie,
That the thief, though ne'er so sly,
With his flesh-hooks, don't come nigh
          To catch it,

From him, who alone sits there,
Having his eyes still in his ear,
And a deal of nightly fear
          To watch it !

II.

Wash your hands, or else the fire
Will not teend* to your desire ;
Unwashed hands, ye maidens, know,
Dead the fire, though ye blow.

                Robert Herrick.

---

* Burn.

MERRY SOULS.

O you merry, merry Souls,
　　Christmas is a-coming,
We shall have flowing bowls,
　　Dancing, piping, drumming.

Delicate minced pies
　　To feast every virgin,
Capon and goose likewise,
　　Brawn and a dish of sturgeon.

Then, for your Christmas box,
　　Sweet plum-cakes and money,
Delicate Holland smocks,
　　Kisses sweet as honey.

Hey for the Christmas ball,
　　Where we shall be jolly
Jigging short and tall,
　　Kate, Dick, Ralph, and Molly.

Then to the hop we'll go
　　Where we'll jig and caper;
Maidens all-a-row;
　　Will shall pay the scraper.

Hodge shall dance with Prue,
  Keeping time with kisses;
We'll have a jovial crew
  Of sweet smirking misses.
          Round About Our Coal Fire.

CHRISTMAS IN THE OLDEN TIME.

The damsel donned her kirtle sheen;
The hall was dressed with holly green;
Forth to the wood did merry-men go
To gather in the mistletoe.
Then opened wide the baron's hall
To vassal, tenant, seri, and all;
Power laid his rod of rule aside,
And ceremony doffed his pride.
The heir, with roses in his shoes,
That night might village partner choose;
The lord underogating share
The vulgar game of post-and-pair.
All hailed with uncontrolled delight
And general voice, the happy night,
That to the cottage as the crown
Brought tidings of salvation down.
The fire with well-dried logs supplied
Went roaring up the chimney wide;
The huge hall-table's oaken face,
Scrubbed till it shone, the day to grace,
Bore then upon its massive board
No mark to part the squire and lord.
Then was brought in the lusty brawn
By old blue-coated serving-man;

Then the grim boar's head frowned on high,
Crested with bay and rosemary.
Well can the green-garbed ranger tell
How, when, and where the monster fell;
What dogs before his death he tore,
And all the baiting of the boar.
The wassail round, in good brown bowls,
Garnished with ribbons blithely trowls.
There the huge sirloin reeked; hard by
Plum-porridge stood and Christmas-pie;
Nor failed old Scotland to produce
At such high tide her savory goose.
Then came the merry masquers in
And carols roared with blithesome din;
If unmelodious was the song,
It was a hearty note and strong.
Who lists may in their mumming see
Traces of ancient mystery.
While shirts supplied the masquerade,
And smutted cheeks the visors made:
But, oh! what masquers richly dight
Can boast of bosoms half so light!
England was merry England when
Old Christmas brought his sports again.
'Twas Christmas broached the mightiest ale,
'Twas Christmas told the merriest tale;
A Christmas gambol oft would cheer
The poor man's heart through half the year.

Sir Walter Scott.

CEREMONIES FOR CHRISTMAS.

Come, bring with a noise,
My merry, merry boys,
The Christmas-log to the firing,
While my good dame, she
Bids ye all be free,
And drink to your heart's desiring.

With the last year's brand
Light the new block, and,
For good success in his spending,
On your psalteries play,
That sweet luck may
Come while the log is a-teending.*

Drink now the strong beer,
Cut the white loaf here,
The while the meat is a-shredding;
For the rare mince-pie
And the plums stand by,
To fill the paste that's a-kneading.
                              Robert Herrick.

---

* Burning.

BRINGING IN THE BOAR'S HEAD.

Caput apri defero
Reddens laudes domino.
The boar's head in hand bring I,
With garlands gay and rosemary;
I pray you all sing merrily
  Qui estis in convivio.

The boar's head, I understand,
Is the chief service in this land;
Look, wherever it be fand,
  Servite cum cantico.

Be glad, lords, both more and less,
 For this hath ordained our steward
To cheer you all this Christmas,
 The boar's head with mustard.
     Ritson's Ancient Songs.

THE BOAR'S HEAD CAROL.

SUNG AT QUEEN'S COLLEGE, OXFORD.

The boar's head in hand bear I,
Bedecked with bays and rosemary;
And I pray you, my masters, be merry,
        Quot estis in convivo.
        Caput apri defero
        Reddens laudes domino.

The boar's head, as I understand,
Is the rarest dish in all this land,
Which thus bedeck'd with a gay garland
        Let us servire cantico.
        Caput apri defero
        Reddens laudes domino.

Our steward hath provided this
In honor of the King of bliss;
Which on this day to be served is
        In Reginensi Atrio.
        Caput apri defero
        Reddens laudes domino.

TO BE EATEN WITH MUSTARD.

SUNG AT ST. JOHN'S COLLEGE, OXFORD, CHRISTMAS, 1607.

The boar is dead,
So, here is his head;
   What man could have done more
Than his head off to strike,
Meleager-like,
   And bring it as I do before.

He living spoiled
Where good men toiled,
   Which made kind Ceres sorry;
But now dead and drawn
Is very good brawn,
   And we have brought it for ye.

Then set down the swineyard,
The foe to the vineyard,
   Let Bacchus crown his fall;
Let this boar's head and mustard
Stand for pig, goose, and custard,
   And so ye are welcome all.

CHRISTMAS DAY IN THE MORNING.

Maids, get up and bake your pies,
　　Bake your pies, bake your pies;
Maids, get up and bake your pies,
　　'Tis Christmas day in the morning.

See the ships all sailing by,
　　Sailing by, sailing by;
See the ships all sailing by
　　On Christmas day in the morning.

Dame, what made your ducks to die,
　　Ducks to die, ducks to die;
Dame, what made your ducks to die
　　On Christmas day in the morning?

You let your lazy maidens lie,
　　Maidens lie, maidens lie;
You let your lazy maidens lie
　　On Christmas day in the morning.

Bishoprick Garland, A.D. 1834.

PRAISE OF CHRISTMAS.

FIRST PART.

All hail to the days that merit more praise
    Than all the rest of the year,
And welcome the nights that double delights
    As well for the poor as the peer!
Good fortune attend each merry-man's friend,
    That doth but the best that he may;
Forgetting old wrongs, with carols and songs,
    To drive the cold winter away.

Let Misery pack, with a whip at his back,
    To the deep Tantalian flood;
In Lethe profound let envy be drown'd,
    That pines at another man's good;
Let Sorrow's expense be banded from hence,
    All payments have greater delay,
We'll spend the long nights in cheerful delights
    To drive the cold winter away.

'Tis ill for a mind to anger inclined
    To think of small injuries now;
If wrath be to seek, do not lend her thy cheek,
    Nor let her inhabit thy brow,

D   7

Cross out of thy books malevolent looks,
  Both beauty and youth's decay,
And wholly consort with mirth and with sport
  To drive the cold winter away.

The court in all state now opens her gate
  And gives a free welcome to most;
The city likewise, tho' somewhat precise,
  Doth willingly part with her roast:
But yet by report from city and court
  The country will e'er gain the day;
More liquor is spent and with better content
  To drive the cold winter away.

Our good gentry there for costs do not spare,
  The yeomanry fast not till Lent;
The farmers and such think nothing too much,
  If they keep but to pay for their rent.
The poorest of all now do merrily call,
  When at a fit place they can stay,
For a song or a tale or a cup of good ale
  To drive the cold winter away.

Thus none will allow of solitude now
  But merrily greets the time,
To make it appear of all the whole year
  That this is accounted the prime:

December is seen apparell'd in green,
   And January fresh as May
Comes dancing along with a cup and a song
   To drive the cold winter away.

SECOND PART.

This time of the year is spent in good cheer,
   And neighbors together do meet
To sit by the fire, with friendly desire,
   Each other in love to greet;
Old grudges forgot are put in the pot,
   All sorrows aside they lay;
The 'old and the young doth carol this song
   To drive the cold winter away.

Sisley and Nanny, more jocund than any,
   As blithe as the month of June,
Do carol and sing like birds of the spring,
   No nightingale sweeter in tune;
To bring in content, when summer is spent,
   In pleasant delight and play,
With mirth and good cheer to end the whole
     year,
   And drive the cold winter away.

The shepherd, the swain, do highly disdain
   To waste out their time in care;
And Clim of the Clough hath plenty enough
   If he but a penny can spare

To spend at the night, in joy and delight,
　.Now after his labor all day ;
For better than lands is the help of his hands
　To drive the cold winter away.

To mask and to mum kind neighbors will
　　come
　With wassails of nut-brown ale,
To drink and carouse to all in the house
　As merry as bucks in the dale ;
Where cake, bread, and cheese are brought for
　　your fees
　To make you the longer stay ;
At the fire to warm 'twill do you no harm,
　To drive the cold winter away.

When Christmas's tide comes in like a bride
　With holly and ivy clad,
Twelve days in the year much mirth and good
　　cheer
　In every household is had ;
The country guise is then to devise
　Some gambols of Christmas play,
Whereat the young men do best that they can
　To drive the cold winter away.

When white-bearded frost hath threatened his
　　worst,
　And fallen from branch and brier,

Then time away calls from husbandry halls
   And from the good countryman's fire,
Together to go to plough and to sow,
   To get us both food and array,
And thus with content the time we have spent
   To drive the cold winter away.

WINTER'S DELIGHTS.

Now winter nights enlarge
  The number of their hours,
And clouds their storms discharge
  Upon the airy towers.
Let now the chimneys blaze,
  And cups o'erflow with wine;
Let well-tuned words amaze
  With harmony divine.
Now yellow waxen lights
  Shall wait on honey love,
While youthful revels, masques, and courtly
      sights
  Sleep's leaden spells remove.

The time doth well dispense
  With lovers' long discourse;
Much speech hath some defence,
  Though beauty no remorse.
All do not all things well:
  Some, measures comely tread,
Some, knotted riddles tell,
  Some, poems smoothly read.
The summer hath his joys,
  And winter his delights;
Though love and all his pleasures are but toys,
  They shorten tedious nights.

Thomas Campion.

A CHRISTMAS CATCH.

To shorten winter's sadness,
See where the nymphs with gladness
Disguised all are coming,
Right wantonly a-mumming.
Fa la.

Whilst youthful sports are lasting,
To feasting turn our fasting;
With revels and with wassails
Make grief and care our vassals.
Fa la.

For youth it well beseemeth
That pleasure he esteemeth;
And sullen age is hated
That mirth would have abated.
Fa la.

Thomas Weelkes, A.D. 1597.

THE EPIC.

At Francis Allen's on the Christmas eve,—
The game of forfeits done—the girls all kissed
Beneath the sacred bush and past away,—
The parson Holmes, the poet Everard Hall,
The host, and I sat round the wassail-bowl,
Then half-way ebbed: and there we held a talk,
How all the old honor had from Christmas
      gone,
Or gone, or dwindled down to some odd games
In some odd nooks like this; till I, tired out
With cutting eights that day upon the pond,
Where, 'three times slipping from the outer
      edge,
I bumped the ice into three several stars,
Fell in a doze; and, half-awake, I heard
The parson taking wide and wider sweeps,
Now harping on the church-commissioners,
Now hawking at geology and schism;
Until I woke, and found him settled down
Upon the general decay of faith
Right through the world; "at home was little
      left,
And none abroad; there was no anchor, none,
To hold by."   Francis, laughing, clapt his hand
On Everard's shoulder with, " I hold by him."

" And I," quoth Everard, " by the wassail-bowl."
" Why, yes," I said, " we knew your gift that
    way
At college ; but another which you had,
I mean of verse (for so we held it then),
What came of that ?" " You know," said Frank,
    " he burnt
His epic, his King Arthur, some twelve books,"—
And then to me demanding why ? " Oh, sir,
He thought that nothing new was said, or else
Something so said 'twas nothing—that a truth
Looks freshest in the fashion of the day :
God knows, he has a mint of reasons : ask.
It pleased *me* well enough." " Nay, nay," said
    Hall,
" Why take the style of those heroic times ?
For nature brings not back the mastodon,
Nor we those times ; and why should any man
Remodel models ? These twelve books of mine
Were faint Homeric echoes, nothing-worth,
Mere chaff and draff, much better burnt." " But
    I,"
Said Francis, " picked the eleventh from this
    hearth,
And have it : keep a thing, its use will come.
I hoard it as a sugar-plum for Holmes."
He laughed, and I, though sleepy, like a horse
That hears the corn-bin open, pricked my ears ;
For I remembered Everard's college fame
    III.—*f*

When we were freshmen : then, at my request,
He brought it; and the poet, little urged,
But, with some prelude of disparagement,
Read, mouthing out his hollow oes and aes,
Deep-chested music, and to this result :

MORTE D'ARTHUR.

So all day long the noise of battle rolled
Among the mountains by the winter sea;
Until King Arthur's table, man by man,
Had fallen in Lyonesse about their Lord,
King Arthur : then, because his wound was
       deep,
The bold Sir Bedivere uplifted him,
Sir Bedivere, the last of all his knights,
And bore him to a chapel nigh the field,
A broken chancel with a broken cross,
That stood on a dark strait of barren land.
On one side lay the ocean, and on one
Lay a great water, and the moon was full.
   Then spake King Arthur to Sir Bedivere :
" The sequel of to-day unsolders all
The goodliest fellowship of famous knights
Whereof this world holds record.   Such a sleep
They sleep—the men I loved.   I think that we
Shall nevermore, at any future time,
Delight our souls with talk of knightly deeds,
Walking about the gardens and the halls
Of Camelot, as in the days that were.

I perish by this people which I made,—
Tho' Merlin sware that I should come again
To rule once more,—but let what will be, be,
I am so deeply smitten thro' the helm
That without help I cannot last till morn.
Thou, therefore, take my brand, Excalibur,
Which was my pride: for thou rememberest
    how
In those old days, one summer noon, an arm
Rose up from out the bosom of the lake,
Clothed in white samite, mystic, wonderful,
Holding the sword—and how I rowed across
And took it, and have worn it, like a king:
And, whensoever I am sung or told
In after time, this also shall be known:
But now delay not: take Excalibur
And fling him far into the middle mere:
Watch what thou seest, and lightly bring me
    word."
  To him replied the bold Sir Bedivere:
"It is not meet, Sir King, to leave thee thus,
Aidless, alone, and smitten through the helm.
A little thing may harm a wounded man,
Yet I thy hest will all perform at full,
Watch what I see, and lightly bring thee word."
  So saying, from the ruined shrine he stept
And in the moon athwart the place of tombs,
Where lay the mighty bones of ancient men,
Old knights, and over them the sea-wind sang

Shrill, chill, with flakes of foam.   He, stepping
 down
By zigzag paths and juts of pointed rock,
Came on the shining levels of the lake.
There drew he forth the brand Excalibur,
And o'er him, drawing it, the winter moon
Brightening the skirts of a long cloud, ran forth
And sparkled keen with frost against the hilt :
For all the haft twinkled with diamond sparks,
Myriads of topaz-lights and jacinth-work
Of subtlest jewelry.   He gazed so long
That both his eyes were dazzled, as he stood,
This way and that dividing the swift mind,
In act to throw : but at the last it seemed
Better to leave Excalibur concealed
There in the many-knotted water-flags
That whistled stiff and dry about the marge.
So strode he back slow to the wounded King.

 Then spake King Arthur to Sir Bedivere :
"Hast thou performed my mission which I gave ?
What is it thou hast seen ? or what hast heard ?"

 And answer made the bold Sir Bedivere :
" I heard the ripple washing in the reeds,
And the wild water lapping on the crag."

 To whom replied King Arthur, faint and pale :
" Thou hast betrayed thy nature and thy name,
Not rendering true answer, as beseemed
Thy fealty, nor like a noble knight :
For surer sign had followed, either hand,

Or voice, or else a motion of the mere.
This is a shameful thing for men to lie.
Yet now, I charge thee, quickly go again
As thou art lief and dear, and do the thing
I bad thee, watch, and lightly bring me word."

Then went Sir Bedivere the second time
Across the ridge and paced beside the mere,
Counting the dewy pebbles, fixed in thought;
But when he saw the wonder of the hilt,
How curiously and strangely chased, he smote
His palms together, and he cried aloud,
" And if, indeed, I cast the brand away,
Surely a precious thing, one worthy note,
Should thus be lost forever from the earth,
Which might have pleased the eyes of many
    men.
What good should follow this, if this were done ?
What harm, undone ? deep harm to disobey,
Seeing obedience is the bond of rule.
Were it well to obey then, if a king demand
An act unprofitable against himself ?"

   *   *   *   *   *   *

So spake he, clouded with his own conceit,
And hid Excalibur the second time,
And so strode back slow to the wounded King.

Then spoke King Arthur, breathing heavily :
" What is it thou hast ·seen ? or what hast
    heard ?"

And answer made the bold Sir Bedivere :

8

" I heard the water lapping on the crag,
And the long ripple washing in the reeds."
    To whom replied King Arthur much in wrath :
" Ah, miserable and unkind, untrue,
Unknightly, traitor-hearted! Woe is me!
Authority forgets a dying king,
Laid widowed of the power of his eye
That bowed the will.   I see thee what thou art ;
For thou, the latest left of all my knights,
In whom should meet the offices of all,
Thou wouldst betray me for the precious hilt ;
Either from lust of gold, or like a girl
Valuing the giddy pleasure of the eyes.
Yet, for a man may fail in duty twice,
And the third time may prosper, get thee hence ;
But, if thou spare to fling Excalibur,
I will arise and slay thee with my hands."
    Then quickly rose Sir Bedivere and ran,
And, leaping down the ridges lightly, plunged
Among the bulrush-beds, and clutched the sword
And strongly wheeled and threw it.   The great
        brand
Made lightnings in the splendor of the moon,
And flashing round and round, and whirled in an
        arch,
Shot like a streamer of the northern morn,
Seen where the moving isles of winter shock
By night, with noises of the northern sea,
So flashed and fell the brand Excalibur :

But ere he dipt the surface, rose an arm
Clothed in white samite, mystic, wonderful,
And caught him by the hilt and brandished him
Three times, and drew him under in the mere.
And lightly went the other to the King.

* * * * * *

Here ended Hall, and our last light, that long
Had winked, and threatened darkness, flared
  and fell:
At which the Parson, sent to sleep with sound,
And waked with silence, grunted "Good!" but
  we
Sat rapt: it was the tone with which he read—
Perhaps some modern touches here and there
Redeemed it from the charge of nothingness—
Or else we loved the man, and prized his work;
I know not; but we sitting as I said,
The cock crew loud; as at that time of year
The lusty bird takes every hour for dawn:
Then Francis, muttering, like a man ill-used,
"There now—that's nothing!" drew a little back,
And drove his heel into the smouldered log,
That sent a blast of sparkles up the flue:
And so to bed; where yet in sleep I seemed
To sail with Arthur under looming shores,
Point after point; till on to dawn, when dreams
Begin to feel the truth and stir of day,
To me, methought, who waited with a crowd,
Then came a bark that, blowing forward, bore

King Arthur, like a modern gentleman
Of stateliest port; and all the people cried,
" Arthur is come again : he cannot die."
Then those that stood upon the hills behind
Repeated " Come again, and thrice as fair;"
And, further inland, voices echoed, " Come
With all good things, and war shall be no more."
At this a hundred bells began to peal,
That with the sound I woke, and heard indeed
The clear church-bells ring in the Christmas
   morn.

Lord Tennyson.

THE COUNTRY LIFE.

For sports, for pageantries, and plays,
Thou hast thy eves and holidays
On which the young men and maids meet
To exercise their dancing feet,
Tripping the comely country-round,
With daffodils and daisies crowned.
Thy wakes, thy quintals, here thou hast,
Thy May-poles, too, with garlands graced,
Thy morris-dance, thy Whitsun-ale,
Thy shearing-feast, which never fail,
Thy harvest home, thy wassail-bowl,
That's tossed up after fox-i'-th'-hole,
Thy mummeries, thy Twelfthtide kings
And queens, thy Christmas revellings,
Thy nut-brown mirth, thy russet wit,
And no man pays too dear for it.

O happy life! if that their good
The husbandmen but understood,
Who all the day themselves do please
And younglings with such sports as these,
And, lying down, have naught t' affright
Sweet sleep, that makes more short the night.

Robert Herrick.

8*

CHRISTMAS OMNIPRESENT.

Christmas comes! He comes, he comes,
Ushered with a rain of plums;
Hollies in the windows greet him;
Schools come driving post to meet him;
Gifts precede him, bells proclaim him,
Every mouth delights to name him;
Wet, and cold, and wind, and dark
Make him but the warmer mark;
And yet he comes not one-embodied,
Universal 's the blithe godhead,
And in every festal house
Presence hath ubiquitous.
Curtains, those snug room-enfolders,
Hang upon his million shoulders,
And he has a million eyes
Of fire, and eats a million pies,
And is very merry and wise;
Very wise and very merry,
And loves a kiss beneath the berry.
Then full many a shape hath he,
All in said ubiquity:
Now is he a green array,
And now an " eve," and now a " day;"
Now he's town gone *out* of town,
And now a feast in civic gown,
And now the pantomime and clown

With a crack upon the crown,
And all sorts of tumbles down;
And then he's music in the night,
And the money gotten by't:
He's a man that can't write verses,
Bringing some to ope your purses:
He's a turkey, he's a goose,
He's oranges unfit for use;
He's a kiss that loves to grow
Underneath the mistletoe;
And he's forfeits, cards, and wassails,
And a king and queen with vassals,
All the "quizzes" of the time
Drawn and quarter'd with a rhyme;
And then, for their revival's sake,
Lo! he's an enormous cake,
With a sugar on the top,
Seen before in many a shop,
Where the boys could gaze forever,
They think the cake so very clever.
Then, some morning, in the lurch
Leaving romps, he goes to church,
Looking very grave and thankful,
After which he's just as prankful.
Now a saint, and now a sinner,
But, above all, he's a dinner;
He's a dinner, where you see
Everybody's family;

Beef, and pudding, and mince-pies,
And little boys with laughing eyes,
Whom their seniors ask arch questions,
Feigning fears of indigestions
As if they, forsooth, the old ones,
Hadn't, privately, tenfold ones:
He's a dinner and a fire,
Heap'd beyond your heart's desire,—
Heap'd with log, and bak'd with coals,
Till it roasts your very souls,
And your cheek the fire outstares,
And you all push back your chairs,
And the mirth becomes too great,
And you all sit up too late,
Nodding all with too much head,
And so go off to too much bed.

O plethora of beef and bliss!
Monkish feaster, sly of kiss!
Southern soul in body Dutch!
Glorious time of great Too-Much!
Too much heat and too much noise,
Too much babblement of boys;
Too much eating, too much drinking,
Too much ev'rything but thinking;
Solely bent to laugh and stuff,
And trample upon base Enough.
Oh, right is thy instructive praise
Of the wealth of Nature's ways!

Right thy most unthrifty glee,
And pious thy mince-piety!
For, behold! great Nature's self
Builds her no abstemious shelf,
But provides (her love is such
For all) her own great, good Too-Much,—
Too much grass, and too much tree,
Too much air, and land, and sea,
Too much seed of fruit and flower,
And fish, an unimagin'd dower!
(In whose single roe shall be
Life enough to stock the sea,—
Endless ichthyophagy!)
Ev'ry instant through the day
Worlds of life are thrown away;
Worlds of life, and worlds of pleasure,
Not for lavishment of treasure,
But because she's so immensely
Rich, and loves us so intensely.
She would have us, once for all,
Wake at her benignant call,
And all grow wise, and all lay down
Strife, and jealousy, and frown,
And, like the sons of one great mother,
Share, and be blest, with one another.

Leigh Hunt.

AN OLD ENGLISH CHRISTMAS-TIDE.

Thrice holy ring, afar and wide,
The merry bells this Christmas-tide ;
Afar and wide, through hushed snow,
From ivied minster-portico,
Sweet anthems swell to tell the tale
Of that young babe the shepherds hail
Sitting amid their nibbling flocks
What time the Hallelujah shocks
The drowsy earth, and Cherubim
Break through the heaven with harp and hymn.

Belated birds sing tingling notes
To warm apace their chilly throats,
Or they. mayhap, have caught the story
And pipe their part from branches hoary ;
While up aloft, his tempered beams
The sun has poured in gentle streams,
Sending o'er snowy hill and dell
A pleasance to greet the Christmas bell !
Now every yeoman starts abroad
For holly green and the ivy-tod ;
Good folk to kirk are soon atrip
Mellow with cheer and good-fellowship,
And cosey chimneys, here and there
Puff forth the sweets o' Christmas fare.

Ho! rosy wenches and merry men
From over the hill and field and fen,
Great store is here, the drifts between
Of myrtle red-berried, and mistletoe green!
Ho, Phyllis and Kate and bonny Nell
Come hither, and buffet the goodmen well,
An they gather not for hall and hearth,
Fair bays to grace the evening mirth.
Aye, laugh ye well! and echoed wide
Your voices sing through the Christmas-tide,
And wintry winds emblend their tones
At the minster-eaves with the organ groans:
The carols meet with laughter sweet
In a gay embrace mid the drifting sleet.

Anon the weary sun's at rest,
And clouds that hovered all day by,
Like silver arras down the sky
Enfold him—while the winds are whist—
But not the Christmas jollity,
For, little space, and wassail high
Flows at the board; and hautboys sound
The tripping dance and merry round.
Here youths and maidens stand in row
Kissing beneath the mistletoe;
And many a tale of midnight rout
O' Christmas-tide the woods about,
Of faery meetings beneath the moon
In wintry blast or summer swoon,

Goes round the hearth, while all aglow
The yule-log crackles the crane below.

Drink hael! good folk, by the chimney side,
O sweet's the holy Christmas-tide!
Drink hael! Drink hael! and pledge again :
" Here's peace on earth, good-will to men !"

H. S. M.

SIGNS OF CHRISTMAS.

When on the barn's thatch'd roof is seen
The moss in tufts of liveliest green;
When Roger to the wood pile goes,
And, as he turns, his fingers blows;
When all around is cold and drear,
Be sure that Christmas-tide is near.

When up the garden walk in vain
We seek for Flora's lovely train;
When the sweet hawthorn bower is bare,
And bleak and cheerless is the air;
When all seems desolate around,
Christmas advances o'er the ground.

When Tom at eve comes home from plough,
And brings the mistletoe's green bough,
With milk-white berries spotted o'er,
And shakes it the sly maids before,
Then hangs the trophy up on high,
Be sure that Christmas-tide is nigh.

When Hal, the woodman, in his clogs,
Bears home the huge unwieldly logs,
That, hissing on the smould'ring fire,
Flame out at last a quiv'ring spire;

III.—E   *g*   9

When in his hat the holly stands,
Old Christmas musters up his bands.

When cluster'd round the fire at night,
Old William talks of ghost and sprite,
And, as a distant out-house gate
Slams by the wind, they fearful wait,
While some each shadowy nook explore,
Then Christmas pauses at the door.

When Dick comes shiv'ring from the yard,
And says the pond is frozen hard,
While from his hat, all white with snow,
The moisture, trickling, drops below,
While carols sound, the night to cheer,
Then Christmas and his train are here.

Edwin Lees.

THE MISTLETOE.

When winter nights grow long,
  And winds without blow cold,
We sit in a ring round the warm wood-fire,
  And listen to stories old!
And we try to look grave, (as maids should be,)
When the men bring in boughs of the Laurel-
    tree.
   O the Laurel, the evergreen tree!
   The poets have laurels, and why not we?

How pleasant, when night falls down
  And hides the wintry sun,
To see them come in to the blazing fire,
  And know that their work is done;
Whilst many bring in, with a laugh or rhyme,
Green branches of Holly for Christmas time!
   O the Holly, the bright green Holly,
   It tells (like a tongue) that the times are jolly!

Sometimes—(in our grave house,
  Observe, this happeneth not;)
But, at times, the evergreen laurel boughs
  And the holly are all forgot!

And then ! what then ? why, the men laugh low,
And hang up a branch of the Mistletoe !
  O brave is the Laurel ! and brave is the Holly !
  But the Mistletoe banisheth melancholy !
  Ah, nobody knows, nor ever shall know,
  What is done—under the Mistletoe.
                    Bryan Waller Proctor.

CHRISTMAS OF OLD.

IN GERMANY.

Three weeks before the day whereon was born
    the Lord of grace,
And on the Thursday, boys and girls do run in
    every place,
And bounce and beat at every door, with blows
    and lusty snaps,
And cry the advent of the Lord, not born as
    yet, perhaps:
And wishing to the neighbors all, that in the
    houses dwell,
A happy year, and everything to spring and
    prosper well:
Here have they pears, and plums, and pence;
    each man gives willingly,
For these three nights are always thought un-
    fortunate to be,
Wherein they are afraid of sprites and cankered
    witches' spite,
And dreadful devils, black and grim, that then
    have chiefest might.

In these same days, young, wanton girls that
    meet for marriage be,

9*

Do search to know the names of them that
  shall their husbands be.
Four onions, five, or eight they take, and make
  in every one
Such names as they do fancy most and best do
  think upon.
Thus near the chimney then they set, and that
  same onion than
The first doth sprout doth surely bear the name
  of their good man.
Their husband's nature eke they seek to know
  and all his guise :
When as the sun hath hid himself, and left the
  starry skies,
Unto some woodstack do they go, and while
  they there do stand,
Each one draws out a fagot stick, the next
  that comes to hand,
Which if it straight and even be, and have no
  knots at all,
A gentle husband then they think shall surely
  to them fall ;
But, if it foul and crooked be, and knotty here
  and there,
A crabbed, churlish husband then they earnestly
  do fear.

Then comes the day wherein the Lord did bring
  his birth to pass,

Whereas at midnight up they rise, and every
 man to Mass.
This time so holy counted is, that divers
 earnestly
Do think the waters all to wine are changèd
 suddenly
In that same hour that Christ himself was
 born and came to light,
And unto water straight again transformed and
 altered quite.
There are beside that mindfully the money still
 do watch
That first to altar comes, which then they
 privily do snatch.
The priests, lest other should it have, take oft
 the same away,
Whereby they think throughout the year to
 have good luck in play,
And not to lose : then straight at game till daylight do they strive
To make some present proof how well their
 hallowed pence will thrive.

This done, a wooden child in clouts is on the
 altar set,
About the which both boys and girls do dance
 and trimly get,
And carols sing in praise of Christ, and for to
 help them here,

The organs answer every verse with sweet and
    solemn cheer.
The priests do roar aloud, and round about the
    parents stand,
To see the sport, and with their voice do help
    them and their hand.
Thus wont the Coribants perhaps upon the
    mountain Ide,
The crying noise of Jupiter, new born, with
    song to hide,
To dance about him round, and on their brazen
    pans to beat,
Lest that his father, finding him, should him
    destroy and eat.

Then followeth Saint Stephen's Day, whereon
    doth every man
His horses jaunt and course abroad, as swiftly
    as he can.
Until they do extremely sweat, and then they
    let them blood,
For this being done upon this day, they say
    doth do them good,
And keeps them from all maladies and sickness
    through the year,
As if that Stephen any time took charge of
    horses here.
Next, John, the son of Zebedee, hath his ap-
    pointed day,

Who once, by cruel tyrant's will, constrained
    was, they say,
Strong poison up to drink, therefore the Papists
    do believe
That whoso puts their trust in him, no poison
    them can grieve.
The wine beside that hallowed is, in worship of
    his name,
The priests do give the people that bring money
    for the same.
And after with the selfsame wine are little
    manchets* made,
Against the boisterous winter storms, and sun-
    dry such like trade.
The men upon this solemn day do take this
    holy wine,
To make them strong, so do the maids to make
    them fair and fine.

Then comes the day that calls to mind the cruel
    Herod's strife,
Who seeking Christ to kill, the King of ever-
    lasting life,
Destroyèd all the infants young, a beast un-
    merciless,
And put to death all such as were of two years
    age or less.

---

* White bread.

To them the sinful wretches cry and earnestly
    do pray
To get them pardon for their faults, and wipe
    their sins away.
The parents, when this day appears, do beat
    their children all
Though nothing they deserve, and servants all
    to beating fall,
And monks do whip each other well, or else
    their Prior great,
Or Abbot mad, doth take in hand their breeches
    all to beat
In worship of these Innocents, or rather, as we
    see,
In honor of the curséd king that did this
    cruelty.

The next to this is New-Year's Day, whereon
    to every friend
They costly presents in do bring and New-
    Year's gifts do send.
These gifts the husband gives his wife, and
    father eke the child,
And master on his men bestows the like, with
    favor mild,
And good beginning of the year they wish and
    wish again,
According to the ancient guise of heathen people
    vain.

These eight days no man doth require his debts
of any man,
Their tables do they furnish out with all the
meat they can:
With marchpanes, tarts, and custards great they
drink with staring eyes,
They rout and revel, feed and feast as merry
all as pies,
As if they should at the entrance of this New
Year have to die,
Yet would they have their bellies full and
ancient friends ally.

The Wise Men's day here followeth, who out
from Persia far,
Brought gifts and presents unto Christ, con-
ducted by a star.
The Papists do believe that these were kings,
and so them call,
And do affirm that of the same there were but
three in all.
Here sundry friends together come, and meet
in company,
And make a king amongst themselves by voice
or destiny;
Who, after princely guise, appoints his officers
alway,
Then unto feasting do they go, and long time
after play:

Upon their boards, in order thick, their dainty
      dishes stand,
Till that their purses empty be and creditors at
      hand.
Their children herein follow them, and choosing
      princes here,
With pomp and great solemnity, they meet and
      make good cheer
With money either got by stealth, or of their
      parents eft,
That so they may be trained to know both riot
      here and theft.
Then, also, every householder, to his ability,
Doth make a mighty cake that may suffice his
      company :
Herein a penny doth he put, before it comes to
      fire,
This he divides according as his household doth
      require ;
And every piece distributeth, as round about
      they stand,
Which in their names unto the poor is given
      , out of hand.
But whoso chanceth on the piece wherein the
      money lies
Is counted king amongst them all, and is with
      shouts and cries
Exalted to the heavens up, who, taking chalk
      in hand,

Doth make a cross on every beam and rafters
    as they stand:
Great force and power have these against all
    injuries and harms,
Of cursed devils, sprites and bugs, of conjurings
    and charms.
So much this king can do, so much the crosses .
    bring to pass,
Made by some servant, maid or child, or by
    some foolish ass!

Twice six nights then from Christmas they do
    count with diligence,
Wherein each master in his house doth burn up
    frankincense:
And on the table sets a loaf, when night ap-
    proacheth near,
Before the coals and frankincense to be per-
    fumed there:
First bowing down his head he stands, and nose,
    and ears, and eyes
He smokes, and with his mouth receives the
    fume that doth arise; .
Whom followeth straight his wife, and doth the
    same full solemnly,
And of their children every one, and all their
    family:
Which doth preserve, they say, their teeth, and
    nose, and eyes, and ear
10

From every kind of malady and sickness all
the year.

When every one receivéd hath this odor great
and small,

Then one takes up the pan with coals, and
frankincense and all.

Another takes the loaf, whom all the rest do
follow here,

And round about the house they go, with torch
or taper clear,

That neither bread nor meat do want; nor
witch with dreadful charm

Have power to hurt their children, or to do their
cattle harm.

There are that three nights only do perform
this foolish gear,

To this intent, and think themselves in safety
all the year.

To Christ dare none commit himself.   And in
these days beside

They judge what weather all the year shall
happen and betide:

Ascribing to .each day a month, and at this
present time

The youth in every place do flock, and all
apparelled fine,

With pipers through the streets they run, and
sing at every door

In commendation of the man, rewarded well
    therefore,
Which on themselves they do bestow, or on the
    church as though
The people were not plagued with rogues and
    begging friars enow.
There cities are where boys and girls together
    still do run
About the streets with like as soon as night
    begins to come,
And bring abroad their wassail-bowls, who well
    rewarded be
With cakes, and cheese, and great good cheer,
    and money plenteously.

From the German of Thos. Kirchmaier, A.D. 1553.

A PLEA FOR A PRESENT.

Father John Burges,
Necessity urges
My woeful cry
To Sir Robert Pie:
And that he will venture
To send my debenture.
Tell him his Ben
Knew the time when
He loved the Muses;
Though now he refuses
To take apprehension
Of a year's pension,
And more is behind;
Put him in mind
Christmas is near,
And neither good cheer,
Mirth, fooling, nor wit,
Nor any least fit
Of gambol or sport
Will come to the court
If there be no money,
No plover or cony
Will come to the table,
Or wine to enable

The muse, or the poet,
The parish will know it
Nor any quick warming-pan help him to bed;
If the 'Chequer be empty, so will be his head.

Ben Jonson.

A NEW-YEAR'S GIFT SENT TO SIR SIMEON STEWARD.

No news of navies burnt at sea,
No noise of late-spawned Tityries,
No closet plot or open vent
That frights men with a Parliament:
No new device or late-found trick,
To read by the stars the kingdom's sick;
No gin to catch the State, or wring
The free-born nostrils of the king,
We send to you, but here a jolly
Verse crowned with ivy and with holly;
That tells of winter's tales and mirth
That milkmaids make about the hearth,
Of Christmas sports. the wassail-bowl,
That's tost up after fox-i'-th'-hole;
Of Blindman-buff, and of the care
That young men have to shoe the mare;
Of Twelve-tide cake, of peas and beans,
Wherewith ye make those merry scenes,
When as ye choose your king and queen,
And cry out: Hey, for our town green!
Of ash-heaps, in the which ye use
Husbands and wives by streaks to choose;
Of crackling laurel, which foresounds
A plenteous harvest to your grounds;

Of these and such like things, for shift,
We send instead of New-Year's gift:
Read then, and when your faces shine
With buxom meat and cap'ring wine,
Remember us in cups full-crowned,
And let our city-health go round,
Quite through the young maids and the men
To the ninth number, if not ten;
Until the fired chestnuts leap
For joy to see the fruits ye reap
From the plump chalice and the cup
That tempts till it be tosséd up.
Then, as ye sit about your embers,
Call not to mind those fled Decembers;
But think on these that are to appear
As daughters to the instant year;
Sit crowned with rose-buds, and carouse,
Till *Liber Pater* twirls the house
About your ears; and lay upon
The year, your cares, that's fled and gone.
And let the russet swains the plough
And harrow hang up resting now;
And to the bagpipe all address
Till sleep takes place of weariness;
And thus, throughout, with Christmas plays
Frolic the full twelve holydays.

Robert Herrick.

THE NEW-YEAR'S GIFT.

Let others look for pearl and gold
Tissues, or tabbies manifold;
One only lock of that sweet hay
Whereon the Blessed Baby lay,
Or one poor swaddling-clout, shall be
The richest New-Year's gift to me.

Robert Herrick.

AN INVITATION TO THE REVEL.

Come follow, follow me,
Those that good fellows be,
Into the buttery
Our manhood for to try ;
The master keeps a bounteous house,
And gives leave freely to carouse.

Then wherefore should we fear,
Seeing here is store of cheer ?
It shows but cowardice
At this time to be nice.
Then boldly draw your blades and fight,
For we shall have a merry night.

When we have done this fray,
Then we will go to play
At cards or else at dice,
And be rich in a trice ;
Then let the knaves go round apace,
I hope each time to have an ace.

Come, maids, let's want no beer
After our Christmas cheer,
And I will duly crave
Good husbands you may have,

And that you may good houses keep,
When we may drink carouses deep.

And when that's spent the day
We'll Christmas gambols play,
At hot cockles beside
And then go to all-hide,
With many other pretty toys,
Men, women, youths, maids, girls, and boys.

Come, let's dance round the hall,
And let's for liquor call;
Put apples in the fire,
Sweet maids, I you desire;
And let a bowl be spiced well
Of happy stuff that doth excel.

Twelve days we now have spent
In mirth and merriment,
And daintily did fare,
For which we took no care:
But now I sadly call to mind
What days of sorrow are behind.

We must leave off to play,
To-morrow's working-day;
According to each calling
Each man must now be falling,

And ply his business all the year
Next Christmas for to make good cheer.

Now of my master kind
Good welcome I did find,
And of my loving mistress
This merry time of Christmas;
For which to them great thanks I give,
God grant they long together live.

A CHRISTMAS DITTY.

Sweep the ingle, froth the beer,
Tiptoe on till chanticleer,
Loose the laugh, dry the tear,—
    Crack the drums
    When Christmas comes!

AT THE END OF THE FEAST.

Mark well my heavy, doleful tale,
   For Twelfth-day now is come,
And now I must no longer sing,
   And say no words but mum ;
For I perforce must take my leave
   Of all my dainty cheer,
Plum-porridge, roast-beef, and minced-pies,
   My strong ale and my beer.

Kind-hearted Christmas, now adieu,
   For I with thee must part,
And for to take my leave of thee
   Doth grieve me at the heart ;
Thou wert an ancient housekeeper,
   And mirth with meat didst keep,
But thou art going out of town,
   Which makes me for to weep.

God knoweth whether I again
   Thy merry face shall see,
Which to good fellows and the poor
   That was so frank and free.
Thou lovedst pastime with thy heart,
   And eke good company ;
Pray hold me up for fear I swoon,
   For I am like to die.

F   11

Come, butler, fill a brimmer up
　　To cheer my fainting heart,
That to old Christmas I may drink
　　Before he doth depart ;
And let each one that's in this room
　　With me likewise condole,
And for to cheer their spirits sad
　　Let each one drink a bowl.

And when the same it hath gone round
　　Then fall unto your cheer,
For you do know that Christmas time
　　It comes but once a year.
But this good draught which I have drunk
　　Hath comforted my heart,
For I was very fearful that
　　My stomach would depart.

Thanks to my master and my dame
　　That doth such cheer afford ;
God bless them, that each Christmas they
　　May furnish thus their board.
My stomach having come to me,
　　I mean to have a bout,
Intending to eat most heartily ;
　　Good friends, I do not flout.

New Christmas Carols, A. D. 1642.

TWELFTH NIGHT; OR, KING AND QUEEN.

Now, now the mirth comes
With the cake full of plums,
Where bean's the king of the sport here;
Beside, we must know
The pea also
Must revel as queen in the court here.

Begin then to choose,
This night, as ye use,
Who shall for the present delight here;
Be a king by the lot,
And who shall not
Be Twelve-day queen for the night here!

Which known, let us make
Joy-sops with the cake;
And let not a man then be seen here,
Who unurged will not drink,
To the base from the brink,
A health to the king and the queen here!

Next crown the bowl full
With gentle lamb's wool,
And sugar, nutmeg, and ginger,

With store of ale, too ;
And this ye must do
To make the wassail a swinger.

Give then to the king
And queen, wassailing,
And though with ale ye be wet here,
Yet part ye from hence
As free from offence
As when ye innocent met here

Robert Herrick.

CEREMONIES FOR CANDLEMAS EVE.

Down with the rosemary and bays,
  Down with the mistletoe ;
Instead of holly, now upraise
  The greener box for show.

The holly hitherto did sway ;
  Let box now domineer
Until the dancing Easter day
  Or Easter's eve appear.

Then youthful box, which now hath grace
  Your houses to renew,
Grown old, surrender must his place
  Unto the crispéd yew.

When yew is out, then birch comes in,
  And many flowers beside,
Both of a fresh and fragrant kin,
  To honor Whitsuntide.

Green rushes then, and sweetest bents,
  With cooler oaken boughs,
Come in for comely ornaments,
  To readorn the house.
Thus times do shift, each thing his turn does hold;
New things succeed as former things grow old.
                              Robert Herrick.

11*

ANOTHER CEREMONY.

Down with the rosemary, and so
Down with the bays and mistletoe;
Down with the holly, ivy, all
Wherewith ye dressed the Christmas hall,
That so the superstitious find
No one last branch there left behind;
For, look! how many leaves there be
Neglected there, maids, trust to me
So many goblins you shall see.

Robert Herrick.

THE CEREMONIES FOR CANDLEMAS DAY.

Kindle the Christmas brand, and then
   Till sunset let it burn,
Which quenched, then lay it up again
   Till Christmas next return.   .

Part must be kept, wherewith to teend
   The Christmas log next year,
And where 'tis safely kept, the fiend
   Can do no mischief there.
                    Robert Herrick.

ANOTHER CEREMONY.

End now the white-loaf and the pie,
And let all sports with Christmas die.
                    Robert Herrick.

SAINT DISTAFF'S DAY, THE MORROW
AFTER TWELFTH DAY.

Partly work and partly play
Ye must on St. Distaff's day;
From the plough soon free your team,
Then come home and fodder them;
If the maids a-spinning go,
Burn the flax and fire the tow;
Scorch their plackets, but beware
That ye singe no maiden-hair;
Bring in pails of water then,
Let the maids bewash the men;
Give St. Distaff all the right,
Then bid Christmas sport good-night,
And next morrow every one
To his own vocation.

Robert Herrick.

The Shepherds.

"His place of birth a solemn
        angel tells
To   simple   shepherds   keeping
        watch by night."

Milton.

III.—*i*

❦

ON OATEN PIPES.

As I rode out this enderes night,
Of three ioli sheppardes I saw a sight,
And all abowte there fold a star shone bright ;
 They sang, terli, terlow ;
So mereli the sheppardes their pipes can blow.

Doune from heaven, from heaven so hie,
Of angeles ther came a great companie,
With mirthe, and joy, and great solemnitye,
 The sange, terly, terlow ;
So mereli the sheppardes their pipes can blow.
Coventry Mysteries.

PIPE-PLAYING.

*Tyrle, Tyrle, so Merrily the Shepherds began
to Blow.*

About the field they piped full right,
Even about the midst of the night;
Adown from heaven they saw come a light,
    Tyrle, tyrle.

Of angels there came a company
With merry songs and melody,
The shepherds anon gan them espy,
    Tyrle, tyrle.

Gloria in excelsis the angels sung,
And said how peace was present among,
To every man that to the faith would 'long,
    Tyrle, tyrle.

The shepherds hied them to Bethlehem
To see that blessed sun's beam;
And there they found that glorious stream,
    Tyrle, tyrle.

Now pray we to that meek Child,
And to his mother that is so mild,
The which was never defiled,
    Tyrle, tyrle.

That we may come unto his bliss,
Where joy shall never miss;
That we may sing in Paradise,

     Tyrle, tyrle.

I pray you all that be here
For to sing and make good cheer,
In the worship of God this year,

     Tyrle, tyrle.
   Wright's Songs and Carols.

12

THE FIRST CAROL.

The first Nowell the Angel did say
Was to three poor Shepherds in the fields as
    they lay;
In fields where they lay keeping their sheep,
In a cold winter's night that was so deep.
    Nowell, Nowell, Nowell, Nowell,
    Born is the King of Israel.

They looked up and saw a Star
Shining in the East beyond them far;
And to the earth it gave great light,
And so it continued both day and night.
    Nowell, Nowell, Nowell, Nowell,
    Born is the King of Israel.

And by the light of that same Star
Three Wise Men came from country far;
To seek for a King was their intent,
And to follow the Star wherever it went.
    Nowell, Nowell, Nowell, Nowell,
    Born is the King of Israel.

The Star drew nigh to the northwest,
O'er Bethlehem it took its rest,

And there it did both stop and stay
Right over the place where Jesus lay.
    Nowell, Nowell, Nowell, Nowell,
    Born is the King of Israel.

Then did they know assuredly
Within that house the King did lie:
One enter'd in then for to see,
And found the Babe in poverty.
    Nowell, Nowell, Nowell, Nowell,
    Born is the King of Israel.

Then enter'd in those Wise Men three
Most reverently upon their knee,
And offer'd there in his presence
Both gold, and myrrh, and frankincense.
    Nowell, Nowell, Nowell, Nowell,
    Born is the King of Israel.

Between an ox-stall and an ass
This Child truly there born he was;
For want of clothing they did him lay
All in the manger among the hay.
    Nowell, Nowell, Nowell, Nowell,
    Born is the King of Israel.

Then let us all with one accord
Sing praises to our Heavenly Lord,

That hath made heaven and earth of naught,
And with his blood mankind hath bought.
    Nowell, Nowell, Nowell, Nowell,
    Born is the King of Israel.

If we in our time shall do well,
We shall be free from death and hell;
For God hath prepared for us all
A resting-place in general.
    Nowell, Nowell, Nowell, Nowell,
    Born is the King of Israel.

IN BETHLEHEM.

In Bethlehem, that noble place,
As by the Prophet said it was,
Of the Virgin Mary, filled with grace.
  Salvator mundi natus est.
  Be we merry in this feast,
  In quo Salvator natus est.

On Christmas night an Angel told
The shepherds watching by their fold,
In Bethlehem, full nigh the wold,
  " *Salvator mundi natus est.*"
  Be we merry in this feast,
  In quo Salvator natus est.

The shepherds were encompassed right,
About them shone a glorious light,
" Dread ye naught," said the Angel bright,
  " *Salvator mundi natus est.*"
  Be we merry in this feast,
  In quo Salvator natus est.

" No cause have ye to be afraid,
For why ? this day is Jesus laid
On Mary's lap, that gentle maid :
  12*

Salvator mundi natus est.
Be we merry in this feast,
In quo Salvator natus est.

" And thus in faith find him ye shall
Laid poorly in an ox's stall."
The shepherds then lauded God all,
Quia Salvator natus est.
Be we merry in this feast,
In quo Salvator natus est.

Christmas Carolles, A.D. 1550.

A CAROL IN THE PASTURES.

Sweet music, sweeter far
 Than any song is sweet:
Sweet music, heavenly rare,
 Mine ears, O peers, doth greet.
You gentle flocks, whose fleeces, pearled with
 dew,
 Resemble heaven, whom golden drops make
 bright,
Listen, O listen, now, O not to you
 Our pipes make sport to shorten weary night;
 But voices most divine
  Make blissful harmony:
 Voices that seem to shine,
  For what else clears the sky?
Tunes can we hear, but not the singers see,
The tunes divine, and so the singers be.

 Lo, how the firmament
  Within an azure fold
 The flock of stars hath pent,
  That we might them behold;
Yet from their beams proceedeth not this light,
 Nor can their crystals such reflection give.
What then doth make the element so bright?
 The heavens are come down upon earth to
 live.

But hearken to the song,
    Glory to glory's king,
And peace all men among,
    These quiristers do sing.
Angels they are, as also (Shepherds) he
Whom in our fear we do admire to see.

Let not amazement blind
    Your souls, said he, annoy:
To you and all mankind
    My message bringeth joy.
For lo, the world's great Shepherd now is born,
    A blessed babe, an infant full of power:
After long night uprisen is the morn,
    Renowning Bethl'em in the Saviour.
Sprung is the perfect day,
    By prophets seen afar:
Sprung is the mirthful May,
    Which winter cannot mar.
In David's city doth this sun appear
Clouded in flesh, yet, shepherds, sit we here?

Edward Bolton.

THE SHEPHERDS.

Sweet, harmless livers! on whose holy leisure
  Waits innocence and pleasure;
Whose leaders to those pastures and clear
    springs
  Were patriarchs, saints, and kings;
How happened it that in the dead of night
  You only saw true light,
While Palestine was fast asleep and lay
  Without one thought of day?
Was it because those first and blesséd swains
  Were pilgrims on those plains
When they received the promise, for which now
  'Twas there first shown to you?
'Tis true he loves that dust whereon they go
  That serve him here below,
And therefore might for memory of those
  His love then first disclose;
But wretched Salem, once his love, must now
  No voice nor vision know;
Her stately piles with all their height and pride
  Now languishéd and died,
And Bethl'em's humble cots above them stept
  While all her seers slept;
Her cedar fir, hewed stones, and gold were all
  Polluted through their fall;

And those once sacred mansions were now
    Mere emptiness and show.
This made the angel call at reeds and thatch,
    Yet where the shepherds watch,
And God's own lodging, though he could not
    lack,
    To be a common rack.
No costly pride, no soft-clothed luxury
    In those thin cells could lie ;
Each stirring wind and storm blew through
    their cots,
    Which never harbored plots ;
Only content and love and humble joys
    Lived there without all noise ;
Perhaps some harmless cares for the next day
    Did in their bosoms play :
As where to lead their sheep, what silent nook,
    What springs or shades to look ;
But that was all ; and now with gladsome
    care
    They for the town prepare ;
They leave their flock, and in a busy talk
    All towards Bethl'em walk,
To seek their soul's great Shepherd who was
    come
    To bring all stragglers home ;
Where now they find him out, and, taught
    before,
    The Lamb of God adore,

That Lamb, whose days great kings and proph-
    ets wished
  And longed to see, but missed.
The first light they beheld was bright and gay,
  And turned their night to day ;
But to this later light they saw in him,
  Their day was dark and dim.
Henry Vaughan.

ON SHEPHERDS' PIPES.

O than the fairest day, thrice fairer night!
  Night to blest days in which a sun doth rise
  Of which that golden age which clears the
      skies
Is but a sparkling ray, a shadow-light!
And blessed ye, in silly pastors' sight,
  Mild creatures, in whose warm crib now lies
  That heaven-sent youngling, holy-maid-born
      wight:
Midst, end, beginning of our prophecies!
Blest cottage that hath flowers in winter spread,
  Though withered—blessed grass that hath the
      grace
  To deck and be a carpet to that place!
Thus sang, unto the sounds of oaten reed,
  Before the Babe, the shepherds bowed on
      knees;
  And springs ran nectar, honey dropped from
      trees.

William Drummond.

ANGEL TIDINGS.

Run, shepherds, run where Bethlehem blest
   appears.
We bring the best of news ; be not dismayed ;
A Saviour there is born more old than years,
Amidst heaven's rolling height this earth who
   stayed.
In a poor cottage inned, a virgin maid
   A weakling did him bear, who all upbears ;
There is he poorly swaddled, in manger laid,
To whom too narrow swaddlings are our
   spheres :
Run, shepherds, run, and solemnize his birth.
   This is that night—no, day, grown great with
   bliss,
   In which the power of Satan broken is :
In Heaven be glory, peace unto the earth !
   Thus singing, through the air the angels
   swam,
   And cope of stars re-echoéd the same.
              William Drummond.

THE NEWS-BEARERS.

The shepherds went their hasty way,
  And found the lowly stable-shed
Where the Virgin-Mother lay ;
  And now they checked their eager tread,
For to the Babe that at her bosom clung,
A mother's song the Virgin-Mother sung.

They told her how a glorious light,
  Streaming from a heavenly throng,
Around them shone, suspending night!
  While sweeter than a mother's song,
Blest angels heralded the Saviour's birth,
Glory to God on high ! and peace on earth !

She listened to the tale divine,
  And closer still the Babe she prest;
And while she cried, the Babe is mine !
  The milk rushed faster to her breast ;
Joy rose within her like a summer's morn ;
Peace, peace on earth ! the Prince of peace is
    born.

Thou Mother of the Prince of peace,
  Poor, simple, and of low estate !

That strife should vanish, battle cease,
  O why should this thy soul elate?
Sweet music's loudest note, the poet's story,—
Didst thou ne'er love to hear of fame and
    glory?

And is not war a youthful king,
  A stately hero ciad in mail?
Beneath his footsteps laurels spring;
  Him earth's majestic monarchs hail
Their friend, their playmate! and his bold
    bright eye
Compels the maiden's love-confessing sigh.

"Tell this in some more courtly scene,
  To maids and youths in robes of state!
I am a woman poor and mean,
  And therefore is my soul elate;
War is a ruffian all with guilt defiled,
That from the aged father tears his child.

"A murderous fiend by fiends adored,
  He kills the sire and starves the son;
The husband kills and from her board
  Steals all his widow's toil had won;
Plunders God's world of beauty; rends away
All safety from the night, all comfort from
    the day.

" Then wisely is my soul elate
   That strife should vanish, battle cease;
I'm poor and of a low estate,
   The Mother of the Prince of peace,
Joy rises in me, like a summer's morn :
Peace, peace on earth ! the Prince of peace is
    born !"

Samuel Taylor Coleridge.

HYMN FOR CHRISTMAS-DAY.

(BEING A DIALOGUE BETWEEN THREE SHEPHERDS.)

Where is this blessed Babe
        That hath made
All the world so full of joy
        And expectation;
        That glorious boy
        That crowns each nation
With a triumphant wreath of blessedness?

Where should he be but in the throng,
        And among
His angel ministers, that sing
        And take wing
Just as may echo to his voice,
        And rejoice,
When wing and tongue and all
May so procure their happiness?

But he hath other waiters now:
        A poor cow,
An ox and mule, stand and behold,
        And wonder
That a stable should enfold
        Him that can thunder.

O what a gracious God have we,
How good! how great! even as our misery.
Jeremy Taylor.

13*

A HYMN OF THE NATIVITY.

(SUNG AS BY THE SHEPHERDS.)

Come we shepherds whose blest sight
Hath met Love's noon in Nature's night;
Come, lift we up our loftier song,
And wake the sun that lies too long.

To all our world of well-stol'n joy,
 He slept and dreamt of no such thing,
While we found out heaven's fairer eye
 And kist the cradle of our King; ´
Tell him he rises now too late
To show us aught worth looking at.

Tell him we now can show him more
 Then e'er he showed to mortal sight,
Than he himself e'er saw before,
 Which to be seen needs not his light.
Tell him, Tityrus, where th' hast been,
Tell him, Thyrsis, what th' hast seen.

Tityrus.

Gloomy night embraced the place
 Where the noble Infant lay,
The Babe looked up and showed his face;
 In spite of darkness it was day:

It was thy day, Sweet, and did rise
Not from the East, but from thine eyes.
      CHORUS.—It was thy day, Sweet, etc.

Thyrsis.

Winter chid aloud and sent
  The angry North to wage his wars ;
The North forgot his fierce intent,
  And left perfumes instead of scars ;
By those sweet eyes' persuasive powers,
Where he meant frost he scattered flowers.
      CHORUS.—By those sweet eyes, etc.

Both.

We saw thee in thy balmy nest,
  Bright dawn of our eternal day !
We saw thine eyes break from their East
  And chase the trembling shades away ;
We saw thee, and we blest the sight,
We saw thee by thine own sweet light.

Tityrus.

Poor world (said I), what wilt thou do
  To entertain this starry stranger ?
Is this the best thou canst bestow,
  A cold and not too cleanly manger.
Contend, ye powers of heaven and earth,
To fit a bed for this huge birth.
      CHORUS.—Contend, ye powers, etc.

Thyrsis.

Proud world (said I), cease your contest,
  And let the mighty Babe alone ;
The Phœnix builds the Phœnix nest,
  Love's architecture is all one.
The Babe whose birth embraves this morn
Made his own bed ere he was born.
      CHORUS.—The Babe whose birth, etc.

Tityrus.

I saw the curl'd drops, soft and slow,
  Come hovering o'er the place's head,
Offering their whitest sheets of snow
  To furnish the fair Infant's bed :
Forbear (said I), be not too bold ;
Your fleece is white, but 'tis too cold.
      CHORUS.—Forbear (said I), etc.

Thyrsis.

I saw the obsequious seraphins
  Their rosy fleece of fire bestow ;
For well they now can spare their wings,
  Since heaven itself lies here below :
Well done (said I), but are you sure
Your down so warm will pass for pure.
      CHORUS.—Well done (said I), etc.

Tityrus.

No, no, your king's not yet to seek
  Where to repose his royal head ;

See, see, how soon his new-bloom'd cheek
　Twixt's mother's breasts is gone to bed :
Sweet choice (said I), no way but so,
Not to lie cold, yet sleep in snow.
　　　　CHORUS.—Sweet choice (said I), etc.

Both.

We saw thee in thy balmy nest,
　Bright dawn of our eternal day !
We saw thine eyes break from their East
　And chase the trembling shades away ;
We saw thee, and we blest the sight,
We saw thee by thine own sweet light.
　　　　CHORUS.—We saw thee, etc.

Full Chorus.

Welcome, all wonder in one sight,
　Eternity shut in a span,
Summer in winter, day in night,
　Heaven in earth and God in man !
Great little One ! whose all-embracing birth
Lifts earth to heaven, stoops heaven to earth.

Welcome, though not to gold nor silk,
　To more than Cæsar's birthright is,
Two Sister Seas of Virgin milk
　With many a rarely-tempered kiss,
That breathes at once both Maid and Mother,
Warms in the one and cools in the other.

She sings thy tears asleep, and dips
    Her kisses in thy weeping eye;
She spreads the red leaves of thy lips
    That in their buds yet blushing lie:
She 'gainst those mother-diamonds tries
The points of her young eagle's eyes.

Welcome, though not to those gay flies
    Gilded i' the beams of earthly kings,
Slippery souls in smiling eyes,
    But to poor shepherds' homespun things;
Whose wealth's their flock, whose wit to be
Well read in their simplicity.

Yet when young April's husband-showers
    Shall bless the fruitful Maia's bed,
We'll bring the first-born of her flowers
    To kiss thy feet and crown thy head:
To thee, dread Lamb, whose love must keep
The shepherds more than they their sheep.

To thee, meek Majesty! soft King
    Of simple graces and sweet loves,
Each of us his lamb will bring,
    Each his pair of silver doves,
Till burnt at last in fire of thy fair eyes
Ourselves become our own best sacrifice.

                            Richard Crashaw.

SUNG BY THE SHEPHERD.

The New Year is begun,
   Good-morrow, my masters all!
The cheerful rising sun
   Now shining in this hall,
      Brings mirth and joy
      To man and boy.
With all that here doth dwell;
     Whom Jesus bless
     With love's increase,
So all things shall prosper well.

A New-Year's gift I bring
   Unto my master here,
Which is a welcome thing
   Of mirth and merry cheer.
     A New-Year's lamb
     Come from thy dam
An hour before daybreak,
     Your noted ewe
     Doth this bestow,
Good master, for your sake.

And to my dame so kind
   This New-Year's gift I bring;

I'll bear an honest mind
　　Unto her whilst I live.
　　　　Your white-woolled sheep
　　　　I'll safely keep
From harm of bush or brere,
　　　　That garments gay
　　　　For your array
May clothe you the next New Year.

And to your children all,
　　These New-Year's gifts I bring;
And though the price be small,
　　They're fit for queen or king:
　　　　Fair pippins red
　　　　Kept in my bed
A-mellowing since last year,
　　　　Whose beauty bright
　　　　So clear of sight
Their hearts will glad and cheer.

And to your maids and men
　　I bring both points and pins;
Come bid me welcome then,
　　The good New Year begins:
　　　　And for my love
　　　　Let me approve
The friendship of your Maid,
　　　　Whose nappy ale,
　　　　So good and stale,
Will make my wits afraid.

I dare not with it deal
   But in a sober diet:
If I, poor shepherd, steal
   A draught to be unquiet,
      And lose my way
      This New-Year's day
As I go to my fold,
      You'll surely think
      My love of drink
This following year will hold.

Here stands my bottle and hook,
   Good kitchen-maid, draw near,
Thou art an honest cook,
   And canst brew ale and beer;
      Thy office show,
      Before I go,
My bottle and bag come fill,
      And for thy sake
      I'll merry make
Upon the next green hill.
               New Christmas Carols.

14

FROM "THE LIGHT OF THE WORLD."

AT BETHLEHEM.

So many hills arising, green and gray,
On Earth's large round, and that one hill to
    say:
"I was his bearing-place!"   On Earth's wide
    breast
So many maids! and she—of all most blest—
Heavily mounting Bethlehem, to be
His Mother!—Holy Maid of Galilee!
Hill, with the olives, and the little town!
If rivers from their crystal founts flow down,
If 'twas the dawn which did day's gold unbar,
Ye were beginnings of the best we are,
The most we see, the highest that we know,
The lifting heavenward of man's life below.
Therefore, though better lips ye shall not lack,
Suffer if one of modern mood steals back—
Weary and wayworn from the desert-road
Of barren thought; from Hope's Dead Sea,
    which glowed
With Love's fair mirage; from the poet's haunt,
The scholar's lamp, the statesman's scheme, the
    vaunt,

The failure, of all fond philosophies,—
Back unto Thee, back to thy olive-trees,
Thy people, and thy story, and thy Son,
Mary of Nazareth! So long agone
Bearing us Him who made our christendom,
And came to save the earth, from heav'n, His
      home.

So many hill-sides, crowned with rugged rocks!
So many simple shepherds keeping flocks
In many moonlit fields! but, only they—
So lone, so long ago, so far away—
On that one winter's night, at Bethlehem,
To have white angels singing lauds for them!
They only—hinds wrapped in the he-goat's
      skin—
To hear heaven's music, bidding peace begin!
Only for those, of countless watching eyes,
The "Glory of the Lord" glad to arise;
The skies to blaze with gold and silver light
Of seraphs by strong joy flashed into sight;
The wind, for them, with that strange song to
      swell,—
By too much happiness incredible—
That tender anthem of good times to be,
Then at their dawn—not daylight yet, ah me!
"Peace upon earth! Good-will!" sung to the
      strings
Of lutes celestial. Nay, if these things

Too blessëd to believe have seemed, or seem,
Not ours the fault, dear angels!   Prove the
    dream
Waking and true! sing once again, and make
Moonlight and starlight sweet for earth's sad
    sake!
Or, if heaven bids ye lock in silence still
Conquest of peace, and coming of good-will,
Till times to be, then—oh, you placid sheep!
Ah, thrice-blest shepherds! suffer if we creep
Back through the tangled thicket of the years
To graze in your fair flock, to strain our ears
With listening herdsmen, if, perchance, one
    note
Of such high singing in the fine air float;
If any rock thrills yet with that great strain
We did not hear, and shall not hear, again;
If any olive-leaf at Bethlehem
Lisps still one syllable vouchsafed to them;
If some stream, conscious still—some breeze—
    be stirred ·
With echo of th' immortal words ye heard.

What was it that ye heard? the wind of night
Playing in cheating tones, with touches light,
Amid the palm-plumes? or, one stop outblown
Of planetary music, so far flown
Earthwards, that to those innocent ears 'twas
    brought

Which bent the mighty measure to their
    thought?
Or, haply, from breast-shaped Beth-Haccarem,
The hill of Herod, some waft sent to them
Of storming drums and trumps, at festival
Held in the Idumæan's purple hall?
Or, it may be, some Aramaic song
Of country lovers, after partings long
Meeting anew, with much "good will" indeed,
Blown by some swain upon his Jordan reed?
Nay, nay! your abbas back ye did not fling,
From each astonished ear, for swains to sing
Their village-verses clear; for sounds well-
    known
Of wandering breeze, or whispering trees, or
    tone
Of Herod's trumpets.   And ye did not gaze
Heart-startled on the stars (albeit the rays
Of that lone orb shot, sparkling, from the east
Unseen before), for these, largest and least,
Were fold-lamps, lighted nightly: and ye knew
Far differing glory in the night's dark blue
Suddenly lit with rose, and pierced with spike
Of golden spear-beam.   Oh, a dream, belike!
Some far-fetched vision, new to peasant's sleep,
Of paradise stripped bare!—But, why thus
    keep
Secrets for them?   This bar, which doth enclose
Better and nobler souls, why burst for those

III.—*l*   14*

Who supped on the parched pulse, and lapped
    the stream,
And each, at the same hour, dreams the same
    dream!
Or, easier still, they lied!   Yet, wherefore, then
"Rise, and go up to Bethlehem," and unpen
To wolf and jackal all their hapless fold
So they might "see these things which had
    been told
In heaven's own voice"?   And heaven, what-
    e'er betide,
Spreads surely somewhere, on death's farther
    side!

And, truly, if joy's music once hath rung
From lips of bands invisible, if any—
(Be they the dead, or of the deathless many)—
Love and serve man, angelical befrienders,
Glad of his weal, and from his woe defenders,—
If such, in heaven, have pity on our tears,
Forever falling with the unmending years,
High cause had they, at Bethlehem, that
    night,
To lift the curtain of hope's hidden light,
To break decree of silence with love's cry,
Foreseeing how this Babe, born lowlily,
Should—past dispute, since now achieved is
    this—
Bring earth great gifts of blessing and of bliss;

Date, from that crib, the dynasty of love ;
Strip his misused thunderbolts from Jove ;
Bend to their knee Rome's Cæsars, break the
    chain
From the slave's neck ; set sick hearts free
    again
Bitterly bound by priests, and scribes, and
    scrolls ;
And heal, with balm of pardon, sinking souls :
Should mercy to her vacant throne restore,
Teach right to kings, and patience to the poor ;
Should, from that bearing-cave, outside the
    khan,
Amid the kneeling cattle, rise, and be
Light of all lands, and splendor of each sea,
The sun-burst of a new morn come to earth,
Not yet, alas ! broad day, but day's white birth
Which promiseth ; and blesseth, promising.
These from that night ! What cause of won-
    dering
If that one silence of all silences
Brake into music ? if, for hopes like these
Angels, who love us, sang that song, and show
Of time's far purpose made the " great light"
    glow ?

Wherefore, let whosoever will drink dry
His cup of faith ; and think that, verily,

Not in a vision, no way otherwise
Than those poor shepherds told, there did arise
This portent. Being amidst their sheep and
      goats,
Lapped careless in their pasture-keeping coats,
Blind as their drowsy beasts to what drew nigh,
(Such the lulled ear, and such th' unbusied eye
Which ofttimes hears and sees hid things!) there
      spread
The " Glory of the Lord" around each head :
Broke, be it deemed, o'er hill and over hollow,
On the inner seeing, the sense concealed, un-
      known,
Of those plain hinds—glad, humble, and alone—
Flooding their minds, filling their hearts; around,
Above, below, disclosing grove and ground,
The rocks, the hill, the town, the solitude,
The wondering flocks,—agaze with grass half-
      chewed,—
The palm-crowns, and the path to Bethlehem,
As sight angelic spies.   And, came to them
The " Angel of the Lord," visible, sure,
Known for the angel by his presence pure
Whereon was written love, and peace, and
      grace,
With beauty passing mortal mien and face.

So when the Angels were no more to see,
Re-entering those gates of space,—whose key

Love keeps on that side, and on this side death—
Each shepherd to the other whispering saith,
Lest he should miss some lingering symphonies
Of that departing music, " Let us rise
And go even now to Bethlehem, and spy
This which is come to pass, shewed graciously
By the Lord's angels." Therewith hasted they
By olive-yards, and old walls mossed and gray
Where, in close chinks, the lizard and the snake,
Thinking the sunlight come, stirred, half-awake :
Across the terraced levels of the vines,
Under the pillared palms, along the lines
Of lance-leaved oleanders, scented sweet,
Through the pomegranate-gardens sped their
      feet ;
Over the causeway, up the slope, they spring,
Breast the steep path, with steps not slacken-
      ing ;
Past David's well, past the town-wall they ran,
Unto the House of Chimham, to the khan,
Where mark them peering in, the posts be-
      tween,
Questioning—all out of breath—if birth hath
      been
This night, in any guest-room, high or low ?
The drowsy porter at the gate saith, " No !"—
Shooting the bars ; while the packed camels
      shake
Their bells to listen, and the sleepers wake,

And to their feet the ponderous steers slow
    rise,
Lifting from trampled fodder large mild eyes ;—
" Nay ! Brothers ! no such thing ! yet there is
    gone
Yonder, one nigh her time, a gentle one !
With him that seemed her spouse—of Galilee ;
They toiled at sundown to our doors—but,
    see !
No nook was here ! Seek at the cave instead ;
We shook some barley-straw to make their
    bed."

Then to the cave they wended, and there spied
That which was more, if truth be testified,
Than all the pomp seen thro' proud Herod's
    porch
Ablaze with brass, and silk, and scented torch,
High on Beth-Haccarem ; more to behold,
If men had known, than all the glory told
Of splendid Cæsar in his marbled home
On the white Isle ; or audience-hall at Rome
With trembling princes thronged.   A clay lamp
    swings
By twisted camel-cords, from blackened rings,
Shewing with flickering gleams, a Child new-
    born
Wrapped in a cloth, laid where the beasts at
    morn

Will champ their bean-straw : in the lamp-ray
    dim
A fresh-made Mother by Him, fostering Him
With face and mien to worship, speaking
    naught ;
Close at hand Joseph, and the ass, hath brought
That precious twofold burden to the gate ;
With goats, sheep, oxen, driven to shelter late :
No mightier sight ! Yet all sufficeth it—
If we will deem things be beyond our wit—
To prove heaven's music true, and show heav-
    en's way,
How, not by famous kings, nor with array
Of brazen letters on the boastful stone,
But " by the mouth of babes," quiet, alone,
Little beginnings planning for large ends,
With other purpose than fond man attends,
Wisdom and love, in secret fellowship
Guide our world's wandering with a finger-tip ;
And how, that night, as these did darkly
    see,
They sealed the first scrolls of earth's his-
    tory,
And opened what shall run till death be dead.

Which babe they reverenced, bending low the
    head,
First of all worshippers ; and told the things
Done in the plain, and played on angel's strings.

Then those around wondered and worshipped,
        too,
And Mary heard—but wondered not—anew
Hiding this in her heart, the heart which
        beat
With blood of Jesus Christ, holy and sweet.

Also, not marvelling, albeit they heard,
Stood certain by—those three swart ones—ap-
        peared
From climes unknown; yet, surely, on high
        quest
Of what that star proclaimed, bright on the
        breast
First of the Ram, afterwards glittering thence
Into the watery Trigon, where, intense,
It lit the Crab, and burned the Fishes pale.
Three Signiors, owning many a costly bale;
Three travelled masters, by their bearing lords
Of lands and slaves. The Indian silk affords,
With many a folded braid of white and gold,
Shade to their brows; rich goat-hair shawls did
        fold
Their gowns of flow'r'd white muslin, midway
        tied ;
And ruby, turkis, emerald—stones of pride—
Blazed on their thumb-rings; and a pearl
        gleamed white
In every ear; and silver belts, clasped tight,

Held ink-box, reeds, and knives, in scabbards
    gemmed ;
Curled shoes of goat-skin dyed, with seed-
    pearls hemmed,
Shod their brown feet; hair shorn; lids low, to
    think—
Eyes deep and wistful, as of those who drink
Waters of hidden wisdom, night and day,
And live twain lives, conforming as they
    may,
In diligence, and due observances
To ways of men ; yet, not at one with these ;
But ever straining past the things that seem
To that which is—the truth behind the dream.
Three princely wanderers of the Asian blood
Perchance, by Indus dwellers ; or some flood,
That feeds her from Himâla's icy dome ;
Or, haply, to those Syrian palm-trees come
From Gunga's banks, or mounts of Malabar
Which lift the Deccan to its sun, and far—
Rampart-like—fringe the blue Arabian Sea.
True followers of the Buddh they seemed to be,
The better arm and shoulder showing bare
With each ; and on the neck of each, draped fair
A scarf of saffron, patched ; and, 'twixt the
    eyes,
In saffron stamped, the Name of mysteries
OM ; and the Swastika, with secrets rife
How man may 'scape the dire deceits of life.

H   15

These three stood by, as who would entrance
    make;
And heard the shepherd's tale; and, hearing,
    spake
Strange Indian words one to another; then
    sent
Command.   Their serving-men, obedient,
Cast loose from off the camels, kneeling nigh,
Nettings and mats, and made the fastenings fly
From belly-band, and crupper-rope, and tail;
And broke the knots, and let each dusty bale
Slide from the saddle-horns, and give to see
Long-hoarded treasure of great jewelry,
And fragrant secrets of the Indian grove,
And splendors of the Indian looms, inwove
With gold and silver flowers: "for, now," said
    they,
" Our eyes have seen this thing sought day by
    day;
By the all-conscious, silent sky well-known,
And, specially, of yon white star fore-shown
Which, bursting magically on the sight,
Beckoned us from our homes, shining aright,
The silver beacon to this holy hill:
Mark if it sparkles not, aware and still,
Over the place: The astral houses, see !
Spake truth: Our feet were guided faithfully.
'Tis the Star-Child, who was to rise, and wear
A crown than Suleiman's more royal and rare,

' King of the Jews !' Grant an approach to us
Who crave to worship Him."

                          Now, it fell thus
That these first to Jerusalem had passed,
And sojourned there, observing feast and fast
In the thronged city ; oft of townsmen seen
In market and bazaar ; and, by their mien
Noted for lordliest of all strangers there,
Much whispered of, in sooth, as who saw clear
Shadows of times to come, and secrets bright
Writ in the jewelled cipher of the night.
So that the voice of this to Herod went
Feastful and fearful ; ever ill-content
Mid plots and perils ; girt with singing boys,
And dancing girls of Tyre, and armored noise
Of Cæsar's legionaries.   Long and near,
In audience hall, each dusky wayfarer
Questioned he of their knowledge, and the star,
What message flashed it ?   Whether near or far
Would rise this portent of a Babe to reign
King of the Jews, and bring a crown again
To weeping Zion, and cast forth from them
The Roman scourge ?   And if at Bethlehem,
As, with one voice, priests, elders, scribes aver,
Then, let them thither wend, and spy the stir,
And find this Babe, and come anew to him,
Declaring where the wonder.   " 'Twas his
    whim"

Quotha " to be of fashion with the stars,
(Weary, like them, of gazing upon wars)
To shine upon this suckling, bending knee
Save unto Cæsar uncrooked latterly."

Thence came it those three stood at entering
Before the door ; and their rich gifts did bring,
Red gold from the Indian rocks, cunningly
    beat
To plate and chalice, with old fables sweet
Of Buddh's compassion, and dark Mara's powers
Round the brims glittering ; and a riot of
    flowers
Done on the gold, with gold script to proclaim
The Noble Truths, and Threefold mystic Name
OM, and the Swastika, and how man wins
Blessed Nirvana's rest, being quit of sins,
And, day and night, reciting, " Oh, the Gem !
Upon the Lotus ! Oh, the Lotus-stem !"
Also, more precious than much gold, they
    poured
Rare spices forth, unknitting cord on cord ;
And, one by one, unwinding cloths, as though
The merchantmen had sought to shut in so
The breath of those distillings : in such kind
As when Nile's black embalming slaves would
    bind
Sindon o'er sindon, cere-cloth, cinglets, bands
Roll after roll, on head, breast, feet, and hands,

Round some dead king, whose cold and withered
    palm
Had dropped the sceptre; drenched with musk
    and balm,
And natron, and what keeps from perishing;
So they might save—after long wandering—
The body for the spirit, and hold fast
Life's likeness, till the dead man lived at last.
Thus, from their coats involved of leaves and
    silk,
Slowly they freed the odorous thorn-tree's
    milk,
The gray myrrh, and the cassia, and the spice,
Filling the wind with frankincense past price,
With hearts of blossoms from a hundred glens
And essence of a thousand rose-gardens,
Till the night's gloom like a royal curtain hung
Jewelled with stars, and rich with fragrance
    flung
Athwart the arch; and, in the cavern there
The air around was as the breathing-air
Of a queen's chamber, when she comes to bed,
And all that glad earth owns gives goodlihead.

Witness them entering,—these three from afar—
Who knew the skies, and had the strange white
    star
To light their nightly lamp, thro' deserts wide
Of Bactria, and the Persic wastes, and tide

Of Tigris and Euphrates; past the snow
Of Ararat, and where the sand-winds blow
O'er Ituræa; and the crimson peaks
Of Moab, and the fierce, bright, barren reeks
From Asphaltitics; to this hill—to thee
Bethlehem-Ephrata! Witness these three
Gaze, hand in hand, with faces grave and mild,
Where, 'mid the gear and goats, Mother and
        Child
Make state and splendor for their eyes. Then
        lay
Each stranger on the earth, in the Indian way,
Paying the "eight prostrations;" and was heard
Saying softly, in the Indian tongue, that word
Wherewith a Prince is honored. Humbly ran,
On this, the people of their caravan
And fetch the gold, and—laid on gold—the spice,
Frankincense, myrrh: and next, with reverence
        nice,
Foreheads in dust, they spread the precious
        things
At Mary's feet, and worship Him who clings
To Mary's bosom drinking soft life so
Who shall be life and light to all below.
" For, now we see," say they, departing: " plain
The star's word comes to pass! The Buddh
        again
Appeareth, or some Bôddhisat of might
Arising for the west, who shall set right,

And serve and reconcile; and, maybe, teach
Knowledge to those who know.   We, brothers,
    each,
Have heard yon shepherds babbling: if the sky
Speaketh with such, heaven's mercy is drawn
    nigh!
Well did we counsel, journeying to this place!
Yon hour-old Babe, milking that breast of grace,
The world will praise and worship, well-con-
    tent."

Then, fearing Herod, to their homes they went
Musing along the road.   But he alway
Angered and troubled, bade his soldiers slay
Whatever man-child sucked in Bethlehem.
Lord! had'st Thou been all God, as pleaseth
    them
Who poorly see Thy godlike self, and take
True glory from Thee for false glory's sake:
Co-equal power, as these—too bold—blaspheme,
Ruler of what Thou camest to redeem;
Not Babe Divine, feeling with touch of silk
For fountains of a mortal Mother's milk
With sweet mouth buried in the warm feast
    thus,
And dear heart growing great to beat for us,
And soft feet waiting till the way was spread
Whereby what was true God in Thee should
    tread

Triumphant over woe and death to bliss,—
Thou, from Thy cradle would'st have stayed in
    this
Those butchers!   With one angel's swift decree,
Out of the silver cohorts lackeying Thee,
Thou had'st thrust down the bitter prince who
    killed
Thine innocents!   Would'st Thou not?   Was't
    not willed?
Alas! "Peace and good-will" in agony
Found first fruits!   Rama heard that woful cry
Of Rachel weeping for the children; lone,
Uncomforted, because her babes are gone.
Herod the King!   hast thou heard Rachel's
    wail
Where restitution is?   Did aught avail
Somewhere? at last? past life? after long stress
Of heavy shame to bring forgetfulness?
If such grace be, no hopeless sin is wrought;
Thy bloody blade missed what its vile edge
    sought;
Mother, and Child, and Joseph—safe from thee—
Journey to Egypt, while the eastern Three
Wind homewards, lightened of their spice and
    gold;
And those great days, that were to be, unfold
In the fair fields beside the shining sea
Which rolls, 'mid palms and rocks, in Galilee.

                    Sir Edwin Arnold.

It Brings Good Cheer.

" You may talk of Country Christ-
    masses,
Their thirty pound butter'd eggs,
    their pies of carps' tongues ;
Their pheasants drench'd with
    ambergris ; the carcasses of three
    fat wethers bruised for gravy to
    make sauce for a single pea-
    cock !"

Massinger.

OLD CHRISTMAS RETURNED.

All you that to feasting and mirth are inclined,
Come, here is good news for to pleasure your
    mind;
Old Christmas is come for to keep open house,
He scorns to be guilty of starving a mouse.
Then come, boys, and welcome for diet th''
    chief,
Plum-pudding, goose, capon, minced-pies, and
    roast-beef.

A long time together he hath been forgot,
They scarce could afford to hang on the pot;
Such miserly sneaking in England hath been,
As by our forefathers ne'er us'd to be seen;
But now he's returned, you shall have in brief,
Plum-pudding, goose, capon, minced-pies, and
    roast-beef.

The times were ne'er good since Old Christmas
    was fled,
And all hospitality hath been so dead;
No mirth at our festivals late did appear,
They scarcely would part with a cup of March
    beer;

But now you shall have for the ease of your
    grief,
Plum-pudding, goose, capon, minced-pies, and
    roast-beef.

The butler and baker, they now may be glad,
The times they are mended, though they have
    been bad;
The brewer, he likewise may be of good cheer,
He shall have good trading for ale and strong
    beer;
All trades shall be jolly, and have for relief,
Plum-pudding, goose, capon, minced-pies, and
    roast-beef.

The holly and ivy about the walls wind,
And show that we ought to our neighbors be
    kind,
Inviting each other for pastime and sport,
And where we best fare, there we most do
    resort;
We fail not of victuals, and that of the chief,
Plum-pudding, goose, capon, minced-pies, and
    roast-beef.

The cooks shall be busied by day and by night,
In roasting and boiling, for taste and delight;
Their senses in liquor that's nappy they'll steep,
Though they be afforded to have little sleep;

They still are employed for to dress us in brief,
Plum-pudding, goose, capon, minced-pies, and
    roast-beef.

Although the cold weather doth hunger pro-
    voke,
'Tis a comfort to see how the chimneys do
    smoke;
Provision is making for beer, ale, and wine,
For all that are willing or ready to dine :
Then haste to the kitchen for diet the chief,
Plum-pudding, goose, capon, minced-pies, and
    roast-beef.

All travellers, as they do pass on their way,
At gentlemen's halls are invited to stay,
Themselves to refresh, and their horses to rest,
Since that he must be Old Christmas's guest ;
Nay, the poor shall not want, but have for re-
    lief,
Plum-pudding, goose, capon, minced-pies, and
    roast-beef.

Now Mock-beggar-hall it no more shall stand
    empty,
But all shall be furnisht with freedom and
    plenty;
The hoarding old misers, who us'd to preserve
The gold in their coffers, and see the poor
    starve,

Must now spread their tables, and give them in
    brief,
Plum-pudding, goose, capon, minced-pies, and
    roast-beef.

The court, and the city, and country are glad,
Old Christmas is come to cheer up the sad ;
Broad pieces and guineas about now shall fly,
And hundreds be losers by cogging a die,
Whilst others are feasting with diet the chief,
Plum-pudding, goose, capon, minced-pies, and
    roast-beef.

Those that have no coin at the cards for to play,
May sit by the fire and pass time away,
And drink of their moisture contented and free,
" My honest, good fellow, come, here is to thee !"
And when they are hungry, fall to their relief,
Plum-pudding, goose, capon, minced-pies, and
    roast-beef.

Young gallants and ladies shall foot it along,
Each room in the house to the music shall
    throng,
Whilst jolly carouses about they shall pass,
And each country swain trip about with his lass ;
Meantime goes the caterer to fetch in the chief,
Plum-pudding, goose, capon, minced-pies, and
    roast-beef.

The cooks and the scullion, who toil in their
      frocks,
Their hopes do depend upon their Christmas-box;
There is very few that do live on the earth
But enjoy at this time either profit or mirth ;
Yea, those that are charged to find all relief,
Plum-pudding, goose, capon, minced-pies, and
      roast-beef.

Then well may we welcome Old Christmas to
      town,
Who brings us good cheer and good liquor so
      brown ;
To pass the cold winter away with delight,
We feast it all day, and we frolic all night ;
Both hunger and cold we keep out with relief,
Plum-pudding, goose, capon, minced-pies, and
      roast-beef.

Then let all curmudgeons who dote on their
      wealth,
And value their treasure much more than their
      health,
Go hang themselves up, if they will be so kind ;
Old Christmas with them but small welcome
      shall find ;
They will not afford to themselves without grief,
Plum-pudding, goose, capon, minced-pies, and
      roast-beef.

Evans' Old Ballads.

THE TRENCHERMAN.

My master and dame, I well perceive,
   Are purposed to oe merry to-night,
And willingly hath given me leave
   To combat with a Christmas Knight.
Sir Pig, I see, comes prancing in
   And bids me draw if that I dare;
I care not for his valor a pin,
   For Jack of him will have a share.

My lady goose among the rest
   Upon the table takes her place,
And piping-hot bids do my best,
   And bravely looks me in the face;
For pigs and geese are gallant cheer,
   God bless my master and dame therefore!
I trust before the next New Year
   To eat my part of half a score.

I likewise see good minced-pie
   Here standing swaggering on the table;
The lofty walls so large and high
   I'll level down if I be able;
For they be furnished with good plums,
   And spiced well with pepper and salt,

Every prune as big as both my thumbs
To drive down bravely the juice of malt.

Fill me some of your Christmas beer,
Your pepper sets my mouth on heat,
And Jack's a-dry with your good cheer,
Give me some good ale to my meat.
And then again my stomach I'll show,
For good roast-beef here stoutly stands;
I'll make it stoop before I go,
Or I'll be no man of my hands.

And for the plenty of this house
God keep it thus well-stored alway;
Come, butler, fill me a good carouse,
And so we'll end our Christmas day.
New Christmas Carols.

16*

BAN AND BLESSING.

Now Christmas comes, 'tis fit that we
Should feast and sing and merry be,
Keep open house, let fiddlers play ;
A fig for cold, sing care away !
And may they who thereat repine,
On brown bread and on small beer dine.
Make fires with logs, let the cooks sweat
With boiling and with roasting meat ;
Let ovens be heat for fresh supplies
Of puddings, pasties, and minced-pies.
And whilst that Christmas doth abide
Let butt'ry-door stand open wide.
Hang up those churls that will not feast
Or with good fellows be a guest,
And hang up those would take away
The observation of that day ;
O may they never minced-pies eat,
Plum-pudding, roast-beef, nor such meat.
But blest be they, awake and sleep,
Who at that time a good house keep ;
May never want come nigh their door,
Who at that time relieve the poor ;
Be plenty always in their house
Of beef, veal, lamb, pork, mutton, souse.

Poor Robin's Almanac.

THRICE WELCOME!

Now thrice welcome, Christmas,
  Which brings us good cheer,
Minced-pies and plum porridge,
  Good ale and strong beer;
With pig, goose, and capon,
  The best that may be,
So well doth the weather
  And our stomachs agree.

Observe how the chimneys
  Do smoke all about;
The cooks are providing
  For dinner, no doubt;
But those on whose tables
  No victuals appear,
O may they keep Lent
  All the rest of the year.

With holly and ivy
  So green and so gay,
We deck up our houses
  As fresh as the day;
With bay and rosemary
  And laurel complete;
And every one now
  Is a king in conceit.

Poor Robin's Almanac.

CHRISTMAS PROVENDER.

Provide for Christmas ere that it do come,
To feast thy neighbor good cheer to have some;
Good bread and drink, a fire in the hall,
Brawn, pudding, souse, and good mustard withal.
Beef, mutton, pork, and shred pies of the best,
Pig, veal, goose, capon, and turkey well drest;
Apples and nuts to throw about the hall,
That boys and girls may scramble for them all.
Sing jolly carols, make the fiddlers play,
Let scrupulous fanatics keep away;
For oftentimes seen no arranter knave
Than some who do counterfeit most to be grave.
                                        Poor Robin's Almanac.

GLEE AND SOLACE.

With merry glee and solace ·
This second day of Christmas
　Now comes in bravely to my master's house,
Where plenty of good cheer I see,
With that which most contenteth me,
　　As brawn and bacon, powdered beef, and
　　souse.

For the love of Stephen,
That blessed saint of heaven,
　Which stonéd was for Jesus Christ his sake,
Let us all, both more and less,
Cast away all heaviness,
　And in a sober manner merry make.

He was a man belovéd,
And his faith approvéd
　By suffering death on this holy day,
Where he with gentle patience
And a constant sufferance,
　Hath taught us all to heaven the ready way.

So let our mirth be civil,
That not one thought of evil
　May take possession of our hearts at all,

So shall we love and favor get
Of them that kindly thus do set
   Their bounties here so freely in this hall.

Of delicates so dainty,
I see now here is plenty
   Upon this table ready here prepared;
Then let us now give thanks to those
That all things friendly thus bestows,
   Esteeming not this world that is so hard.

For of the same my master
Hath made me here a taster;
   The Lord above requite him for the same!
And so to all within this house
I will drink a full carouse,
   With leave of my good master and my dame.

And the Lord be praised
My stomach is well eased,
   My bones at quiet may go take their rest;
'Good fortune surely follow me
To bring me thus so luckily
   To eat and drink so freely of the best.

          New Christmas Carols, A.D. 1661.

ON SAINT JOHN'S DAY.

In honor of Saint John we thus
    Do keep good Christmas cheer ;
And he that comes to dine with us,
    I think he need not spare.
The butcher he hath killed good beef,
    The caterer brings it in ;
But Christmas pies are still the chief,
    If that I durst begin.

Our bacon-hogs are full and fat
    To make us brawn and souse ;
Full well may I rejoice thereat
    To see them in the house.
But yet the minced-pie it is
    That sets my teeth on water;
Good mistress, let me have a bit,
    For I do long thereafter.

And I will fetch you water in
    To brew and bake withal,
Your love and favor still to win
    When as you please to call.
Then grant me, dame, your love and leave
    To taste your pie-meat here ;
It is the best, in my conceit,
    Of all your Christmas-cheer.

The cloves, and mace, and gallant plums
 That here on heaps do lie,
And prunes as big as both my thumbs,
 Enticeth much mine eye.
Oh, let me eat my belly-full
 Of your good Christmas-pie;
Except thereat I have a pull,
 I think I sure shall die.

Good master, stand my loving friend,
 For Christmas-time is short,
And when it comes unto an end
 I may no longer sport;
Then while it doth continue here,
 Let me such labor find
To eat my fill of that good cheer
 That best doth please my mind.

Then I shall thank my dame therefore,
 That gives her kind consent
That Jack, your boy, with others more,
 May have this Christmas spent
In pleasant mirth and merry glee,
 As young men most delight;
For that's the only sport for me,
 And so God give you all good-night.

    New Christmas Carols, A.D. 1661.

CHRISTMAS ALMS.

Now that the time is come wherein
  Our Saviour Christ was born,
The larders full of beef and pork,
  The garners filled with corn;
As God hath plenty to thee sent,
  Take comfort of thy labors,
And let it never thee repent
  To feast thy needy neighbors.

Let fires in every chimney be
  That people they may warm them;
Tables with dishes covered,—
  Good victuals will not harm them.
With mutton, veal, beef, pig, and pork,*
  Well furnish every board;
Plum-pudding, furmety, and what
  Thy stock will them afford.

No niggard of thy liquor be,
  Let it go round thy table;
People may freely drink, but not
  So long as they are able.
Good customs they may be abused,
  Which makes rich men to slack us;

III.—I   *n*   17

This feast is to relieve the poor,
 And not to drunken Bacchus.

This, if thou doest,
 'Twill credit raise thee;
God will thee bless,
 And neighbors praise thee.
                    Poor Robin's Almanac.

CHRISTMAS AT THE ROUND TABLE.

The great King Arthur made a royal feast,
    And held his Royal Christmas at Carlisle,
And thither came the vassals, most and least,
    From every corner of the British Isle ;
And all were entertained, both man and beast,
    According to their rank, in proper style ;
The steeds were fed and littered in the stable,
The ladies and the knights sat down to table.

The bill of fare (as you may well suppose)
    Was suited to those plentiful old times,
Before our modern luxuries arose,
    With truffles, and ragouts, and various crimes ;
And, therefore, from the original in prose
    I shall arrange the catalogue in rhymes :
They served up salmon, venison and wild boars
By hundreds, and by dozens, and by scores.

Hogsheads of honey, kilderkins of mustard,
    Muttons, and fatted beeves, and bacon swine ;
Herons and bitterns, peacocks, swan, and bus-
        tard,
    Teal, mallard, pigeons, widgeons, and, in fine,
Plum-puddings, pancakes, apple-pies, and cus-
        tard,

And therewithal they drank good Gascon
    wine,
With mead, and ale, and cider of our own ;
For porter, punch, and negus were not known.

All sorts of people there were seen together,
    All sorts of characters, all sorts of dresses ;
The fool with fox's tail and peacock feather,
    Pilgrims, and penitents, and grave burgesses ;
The country people with their coats of leather,
    Vintners and victuallers with cans and messes,
Grooms, archers, varlets, falconers, and yeomen,
Damsels, and waiting-maids, and waiting-women.

John Hookham Frere.

Lullaby.

"Sleep, my little one,
Sleep, my pretty one,
Sleep."

Tennyson.

17*

A CAROL AT THE MANGER.

Lully, lulla, thow littel tine child;
By, by, lully, lullay, thow littell tyne child;
By, by, lully, lullay.

O sisters too! how may we do,
For to preserve this day
This pore yongling, for whom we do sing
By, by, lully, lullay.

Herod the King, in his raging,
Chargid he hath this day
His men of might, in his owne sight,
All yonge children to slay.

That wo is me, pore child for the!
And ever morne and day,
For the parting nether say nor singe
By, by, lully, lullay.

Coventry Mysteries.

A DREAM CAROL.

Ah, my dear Son, said Mary, ah, my dear,
Kiss thy mother, Jesu, with a laughing cheer!

    This endnes* night I saw a sight
      All in my sleep, ·
    Mary, that May, she sung lullay
      And sore did weep;
    To keep, she sought, full fast about
      Her Son from cold.
    Joseph said, Wife, my joy, my life,
      Say what ye would.
    Nothing, my spouse, is in this house
      Unto my pay ;†
    My Son a king, that made all thing,
      Lieth in hay.
          Ah, my dear Son! etc.

    My mother dear, amend your cheer
      And now be still;
    Thus for to lie it is soothly
      My Father's will.

---

* Last.   † Content.

Derision, great passion,
  Infinitely,
As it is found many a wound
  Suffer shall I ;
On Calvary that is so high
  There shall I be,
Man to restore, nailéd full sore
  Upon a tree.
      Ah, my dear Son! etc.

Sandy's Christmas Carols.

THE KING IN THE CRADLE.

My sweet little baby, what meanest thou to
    cry?
Be still, my blesséd babe, though cause thou
    hast to mourn,
Whose blood most innocent to shed the cruel
    king hath sworn;
And lo, alas! behold what slaughter he doth
    make,
Shedding the blood of infants all, sweet Saviour,
    for thy sake.
A King, a King is born, they say, which King
    this king would kill:
O woe and woful heavy day when wretches
    have their will!
           Lulla, la lulla, lulla lullaby.

Three kings this King of kings to see are come
    from far,
To each unknown, with offerings great, by
    guiding of a star;
And shepherds heard the song, which angels
    bright did sing,
Giving all glory unto God for coming of this
    King,

Which must be made away—King Herod would
    him kill;
O woe and woful heavy day when wretches
    have their will?

                ·   Lulla, etc.

Lo, lo, my little babe, be still, lament no more;
From fury thou shalt step aside, help have we
    still in store:
We heavenly warning have some other soil to
    seek;
From death must fly the Lord of life, as lamb
    both mild and meek:
Thus must my babe obey the king that would
    him kill;
O woe and woful heavy day when wretches
    have their will!

                   Lulla, etc.

But thou shalt live and reign, as sibyls hath
    foresaid,
As all the prophets prophesy, whose mother,
    yet a maid
And perfect virgin pure, with her breasts shall
    upbreed
Both God and man that all hath made, the son
    of heavenly seed:

Whom caitives none can 'tray, whom tyrants
    none can kill:
O joy and joyful happy day when wretches
    want their will!

Lulla, etc.

Byrd's Psalmes, Sonets, etc., A.D. 1588.

MADONNA AND CHILD.

This endris night *
I saw a sight,
  A star as bright as day ;
And ever among
A maiden sung,
  Lullay, by by, lullay.

This lovely lady sat and sang, and to her child
  she said,—
" My son, my brother, my father dear, why
  liest thou thus in hayd ?†
    My sweet bird,
    Thus it is betide
      Though thou be king veray ;
    But, nevertheless,
    I will not cease
      To sing, by by, lullay."

The child then spake ; in his talking he to his
  mother said,—
" I bekid ‡ am king, in crib though I be laid ;

---

    * Endris night : last night.   † Hay.
    ‡ Nevertheless.

For angels bright
Down to me light,
  Thou knowest it is no nay,
And of that sight
Thou mayest be light
  To sing, by by, lullay."

"Now, sweet Son, since thou art king, why art
  thou laid in stall ?
Why not thou ordain thy bedding in some great
  kingès hall ?
      Methinketh it is right
      That king or knight
        Should be in good array ;
      And them among
      It were no wrong
        To sing, by by, lullay."

"Mary, mother, I am thy child, though I be laid
  in stall,
Lords and dukes shall worship me and so shall
  kingès all.
      Ye shall well see
      That kingès three
        Shall come on the twelfth day ;
      For this behest
      Give me thy breast
        And sing, by by, lullay."

"Now tell me, sweet Son, I thee pray, thou art
    my love and dear,
How should I keep thee to thy pay * and make
    thee glad of cheer?
        For all thy will
        I would fulfil
          Thou weet'st full well in fay,
        And for all this
        I will thee kiss,
          And sing, by by, lullay."

"My dear mother, when time it be, take thou
    me up aloft,
And set me upon thy knee and handle me full
    soft.
        And in thy arm
        Thou wilt me warm,
          And keep me night and day;
        If I weep
        And may not sleep
          Thou sing, by by, lullay."

"Now, sweet Son, since it is so, all things are at
    thy will,
I pray thee grant to me a boon if it be right
    and skill,

---

* Peace.

That child or man,
That will or can,
   Be merry upon my day;
To bliss them bring,
And I shall sing,
   Lullay, by by, lullay."

A ROCKING HYMN.

Sweet baby, sleep; what ails my dear?
  What ails my darling thus to cry?
Be still, my child, and lend thine ear
  To hear me sing thy lullaby.
    My pretty lamb, forbear to weep;
    Be still, my dear; sweet baby, sleep.

Thou blessed soul, what canst thou fear?
  What things to thee can mischief do?
Thy God is now thy Father dear;
  His holy Spouse thy Mother, too.
    Sweet baby, then, forbear to weep;
    Be still, my babe; sweet baby, sleep.

Whilst thus thy lullaby I sing,
  For thee great blessings ripening be;
Thine eldest brother is a king,
  And hath a kingdom bought for thee.
    Sweet baby, then, forbear to weep;
    Be still, my babe; sweet baby, sleep.

Sweet baby, sleep, and nothing fear,
  For whosoever thee offends,
By thy protector threatened are,
  And God and angels are thy friends.
III.—o   18*

Sweet baby, then, forbear to weep;
Be still, my babe; sweet baby, sleep.

When God with us was dwelling here,
In little babes he took delight:
Such innocents as thou, my dear,
Are ever precious in his sight.
Sweet baby, then, forbear to weep;
Be still, my babe; sweet baby, sleep.

A little infant once was he,
And Strength-in-Weakness then was laid
Upon his Virgin-Mother's knee,
That power to thee might be conveyed.
Sweet baby, then, forbear to weep;
Be still, my babe; sweet baby, sleep.

In this thy frailty and thy need
He friends and helpers doth prepare,
Which thee shall cherish, clothe, and feed,
For of thy weal they tender are.
Sweet baby, then, forbear to weep;
Be still, my babe; sweet baby, sleep.

The King of kings, when he was born,
Had not so much for outward ease;
By him such dressings were not worn,
Nor such-like swaddling-clothes as these.
Sweet baby, then, forbear to weep;
Be still, my babe; sweet baby, sleep.

Within a manger lodged thy Lord,
  Where oxen lay and asses fed ;
Warm rooms we do to thee afford,
  An easy cradle or a bed.
    Sweet baby, then, forbear to weep ;
    Be still, my babe ; sweet baby, sleep.

The wants that he did then sustain
  Have purchased wealth, my babe, for thee,
And by his torments and his pain
  Thy rest and ease secured be.
    My baby, then, forbear to weep ;
    Be still, my babe ; sweet baby, sleep.

Thou hast (yet more), to perfect this,
  A promise and an earnest got
Of gaining everlasting bliss,
  Though thou, my babe, perceiv'st it not.
    Sweet baby, then, forbear to weep ;
    Be still, my babe ; sweet baby, sleep.
                George Wither.

A CRADLE-SONG OF THE VIRGIN.

The Virgin stills the crying
Of Jesus, sleepless lying;
And singing for his pleasure,
Thus calls upon her treasure,
"My darling, do not weep, my Jesu, sleep!"

O lamb, my love inviting,
O star, my soul delighting,
O flower of mine own bearing,
O jewel past comparing!
       My darling, etc.

My Child, of might indwelling,
My sweet, all sweets excelling,
Of bliss the fountain flowing,
The dayspring ever glowing
       My darling, etc.

My joy, my exultation,
My spirit's consolation;
My son, my spouse, my brother,
O listen to thy mother!
       My darling, etc.

Say, would'st thou heavenly sweetness,
Or love of answering meetness?
Or is fit music wanting?
Ho! angels, raise your chanting!
            My darling, etc.
Translated from the Latin by Rev. H. R. Bramley.

WHISPERING PALMS.

Holy angels and blest,
  Through these Palms as ye sweep,
Hold their branches at rest,
  For my Babe is asleep.

And ye, Bethlehem palm-trees,
  As stormy winds rush
In tempest and fury
  Your angry noise hush;—
Move gently, move gently,
  Restrain your wild sweep;
Hold your branches at rest—
  My Babe is asleep.

Lope de Veaa.

A CHRISTMAS LULLABY.

Sleep, baby, sleep! The Mother sings;
Heaven's angels kneel and fold their wings:
    Sleep, baby, sleep!

With swathes of scented hay thy bed
By Mary's hand at eve was spread.
    Sleep, baby, sleep!

At midnight came the shepherds, they
Whom seraphs wakened by the way.
    Sleep, baby, sleep!

And three kings from the East afar
Ere dawn came, guided by thy star.
    Sleep, baby, sleep!

They brought thee gifts of gold and gems,
Pure orient pearls, rich diadems.
    Sleep, baby, sleep!

But thou who liest slumbering there,
Art King of kings, earth, ocean, air.
    Sleep, baby, sleep!

Sleep, baby, sleep! The shepherds sing:
Through heaven, through earth, hosannas ring.
    Sleep, baby, sleep!

            John Addington Symonds.

THE VIRGIN'S CRADLE-HYMN.

Dormi, Jesu! Mater ridet
Quæ tam dulcem somnum videt,
   Dormi, Jesu! blandule!
Si non dormis, Mater plorat
Inter fila cantans orat,
   Blande, veni, somnule.

Translation.

Sleep, sweet babe! my cares beguiling :
Mother sits beside thee smiling ;
   Sleep, my darling, tenderly !
If thou sleep not, mother mourneth,
Singing as her wheel she turneth :
   Come soft slumber, balmily !

              Samuel Taylor Coleridge.

THE SOVEREIGN.

Upon my lap my sovereign sits
And sucks upon my breast;
Meantime his love maintains my life
And gives my sense her rest.
   Sing lullaby, my little boy,
   Sing lullaby, mine only joy!

When thou hast taken thy repast,
Repose, my babe, on me;
So may thy mother and thy nurse
Thy cradle also be.
   Sing lullaby, my little boy,
   Sing lullaby, mine only joy!

I grieve that duty doth not work
All that my wishing would,
Because I would not be to thee
But in the best I should.
   Sing lullaby, my little boy,
   Sing lullaby, mine only joy!

Yet as I am, and as I may
I must and will be thine,

Though all too little for thyself
Vouchsafing to be mine.
  Sing lullaby, my little boy,
  Sing lullaby, mine only joy!

                    Martin Peerson, A.D. 1620.

BY THE CRADLE-SIDE.

Sweet dreams, form a shade
O'er my lovely infant's head!
Sweet dreams of pleasant streams
By happy, silent, moony beams!

Sweet sleep, with soft down
Weave thy brows an infant crown!
Sweet sleep, angel mild,
Hover o'er my happy child!

Sweet smiles, in the night
Hover over my delight!
Sweet smiles, mother's smile
All the livelong night beguile.

Sweet moans, dovelike sighs,
Chase not slumber from thine eyes!
Sweet moan, sweeter smile,
All the dovelike moans beguile!

Sleep, sleep, happy child!
All creation slept and smiled.
Sleep, sleep, happy sleep,
While o'er thee doth mother weep.

Sweet babe, in thy face
Holy image I can trace;
Sweet babe, once like thee
Thy Maker lay and wept for me:

Wept for me, for thee, for all,
When he was an infant small;
Thou his image ever see,
Heavenly face that smiles on thee!

Smiles on thee, on me, on all,
Who became an infant small,
Infant smiles are his own smiles:
Heaven and earth to peace beguiles.

William Blake.

THE VIRGIN MARY TO THE CHILD JESUS.

> But see, the Virgin blest
> Hath laid her babe to rest.
>
> *Milton.*

I.

Sleep, sleep, mine Holy One!
My flesh, my Lord!—what name? I do not
    know
A name that seemeth not too high or low,
  Too far from me or heaven.
My Jesus, that is best! that word being given
By the majestic angel whose command
Was softly as a man's beseeching said,
When I and all the earth appeared to stand
  In the great overflow
Of light celestial from his wings and head.
  Sleep, sleep, my saving One!

II.

And art Thou come for saving, baby-browed
And speechless Being—art Thou come for sav-
    ing?
The palm that grows beside our door is bowed
By treadings of the low wind from the south,
A restless shadow through the chamber waving:
19*

Upon its bough a bird sings in the sun ;
But Thou, with that close slumber on thy
     mouth,
Dost seem of wind and sun already weary.
Art come for saving, O my weary One ?

III,

Perchance this sleep that shutteth out the
     dreary
Earth-sounds and motions, opens on Thy soul
High dreams on fire with God ;
High songs that make the pathways where they
     roll
More bright than stars do theirs; and visions
     new
Of Thine eternal nature's old abode.
   Suffer this mother's kiss,
   Best thing that earthly is,
To guide the music and the glory through,
Nor narrow in Thy dream the broad upliftings
   Of any seraph wing!
Thus, noiseless, thus. Sleep, sleep, my dream-
     ing One!

IV.

The slumber of His lips meseems to run
Through my lips to mine heart; to all its shift-
     ings

Of sensual life, bring contrariousness
In a great calm. I feel, I could lie down
As Moses did, and die,*—and then live most.
I am 'ware of you, heavenly Presences,
That stand with your peculiar light unlost,
Each forehead with a high thought for a crown,
Unsunned i' the sunshine! I am 'ware. Yet
     throw
No shade against the wall! How motionless
Ye round me with your living statuary,
While through your whiteness, in and out·
    wardly,
Continual thoughts of God appear to go,
Like light's soul in itself! I bear, I bear,
To look upon the dropt lids of your eyes,
Though their external shining testifies
To that beatitude within, which were
Enough to blast an eagle at his sun.
I fall not on my sad clay face before ye ;
   I look on His. I know
My spirit which dilateth with the woe
   Of His mortality,
   May well contain your glory.
   Yea, drop your lids more low,
Ye are but fellow-worshippers with me!
   Sleep, sleep, my worshipped One!

---

  * It is a Jewish tradition that Moses died of the kisses
of God's lips.

v.

We sate among the stalls at Bethlehem.
The dumb kine from their fodder turning them,
  Softened their horned faces
  To almost human gazes
  Towards the newly born.
The simple shepherds from the star-lit brooks
  Brought visionary looks,
As yet in their astonished hearing rung
  The strange, sweet angel-tongue.
The magi of the East, in sandals worn,
  Knelt reverent, sweeping round,
With long pale beards their gifts upon the
    ground,
  The incense, myrrh and gold,
These baby hands were impotent to hold.
So, let all earthlies and celestials wait
  Upon thy royal state!
  Sleep, sleep, my kingly One!

vi.

I am not proud—meek angels, ye invest
New meeknesses to hear such utterance rest
On mortal lips,—" I am not proud"—not proud!
Albeit in my flesh God sent His Son,
Albeit over Him my head is bowed
As others bow before Him, still mine heart
Bows lower than their knees.   O centuries
That roll, in vision, your futurities

My future grave athwart,—
Whose murmurs seem to reach me while I keep
   Watch o'er this sleep,—
Say of me as the heavenly said,—" Thou art
The blessedest of women !"—blessedest,
Not holiest, not noblest,—no high name,
Whose height misplaced may pierce me like a
    shame,
When I sit meek in heaven !

VII.

    For me—for me—
God knows that I am feeble like the rest !—
I often wandered forth, more child than maiden,
Among the midnight hills of Galilee,
   Whose summits looked heaven-laden ;
Listening to silence as it seemed to be
God's voice, so soft yet strong—so fain to press
Upon my heart as heaven did on the height,
And waken up its shadows by a light,
And show its vileness by a holiness.
Then I knelt down most silent like the night,
   Too self-renounced for fears,
Raising my small face to the boundless blue
Whose stars did mix and tremble in my tears.
God heard them falling after—with His dew.

VIII.

So, seeing my corruption, can I see
This Incorruptible now born of me—
   III.—*p*

This fair new Innocence no sun did chance
To shine on, (for even Adam was no child,)
Created from my nature all defiled,
This mystery from out mine ignorance—
Nor feel the blindness, stain, corruption, more
Than others do, or I did heretofore?—
Can hands wherein such burden pure has
        been,
Not open with the cry, " Unclean, unclean!"
More oft than any else beneath the skies?
    Ah King, ah Christ, ah Son!
The kine, the shepherds, the abased wise,
    Must all less lowly wait
    Than I, upon thy state!—
    Sleep, sleep, my kingly One!

                    IX.

Art Thou a King, then?   Come, His universe,
    Come, crown me Him a king!
Pluck rays from all such stars as never fling
    Their light where fell a curse.
And make a crowning for this kingly brow!—
What is my word?—Each empyreal star
    Sits in a sphere afar
    In shining ambuscade :
    The child-brow, crowned by none,
    Keeps its unchildlike shade.
    Sleep, sleep, my crownless One!

X.

Unchildlike shade!—no other babe doth wear
An aspect very sorrowful, as Thou.—
No small babe-smiles, my watching heart has
 seen,
To float like speech the speechless lips between ;
No dovelike cooing in the golden air,
No quick short joys of leaping babyhood.
 Alas, our earthly good
In heaven thought evil, seems too good for Thee :
 Yet, sleep, my weary One !

XI.

And then the drear, sharp tongue of prophecy,
With the dread sense of things which shall be
 done,
Doth smite me inly, like a sword—a sword ?—
(That "smites the Shepherd!") then I think
 aloud
The words "despised," — "rejected," — every
 word
Recoiling into darkness as I view
 The darling on my knee.
Bright angels,—move not!—lest ye stir the
 cloud
Betwixt my soul and His futurity !
I must not die, with mother's work to do,
 And could not live—and see.

XII.

It is enough to bear
This image still and fair—
This holier in sleep,
Than a saint at prayer:
This aspect of a child
Who never sinned or smiled—
This presence in an infant's face:
This sadness most like love,
This love than love more deep,
This weakness like omnipotence,
It is so strong to move!
Awful is this watching place,
Awful what I see from hence—
A king, without regalia,
A God, without the thunder,
A child, without the heart for play;
Ay, a Creator rent asunder
From His first glory and cast away
On His own world, for me alone
To hold in hands created, crying—Son!

XIII.

That tear fell not on Thee
Beloved, yet Thou stirrest in Thy slumber!
Thou, stirring not for glad sounds out of num-
ber

Which through the vibratory palm-trees run
  From summer wind and bird,
  So quickly hast Thou heard
  A tear fall silently ?—
Wak'st Thou, O loving One ?
        Elizabeth Barrett Browning.

A BEDSIDE DITTY.

Baby, baby dear,
Earth and heaven are near
Now, for heaven is here.

Heaven is every place
Where your flower-sweet face
Fills our eyes with grace.

Till your own eyes deign
Earth a glance again,
Earth and heaven are twain.

Now your sleep is done,
Shine, and show the sun
Earth and heaven are one.

Algernon Charles Swinburne.

GIVEN BACK ON CHRISTMAS MORN.

(A MOTHER WATCHES BY HER SICK BABE.)

Round about the casement
  Wail the winds of winter;
Shaken from the frozen eaves
  Many an icy splinter.
On the hillside, in the hollow,
  Weaving wreaths of snow:
Now in gusts of solemn music
  Lost in murmurs low;
Howling now across the wold
  In its shroudlike vastness,
Like the wolves about a fold
  In some Alpine fastness,
Hungered by the cold.

(THE MOTHER SINGS.)

Babe of mine—babe of mine,
  Must I lose you?
Dare I weep if the Divine
  Will should choose you?—
Ah, to mourn, as I have smiled,
At the thought of you, my child!
  Ah, my child—my child!

Babe of mine—you entwine
　　With existence!
If one strips the clinging vine
　　There's resistance—
Shall not I then——? I talk wild,
Seeing Death so near my child:—
　　Ah, my child—my child!

Babe of mine—heart's best wine—
　　Life's pure essence!
Gloomy shadows, that define
　　Death's near presence.
Dim those dear eyes, undefiled
As God's violets—ah, my child:
　　Ah, my child—my child!

The imperial purple of the night
　　Is spread, wine-dark, above,
But glistens with no gems of light,
　　To hint of Heaven's love.
A sombre pall hangs overhead,
Fringed with lurid clouds of lead,—
O'er the sleeping earth below
One long, wide waste of silent snow,
And the wind moans drearily
　　As it wanders by,
And the night wanes wearily
　　In the starlight sky.

(THE MOTHER SINGS.)

Must the dear eyes close?
　Must the lips be still?—
How I love their speech that flows
　Like a wanton rill!
Must those cheeks, soft-tinged with rose,
　Pallid grow and chill?
Give her back to me, angel in disguise!
So your mystery I shall learn—yet with tear-
　　　less eyes.
　By the pangs, the prayers,
　　By the mother's glee,
　By her hopes, her fears, her cares,
　　Give my child to me—
　　　Give it back to me!

　Quenched the eye's soft light,
　　Hushed the cowslip breath!
　Going, darling, in the night?
　　Spare—oh, spare her, Death!
　Dying—is it so?
　　Oh, it must not be!
　Can my one poor treasure go?
　　Give her back to me,
　　Give her back to me:
Or take me too,—left alone,
Now my little one is gone;
　Ah, my child, my child!
　　　　　20*

Among the clouds that sail o'erhead
A yellow radiance is shed ;
And o'er the hill-tops wrapt in snow,
Is born a tinge of rosy glow.
Within the air a stir—like wings
Of angels in their minist'rings ;
A tremulous motion, and a thrill,
As with faint light the heavens fill.
Night's sombre clouds are slow withdrawn,
And nature cries, Awake, 'tis dawn.

About the lonely casement
    Blows fresh the breath of day ;—
The mother, in amazement,
    Sees death-glooms fade away !

The blue eyes open once again,
    Once more the lips have smiled—
Her tears fell like the spring-time rain :
    God gives her back her child !

Hush, there are footsteps on the snow,
That pause the lattice-pane below ;
While voices chant the carol-rhymes,
The Christmas song of olden times :

Awake, good Christians ! Long ago
    The shepherds waked at night,

And saw the heavens with glory glow,
  And angels in the light.
    Hosanna ! sing, Hosanna ! sing,
    Hosanna in the height !

New life they told to all on earth,
  New life and blessing bright,
Forewarning of the Saviour's birth,
  In Bethlehem this night.
    Hosanna ! sing, Hosanna ! sing,
    Hosanna in the height !

New life to all,—new life to all,—
  The tidings good recite !
New life to all, which did befall
  At Bethlehem this night.
    Hosanna ! sing, Hosanna ! sing,
    Hosanna in the height !

The voices hushed—the footsteps died
  In distance far aloof,
It seemed a blessing did abide
  Upon that silent roof,
As far away their cheery singing
Upon the frosty air came ringing.

Among the clouds that sail o'erhead
A yellow glory is outspread ;

And on the hill-tops crowned with snows,
A rosy blushing radiance grows,
As wider still the warm light glows:
And flooding daylight falls again
From cloud to hill—from hill to plain.

A golden sea of swimming light
Poured o'er the sombre shores of night,
While the glad mother, to her breast
Her child yet close and closer pressed,
Her rescued treasure—newly born—
Her babe—given back on Christmas morn.

Thomas Hood

A LULLING SONG.

Hush! my dear, lie still and slumber,
   Holy Angels guard thy bed;
Heavenly blessings without number
   Gently falling on thy head.

Sleep, my babe; thy food and raiment,
   House and home, thy friends provide;
All without thy care or payment,
   All thy wants are well supplied.

How much better thou'rt attended
   Than the Son of God could be,
When from heaven He descended,
   And became a child like thee!

Soft and easy is thy cradle:
   Coarse and hard thy Saviour lay,
When His birthplace was a stable,
   And His softest bed was hay.

See the kinder shepherds round Him,
   Telling wonders from the sky!
Where they sought Him, there they found Him
   With His Virgin-Mother by.

See the lovely Babe a-dressing;
　Lovely Infant, how He smiled!
When He wept, the Mother's blessing
　Soothed and hush'd the holy Child.

Lo, He slumbers in His manger,
　Where the hornéd oxen fed;
—Peace, my darling, here's no danger;
　Here's no ox a-near thy bed!

May'st thou live to know and fear Him,
　Trust and love Him all thy days;
Then go dwell forever near Him,
　See His face and sing His praise!

I could give thee thousand kisses,
　Hoping what I most desire;
Not a mother's fondest wishes
　Can to greater joys aspire.

Isaac Watts.

GOOD-NIGHT.

Good-night, good-night, the day is done;
Rock, rock the cradle, little one;
The lamp is low, and low the sun,
Good-night!

Good-night, good-night, the Christmas bough
Bends to the rocking wind, and thou
To mother's ditty noddest now,
Good-night!

Good-night, good-night, the holy day
Bring baby sweets, and sweets alway!
Rock, rock—then, tiptoe, steal away,
Good-night!
H. S. M.

END OF BOOK III.

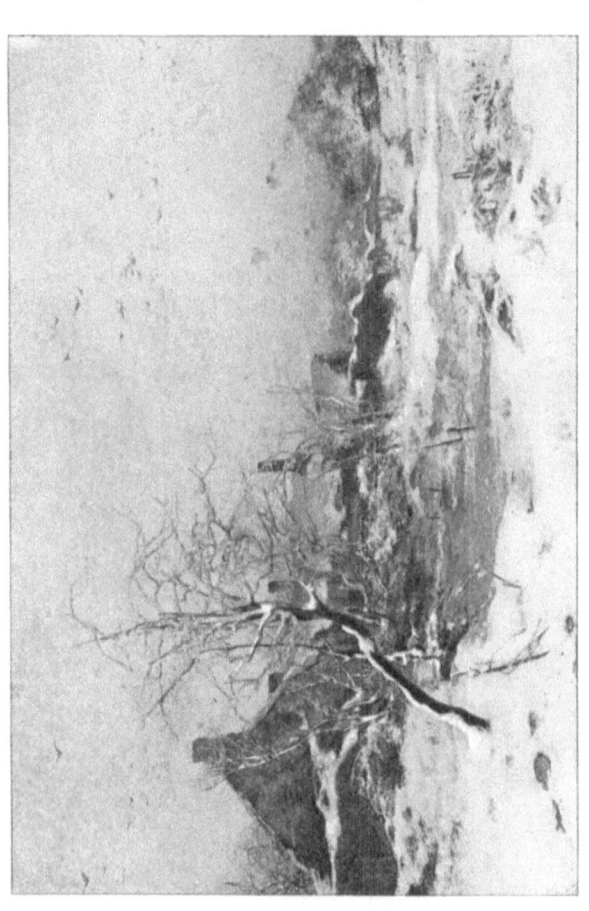

IN THE
YULE-LOG GLOW

CHRISTMAS POEMS FROM
'ROUND THE WORLD

"Sic as folk tell ower at a winter ingle"

Scott

EDITED BY

HARRISON S. MORRIS

IN FOUR BOOKS

Book IV.

PHILADELPHIA

J. B. LIPPINCOTT COMPANY

1900.

Copyright, 1891, by J. B. Lippincott Company.

Printed by J. B. Lippincott Company, Philadelphia.

ILLUSTRATIONS, BOOK IV.

CHRISTMAS WEATHER . . . . Frontispiece.

"WHAT CAN I GIVE HIM?" . . . . Page 90

THE SEASON'S REVERIES . . . . " 174

"TOO HAPPY, HAPPY TREE" . . . . " 212

CONTENTS OF BOOK IV.

SUNG UNDER THE WINDOW.   PAGE

Who's There?   9
God Rest You Merry, Gentlemen   10
Welcome Yule   12
Angel Heralds   14
The Matchless Maiden   15
Remember, O Thou Man   16
The Singers in the Snow   19
A Christmas Chorus   21
Three Ships   22
Jacob's Ladder   24
Saint Stephen, the Clerk   26
The Carnal and the Crane   29
The Holy Well   35
The Holly and the Ivy   38
The Contest of the Vines   39
Ane Sang of the Birth of Christ   41
Christmas Minstrelsy   43
The Old, Old Story   47
A Christmas Ballad   49
A French Noel *   52
Masters, in this Hall 54

* By the courtesy of Messrs. Houghton, Mifflin & Co.

THE WORSHIP OF THE BABE. PAGE

To His Saviour, a Child; a Present, by a Child 59
Honor to the King 60
New Prince, New Pomp 62
Of the Epiphany 64
A Hymn for the Epiphany 66
A Hymn on the Nativity of My Saviour . . . 68
At Christmas 70
New Heaven, New War 72
For Christmas Day 73
Sung to the King in the Presence at Whitehall 75
And They Laid Him in a Manger 77
The Burning Babe 79
Christ's Nativity 81
An Ode on the Birth of Our Saviour 83
Who Can Forget? 85
The Child Jesus 87
Long Ago 89
Star of Bethlehem 91
No Room 92
On Christmas Day 94
The Heavenly Choir 96

THE WASSAIL-BOWL.

Wassail 103
Invitation à Faire Noël 105
A Thanksgiving 107
Around the Wassail-Bowl 108
From Door to Door 111
Wassailing Carol 113

Contents of Book IV.   5

PAGE

A Carol at the Gates 116
Wandering Wassailers 118
Bring Us in Good Ale 120
About the Board 122
Before the Feast 123
A Bill of Christmas Fare 125
The Mahogany-Tree 126
A Christmas Ceremony 129
With Cakes and Ale 129
The Masque of Christmas 130

SANTA CLAUS.

A Visit from St. Nicholas . . . . : . 145
The Hard Times in Elfland * 148
Old Christmas 156
Mrs. Santa Claus 158
Santa Claus to Little Ethel 163

THE SEASON'S REVERIES.

Guests at Yule 169
Christmas in India 171
Christmas Violets 174
Dickens Returns on Christmas Day 175
A Grief at Christmas 176
My Sister's Sleep 183
Christmas in Edinborough. I. 186
Christmas in Edinborough. II. 187
Around the Christmas Lamp 188
Christmas Eve 189
Wonderland 190

* By the courtesy of Messrs. Charles Scribners' Sons.
1*

6 *Contents of Book IV.*

PAGE

Waiting 192
Aunt Mary 193
The Glad New Day 195
Under the Holly Bough 196
The Dawn of Christmas 198
Ballade of Christmas Ghosts 200
The Village Christmas 202
Winter 203
December 204
Christmas Weather in Scotland 205
Sir Galahad 212
A Thought for the Time 213
Ballade of the Winter Fireside 214
A Catch by the Hearth 216
Sally in Our Alley 217
Little Mother 218
Occident and Orient 220
The Blessed Day 225
Christmas in Cuba * 227
Farewell to Christmas 229
The New Year 231
A Happy New Year . . . . · . 234
New-Year's Gifts 236
The End of the Play 238
Finis 240

* By the courtesy of Messrs. Harper & Bros.

Sung Under The Window.

> "This carol they began that hour
> With a hey, and a ho, and a hey
>   nonino!"
>
> *Shakespeare.*

WHO'S THERE?

Nowell, nowell, nowell, nowell,
Who ys there that syngith so, nowell, nowell,
 nowell?

I am here, syre Christmasse!
Well come, my lord syre Christmasse,
Welcome to us all, bothe more and lesse,
                                        Come nere, nowell!

Dieu vous garde, beau syre, tydinges you bryng:
A mayd hath born a chylde full yong,
The weche causeth yew for to syng,
                                        Nowell!

Criste is now born of a pure mayde,
In an oxe stalle he ys layde,
Wher'for syng we alle atte abrayde
                                        Nowell!

Bebbex bien par tutte la company,
Make gode chere and be right mery,
And syng with us now joyfully,
                                        Nowell!

GOD REST YOU MERRY, GENTLEMEN.

God rest you merry, gentlemen,
　Let nothing you dismay,
For Jesus Christ our Saviour
　Was born upon this day
To save us all from Satan's power
　When we were gone astray.
　　O tidings of comfort and joy,
　　For Jesus Christ our Saviour was born
　　　on Christmas day.

In Bethlehem in Jewry
　This blessed babe was born,
And laid within a manger
　Upon this blessed morn ;
The which His mother Mary
　Nothing did take in scorn.
　　　　　　　　O tidings, etc.

From God our Heavenly Father
　A blessed angel came,
And unto certain shepherds
　Brought tidings of the same,
How that in Bethlehem was born
　The Son of God by name.
　　　　　　　　O tidings, etc.

Fear not, then said the angel,
  Let nothing you affright,
This day is born a Saviour
  Of virtue, power, and might ;
So frequently to vanquish all
  The friends of Satan quite.
                         O tidings, etc.

The shepherds at those tidings
  Rejoicéd much in mind,
And left their flocks a-feeding
  In tempest, storm, and wind,
And went to Bethlehem straightway
  This blessed babe to find.
                         O tidings, etc.

But when to Bethlehem they came,
  Whereat this infant lay,
They found Him in a manger
  Where oxen feed on hay ;
His mother Mary kneeling
  Unto the Lord did pray.
                         O tidings, etc.

Now to the Lord sing praises,
  All you within this place,
And with true love and brotherhood
  Each other now embrace ;
This holy tide of Christmas
  All others doth deface.
                         O tidings, etc.

WELCOME YULE.

Welcome Yule, thou merry man,
In worship of this holy day.

Welcome be thou, heaven-king,
Welcome born in one morning,
Welcome for whom we shall sing,
    Welcome Yule.

Welcome be ye, Stephen and John,
Welcome Innocents, every one,
Welcome Thomas Martyr one,
    Welcome Yule.

Welcome be ye, good New Year,
Welcome Twelfth Day, both in fere,*
Welcome saintés lef† and dear,
   ' Welcome Yule.

Welcome be ye, Candlemas,
Welcome be ye, Queen of Bliss,
Welcome both to more and less,
    Welcome Yule.

---

* Together.   † Loved.

Welcome be ye that are here,
Welcome all and make good cheer ;
Welcome all, another year,
    Welcome Yule.

Ritson's Ancient Songs.

ANGEL HERALDS.

As Joseph was a-walking,
　He heard an angel sing:
" This night shall be born
　Our Heavenly King;

" He neither shall be born
　In housen nor in hall,
Nor in the place of Paradise,
　But in an ox's stall;

" He neither shall be clothéd
　In purple nor in pall,
But all in fair linen,
　As we were babies all.

" He neither shall be rocked
　In silver nor in gold,
But in a wooden cradle
　That rocks on the mould.

" He neither shall be christened
　In white wine nor in red,
But with fair spring-water
　With which we were christenéd."

THE MATCHLESS MAIDEN.

I sing of a maiden
    That is makeless ;*
King of all kings
    To her son she ches ;†

He came also‡ still
    There His mother was,
As dew in April
    That falleth on the grass.

He came also still
    To His mother's bower,
As dew in April
    That falleth on the flower.

He came also still
    There His mother lay,
As dew in April
    That falleth on the spray.

Mother and maiden
    Was never none but she ;
Well may such a lady
    God's mother be.

Wright's Songs and Carols.

---

* Matchless.   † Chose.   ‡ As.

REMEMBER, O THOU MAN.

Remember, O thou Man,
O thou Man, O thou Man;
Remember, O thou Man,
    Thy time is spent.
Remember, O thou Man,
How thou camest to me then,
And I did what I can,
    Therefore repent.

Remember Adam's fall,
O thou Man, O thou Man;
Remember Adam's fall
    From Heaven to Hell.
Remember Adam's fall,
How we were condemnéd all
To Hell perpetual,
    There for to dwell.

Remember God's goodness,
O thou Man, O thou Man;
Remember God's goodness
    And promise made.
Remember God's goodness,
How His only Son He sent
Our sins for to redress,
    Be not afraid.

The Angels all did sing,
O thou Man, O thou Man;
The Angels all did sing
   On Sion hill.
The Angels all did sing
Praises to our heavenly king,
And peace to man living,
   With right good-will.

The Shepherds amazed was,
O thou Man, O thou Man;
The Shepherds amazed was
   To hear the angels sing.
The Shepherds amazed was
How this should come to pass,
That Christ our Messias
   Should be our King.

To Bethlehem did they go,
O thou Man, O thou Man;
To Bethlehem did they go
   This thing to see.
To Bethlehem did they go
To see whether it was so,
Whether Christ was born or no,
   To set us free.

As the Angels before did say,
O thou Man, O thou Man;
As the Angels before did say,
   So it came to pass.

As the Angels before did say,
They found Him wrapt in hay
In a manger where He lay,
    So poor He was.

In Bethlehem was He born,
O thou Man, O thou Man;
In Bethlehem was He born
    For mankind dear.
In Bethlehem was He born
For us that were forlorn,
And therefore took no scorn
    Our sins to bear.

In a manger laid He was,
O thou Man, O thou Man;
In a manger laid He was
    At this time present.
In a manger laid He was
Between an ox and an ass,
And all for our trespass,
    Therefore repent.

Give thanks to God always,
O thou Man, O thou Man;
Give thanks to God always
    With hearts most jolly.
Give thanks to God always
Upon this blessed day,
Let all men sing and say,
    Holy, Holy.

            Ravenscroft's Melismata, A.D 1611.

THE SINGERS IN THE SNOW.

God bless the master of this house
    And all that are therein,
And to begin this Christmas tide
    With mirth now let us sing.
For the Saviour of all people
    Upon this time was born,
Who did from death deliver us,
    When we were left forlorn.

Then let us all most merry be,
    And sing with cheerful voice,
For we have good occasion now
    This time for to rejoice.
                    For, etc.

Then put away contention all,
    And fall no more at strife,
Let every man with cheerfulness
    Embrace his loving wife.
                    For, etc.

With plenteous food your houses store,
    Provide some wholesome cheer,
And call your friends together
    That live both far and near.
                    For, etc.

Then let us all most merry be,
　　Since that we are come here,
And we do hope before we part
　　To taste some of your beer.

　　　　　　　　　　For, etc.

Your beer, your beer, your Christmas beer,
　　That seems to be so strong;
And we do wish that Christmas-tide
　　Was twenty times so long.

　　　　　　　　　　For, etc.

Then sing with voices cheerfully,
　　For Christ this time was born,
Who did from death deliver us,
　　When we were left forlorn.

　　　　　　　　　　For, etc.

A CHRISTMAS CHORUS.

Here is joy for every age—
Every generation ;
Prince and peasant, chief and sage,
Every tongue and nation,
Every tongue and nation,
Every rank and station,
Hath to-day salvation.
   Alleluia !

When the world drew near its close,
Came our Lord and leader ;
From the lily came the rose,
From the bush the cedar,
From the bush the cedar,
From the judge the pleader,
From the saint the feeder.
   Alleluia !

God, that came on earth this morn,
In a manger lying,
Hallow'd birth by being born,
Vanquished death by dying,
Vanquished death by dying,
Rallied back the flying,
Ended sin and sighing.
   Alleluia !

THREE SHIPS.

I saw three ships come sailing in,
　On Christmas day, on Christmas day;
I saw three ships come sailing in,
　On Christmas day in the morning.

And what was in those ships all three,
　On Christmas day, on Christmas day?
And what was in those ships all three,
　On Christmas day in the morning?

Our Saviour Christ and His lady,
　On Christmas day, on Christmas day;
Our Saviour Christ and His lady,
　On Christmas day in the morning.

Pray whither sailed those ships all three,
　On Christmas day, on Christmas day?
Pray whither sailed those ships all three,
　On Christmas day in the morning?

O they sailed into Bethlehem,
　On Christmas day, on Christmas day,
O they sailed into Bethlehem,
　On Christmas day in the morning.

And all the bells on earth shall ring,
  On Christmas day, on Christmas day;
And all the bells on earth shall ring,
  On Christmas day in the morning.

And all the angels in heaven shall sing,
  On Christmas day, on Christmas day;
And all the angels in heaven shall sing,
  On Christmas day in the morning.

And all the souls on earth shall sing,
  On Christmas day, on Christmas day;
And all the souls on earth shall sing,
  On Christmas day in the morning.

Then let us all rejoice amain,
  On Christmas day, on Christmas day;
Then let us all rejoice amain,
  On Christmas day in the morning.

JACOB'S LADDER.

As Jacob with travel was weary one day,
At night on a stone for a pillow he lay;
He saw in a vision a ladder so high
That its foot was on earth and its top in the
     sky.
  Hallelujah to Jesus, who died on the tree,
  And hath rais'd up a ladder of mercy for me.

This ladder is high, it is strong and well made,
Hath stood hundreds of years and is not yet
     decayed;
Many millions have climbed it and reached
     Zion's hill,
And thousands, by faith, are climbing it still.
                 Hallelujah, etc.

Come, let us ascend, all may climb it who will,
For the angels of Jacob are guarding it still;
And remember each step that by faith we pass
     o'er,
Some prophet or martyr hath trod it before.
                 Hallelujah, etc.

And when we arrive at the haven of rest,
We shall hear the glad word : Come up hither,
    ye blest !
Here are regions of light, here are mansions of
    bliss,
Oh, who would not climb such a ladder as this ?
               Hallelujah, etc.

B

SAINT STEPHEN, THE CLERK.

Saint Stephen was a clerk
    In King Herod's hall,
And servéd him of bread and cloth
    As ever king befall.

Stephen out of kitchen came
    With boar's head on hand,
He saw a star was fair and bright
    Over Bethlehem stand.

He kist adown the boar's head
    And went into the hall :
" I forsake thee, King Herod,
    And thy workés all.

" I forsake thee, King Herod,
    And thy workés all ;
There is a child in Bethlehem born
    Is better than we all."

" What aileth thee, Stephen ?
    What is thee befall ?
Lacketh thee either meat or drink
    In King Herod's hall ?"

" Lacketh me neither meat ne drink
  In King Herod's hall ;
There is a child in Bethlehem born
  Is better than we all."

" What aileth thee, Stephen ?
  Art thou wode,* or thou ginnest to breed ?†
Lacketh thee either gold or fee,
  Or any rich weed ?"‡

" Lacketh me neither gold nor fee,
  Ne none rich weed ;
There is a child in Bethlehem born
  Shall helpen us at our need."

" That is also sooth,§ Stephen,
  Also sooth i-wis
As this capon crowé shall
  That lieth here in my dish."

That word was not so soon said,
  That word in that hall,
The capon crew *Christus natus est*
  Among the lordés all.

" Riseth up, my tormentors,
  By two and all by one,

And leadeth Stephen out of this town,
    And stoneth him with stone."

Tooken they Stephen
    And stoned him in the way,
And therefore is his even
    On Christés own day.

THE CARNAL AND THE CRANE.

As I pass'd by a riverside,
  And there as I did reign,*
In argument I chanced to hear
  A Carnal† and a Crane.

The Carnal said unto the Crane,
  If all the world should turn,
Before we had the Father,
  But now we have the Son!

From whence does the Son come?
  From where and from what place?
He said, In a manger,
  Between an ox and ass!

I pray thee, said the Carnal,
  Tell me before thou go,
Was not the mother of Jesus
  Conceived by the Holy Ghost?

She was the purest Virgin,
  And the cleanest from sin;
She was the handmaid of our Lord,
  And mother of our King.

---

* Run.   † Crow.

3*

Where is the golden cradle
    That Christ was rockéd in?
Where are the silken sheets
    That Jesus was wrapt in?

A manger was the cradle
    That Christ was rockéd in;
The provender the asses left
    So sweetly He slept on.

There was a star in the West-land,
    So bright did it appear
Into King Herod's chamber,
    And where King Herod were.

The Wise Men soon espied it,
    And told the king on high,
A princely babe was born that night
    No king could e'er destroy.

If this be true, King Herod said,
    As thou tellest unto me,
This roasted cock that lies in the dish
    Shall crow full fences* three.

The cock soon freshly feathered was
    By the work of God's own hand,

---

* Rounds.

And then three fences crowéd he
  In the dish where he did stand.

Rise up, rise up, you merry men all,
  See that you ready be,
All children under two years old
  Now slain they all shall be.

Then Jesus, ah! and Joseph,
  And Mary that was so pure,
They travelled into Egypt,
  As you shall find it sure.

And when they came to Egypt's land,
  Amongst those fierce wild beasts,
Mary, she being weary,
  Must needs sit down to rest.

Come sit thee down, says Jesus,
  Come sit thee down by me,
And thou shalt see how these wild beasts
  Do come and worship me.

First came the lovely lion,
  Which Jesu's grace did spring,
And of the wild beasts in the field,
  The lion shall be the king.

We'll choose our virtuous princes,
  Of birth and high degree,

In every sundry nation,
  Where'er we come and see.

Then Jesus, ah! and Joseph,
  And Mary, that was unknown,
They travelled by a husbandman,
  Just while his seed was sown.

God speed thee, man! said Jesus,
  Go fetch thy ox and wain,
And carry home thy corn again
  Which thou this day hast sown.

The husbandman fell on his knees,
  Even before his face ;
Long time hast Thou been looked for,
  But now Thou art come at last.

And I myself do now believe
  Thy name is Jesus called ;
Redeemer of mankind Thou art,
  Though undeserving all.

The truth, man, thou hast spoken,
  Of it thou may'st be sure,
For I must lose my precious blood
  For thee and thousands more.

If any one should come this way,
  And inquire for me alone,

Tell them that Jesus passed by,
   As thou thy seed did sow.

After that there came King Herod,
   With his train so furiously,
Inquiring of the husbandman,
   Whether Jesus passed by.

Why, the truth it must be spoke,
   And the truth it must be known,
For Jesus passéd by this way
   When my seed was sown.

But now I have it reapen,
   And some laid on my wain,
Ready to fetch and carry
   Into my barn again.

Turn back, says the captain,
   Your labor and mine's in vain,
It's full three-quarters of a year
   Since he his seed sown.

So Herod was deceivéd
   By the work of God's own hand,
And further he proceeded
   Into the Holy Land.

There's thousands of children young,
   Which for His sake did die;

IV.—c

Do not forbid those little ones,
   And do not them deny.

The truth now I have spoken,
   And the truth now I have shown,
Even the blessed Virgin,
   She's now brought forth a Son.

THE HOLY WELL.

As it fell out one May morning,
  And upon one bright holiday,
Sweet Jesus asked of His dear mother,
  If He might go to play.

To play, to play, sweet Jesus shall go,
  And to play pray get you gone;
And let me hear of no complaint
  At night when you come home.

Sweet Jesus went down to yonder town
  As far as the Holy Well,
And there did see as fine children
  As any tongue can tell.

He said, God bless you every one,
  And your bodies Christ save and see:
Little children, shall I play with you,
  And you shall play with me?

But they made answer to Him, No:
They were lords' and ladies' sons;
And He, the meanest of them all,
Was but a maiden's child, born in an ox's
    stall.

Sweet Jesus turned Him around,
And He neither laughed nor smiled,
But the tears came trickling from His eyes
Like water from the skies.

Sweet Jesus turned Him about,
   To His mother's dear home went He,
And said, I have been in yonder town,
   As far as you can see.

I have been down in yonder town
   As far as the Holy Well,
There did I meet as fine children
   As any tongue can tell.

I bid God bless them every one,
   And their bodies Christ save and see :
Little children, shall I play with you,
   And you shall play with me?

But they made answer to me, No:
They were lords' and ladies' sons ;
And I, the meanest of them all,
Was but a maiden's child, born in an ox's
   stall.

Though you are but a maiden's child,
   Born in an ox's stall,
Thou art the Christ, the King of heaven,
   And the Saviour of them all.

Sweet Jesus, go down to yonder town
  As far as the Holy Well,
And take away those sinful souls,
  And dip them deep in hell.

Nay, nay, sweet Jesus said,
  Nay, nay, that may not be ;
For there are too many sinful souls
  Crying out for the help of me.

4

THE HOLLY AND THE IVY.

The Holly and the Ivy,
Now both are full well grown ;
Of all the trees that spring in wood,
The holly bears the crown.
The holly bears a blossom
As white as a lily flow'r ;
And Mary bore sweet Jesus Christ
To be our sweet Saviour.

The holly bears a berry
As red as any blood,
And Mary bore sweet Jesus Christ
To do poor sinners good.
The holly bears a prickle
As sharp as any thorn,
And Mary bore sweet Jesus Christ
On Christmas Day in the morn.

The holly bears a bark
As bitter as any gall,
And Mary bore sweet Jesus Christ
For to redeem us all.
The holly and the ivy
Now are both well grown ;
Of all the trees that are in the wood,
The holly bears the crown.

THE CONTEST OF THE VINES.

Nay, ivy, nay,
  It shall not be, I wis;
Let holly have the mastery,
  As the manner is.

Holly stand in the hall,
  Fair to behold;
Ivy stand without the door,
  She is full sore a-cold.
            Nay, ivy, nay, etc.

Holly and his merry men
  They dancen and they sing;
Ivy and her maidens
  They weepen and they wring.
            Nay, ivy, nay, etc.

Ivy hath a kybe,*
  She caught it with the cold;
So mot they all have ae,†
  That with ivy hold.
            Nay, ivy, nay, etc.

---

* Chapped skin.　　　† So may all have.

Holly hath berries
  As red as any rose,
The forester and the hunters
  Keep them from the does.
                    Nay, ivy, nay, etc.

Ivy hath berries
  As black as any sloe;
There come the owl
  And eat him as she go.
                    Nay, ivy, nay, etc.

Holly hath birdés
  A full fair flock,
The nightingale, the popinjay,
  The gentle laverock.
                    Nay, ivy, nay, etc.

Good ivy,
  What birdés hast thou?
None but the howlet
  That krey * " How, how."

Nay, ivy, nay,
  It shall not be, I wis;
Let holly have the mastery,
  As the manner is.

----

* Cries.

ANE SANG OF THE BIRTH OF CHRIST.

A SCOTCH CAROL.

I come from hevin to tell
The best nowellis that ever befell ;
To you this tythinges trew I bring,
And I will of them say and sing :

This day to yow is borne ane childe
Of Marie meike and Virgine mylde,
That blessit barne, bining and kynde,
Sall yow rejoyce baith heart and mynd.

My saull and lyfe, stand up and see
Quha lyes in ane cribe of tree,
Quhat babe is that, so gude and faire ?
It is Christ, God's sonne and aire.

O God, that made all creature,
How art Thow becum so pure,
That on the hay and stray will lye
Amang the asses, oxin, and kye !

O my deir hert, young Jesus sweit,
Prepare Thy creddill in my spreit,

4*

And I sall rocke Thee in my hert,
And never mair from Thee depart.

But I sall praise Thee evermoir
With sangs sweit unto Thy gloir,
The knees of my hert sall I bow,
And sing that right Balululow.

CHRISTMAS MINSTRELSY.

The minstrels played their Christmas tune
To-night beneath my cottage eaves;
While smitten by a lofty moon,
The encircling laurels thick with leáves,
Gave back a rich and dazzling sheen,
That overpowered their natural green.

Through hill and valley every breeze
Had sunk to rest with folded wings:
Keen was the air, but could not freeze
Nor check the music of the strings;
So stout and hardy were the band
That scraped the chords with strenuous hand.

And who but listened?—till was paid
Respect to every inmate's claim,
The greeting given, the music played
In honor of each household name,
Duly pronounced with lusty call,
And a merry Christmas wished to all.

O Brother! I revere the choice
That took thee from thy native hills;
And it is given thee to rejoice:
Though public care full often tills

(Heaven only witness of the toil)
A barren and ungrateful soil.

Yet would that thou, with me and mine,
Hadst heard this never-failing rite ;
And seen on other faces shine
A true revival of the light
Which nature, and these rustic powers,
In simple childhood, spread through ours!

For pleasure hath not ceased to wait
On these expected annual rounds,
Whether the rich man's sumptuous gate
Call forth the unelaborate sounds,
Or they are offered at the door
That guard the lowliest of the poor.

How touching, when at midnight sweep
Snow-muffled winds, and all is dark,
To hear—and sink again in sleep!
Or at an earlier call, to mark,
By blazing fire, the still suspense
Of self-complacent innocence ;

The mutual nod—the grave disguise
Of hearts with gladness brimming o'er,
And some unhidden tears that rise
For names once heard, and heard no more ;

Tears brightened by the serenade
For infant in the cradle laid!

Ah! not for emerald fields alone,
With ambient streams more pure and bright
Than fabled Cytherea's zone
Glittering before the Thunderer's sight,
Is to my heart of hearts endeared,
The ground where we were born and reared!

Hail, ancient manners! sure defence,
Where they survive, of wholesome laws:
Remnants of love whose modest sense
Thus into narrow room withdraws;
Hail, usages of pristine mould,
And ye that guard them, Mountains old!

Bear with me, Brother! quench the thought
That slights this passion or condemns;
If thee fond fancy ever brought
From the proud margin of the Thames,
And Lambeth's venerable towers,
To humble streams and greener bowers.

Yes, they can make, who fail to find
Short leisure even in busiest days,
Moments to cast a look behind,
And profit by those kindly rays

That through the clouds do sometimes steal,
And all the far-off past reveal.

Hence, while the imperial city's din
Beats frequent on thy satiate ear,
A pleased attention I may win
To agitations less severe,
That neither overwhelm nor cloy,
But fill the hollow vale with joy!

William Wordsworth.

THE OLD, OLD STORY.

Listen, Lordings, unto me, a tale I will you
tell,
Which, as on this night of glee, in David's town
befell.
Joseph came from Nazareth, with Mary that
sweet maid ;
Weary were they, nigh to death; and for a
lodging pray'd.
Sing high, sing high, sing low, sing low,
Sing high, sing low, sing to and fro,
    Go tell it out with speed,
    Cry out and shout all round about,
    That Christ is born indeed.

In the inn they found no room ; a scanty bed
they made :
Soon a Babe from Mary's womb was in the
manger laid.
Forth He came as light through glass : He came
to save us all,
In the stable ox and ass before their Maker
fall.

          Sing high, sing low, etc.

Shepherds lay afield that night, to keep the
    silly sheep,
Hosts of angels in their sight came down from
    heaven's high steep.
Tidings! tidings! unto you: to you a Child is
    born,
Purer than the drops of dew, and brighter than
    the morn.
               Sing high, sing low, etc.

Onward then the angels sped, the shepherds
    onward went,
God was in His manger bed, in worship low
    they bent.
In the morning see ye mind, my masters one
    and all,
At the altar Him to find who lay within the
    stall.
               Sing high, sing low, etc.
                    H. R. Bramley.

A CHRISTMAS BALLAD.

Outlanders, whence come ye last?
The snow in the street and the wind on the door.
Through what green sea and great have ye
    past?
Minstrels and maids, stand forth on the floor.

From far away, O masters mine,
The snow in the street and the wind on the door.
We come to bear you goodly wine :
Minstrels and maids, stand forth on the floor.

From far away we come to you,
The snow in the street and the wind on the door.
To tell of great tidings strange and true:
Minstrels and maids, stand forth on the floor.

News, news of the Trinity,
The snow in the street and the wind on the door.
And Mary and Joseph from over the sea:
Minstrels and maids, stand forth on the floor.

For as we wandered far and wide,
The snow in the street and the wind on the door.
What hope do ye deem there should us betide?
Minstrels and maids, stand forth on the floor.

Under a bent when the night was deep,
The snow in the street and the wind on the door.
There lay three shepherds tending their sheep:
Minstrels and maids, stand forth on the floor.

" O ye shepherds, what have ye seen,
The snow in the street and the wind on the door.
To slay your sorrow and heal your teen ?"
Minstrels and maids, stand forth on the floor.

" In an ox-stall this night we saw,
The snow in the street and the wind on the door.
A Babe and a maid without a flaw.
Minstrels and maids, stand forth on the floor.

" There was an old man there beside,
The snow in the street and the wind on the door.
His hair was white, and his hood was wide.
Minstrels and maids, stand forth on the floor.

" And as we gazed this thing upon,
The snow in the street and the wind on the door.
Those twain knelt down to the Little One.
Minstrels and maids, stand forth on the floor.

" And a marvellous song we straight did hear,
The snow in the street and the wind on the door.
That slew our sorrow and healed our care."
Minstrels and maids, stand forth on the floor

News of a fair and a marvellous thing,
  The snow in the street and the wind on the door.
Nowell, nowell, nowell, we sing!
  Minstrels and maids, stand forth on the floor.
                              William Morris.

A FRENCH NOËL.

(TRANSLATED FROM GUI BARÔZAI.)

I hear along our street
 Pass the minstrel throngs ;
Hark ! they play so sweet,
 On their hautboys, Christmas songs !
  Let us by the fire
  Ever higher
  Sing them till the night expire !

In December ring
 Every day the chimes ;
Loud the gleemen sing
 In the streets their merry rhymes.
    Let us by the fire, etc.

Shepherds at the grange,
 Where the Babe was born,
Sang, with many a change,
 Christmas carols until morn.
    Let us by the fire, etc.

These good people sang
 Songs devout and sweet ;
While the rafters rang
 There they stood with freezing feet.
    Let us by the fire, etc.

Nuns in frigid cells
  At this holy tide
For want of something else
  Christmas songs at times have tried.
    ·   Let us by the fire, etc.

Washerwomen old,
  To the sound they beat,
Sing by rivers cold
  With uncovered heads and feet.
    ·   Let us by the fire, etc.

Who by the fireside stands
  Stamps his feet and sings;
But he who blows his hands
  Not so gay a carol brings.
       Let us by the fire, etc.
Henry Wadsworth Longfellow.

MASTERS, IN THIS HALL.

" To Bethl'em did they go, the shepherds three ;
To Bethl'em did they go to see whe'r it were
        so or no,
Whether Christ were born or no
        To set men free."

Masters, in this hall,
        Hear ye news to-day
Brought over sea,
        And ever I you pray.
            Nowell ! Nowell ! Nowell ! Nowell !
                Sing we clear !
            Holpen are all folk on earth,
                Born is God's Son so dear.

Going over the hills,
        Through the milk-white snow,
Heard I ewes bleat
        While the winds did blow.
                    Nowell, etc.

Shepherds many an one
        Sat among the sheep ;

No man spake more word
  Than they had been asleep.
                  Nowell, etc.

Quoth I, " Fellows mine,
  Why this guise sit ye ?
Making but dull cheer,
  Shepherds though ye be ?
                  Nowell, etc.

" Shepherds should of right
  Leap, and dance, and sing ;
Thus to see you sit
  Is a right strange thing."
                  Nowell, etc.

Quoth these fellows three,
  " To Bethl'em town we go,
To see a Mighty Lord
  Lie in manger low."
                  Nowell, etc.

" How name ye this Lord,
  Shepherds ?" then said I.
" Very God," they said,
  " Come from Heaven high."
                  Nowell, etc.

Then to Bethl'em town
  We went two and two,

And in a sorry place
  Heard the oxen low.

Nowell, etc.

Therein did we see
  A sweet and goodly May,
And a fair old man ;
  Upon the straw she lay.

Nowell, etc.

And a little Child
  On her arm had she ;
" Wot ye who is this ?"
  Said the hinds to me.

Nowell, etc.

Ox and ass Him know,
  Kneeling on their knee :
Wondrous joy had I
  This little Babe to see.

Nowell, etc.

This is Christ the Lord :
  Masters, be ye glad !
Christmas is come in,
  And no folk should be sad.

Nowell, etc.
William Morris.

The Worship Of The Babe.

" Rejoice, our Saviour He was born
On Christmas day in the morning."

Old Carol.

TO HIS SAVIOUR, A CHILD; A PRESENT,
BY A CHILD.

Go, pretty child, and bear this flower
Unto thy little Saviour;
And tell Him by that bud now blown,
He is a Rose of Sharon known.
When thou hast said so, stick it there
Upon His bib or stomacher;
And tell Him, for good handsel too,
That thou hast brought a whistle new,
Made of a clean, strait oaten reed
To charm His cries at time of need.
Tell Him for coral thou hast none,
But if thou had'st He should have one;
But poor thou art, and known to be
Even as moneyless as He.
Lastly, if thou can'st win a kiss
From those mellifluous lips of His,
Then never take a second on
To spoil the first impression.

Robert Herrick.

HONOR TO THE KING.

Yet if his majesty our sovereign lord
Should of his own accord
Friendly himself invite,
And say, " I'll be your guest to-morrow night,"
How should we stir ourselves, call and com-
      mand
All hands to work : " Let no man idle stand.
Set me fine Spanish tables in the hall,
See they be fitted all ;
Let there be room to ea ,
And order taken that there want no meat.
See every sconce and candlestick made bright,
That without tapers they may give a light.
Look to the presence ; are the carpets spread,
The dais o'er the head,
The cushions in the chairs,
And all the candles lighted on the stairs ?
Perfume the chambers, and in any case
Let each man give attendance in his place."
Thus if the king were coming would we do,
And 'twere good reason too ;
For 'tis a duteous thing
To show all honor to an earthly king,
And after all our travail and our cost,
So he be pleased, to think no labor lost.

But at the coming of the King of Heaven,
All's set at six and seven:
We wallow in our sin,
Christ cannot find a chamber in the inn.
We entertain Him always like a stranger,
And, as at first, still lodge Him in the manger.

Christ Church, Oxford, MS.

NEW PRINCE, NEW POMP.

Behold a silly, tender Babe,
  In freezing winter night,
In homely manger trembling lies ;
  Alas ! a piteous sight.

The inns are full, no man will yield
  This little pilgrim bed ;
But forced He is with silly beasts
  In crib to shroud His head.

Despise Him not for lying there,
  First what He is inquire ;
An orient pearl is often found
  In depth of dirty mire.

Weigh not His crib, His wooden dish,
  Nor beast that by Him feed ;
Weigh not His mother's poor attire,
  Nor Joseph's simple weed.

This stable is a prince's court,
  This crib His chair of state ;
The beasts are parcel of His pomp,
  The wooden dish His plate.

The persons in that poor attire
  His royal liveries wear;
The Prince himself is come from heaven,
  This pomp is praiséd there.

With joy approach, O Christian wight!
  Do homage to thy King;
And highly praise this humble pomp
  Which He from heaven doth bring.

Robert Southwell.

OF THE EPIPHANY.

Fair eastern star, that art ordained to run
Before the sages, to the rising sun,
Here cease thy course, and wonder that the
    cloud
Of this poor stable can thy Maker shroud:
Ye heavenly bodies glory to be bright,
And are esteemed as ye are rich in light;
But here on earth is taught a different way,
Since under this low roof the Highest lay.
Jerusalem erects her stately towers,
Displays her windows and adorns her bowers;
Yet there thou must not cast a trembling spark,
Let Herod's palace still continue dark;
Each school and synagogue thy force repels,
There pride enthroned in misty error dwells;
The temple, where the priests maintain their
    quire,
Shall taste no beam of thy celestial fire,
While this weak cottage all thy splendor takes:
A joyful gate of every chink it makes.
Here shines no golden roof, no ivory stair,
No king exalted in a stately chair,
Girt with attendants, or by heralds styled,
But straw and hay enwrap a speechless child.

Yet Sabæ's lords before this babe unfold
Their treasures, offering incense, myrrh, and
     gold.
The crib becomes an altar; therefore dies
No ox nor sheep; for in their fodder lies
The Prince of Peace, who, thankful for His bed,
Destroys those rites in which their blood was
     shed:
The quintessence of earth He takes, and fees,
And precious gums distilled from weeping trees;
Rich metals and sweet odors now declare
The glorious blessings which His laws prepare,
To clear us from the base and loathsome flood
Of sense and make us fit for angel's food,
Who lift to God for us the holy smoke
Of fervent prayers with which we Him invoke,
And try our actions in the searching fire
By which the seraphims our lips inspire:
No muddy dross pure minerals shall infect,
We shall exhale our vapors up direct:
No storm shall cross, nor glittering lights deface
Perpetual sighs which seek a happy place.

                   Sir John Beaumont.

A HYMN FOR THE EPIPHANY.

SUNG AS BY THE THREE KINGS.

1 *King.*   Bright Babe ! whose awful beauties
                make
             The morn incur a sweet mistake ;
2 *King.*   For whom the officious heavens devise
             To disinherit the sun's rise ;
3 *King.*   Delicately to displace
             The day, and plant it fairer in Thy
                face ;
1 *King.*   O Thou born King of loves !
2 *King.*   Of lights !
3 *King.*   Of joys !

Chorus.   Look up, sweet Babe, look up and see !
             For love of Thee,
             Thus far from home
             The East is come
             To seek herself in Thy sweet eyes.

1 *King.*   We who strangely went astray,
             Lost in a bright
             Meridian night ;
2 *King.*   A darkness made of too much day ;
3 *King.*   Beckoned from far
             By Thy fair star,
             Lo, at last have found our way.

Chorus. To Thee, Thou Day of Night! Thou
      East of West!
      Lo, we at last have found the way
      To Thee, the world's great universal
      East,
      The general and indifferent day.

1 *King.* All circling point! all-centring sphere!
      The world's one round eternal year:
2 *King.* Whose full and all-unwrinkled face
      Nor sinks nor swells with time or
      place;
3 *King.* But everywhere and every while
      Is one consistent solid smile,
1 *King.* Not vexed and tost,
2 *King.* 'Twixt spring and frost;
3 *King.* Nor by alternate shreds of light;
      Sordidly shifting hands with shades
      and night.

Chorus. O little All, in Thy embrace,
      The world lies warm and likes his
      place;
      Nor does his full globe fail to be
      Kissed on both his cheeks by Thee;
      Time is too narrow for Thy year,
      Nor makes the whole world Thy half-
      sphere.

                   Richard Crashaw.

A HYMN ON THE NATIVITY OF MY
SAVIOUR.

I sing the birth was born to-night,
The author both of life and light;
　The angels so did sound it.
And like the ravished shepherds said,
Who saw the light, and were afraid,
　Yet searched, and true they found it

The Son of God th' eternal king,
That did us all salvation bring,
　And freed the soul from danger ;
He whom the whole world could not take,
The Word, which heaven and earth did make,
　Was now laid in a manger.

The Father's wisdom willed it so,
The Son's obedience knew no No,
　Both wills were in one stature ;
And as that wisdom had decreed,
The Word was now made flesh indeed,
　And took on Him our nature.

What comfort by Him do we win,
Who made himself the price of sin,
　To make us heirs of glory !
To see this babe all innocence ;
A martyr born in our defence ;
　Can man forget the story ?

Ben Jonson.

AT CHRISTMAS.

All after pleasures as I rid one day,
   My horse and I both tried, body and mind,
   With full cry of affections quite astray,
I took up in the next inn I could find.

There, when I came, whom found I but my
      dear—
   My dearest Lord; expecting till the grief
   Of pleasures brought me to Him; ready there
To be all passengers' most sweet relief?

O Thou, whose glorious, yet contracted light,
   Wrapt in night's mantle, stole into a manger;
   Since my dark soul and brutish is Thy right,
To man, of all beasts, be not Thou a stranger;

Furnish and deck my soul, that Thou may'st
      have
A better lodging than a rock or grave.

The shepherds sing; and shall I silent be?
      My God, no hymn for Thee?
My soul's a shepherd too; a flock it feeds
      Of thoughts and words and deeds;
The pasture is Thy word, the stream Thy grace,
      Enriching every place.

Shepherd and flock shall sing, and all my
 powers
  Outsing the daylight hours.
Then we will chide the sun for letting night
  Take up his place and right:
We sing one common Lord; wherefore He
 should
  Himself the candle hold.

I will go searching till I find a sun
  Shall stay till we have done;
A willing shiner, that shall shine as gladly
  As frost-nipt suns look sadly,
Then we will sing and shine all our own day,
  And one another pay.

His beams shall cheer my breast; and both so
 twine,
Till ev'n his beams sing and my music shine.
      George Herbert.

NEW HEAVEN, NEW WAR.

Come to your heaven, you heavenly quires!
Earth hath the heaven of your desires;
Remove your dwelling to your God,
A stall is now His blest abode;
Sith men their homage do deny,
Come, angels, all their fault supply.

This little Babe, so few days old,
Is come to rifle Satan's fold;
All hell doth at His presence quake,
Though He himself for cold do shake;
For in this weak, unarméd wise
The gates of hell He will surprise.

My soul, with Christ join thou in fight;
Stick to the tents that He hath pight;
Within His crib is surest ward,
This little Babe will be thy guard;
If thou wilt foil thy foes with joy,
Then flit not from this heavenly Boy.

Robert Southwell.

FOR CHRISTMAS DAY.

Rejoice, rejoice, with heart and voice!
In Christé's birth this day rejoice!
From Virgin's womb this day did spring
The precious seed that only savéd man ;
This day let man rejoice and sweetly sing,
Since on this day salvation first began.
    This day did Christ man's soul from death re-
       move,
    With glorious saints to dwell in heaven
       above.

This day to man came pledge of perfect peace,
This day to man came perfect unity,
This day man's grief began for to surcease,
This day did man receive a remedy
    For each offence and every deadly sin,
    With guilty heart that erst he wandered in.

In Christé's flock let love be surely placed,
From Christé's flock let concord hate expel,
Of Christé's flock let love be so embraced
As we in Christ and Christ in us may dwell;
    Christ is the author of all unity,
    From whence proceedeth all felicity.

D   7

O sing unto this glittering, glorious king,
O praise His name let every living thing;
Let heart and voice, like bells of silver, ring
The comfort that this day doth bring;
    Let lute, let shawm, with sound of sweet de-
        light,
    The joy of Christé's birth this day recite.

Francis Kinwelmersh, A.D. 1576.

SUNG TO THE KING IN THE PRES-
ENCE AT WHITEHALL.

Chor.—What sweeter music can we bring,
   Than a carol for to sing
  The birth of this our heavenly King?
  Awake the voice! awake the string!
  Heart, ear, and eye, and everything
  Awake! the while the active finger
  Runs divisions with the singer.

  From the flourish they come to the song.

  Dark and dull night, fly hence away,
  And give the honor to this day,
  That sees December turn'd to May.

  If we may ask the reason, say
  The why and wherefore all things here
  Seem like the spring-time of the year?
  Why does the chilling winter's morn
  Smile like a field beset with corn?
  Or smell like to a mead new-shorn,
  Thus on the sudden? Come and see
  The cause why things thus fragrant be:
  'Tis He is born whose quickening birth
  Gives life and lustre public mirth
  To heaven and the under-earth.

Chor.—We see Him come, and know Him ours,
    Who with His sunshine and His showers
    Turns all the patient ground to flowers.

    The darling of the world is come,
    And fit it is we find a room
    To welcome Him.   The nobler part
    Of all the house here is the heart.

Chor.—Which we will give Him ; and bequeath
    This holly and this ivy wreath,
    To do Him honor, who's our King,
    And Lord of all this revelling.
                Robert Herrick.

AND THEY LAID HIM IN A MANGER.

Happy crib, that wert alone
To my God, bed, cradle, throne!
Whilst thy glorious vileness I
View with divine fancy's eye,
Sordid filth seems all the cost,
State, and splendor, crowns do boast.

See heaven's sacred majesty
Humbled beneath poverty;
Swaddled up in homely rags
On a bed of straw and flags!
He whose hands the heavens displayed,
And the world's foundation laid,
From the world 's almost exiled,
Of all ornaments despoiled.
Perfumes bathe Him not, new-born,
Persian mantles not adorn;
Nor do the rich roofs look bright
With the jasper's orient light.
Where, O royal Infant, be
Th' ensigns of Thy majesty;
Thy Sire's equalizing state;
And Thy sceptre that rules fate?
Where's Thy angel-guarded throne,
Whence Thy laws Thou didst make known,

7*

Laws which heaven, earth, hell, obeyed ?
These, ah ! these aside He laid ;
Would the emblem be—of pride
By humility outvied ?

Sir Edward Sherburne.

THE BURNING BABE.

As I in hoary winter's night stood shivering in
　　the snow,
Surprised I was with sudden heat which made
　　my heart to glow；　.
And lifting up a fearful eye to view what fire
　　was near,
A pretty babe all burning bright did in the air
　　appear,
Who, scorchéd with excessive heat, such floods
　　of tears did shed,
As though his floods should quench his flames
　　which with his tears were fed.
Alas！ quoth he, but newly born in fiery heats
　　I fry,
Yet none approach to warm their hearts or feel
　　my fire but I.
My faultless breast the furnace is, the fuel
　　wounding thorns：
Love is the fire and sighs the smoke, the ashes
　　shame and scorns：
The fuel justice layeth on, and mercy blows the
　　coals；
The metal in this furnace wrought are men's
　　defiléd souls；

For which, as now on fire I am, to work them
    to their good,
So will I melt into a bath to wash them in my
    blood.
With that he vanish'd out of sight and swiftly
    shrunk away.
And straight I calléd unto mind that it was
    Christmas Day.

                  Robert Southwell.

CHRIST'S NATIVITY.

Awake, glad heart! get up and sing!
It is the birthday of thy King.
      Awake! awake!
      The sun doth shake
Light from his locks, and, all the way
Breathing perfumes, doth spice the day.

Awake! awake! hark how th' wood rings,
Winds whisper, and the busy springs
      A concert make!
      Awake! awake!
Man is their high-priest, and should rise
To offer up the sacrifice.

I would I were some bird or star
Fluttering in woods, or lifted far
      Above this inn,
      And road of sin!
Then either star or bird should be
Shining or singing still to Thee.

I would I had in my best part
Fit rooms for Thee! or that my heart
      Were so clean as
      Thy manger was!

IV.—*f*

But I am all filth, and obscene ;
Yet, if Thou wilt, Thou canst make clean.

Sweet Jesu! will then.   Let no more
This leper haunt and soil Thy door!
      Cure him, ease him,
       O release him !
And let once more, by mystic birth,
The Lord of life be born in earth.

              Henry Vaughan.

AN ODE ON THE BIRTH OF OUR SAVIOUR.

In numbers, and but these few,
I sing Thy birth, O Jesu!
Thou pretty baby, born here
With sup'rabundant scorn here:
Who, for Thy princely port here,
  Hadst for Thy place
  Of birth a base
Out-stable for Thy court here.

Instead of neat enclosures
Of interwoven osiers,
Instead of fragrant posies
Of daffodils and roses,
Thy cradle, kingly stranger,
  As gospel tells,
  Was nothing else
But here a homely manger.

But we with silks not crewels,
With sundry precious jewels,
And lily work will dress Thee;
And, as we dispossess Thee

Of clouts, we'll make a chamber,
    Sweet babe, for Thee
    Of ivory
And plater'd round with amber.

The Jews they did disdain Thee,
But we will entertain Thee
With glories to await here
Upon Thy princely state here;
And, more for love than pity,
    From year to year
    We'll make Thee here
A free-born of our city.

        Robert Herrick.

WHO CAN FORGET?

Who can forget—never to be forgot—
  The time, that all the world in slumber lies,
When, like the stars, the singing angels shot
    To earth, and heaven awaked all his eyes
    To see another sun at midnight rise
On earth ? Was never sight of pareil fame
For God before, man like himself did frame,
But God himself now like a mortal man became.

A child He was, and had not learnt to speak,
    That with His word the world before did
        make ;
His mother's arms Him bore, He was so weak,
    That with one hand the vaults of heaven
        could shake ;
    See how small room my infant Lord doth
        take,
Whom all the world is not enough to hold !
Who of His years or of His age hath told ?
Never such age so young, never a child so old.

And yet but newly He was infanted,
    And yet already He was sought to die ;
Yet scarcely born, already banished ;
    Not able yet to go, and forced to fly :
    But scarcely fled away, when by and by

8

The tyran's sword with blood is all defiled,
And Rachel, for her sons, with fury wild,
Cries, " O thou cruel king, and O my sweetest
        Child !"

Egypt His nurse became, where Nilus springs,
    Who, straight to entertain the rising sun,
The hasty harvest in his bosom brings ;
    But now for drought the fields were all un-
        done,
    And now with waters all is overrun :
So fast the Cynthian mountains pour'd their
        snow,
When once they felt the sun so near them glow,
That Nilus Egypt lost, and to a sea did grow.

The angels carolled loud their song of peace ;
    The cursed oracles were strucken dumb ;
To see their Shepherd the poor shepherds press ;
    To see their King, the kingly sophies* come ;
    And them to guide unto his Master's home,
A star comes dancing up the orient,
That springs for joy over the strawy tent,
Where gold, to make their prince a crown, they
        all present.

                              Giles Fletcher.

---

* Wise men.

THE CHILD JESUS.

A CORNISH CAROL.

Welcome that star in Judah's sky,
    That voice o'er Bethlehem's palmy glen!
The lamp far sages hailed on high,
    The tones that thrilled the shepherd men:
Glory to God in loftiest heaven!
    Thus angels smote the echoing chord;
Glad tidings unto man forgiven,
    Peace from the presence of the Lord.

The Shepherds sought that birth divine,
    The Wise Men traced their guided way;
There, by strange light and mystic sign,
    The God they came to worship lay.
A human Babe in beauty smiled,
    Where lowing oxen round Him trod:
A maiden clasped her awful Child,
    Pure offspring of the breath of God.

Those voices from on high are mute,
    The star the Wise Men saw is dim;
But hope still guides the wanderer's foot,
    And faith renews the angel hymn:

Glory to God in loftiest heaven!
  Touch with glad hand the ancient chord ;
Good tidings unto man forgiven,
  Peace from the presence of the Lord.

                  Robert Stephen Hawker.

LONG AGO.

In the bleak mid-winter
  Frosty wind made moan,
Earth stood hard as iron,
  Water like a stone ;
Snow had fallen, snow on snow,
  Snow on snow,
In the bleak wind-winter
  Long ago.

Our God, heaven cannot hold Him,
  Nor earth sustain ;
Heaven and earth shall flee away
  When He comes to reign :
In the bleak mid-winter
  A stable-place sufficed
The Lord God Almighty,
  Jesus Christ.

Enough for Him whom cherubim
  Worship night and day,
A breastful of milk
  And a mangerful of hay ;
Enough for Him whom angels
  Fall down before,
The ox and ass and camel
  Which adore.

8*

Angels and archangels
  May have gathered there,
Cherubim and seraphim
  Thronged the air ;
But only His mother,
  In her maiden bliss,
Worshipped the Beloved
  With a kiss.

What can I give Him,
  Poor as I am ?
If I were a shepherd,
  I would bring a lamb ;
If I were a wise man,
  I would do my part :
Yet what I can I give Him,
  Give my heart.

                    Christina G. Rossetti.

STAR OF BETHLEHEM.

When marshalled on the nightly plain
The glitt'ring host bestud the sky,
One star alone of all the train
Can fix the sinner's wandering eye.
Hark! hark! to God the chorus breaks
From ev'ry host, from ev'ry gem;
But one alone the Saviour speaks,—
It is the Star of Bethlehem!

Once on the raging seas I rode;
The storm was loud, the night was dark;
The ocean yawned, and rudely blew
The wind that tossed my found'ring bark.
Deep horror then my vitals froze;
Death-struck, I ceased the tide to stem,
When suddenly a star arose,—
It was the Star of Bethlehem!

It was my guide, my light, my all;
It bade my dark forebodings cease;
And through the storm and danger's thrall,
It led me to the port of peace.
Now safely moored, my perils o'er,
I'll sing first in night's diadem,
Forever and forever more,—
The Star, the Star of Bethlehem!

Henry Kirke White

NO ROOM.

Foot-sore and weary, Mary tried
Some rest to seek, but was denied.
"There is no room," the blind ones cried.

Meekly the Virgin turned away,
No voice entreating her to stay;
There was no room for God that day.

No room for her, round whose tired feet
Angels are bowed in transport sweet
The mother of their God to greet.

No room for Him in whose small hand
The troubled sea and mighty land
Lie cradled like a grain of sand;

No room, O Babe Divine! for Thee
That Christmas night; and even we
Dare shut our hearts and turn the key.

In vain Thy pleading baby cry
Strikes our deaf souls; we pass Thee by,
Unsheltered 'neath the wintry sky.

No room for God! O Christ, that we
Should bar our doors, nor ever see
Our Saviour waiting patiently.

Fling wide the doors! Dear Christ, turn
    back!
The ashes on my hearth lie black—
Of light and warmth a total lack.

How can I bid Thee enter here
Amid the desolation drear
Of lukewarm love and craven fear?

What bleaker shelter can there be
Than my cold heart's tepidity—
Chilled, wind-tossed, as the winter sea?

Dear Lord, I shrink from Thy pure eye,
No home to offer Thee have I;
Yet in Thy mercy pass not by.
               Agnes Repplier.

ON CHRISTMAS DAY.

Assist me, Muse divine! to Sing the Morn
On which the Saviour of Mankind was born;
But oh! what Numbers to the Theme can rise?
Unless kind Angels aid me from the Skies!
Methinks I see the tunefull Host descend,
And with officious Joy the Scene attend!
Hark, by their Hymns directed on the Road,
The Gladsome Shepherds find the nascent God!
And view the Infant conscious of his Birth,
Smiling bespeak Salvation to the Earth!
  For when th' important Æra first drew near
In which the great Messiah should appear;
And to accomplish his redeeming Love;
Beneath our Form should every Woe sustain,
And by triumphant Suffering fix his Reign,
Should for lost Man in Tortures yield his Breath
Dying to save us from eternal Death!
Oh mystick union!—salutary Grace!
Incarnate God our Nature should embrace!
That Deity should stoop to our Disguise!
That man recover'd should regain the Skies!
Dejected Adam! from thy grave ascend,
And view the Serpent's Deadly Malice end,

Adorning bless th' Almighty's boundless Grace
That gave his son a Ransome for thy Race!
Oh never let my Soul this Day forget,
But pay in gratefull praise the annual Debt.

From a manuscript volume, written by
George Washington.

THE HEAVENLY CHOIR.

What sudden blaze of song
  Spreads o'er th' expanse of heaven?
In waves of light it thrills along,
  Th' angelic signal given—
" Glory to God!" from yonder central fire
Flows out the echoing lay beyond the starry
    quire;

Like circles widening round
  Upon a clear blue river,
Orb after orb, the wondrous sound
  Is echoed on forever;
" Glory to God on high, on earth be peace,
And love toward men of love—salvation and
    release."

Yet stay, before thou dare
  To join that festal throng;
Listen and mark what gentle air
  First stirred the tide of song;
'Tis not, " the Saviour born in David's home,
To whom for power and health obedient worlds
    should come:"

'Tis not " the Christ the Lord :"—
　With fix'd adoring look
The choir of angels caught the word,
　Nor yet their silence broke ;
But when they heard the sign, where Christ
　　should be,
In sudden light they shone and heavenly har-
　　mony.

Wrapped in His swaddling-bands,
　And in His manger laid,
The hope and glory of all lands
　Is come to the world's aid :
No peaceful home upon His cradle smiled,
Guests rudely went and came where slept the
　　royal Child.

But where Thou dwellest, Lord,
　No other thought should be ;
Once duly welcomed and adored,
　How should I part with Thee ?
Bethlehem must lose Thee soon, but Thou wilt
　　grace
The single heart to be Thy pure abiding-place.

Thee, on the bosom laid
　Of a pure virgin mind,
In quiet ever, and in shade,
　Shepherd and sage may find ;

They who have bow'd untaught to nature's
    sway,
And they who follow truth along her star-
    paved way.

The pastoral spirits first
    Approach Thee, Babe divine,
For they in lowly thoughts are nursed,
    Meet for Thy lowly shrine :
Sooner than they should miss where Thou dost
    dwell,
Angels from heaven will stoop to guide them
    to Thy cell.

Still, as the day comes round
    For Thee to be revealed,
By wakeful shepherds Thou art found,
    Abiding in the field.
All through the wintry heaven and chill night
    air,
In music and in light Thou dawnest on their
    prayer.

O faint not ye for fear—
    What though your wandering sheep,
Reckless of what they see and hear,
    Lie lost in wilful sleep ?
High heaven in mercy to your sad annoy
Still greets you with glad tidings of immortal
    joy.

Think on th' eternal home
  The Saviour left for you ;
Think on the Lord most holy, come
  To dwell with hearts untrue :
So shall ye tread untired His pastoral ways,
And in the darkness sing your carol of high
    praise.

                      John Keble.

The Wassail-Bowl.

"Wassail, wassail, all over the
    town;
Our toast it is white, our ale it is
    brown,
Our bowl it is made of the mapling
    tree;
With the wassailing bowl we will
    drink to thee."

Old Carol.

9*

WASSAIL.

Give way, give way, ye gates, and win
An easy blessing to your bin
And basket, by our entering in.

May both with manchet* stand replete,
Your larders, too, so hung with meat,
That though a thousand thousand eat,

Yet ere twelve moons shall whirl about
Their silvery spheres, there's none may doubt
But more's sent in than was served out.

Next, may your dairies prosper so
As that your pans no ebb may know;
But if they do, the more to flow,

Like to a solemn, sober stream,
Banked all with lilies, and the cream
Of sweetest cowslips filling them.

Then may your plants be pressed with fruit,
Nor bee or hive you have be mute,
But sweetly sounding like a lute.

---

* White bread.

Last, may your harrows, shares, and ploughs.
Your stacks, your stocks, your sweetest mows.
All prosper by your virgin vows.

Alas! we bless, but see none here,
That brings us either ale or beer;
In a dry house all things are near.

Let's leave a longer time to wait,
Where rust and cobwebs bind the gate;
And all live here with needy fate;

Where chimneys do forever weep
For want of warmth, and stomachs keep
With noise the servants' eyes from sleep.

It is in vain to sing or stay
Our free feet here, but we'll away;
Yet to the Lares this we'll say:

The time will come when you'll be sad,
And reckon this for fortune bad,
T' have lost the good ye might have had.

                                   Robert Herrick.

INVITATION À FAIRE NOËL.

(FROM THE FRENCH OF THE TWELFTH CENTURY.)

Hail, good Masters, let us bide,
Hither come from travel wide,
   This Christmas-tide.
Hearken, give us bed and cheer,
We are weary, life is dear
   This day o' the year!
God send ye joy and peace on earth,
Who broach good cheer for Christé's birth.

Masters, an ye make no feast:
Spicéd ale and meat of beast,
   Nor laugh the least:
If ye fill not pantries high
With bread, and fish, and mammoth pie,
   And sweets, pardie!—
God ordains no peace on earth
To ye who fast at Christé's birth.

Masters, it is writ of old
Who fill the fire for Christmas cold
   And wassail hold,
Shall have of food a double store
And ruddy-blazing ingle roar
   Forevermore.

God sends the peace of heaven and earth
To men who carol Christé's birth.

O Masters! let nor hate nor spite
Mar the tongue of any wight
        'Twixt night and night.
Botun, batun—belabor well
Churls who sleep through matin bell
        And no soothe tell.
God will forfeit peace on earth
If men fall out at Christé's birth.

Christmas tipples every wine,
English, French, and Gascon fine
        And Angevine;
Clinks with neighbor and with guest,
Empties casks with gibe and jest—
        The year's for rest!
God sends to men the joy of earth
Who broach good cheer for Christé's birth.

But hearken, Masters, ere ye drink
While yet the bubbles boil and wink
        At the brink;
Ere ye lift the pot aloft,
Merrily wave it, laughing oft,
        With hood well doft.
And if I cry ye, sad, " Wesseyl!"
Woe's him who answers not " Drinchayl!"
        Translated by H. S. M.

A THANKSGIVING.

Lord, I confess too, when I dine,
  The pulse is Thine,
And all those other bits that be
  There placed by Thee ;
The worts, the purslane, and the mess
  Of water-cress,
Which of Thy kindness Thou hast sent ;
  And my content
Makes those and my belovéd beet
  To be more sweet.
'Tis Thou that crown'st my glittering hearth
  With guiltless mirth,
And giv'st me wassail-bowls to drink
  Spiced to the brink.

       Robert Herrick.

AROUND THE WASSAIL-BOWL.

A jolly wassail-bowl,
　A wassail of good ale;
Well fare the butler's soul
　That setteth this to sale;
　　　　　Our jolly wassail.

Good dame, here at your door
　Our wassail we begin,
We are all maidens poor,
　We pray now let us in
　　　　　With our wassail.

Our wassail we do fill
　With apples and with spice,
Then grant us your good-will
　To taste here once or twice
　　　　　Of our good wassail.

If any maidens be
　Here dwelling in this house,
They kindly will agree
　To take a full carouse
　　　　　Of our wassail.

But here they let us stand
  All freezing in the cold:
Good master, give command
  To enter and be bold,
      With our wassail.

Much joy into this hall
  With us is entered in,
Our master first of all
  We hope will now begin
      Of our wassail.

And after, his good wife
  Our spicéd bowl will try;
The Lord prolong your life!
  Good fortune we espy
      For our wassail.

Some bounty from your hands
  Our wassail to maintain;
We'll buy no house nor lands
  With that which we do gain
      With our wassail.

This is our merry night
  Of choosing king and queen;
Then be it your delight
  That something may be seen
      In our wassail.

It is a noble part
　To bear a liberal mind ;
God bless our master's heart !
　For here we comfort find
　　　　　　With our wassail.

And now we must be gone
　To seek out more good cheer,
Where bounty will be shown
　As we have found it here
　　　　　　With our wassail.

Much joy betide them all,
　Our prayer shall be still,
We hope and ever shall
　For this your great good-will
　　　　　　To our wassail.

FROM DOOR TO DOOR.

Here we come a wassailing
Among the leaves so green,
Here we come a wand'ring,
So fair to be seen.
Love and joy come to you,
And to you your wassail too,
And God bless you and send you a happy New
      Year.

Our wassail-cup is made
Of the rosemary tree,
And so is your beer
Of the best barley.
              Love and joy, etc.

We are not daily beggars
That beg from door to door,
But we are neighbors' children
Whom you have seen before.
              Love and joy, etc.

Good master and good mistress,
As you sit by the fire,
Pray think of us poor children
As wand'ring in the mire.
              Love and joy, etc.

We have a little purse
Made of ratching leather skin;
We want some of your small change
To line it well within.

Love and joy, etc.

Call up the butler of this house,
Put on his golden ring;
Let him bring us a glass of beer,
And the better we shall sing.

Love and joy, etc.

Bring us out a table,
And spread it with a cloth;
Bring us out a mouldy cheese,
And some of your Christmas loaf.

Love and joy, etc.

God bless the master of this house,
Likewise the mistress too
And all the little children
That round the table go.

Love and joy, etc.

WASSAILING CAROL.

We wish you merry Christmas, also a glad New
 Year;
We come to bring you tidings to all mankind so
 dear:
We come to tell that Jesus was born in Beth-
 l'em town,
And now He's gone to glory and pityingly looks
 down
   On us poor wassailers,
   As wassailing we go;
   With footsteps sore
   From door to door
  We trudge through sleet and snow.

A manger was His cradle, the straw it was His
 bed,
The oxen were around Him within that lowly
 shed;
No servants waited on Him with lords and
 ladies gay;
But now He's gone to glory and unto Him we
 pray.
     Us poor wassailers, etc.

IV.—*h*   10*

His mother loved and tended Him and nursed
    Him at her breast,
And good old Joseph watched them both the
    while they took their rest;
And wicked Herod vainly sought to rob them
    of their child,
By slaughtering the Innocents in Bethlehem
    undefiled.
            But us poor wassailers, etc.

Now, all good Christian people, with great con-
    cern we sing
These tidings of your Jesus, the Saviour, Lord
    and King;
In poverty He passed His days that riches we
    might share,
And of your wealth He bids you give and of
    your portion spare
            To us poor wassailers, etc.

Your wife shall be a fruitful vine, a hus'sif
    good and able;
Your children like the olive branches round
    about your table;
Your barns shall burst with plenty and your
    crops shall be secure,
If you will give your charity to us who are so
    poor,
            Us poor wassailers, etc.

And now no more we'll sing to you because the
    hour is late,
And we must trudge and sing our song at many
    another gate;
And so we'll wish you once again a merry
    Christmas time,
And pray God bless you while you give good
    silver for our rhyme.

               Us poor wassailers, etc.

A CAROL AT THE GATES.

Here we come a-whistling through the fields so
      green ;
Here we come a-singing, so fair to be seen.
   God send you happy, God send you happy,
   Pray God send you a happy New Year !

The roads are very dirty, my boots are very
      thin,
I have a little pocket to put a penny in.
                  God send you happy, etc.

Bring out your little table and spread it with a
      cloth,
Bring out some of your old ale, likewise your
      Christmas loaf.
                  God send you happy, etc.

God bless the master of this house, likewise the
      mistress, too,
And all the little children that round the table
      strew.
                  God send you happy, etc.

The cock sat up in the yew-tree, the hen came
     chuckling by,
I wish you a merry Christmas, and a good fat
    pig in the sty.
              God send you happy, etc.

WANDERING WASSAILERS.

Wassail, wassail, all over the town,
Our bread it is white, and our ale it is brown;
Our bowl it is made of the maplin tree,
So here, my good fellow, I'll drink it to thee.

The wassailing bowl, with a toast within,
Come, fill it up unto the brim;
Come fill it up that we may all see;
With the wassailing bowl I'll drink to thee.

Come, butler, come bring us a bowl of your
    best,
And we hope your soul in heaven shall rest;
But if you do bring us a bowl of your small,
Then down shall go butler, the bowl, and all.

O butler, O butler, now don't you be worst,
But pull out your knife and cut us a toast;
And cut us a toast, one that we may all see;
With the wassailing bowl I'll drink to thee.

Here's to Dobbin and to his right eye!
God send our mistress a good Christmas-pie!
A good Christmas-pie as e'er we did see;
With the wassailing bowl I'll drink to thee.

Here's to Broad May and his broad horn,
God send our master a good crop of corn,
A good crop of corn as we all may see;
With the wassailing bowl I'll drink to thee.

Here's to Colly and to her long tail,
We hope our master and mistress heart will
    ne'er fail;
But bring us a bowl of your good strong beer,
And then we shall taste of your happy New
    Year.

Be there here any pretty maids? we hope there
    be some;
Don't let the jolly wassailers stand on the cold
    stone,
But open the door and pull out the pin,
That we jolly wassailers may all sail in.
Chappell's Ancient English Melodies.

BRING US IN GOOD ALE.

Bring us in good ale, and bring us in good ale;
For our blessed Lady's sake, bring us in good ale.

Bring us in no brown bread, for that is made
  of bran,
Nor bring us in no white bread, for therein is
  no game,
    But bring us in good ale.

Bring us in no beef, for there are many bones,
But bring us in good ale, for that goeth down
  at once;
    And bring us in good ale.

Bring us in no bacon, for that is passing fat,
But bring us in good ale, and give us enough
  of that;
    And bring us in good ale.

Bring us in no mutton, for that is often lean,
Nor bring us in no tripes, for they be seldom
  clean;
    But bring us in good ale.

Bring us in no eggs, for there are many shells,
But bring us in good ale, and give us nothing
else ;
> And bring us in good ale.

Bring us in no butter, for therein are many
hairs,
Nor bring us in no pig's flesh, for that will
make us boars ;
> But bring us in good ale.

Bring us in no puddings, for therein is all God's
good,
Nor bring us in no venison, for that is not for
our blood ;
> But bring us in good ale.

Bring us in no capon's flesh, for that is often
dear,
Nor bring us in no duck's flesh, for they slobber
in the mere ;
> But bring us in good ale.
> *Wright's Songs and Carols.*

ABOUT THE BOARD.

Come bravely on, my masters,
For here we shall be tasters
   Of curious dishes that are brave and fine,
Where they that do such cheer afford,
I'll lay my knife upon the board,
   My master and my dame they do not pine.

Who is't will not be merry
And sing down, down, aderry?
   For now it is a time of joy and mirth;
'Tis said 'tis merry in the hall
When as beards they do wag all;
   God's plenty's here, it doth not show a dearth.

Let him take all lives longest,
Come fill us of the strongest,
   And I will drink a health to honest John;
Come, pray thee, butler, fill the bowl,
And let it round the table troll,
   When that is up, I'll tell you more anon.
                New Christmas Carols, A.D. 1642.

BEFORE THE FEAST.

All you that are good fellows,
  Come hearken to my song;
I know you do not hate good cheer
  Nor liquor that is strong.
I hope there is none here
  But soon will take my part,
Seeing my master and my dame
  Say welcome with their heart.

This is a time of joyfulness
  And merry time of year,
Whereas the rich with plenty stored
  Doth make the poor good cheer;
Plum-porridge, roast-beef, and minced-pies
  Stand smoking on the board,
With other brave varieties
  Our master doth afford.

Our mistress and her cleanly maids
  Have neatly played the cooks;
Methinks these dishes eagerly
  At my sharp stomach looks,
As though they were afraid
  To see me draw my blade;
But I revenged on them will be
  Until my stomach's stayed.

Come fill us of the strongest,
  Small drink is out of date ;
Methinks I shall fare like a prince
  And sit in gallant state :
This is no miser's feast,
  Although that things be dear ;
God grant the founder of this feast
  Each Christmas keep good cheer.

This day for Christ we celebrate,
  Who was born at this time ;
For which all Christians should rejoice,
  And I do sing in rhyme.
When you have given God thanks,
  Unto your dainties fall :
Heaven bless my master and my dame,
  Lord bless me and you all.

          New Christmas Carols, A.D. 1642.

A BILL OF CHRISTMAS FARE.

Come, mad boys, be glad, boys, for Christmas is
    here,
And we shall be feasted with jolly good cheer;
Then let us be merry, 'tis Saint Stephen's day,
Let's eat and drink freely, here's nothing to
    pay.

My master bids welcome, and so doth my dame,
And 'tis yonder smoking dish doth me inflame;
Anon I'll be with you, though you me outface,
For now I do tell you I have time and place.

I'll troll the bowl to you, then let it go round,
My heels are so light they can stand on no
    ground;
My tongue it doth chatter, and goes pitter
    patter,
Here's good beer and strong beer, for I will not
    flatter.

And now for remembrance of blessed Saint
    Stephen,
Let's joy at morning, at noon, and at even;
Then leave off your mincing, and fall to mince-
    pies,
I pray take my counsel, be ruled by the wise.

                  New Christmas Carols, A.D. 1642.

THE MAHOGANY-TREE.

Christmas is here :
Winds whistle shrill,
Icy and chill,
Little care we :
Little we fear
Weather without
Sheltered about
The Mahogany-Tree.

Once on the boughs
Birds of rare plume
Sang, in its bloom ;
Night-birds are we :
Here we carouse,
Singing like them,
Perched round the stem
Of the jolly old tree.

Here let us sport,
Boys, as we sit ;
Laughter and wit
Flashing so free,
Life is but short—
When we are gone,

Let them sing on
Round the old tree.

Evenings we knew,
Happy as this;
Faces we miss,
Pleasant to see,
Kind hearts and true,
Gentle and just,
Peace to your dust,
We sing round the tree.

Care, like a dun,
Lurks at the gate :
Let the dog wait;
Happy we'll be!
Drink, every one;
Pile up the coals,
Fill the red bowls,
Round the old tree!

Drain we the cup—
Friend, art afraid?
Spirits are laid
In the Red Sea.
Mantle it up;
Empty it yet;
Let us forget,
Round the old tree.

Sorrow, begone !
Life and its ills,
Duns and their bills,
Bid we to flee.
Come with the dawn,
Blue-devil sprite,
Leave us to-night
Round the old tree.

William Makepeace Thackeray.

A CHRISTMAS CEREMONY.

Wassail the trees, that they may bear
You many a plum and many a pear ;
For more or less fruits they will bring
As you do give them wassailing.

Robert Herrick.

WITH CAKES AND ALE.

With cakes and ale, and antic ring
Well tiptoed to the tabor string,
  And many a buss below the holly,
  And flout at sable melancholy—
So, with a rouse, went Christmassing !

What ! are no latter waits to sing ?
No clog to blaze ? No wit to wing ?
  Are catches gone, and dimpled Dolly,
            With cakes and ale ?

Nay, an you will, behold the thing :
The spicéd meat, the minstreling !
  Undo Misrule, and many a volley
  Of losel snatches born of folly—
Bring back the cheer, be Christmas-king,
            With cakes and ale !

H. S. M.

IV.—*i*

THE MASQUE OF CHRISTMAS.

(AS IT WAS PRESENTED AT COURT, 1616.)

The Court being seated,

Enter CHRISTMAS, *with two or three of the guard,
attired in round hose, long stockings, a close
doublet, a high-crowned hat, with a brooch, a
long, thin beard, a truncheon, little ruffs, white
shoes, his scarfs and garters tied cross, and his
drum beaten before him.*

Why, gentlemen, do you know what you do?
ha! would you have kept me out? Christmas,
old Christmas, Christmas of London, and Captain Christmas? Pray you, let me be brought
before my lord chamberlain, I'll not be answered
else: *'Tis merry in hall, when beards wag all:*
I have seen the time you have wish'd for me
for a merry Christmas; and now you have me,
they would not let me in: *I must come another
time!* a good jest, as if I could come more than
once a year! Why, I am no dangerous person,
and so I told my friends of the guard. I am
old Gregory Christmas still, and though I come
out of Pope's-head alley, as good a Protestant
as any in my parish. The truth is, I have
brought a Masque here, out o' the city, of my
own making, and do present it by a set of my

sons, that come out of the lanes of London, good dancing boys all. It was intended, I confess, for Curriers Hall ; but because the weather has been open, and the Livery were not at leisure to see it till a frost came, that they cannot work, I thought it convenient, with some little alterations, and the groom of the revels' hand to 't, to fit it for a higher place ; which I have done, and though I say it, another manner of device than your New-Year's-night. Bones o' bread, the king! (*seeing King James.*) Son Rowland ! Son Clem ! be ready there in a trice : quick, boys !

Enter his Sons and Daughters, (ten in number,) led in, in a string, by Cupid, who is attired in a flat cap, and a prentice's coat, with wings at his shoulders.

MISRULE, *in a velvet cap, with a sprig, a short cloak, great yellow ruff, like a reveller, his torch-bearer bearing a rope, a cheese, and a basket.*

CAROL, *a long tawny coat, with a red cap, and a flute at his girdle, his torch-bearer carrying a song-book open.*

MINCED-PIE, *like a fine cook's wife, drest neat ; her man carrying a pie, dish, and spoons.*

GAMBOL, *like a tumbler, with a hoop and bells ; his torch-bearer armed with a colt-staff, and a binding cloth.*

Post and Pair, *with a pair-royal of aces in his
hat; his garment all done over with pairs and
purs; his squire carrying a box, cards, and
counters.*

New-Year's-Gift, *in a blue coat, serving-man like,
with an orange, and a sprig of rosemary gilt on
his head, his hat full of brooches, with a collar
of ginger-bread, his torch-bearer carrying a
march-pane with a bottle of wine on either arm.*

Mumming, *in a masquing pied suit, with a vizard,
his torch-bearer carrying the box, and ringing it.*

Wassel, *like a neat sempster and songster; her
page bearing a brown bowl, drest with ribands,
and rosemary before her.*

Offering, *in a short gown, with a porter's staff in
his hand, a wyth born before him, and a bason,
by his torch-bearer.*

Baby-Cake, *drest like a boy, in a fine long coat,
biggin-bib, muckender, and a little dagger; his
usher bearing a great cake, with a bean and a
pease.*
        They enter singing.

Now God preserve, as you do well deserve,
    Your majesties all, two there;
Your highness small, with my good lords all,
    And ladies, how do you do there?

Give me leave to ask, for I bring you a masque
    From little, little, little London;

Which say the king likes, I have passed the
 pikes,
If not, old Christmas is undone.

       [*Noise without.*

Chris. Ho, peace! what's the matter there?

Gam. Here's one o' Friday-street would come
in.

Chris. By no means, nor out of neither of the
Fish-streets, admit not a man; they are not
Christmas creatures: fish and fasting days,
foh! Sons, said I well? look to it.

Gam. No body out o' Friday-street, nor the
two Fish-streets there, do you hear?

Car. Shall John Butter o' Milk-street come
in? Ask him.

Gam. Yes, he may slip in for a torch-bearer, so
he melt not too fast, that he will last till the
masque be done.

Chris. Right, son.

Our dance's freight is a matter of eight;
 And two, the which are wenches:
In all they be ten, four cocks to a hen,
 And will swim to the tune like tenches.

Each hath his knight for to carry his light,
 Which some would say are torches
To bring them here, and to lead them there,
 And home again to their own porches.

Now their intent,—

Enter VENUS, *a deaf tire-woman.*

Ven. Now, all the lords bless me! where am
I, trow? where is Cupid? "Serve the king!"
they may serve the cobbler well enough, some
of 'em, for any courtesy they have, I wisse;
they have need o' mending: unrude people they
are, your courtiers; here was thrust upon thrust
indeed: was it ever so hard to get in before,
trow?

Chris. How now? what's the matter?

Ven. A place, forsooth, I do want a place: I
would have a good place, to see my child act in
before the king and queen's majesties, God bless
'em! to-night.

Chris. Why, here is no place for you.

Ven. Right, forsooth, I am Cupid's mother,
Cupid's own mother, forsooth; yes, forsooth: I
dwell in Pudding-lane: ay, forsooth, he is prentice in Love-lane, with a bugle-maker, that
makes of your bobs, and bird-bolts for ladies.

Chris. Good lady Venus of Pudding-lane, you
must go out for all this.

Ven. Yes, forsooth, I can sit anywhere, so I
may see Cupid act: he is a pretty child, though
I say it, that perhaps should not, you will say.
I had him by my first husband; he was a smith,

forsooth, we dwelt in Do-little-lane then: he came a month before his time, and that may make him somewhat imperfect; but I was a fishmonger's daughter.

Chris. No matter for your pedigree, your house: good Venus, will you depart?

Ven. Ay, forsooth, he'll say his part, I warrant him, as well as e'er a play-boy of 'em all: I could have had money enough for him, an I would have been tempted, and have let him out by the week to the king's players. Master Burbage has been about and about with me, and so has old master Hemings, too, they have need of him; where is he, trow, ha! I would fain see him—pray God they have given him some drink since he came.

Chris. Are you ready, boys? Strike up! nothing will drown this noise but a drum: a'peace, yet! I have not done. Sing,—

Now their intent is above to present—

Car. Why, here be half of the properties forgotten, father.

Offer. Post and Pair wants his pur-chops and his pur-dogs.

Car. Have you ne'er a son at the groom porter's, to beg or borrow a pair of cards quickly?

Gam. It shall not need ; here's your son
Cheater without, has cards in his pocket.

Offer. Ods so! speak to the guards to let him
in, under the name of a property.

Gam. And here's New-Year's-Gift has an
orange and rosemary, but not a clove to stick
in't.

New-Year. Why, let one go to the spicery.

Chris. Fy, fy, fy! it's naught, it's naught, boys.

Ven. Why, I have cloves, if it be cloves you
want. I have cloves in my purse : I never go
without one in my mouth.

Car. And Mumming has not his vizard,
neither.

Chris. No matter! his own face shall serve,
for a punishment, and 'tis bad enough; has
Wassel her bowl, and Minced-pie her spoons?

Offer. Ay, ay : but Misrule doth not like his
suit : he says the players have sent him one too
little, on purpose to disgrace him.

Chris. Let him hold his peace, and his dis
grace will be the less : what! shall we pro
claim where we were furnish'd ? Mum! mum.'
a'peace! be ready, good boys.

> Now their intent is above to present,
>   With all the appurtenances,
> A right Christmas, as of old it was,
>   To be gathered out of the dances.

Which they do bring, and afore the king,
  The queen, and prince, as it were now
Drawn here by love; who over and above,
  Doth draw himself in the geer too.

*Here the drum and fife sound, and they march
about once. In the second coming up,* Christmas *proceeds in his song:*

Hum drum, sauce for a coney;
  No more of your martial music;
Even for the sake o' the next new stake,
  For there I do mean to use it.

And now to ye, who in place are to see
  With roll and farthingale hoopéd:
I pray you know, though he want his bow,
  By the wings, that this is Cupid.

He might go back for to cry, *What you lack?*
  But that were not so witty:
His cap and coat are enough to note
  That he is the love o' the city.

And he leads on, though he now be gone,
  For that was only his-rule:
But now comes in, Tom of Bosoms-inn,
  And he presenteth Mis-rule.

12*

Which you may know, by the very show,
    Albeit you never ask it:
For there you may see what his ensigns be,
    The rope, the cheese, and the basket.

This Carol plays, and has been in his days
    A chirping boy, and a kill-pot:
Kit Cobler it is, I'm a father of his,
    And he dwells in a lane called Fill-pot.

But who is this?   O, my daughter Cis,
    Minced-pie; with her do not dally
On pain o' your life: she's an honest cook's
        wife,
    And comes out of Scalding-alley.

Next in the trace, comes Gambol in place;
    And, to make my tale the shorter,
My son Hercules, tane out of Distaff-lane,
    But an active man, and a porter.

Now Post and Pair, old Christmas's heir,
    Doth make and a gingling sally;
And wot you who, 'tis one of my two
    Sons, card-makers in Pur-alley.

Next in a trice, with his box and his dice,
    Mac-pipin my son, but younger,
Brings Mumming in; and the knave will win,
    For he is a costermonger.

But New-Year's-Gift, of himself makes shift,
　　To tell you what his name is:
With orange on head, and his ginger-bread,
　　Clem Waspe of Honey-lane 'tis.

This, I tell you, is our jolly Wassel,
　　And for Twelfth-night more meet too:
She works by the ell, and her name is Nell,
　　And she dwells in Threadneedle-street too.

Then Offering, he, with his dish and his tree,
　　That in every great house keepeth,
Is by my son, young Little-worth, done,
　　And in Penny-rich street he sleepeth.

Last, Baby-cake that an end doth make
　　Of Christmas, merry, merry vein-a,
Is child Rowlan, and a straight young man,
　　Though he come out of Crooked-lane-a.

There should have been, and a dozen I ween,
　　But I could find but one more
Child of Christmas, and a Log it was,
　　When I them all had gone o'er.

I prayed him, in a time so trim,
　　That he would make one to prance it;
And I myself would have been the twelfth
　　O' but Log he was too heavy to dance it.

Now, Cupid, come you on.

Cup. You worthy wights, king, lords, and knights,
Or queen and ladies bright :
Cupid invites you to the sights
He shall present to-night.

Ven. 'Tis a good child, speak out; hold up
your head, Love.

Cup. And which Cupid—and which Cupid—

Ven. Do not shake so, Robin ; if thou be'st a-
cold, I have some warm waters for thee here.

Chris. Come, you put Robin Cupid out with
your waters and your fisling; will you be gone ?

Ven. Ay, forsooth, he's a child, you must conceive, and must be used tenderly ; he was never
in such an assembly before, forsooth, but once
at the Warmoll Quest, forsooth, where he said
grace as prettily as any of the sheriff's hinch-
boys, forsooth.

Chris. Will you peace, forsooth ?

Cup.   And which Cupid—and which Cupid—

Ven. Ay, that's a good boy, speak plain, Robin ;
how does his majesty like him, I pray ? will he
give eight-pence a day, think you ? Speak out,
Robin.

Chris. Nay, he is out enough. You may take him away, and begin your dance ; this it is to have speeches.

Ven. You wrong the child, you do wrong the infant; I 'peal to his majesty.

Here they dance.

Chris. Well done, boys, my fine boys, my bully boys !

THE EPILOGUE.

Sings. Nor do you think that their legs is all
　　　The commendation of my sons,
　　For at the Artillery garden they shall
　　　As well forsooth use their guns,

　　And march as fine as the Muses nine,
　　　Along the streets of London ;
　　And in their brave tires, to give their false
　　　　fires,
　　　Especially Tom my son.

　　Now if the lanes and the allies afford
　　　Such an ac-ativity as this ,
　　At Christmas next, if they keep their
　　　　word,
　　　Can the children of Cheapside miss ?

　　Though, put the case, when they come in
　　　　place,
　　　They should not dance, but hop :

Their very gold lace, with their silk,
 would 'em grace,
Having so many knights o' the shop.

But were I so wise, I might seem to advise
 So great a potentate as yourself;
They should, sir, I tell ye, spare't out of
 their belly,
 And this way spend some of their pelf.

Ay, and come to the court, for to make
 you some sport,
 At the least once every year,
As Christmas hath done, with his seventh
 or eighth son,
 And his couple of daughters dear.

  And thus it ended.
     Ben Jonson.

Santa Claus.

"His back, or rather burden
     showed
As if it stooped with its own
     load.
To poise this, equally he bore
A paunch of the same bulk be-
     fore,
Which still he had a special care
To keep well crammed with
     thrifty fare."

Butler.

148

A VISIT FROM ST. NICHOLAS.

'Twas the night before Christmas, when all
    through the house
Not a creature was stirring, not even a mouse,
The stockings were hung by the chimney with
    care,
In hopes that St. Nicholas soon would be there.
The children were nestled all snug in their beds,
While visions of sugar-plums danced in their
    heads;
And mamma in her kerchief and I in my cap
Had just settled our brains for a long winter's
    nap,
When out on the lawn there arose such a
    clatter,
I sprang from my bed to see what was the
    matter.
Away to the window I flew like a flash,
Tore open the shutters and threw up the sash;
The moon on the breast of the new-fallen snow
Gave the lustre of day to the objects below;
When what to my wondering eyes should ap-
    pear
But a miniature sleigh and eight tiny reindeer,
With a little old driver so lively and quick
I knew in a moment it must be St. Nick.

More rapid than eagles, his coursers they came,
And he whistled and shouted and called them
        by name :
" Now, Dasher ! now, Dancer ! now, Prancer !
        now, Vixen !
On, Comet ! on, Cupid ! on, Dunder and Blixen !
To the top of the stoop, to the top of the wall !
Now dash away ! dash away ! dash away all !"
As dry leaves before the wild hurricane fly,
When they meet with an obstacle, mount to
        the sky,
So up to the house-top the coursers they flew,
With the sleigh full of toys and St. Nicholas too ;
And then in a twinkling I heard on the roof
The prancing and pawing of each little hoof.
As I drew in my head and was turning around,
Down the chimney St. Nicholas came with a
        bound ;
He was dressed all in furs from his head to his
        foot,
And his clothes were all tarnished with ashes
        and soot.
A bundle of toys he had flung on his back ;
And he looked like a pedler just opening his
        pack.
His eyes, how they twinkled ! his dimples, how
        merry !
His cheeks were like roses, his nose like a
        cherry ;

His droll little mouth was drawn up like a bow,
And the beard on his chin was as white as the
 snow.
The stump of a pipe he held tight in his teeth,
And the smoke, it encircled his head like a
 wreath.
He had a broad face, and a little round belly
That shook when he laughed, like a bowl full
 of jelly.
He was chubby and plump, a right jolly old elf,
And I laughed when I saw him, in spite of my-
 self.
A wink of his eye and a twist of his head
Soon gave me to know I had nothing to dread.
He spoke not a word, but went straight to his
 work,
And filled all the stockings, then turned with a
 jerk,
And laying his finger aside of his nose,
And giving a nod, up the chimney he rose.
He sprang to his sleigh, to his team gave a
 whistle,
And away they all flew like the down of a
 thistle ;
But I heard him exclaim, ere he drove out of
 sight,
" Happy Christmas to all, and to all a good-
 night !"

      Clement C. Moore.

THE HARD TIMES IN ELFLAND.

Strange that the termagant winds should scold
  The Christmas Eve so bitterly!
But Wife, and Harry, the four-year old,
  Big Charley, Nimblewits, and I,

Blithe as the wind was bitter, drew
  More frontward of the mighty fire,
Where wise Newfoundland Fan foreknew
  The heaven that Christian dogs desire—

Stretched o'er the rug, serene and grave,
  Huge nose on heavy paws reclined,
With never a drowning boy to save,
  And warmth of body and peace of mind.

And as our happy circle sat,
  The fire well capp'd the company:
In grave debate or careless chat,
  A right good fellow, mingled he:

He seemed as one of us to sit,
  And talked of things above, below,
With flames more winsome than our wit,
  And coals that burned like love aglow.

While thus our rippling discourse rolled
  Smooth down the channel of the night,
We spoke of Time: thereat, one told
  A parable of the seasons' flight.

Those seasons out, we talked of these:
  And I, with inward purpose sly,
To shield my purse from Christmas-trees,
  And stockings, and wild robbery

When Hal and Nimblewits invade
  My cash in Santa Claus's name,—
In full the hard, hard times surveyed,
  Denounced all waste as crime and shame;

Hinted that "waste" might be a term
  Including skates, velocipedes,
Kites, marbles, soldiers, towers infirm,
  Bows, arrows, cannon, Indian reeds,

Cap-pistols, drums, mechanic toys,
  And all th' infernal host of horns
Whereby to strenuous hells of noise
  Are turned the blessed Christmas morns;

Thus, roused—those horns! to sacred rage,
  I rose, forefinger high in air,
When Harry cried, some war to wage,
  "Papa is hard times ev'ywhere?
           13*

" Maybe in Santa Claus's land
   It isn't hard times none at all!"
Now, blessed vision! to my hand
   Most pat, a marvel strange did fall.

Scarce had my Harry ceased, when " Look !"
   He cried, leapt up in wild alarm,
Ran to my Comrade, shelter took
   Beneath the startled mother's arm,

And so was still : what time we saw
   A foot hang down the fireplace ! Then,
With painful scrambling, scratched and raw,
   Two hands that seemed like hands of men,

Eased down two legs and a body through
   The blazing fire, and forth there came
Before our wide and wondering view
   A figure shrinking half with shame,

And half with weakness. " Sir," I said,
   —But with a mien of dignity
The seedy stranger raised his head :
   " My friends, I'm Santa Claus," said he.

But oh, how changed ! That rotund face
   The new moon rivall'd, pale and thin ;
Where once was cheek, now empty space ;
   Whate'er stood out, did now stand in.

His piteous legs scarce propped him up;
  His arms mere sickles seemed to be:
But most o'erflowed our sorrow's cup
  When that we saw—or did not see—

His belly: we remembered how
  It shook like a bowl of jelly fine:
An earthquake could not shake it now;
  He had no belly—not a sign.

" Yes, yes, old friends, you well may stare:
  I have seen better days," he said:
" But now with shrinkage, loss, and care,
  Your Santa Claus scarce owns his head.

" We've had such hard, hard times this year
  For goblins! Never knew the like.
All Elfland's mortgaged! And we fear
  That gnomes are just about to strike.

" I once was rich, and round, and hale,
  The whole world called me jolly brick;
But listen to a piteous tale,
  Young Harry,—Santa Claus is sick!

" 'Twas thus: a smooth-tongued railroad man
  Comes to my house and talks to me:
' I've got,' says he, ' a little plan
  That suits this nineteenth century.

" ' Instead of driving as you do,
  Six reindeer slow from house to house,
Let's build a Grand Trunk Railway through
  From here to earth's last terminus.

" ' We'll touch at every chimney-top
  An Elevated Track, of course,
Then, as we whisk you by, you'll drop
  Each package down : just think the force

" ' You'll save, the time !   Besides, we'll make
  Our millions: look you, soon we will
Compete for freight—and then we'll take
  Dame Fortune's bales of good and ill—

" ' Why, she's the biggest shipper, sir,
  That e'er did business in this world !
Then Death, that ceaseless traveller,
  Shall on his rounds by us be whirled.

" ' When ghosts return to walk with men,
  We'll bring 'em cheap by steam, and fast :
We'll run a branch to heaven ! and then
  We'll riot, man ; for then, at last,

" ' We'll make with heaven a contract fair
  To call each hour, from town to town,
And carry the dead folks' souls up there,
  And bring the unborn babies down !'

"The plan seemed fair: I gave him cash,
  Nay every penny I could raise.
My wife e'er cried, ' 'Tis rash, 'tis rash :'
  How could I know the stock-thief's ways?

"But soon I learned full well, poor fool!
  My woes began that wretched day.
The President plied me like a tool,
  In lawyer's fees, and rights of way,

"Injunctions, leases, charters, I
  Was meshed as in a mighty maze;
The stock ran low, the talk ran high,
  Then quickly flamed the final blaze.

"With never an inch of track—'tis true!
  The debts were large . . . the oft-told tale.
The President rolled in splendor new,
  —He bought my silver at the sale.

"Yes, sold me out: we've moved away.
  I've had to give up everything;
My reindeer, even, whom I . . . pray,
  Excuse me" . . . here, o'er-sorrowing,

Poor Santa Claus burst into tears,
  Then calmed again: "My reindeer fleet,
I gave them up: on foot, my dears,
  I now must plod through snow and sleet.

" Retrenchment rules in Elfland, now ;
  Yes, every luxury is cut off,
—Which, by the way, reminds me how
  I caught this dreadful hacking cough :

" I cut off the tail of my Ulster furred
  To make young Kris a coat of state
That very night the storm occurred !
  Thus we become the sport of Fate.

" For I was out till after one,
  Surveying chimney-tops and roofs,
A'nd planning how it could be done
  Without any reindeers' bouncing hoofs.

" ' My dear,' says Mrs. Claus, that night,
  A most superior woman she !
' It never, never can be right
  That you, deep sunk in poverty,

" ' This year should leave your poor old bed,
  And trot about, bent down with toys ;
There's Kris a-crying now for bread—
  To give to other people's boys !

" ' Since you've been out, the news arrives
  The Elfs' Insurance Company's gone.
Ah, Claus, those premiums !   Now, our lives
  Depend on yours : thus griefs go on.

" ' And even while you're thus harassed,
   I do believe, if out you went,
You'd go, in spite of all that's passed,
   To the children of that President !'

" Oh, Charley, Harry, Nimblewits,
   These eyes that night ne'er slept a wink ;
My path seemed honeycombed with pits,
   Naught could I do but think and think.

" But, with the day, my courage rose.
   Ne'er shall my boys, my boys, I cried,
When Christmas morns their eyes unclose,
   . Find empty stockings gaping wide !

" Then hewed, and whacked, and whittled I ;
   The wife, the girls, and Kris took fire ;
They spun, sewed, cut,—till by and by
   We made, at home, my pack entire !"

He handed me a bundle here.
   " Now, hoist me up : there, gently : quick !
Dear boys, don't look for much this year :
   Remember, Santa Claus is sick !"

Sidney Lanier.

OLD CHRISTMAS.

Now he who knows Old Christmas,
  He knows a wight of worth,
For he's as good a fellow
  As any on the earth ;
He comes warm-cloaked and coated,
  And buttoned to the chin ;
And ere he is a-nigh the door,
  We ope to let him in.

He comes with voice most cordial,
  It does one good to hear ;
For all the little children
  He asks each passing year:
His heart is warm and gladsome,
  Not like your griping elves,
Who, with their wealth in plenty,
  Think only of themselves.

He tells us witty stories,
  He sings with might and main ;
We ne'er forget his visit
  Till he comes back again.
With laurel green and holly
  We make the house look gay ;
We know that it will please him,
  It was his ancient way.

Oh, he's a rare old fellow ;
  What gifts he gives away !
There's not a lord in England
  Could equal him to-day !
Good luck unto Old Christmas,
  Long life now let us sing ;
He is more kind unto the poor
  Than any crownéd king.

                    Mary Howitt.

MRS. SANTA CLAUS.

The moon was like a frosted cake,
    The stars like flashing beads
That round a brimming punch-bowl break
    'Mid spice and almond seeds;
And here and there a silver beam
    Made bright some curling cloud
Uprising like the wassail's stream,
    Blown off by laughter loud.

It was the night o' Christmas Eve,
    And good old Santa Claus
His door was just about to leave,
    When something made him pause:
" I haven't kissed my wife," quoth he,
    " I haven't said good-by."
So back he went and lovingly
    He kissed her cap awry.

Now Mrs. Claus is just a bit—
    The least bit—of a shrew.
What wonder?   Only think of it—
    She has so much to do.
Imagine all the stocking-legs,
    Of every size and shape,
That hang upon their Christmas pegs
    With greedy mouths agape.

These she must fill, and when you see
　　The northern skies aflame
With quivering light, 'tis only she—
　　This very quaint old dame—
Striking a match against the Pole
　　Her whale-oil lamp to light,
That she may see to work, poor soul,
　　At making toys all night.

" Odd he should kiss me," this she said
　　Before the sleigh had gone ;
" 'Tis many a year since we were wed ;
　　I'll follow him anon.
For faithless husbands, one and all,
　　Ere on their loves they wait,
Their wives' suspicion to forestall
　　Seem most affectionate."

So, pulling on her seal-skin sacque,
　　Into her husband's sleigh
She slipped, and hid behind his pack
　　Just as he drove away.
" Great Bears !" growled Santa in his beard,
　　" A goodly freight have I ;
Were't fouler weather, I had feared
　　The glacier path to try."

Yet none the less they safely sped
　　Across the realms of snow—

The glittering planets overhead,
  The sparkling frost below—
Until the reindeer stopped before
  A mansion tall and fair,
Up to whose wide and lofty door
  Inclined a marble stair.

So soundly all its inmates slept,
  They heard no stroke of hoof;
No fall of foot as Santa leapt
  From pavement unto roof.
So, down the chimney like a sweep
  He crept, and after him
Went Mrs. Claus to have a peep
  At chambers warm and dim.

As luck would have it, there was hung
  A stocking by the fire
To wear which no one over-young
  Could fittingly aspire:
Long, slender, graceful—it was just
  The thing to fill the heart
Of Mrs. C. with deep distrust;
  And—well—it played its part.

Scowling, she watched her husband fill
  The silken foot and leg
With bonbons, fruit, and toys until
  It almost broke its peg.

" My !" whispered Santa, " here's a crop.
  This little boy is wise ;
He knows I fill 'em to the top,
  No matter what the size."

But Mrs. Claus misunderstood,
  Like every jealous wife ;
She *would* make bad things out of good,
  To feed her inward strife.
Snapped she unto herself : " The minx
  Sha'n't have a single thing !
I'll take 'em home again, methinks,
  Nor leave a stick or string !"

So said, so done ; and all that night
  She followed Santa's wake,
And as he stuffed the stockings tight,
  She every one did take,
Stowing them all unseen away,
  In order grimly neat,
Within the dark box of the sleigh,
  All underneath the seat.

And when gray dawn broke, and all
  The bells began to peal,
And tiny forms down many a hall
  And stairway 'gan to steal,
IV.—*l*   14*

In vain each chimney-piece they sought—
Those weeping girls and boys—
For Christmas morn had come and brought
No candy and no toys.

Charles Henry Luders.

SANTA CLAUS TO LITTLE ETHEL.

<small>(IN ANSWER TO HER LETTER, GIVING HIM A LIST OF HER CHRISTMAS WANTS.)</small>

My dear little Ethel,
I fear that the breath'll
Be out of our bodies before we get through ;
Day in and day out
We are rushing about,
And you haven't a notion how much there's to
do.

Ever since last December,
When you may remember
I paid you a visit at dear Elsinore,
There's not been a minute
With a resting-place in it,
And my nose has not once been outside of the
door.

My shop has been going,
My bellows a-blowing,
My hammers and tongs and a thousand odd
tools,
Never give up the battle,
But click, bang, and rattle
Like ten million children in ten thousand
schools.

Dear me, but I'm weary!
And yet, my small deary,
I read all the letters as fast as they come ;
If I didn't,—good gracious!
The house is not spacious,
And the letters would soon squeeze me out of
my home.

" I would like a nice sled,
And a dolly's soft bed,
With a night-gown and bed-clothes of pretty
bright stuffs,
And paints, and a case
Where my books I may place,
And besides all these things, Dolly's collars and
cuffs."

That's a pretty big list!
But may I be kissed
On the back of my head by a crazy mule's
hoof,
If the list I don't fill,
Though it takes all the skill
Of every stout workman beneath my broad
roof.

" Hans, Yakob, and Karl!
Let me not hear a snarl,

Or a growl, or a grumble come out of your
    heads ;
      To work now, instanter !
      Trot, gallop, and canter,
And finish this job ere you go to your beds !"

      So I set them to work
      With a jump and a jerk,
And everything's finished in beautiful style.
      Christmas Eve's here again,
      And I'm off with my train,
Every reindeer prepared for ten seconds a mile.

      I shall slip down the flue
      With this letter for you,
So softly, for fear I your slumbers might break.
      Not a word will I speak,
      But I'll kiss your soft cheek,
And be gone in a jiffy, before you awake.

      Should you find I've forgot
      Any part of the lot
That I ordered prepared and all marked with
    your name,
      Let me just add a word,
      So if that has occurred,
You will know just exactly how I was to blame.

      The fact is, my dear,
      As I go, year by year,

Up and down these straight chimneys, while
　　you are in bed,
　　　　The bumps and the scratches
　　　　That Santa Claus catches
Have rubbed all the hair from the top of his
　　head.

　　　　And my brain being bare
　　　　Of my cover of hair,
Is rapidly losing its power, my pet!
　　　　Sometimes, after all's fixed,
　　　　I get everything mixed,
And you must forgive if I ever forget.

　　　　Good-by, Ethel dear!
　　　　May the coming New Year
Bring all kinds of blessings to you from above;
　　　　Make you happier and better:
　　　　And so my long letter
Must close, with a great deal of Santa Claus's
　　love.

　　　　　　　　　　Francis Wells.

The Season's Reveries.

"How many times have you sat
at gaze
Till the mouldering fire forgot to
blaze,
Shaping among the whimsical
coals
Fancies and figures and shining
goals!"

Lowell.

GUESTS AT YULE.

Noel! Noel!
Thus sounds each Christmas bell
Across the winter snow.
But what are the little footprints all
That mark the path from the churchyard wall?
They are those of the children waked to-night
From sleep by the Christmas bells and light:
      Ring sweetly, chimes!   Soft, soft, my
          rhymes!
      Their beds are under the snow.

Noel! Noel!
Carols each Christmas bell.
    What are the wraiths of mist
That gather anear the window-pane
Where the winter frost all day has lain?
They are soulless elves, who fain would peer
Within and laugh at our Christmas cheer:
      Ring fleetly, chimes!   Swift, swift, my
          rhymes!
      They are made of the mocking mist.

Noel! Noel!
Cease. cease, each Christmas bell!
    Under the holly bough,

Where the happy children throng and shout,
What shadow seems to flit about?
Is it the mother, then, who died
Ere the greens were sere last Christmas-tide?
      Hush, falling chimes!   Cease, cease, my
        rhymes!
      The guests are gathered now.
                Edmund Clarence Stedman.

CHRISTMAS IN INDIA.

Dim dawn the tamarisks—the sky is saffron-
    yellow—
As the women in the village grind the corn, .
And the parrots seek the riverside, each calling
    to his fellow
    That the day, the staring eastern day, is
      born.
    Oh, the white dust on the highway! Oh,
      the stenches in the by-way!
    Oh, the clammy fog that hovers over earth!
And at home they're making merry 'neath the
    white and scarlet berry—
    What part have India's exiles in their mirth?

Full day behind the tamarisks—the sky is blue
    and staring—
As the cattle crawl afield beneath the yoke,
And they bear one o'er the field-path who is
    past all hope or caring,
    To the ghat below the curling wreaths of
      smoke.
    Call on Rama, going slowly, as ye bear a
      brother lowly—
    Call on Rama—he may hear, perhaps, your
      voice!

With our hymn-books and our psalters we ap-
    peal to other altars,
  And to-day we bid " good Christian men re-
    joice !"

High noon above the tamarisks—the sun is hot
    above us—
  As at home the Christmas Day is breaking
    wan,
They will drink our healths at dinner—those
    who tell us how they love us,
  And forget us till another year be gone !
  Oh, the toil that knows no breaking ! Oh!
    the heimweh, ceaseless, aching !
  Oh, the black, dividing sea and alien plain !
Youth was cheap—wherefore we sold it. Gold
    was good—we hoped to hold it,
  And to-day we know the fulness of our gain.

Gray dusk behind the tamarisks—the parrots
    fly together—
  As the sun is sinking slowly over home ;
And his last ray seems to mock us, shackled in
    a lifelong tether
    That drags us back, howe'er so far we roam.
    Hard her service, poor her payment—she in
      ancient, tattered raiment—
    India, she the grim stepmother of our kind.

If a year of life be lent her, if her temple's
    shrine we enter,
  The door is shut—we may not look behind.

Black night behind the tamarisks—the owls
    begin their chorus—
  As the conches from the temple scream and
    bray.
With the fruitless years behind us and the
    hopeless years before us,
  Let us honor, O, my brothers, Christmas
    Day!
  Call a truce, then, to our labors—let us feast
    with friends and neighbors,
  And be merry as the custom of our caste;
For, if "faint and forced the laughter," and if
    sadness follow after,
  We are richer by one mocking Christmas
    past.

                  Rudyard Kipling.

15*

CHRISTMAS VIOLETS.

Last night I found the violets
   You sent me once across the sea;
From gardens that the winter frets,
   In summer lands they came to me.

Still fragrant of the English earth,
   Still humid from the frozen dew,
To me they spoke of Christmas mirth,
   They spoke of England, spoke of you.

The flowers are scentless, black, and sere,
   The perfume long has passed away;
The sea whose tides are year by year
   Is set between us, chill and gray.

But you have reached a windless age,
   The haven of a happy clime;
You do not dread the winter's rage,
   Although we missed the summer-time.

And like the flower's breath over sea,
   Across the gulf of time and pain,
To-night returns the memory
   Of love that lived not all in vain.

Andrew Lang.

DICKENS RETURNS ON CHRISTMAS DAY.

(A ragged girl in Drury Lane was heard to exclaim,
"Dickens dead? Then will Father Christmas die,
too?" June 9, 1870.)

"Dickens is dead!" Beneath that grievous cry
London seemed shivering in the summer heat;
Strangers took up the tale like friends that
 meet:
"Dickens is dead!" said they, and hurried by;
Street children stopped their games—they knew
 not why,
But some new night seemed darkening down
 the street;
A girl in rags, staying her way-worn feet,
Cried, "Dickens dead? Will Father Christmas
 die?"

City he loved, take courage on thy way!
He loves thee still in all thy joys and fears:
Though he whose smiles made bright thine eyes
 of gray—
Whose brave sweet voice, uttering thy tongue-
 less years,
Made laughters bubble through thy sea of tears—
Is gone, Dickens returns on Christmas Day!

     Theodore Watts.

A GRIEF AT CHRISTMAS.

FROM " IN MEMORIAM."

First Year.

The time draws near the birth of Christ
  The moon is hid ; the night is still ;
  The Christmas bells from hill to hill
Answer each other in the mist.

Four voices of four hamlets round,
  From far and near, on mead and moor,
  Swell out and fail, as if a door
Were shut between me and the sound :

Each voice four changes on the wind,
  That now dilate, and now decrease,
  Peace and good-will, good-will and peace,
Peace and good-will, to all mankind.

This year I slept and woke with pain,
  I almost wish'd no more to wake,
  And that my hold on life would break
Before I heard those bells again :

But they my troubled spirit rule,
　For they controll'd me when a boy ;
　They bring me sorrow touched with joy,
The merry merry bells of Yule.

With such compelling cause to grieve
　As daily vexes household peace,
　And chains regret to his decease,
How dare we keep our Christmas-eve ;

Which brings no more a welcome guest
　To enrich the threshold of our night
　With shower'd largess of delight,
In dance and song and game and jest.

Yet go, and while the holly boughs
　Entwine the cold baptismal font,
　Make one wreath more for Use and Wont,
That guard the portals of the house ;

Old sisters of a day gone by,
　Gray nurses, loving nothing new ;
　Why should they miss their yearly due
Before their time ?　They too will die.

With trembling fingers did we weave
　The holly round the Christmas hearth ;
　A rainy cloud possess'd the earth,
And sadly fell our Christmas-eve.
　IV.—*m*

At our old pastimes in the hall
　　We gambol'd, making vain pretence
　　Of gladness, with an awful sense
Of one mute Shadow watching all.

We paused: the winds were in the beech:
　　We heard them sweep the winter land;
　　And in a circle hand-in-hand
Sat silent, looking each at each.

Then echo-like our voices rang;
　　We sung, tho' every eye was dim,
　　A merry song we sang with him
Last year: impetuously we sang:

We ceased: a gentler feeling crept
　　Upon us: surely rest is meet.
　　"They rest," we said, "their sleep is sweet,"
And silence follow'd, and we wept.

Our voices took a higher range;
　　Once more we sang: "They do not die
　　Nor lose their mortal sympathy,
Nor change to us, although they change;

" Rapt from the fickle and the frail
　　With gather'd power, yet the same
　　Pierces the keen seraphic flame
From orb to orb, from veil to veil."

Rise, happy morn, rise, holy morn,
　　Draw forth the cheerful day from night:
　　O Father, touch the east, and light
The light that shone when Hope was born.

Second Year.

Again at Christmas did we weave
　　The holly round the Christmas hearth:
　　The silent snow possessed the earth,
And calmly fell on Christmas-eve:

The yule-clog sparkled keen with frost,
　　No wing of wind the region swept,
　　But over all things brooding slept
The quiet sense of something lost.

As in the winters left behind,
　　Again our ancient games had place,
　　The mimic picture's breathing grace,
And dance and song and hoodman-blind.

Who show'd a token of distress?
　　No single tear, no mark of pain:
　　O sorrow, then can sorrow wane?
O grief, can grief be changed to less?

O last regret, regret can die!
　　No—mixt with all this mystic frame,
　　Her deep relations are the same,
But with long use her tears are dry.

Third Year.

The time draws near the birth of Christ;
   The moon is hid, the night is still;
   A single church below the hill
Is pealing, folded in the mist.

A single peal of bells below,
   That wakens at this hour of rest
   A single murmur in the breast,
That these are not the bells I know.

Like strangers' voices here they sound,
   In lands where not a memory strays,
   Nor landmark breathes of other days,
But all is new unhallow'd ground.

To-night ungather'd let us leave
   This laurel, let this holly stand:
   We live within the stranger's land,
And strangely falls our Christmas-eve.

Our father's dust is left alone
   And silent under other snows:
   There in due time the woodbine blows,
The violet comes, but we are gone.

No more shall wayward grief abuse
   The genial hour with mask and mime;
   For change of place, like growth of time,
Has broke the bond of dying use.

Let cares that petty shadows cast,
  By which our lives are chiefly proved,
  A little spare the night I loved,
And hold it solemn to the past.

But let no footsteps beat the floor,
  Nor bowl of wassail mantle warm;
  For who would keep an ancient form
Thro' which the spirit breathes no more?

Be neither song, nor game, nor feast;
  Nor harp be touch'd, nor flute be blown;
  No dance, no motion, save alone
What lightens in the lucid east

Of rising worlds by yonder wood.
  Long sleeps the summer in the seed;
  Run out your measured arcs, and lead
The closing cycle rich in good.

Ring out wild bells, to the wild sky,
  The flying cloud, the frosty light:
  The year is dying in the night:
Ring out, wild bells, and let him die.

Ring out the old, ring in the new,
  Ring, happy bells, across the snow;
  The year is going, let him go;
Ring out the false, ring in the true.

16

Ring out the grief that saps the mind,
  For those that here we see no more;
  Ring out the feud of rich and poor;
Ring in redress of all mankind.

Ring out the slowly dying cause,
  And ancient forms of party strife;
  Ring in the nobler modes of life,
With sweeter manners, purer laws.

Ring out the want, the care, the sin,
  The faithless coldness of the times;
  Ring out, ring out, my mournful rhymes,
But ring the fuller minstrel in.

Ring out false pride in place and blood,
  The civic slander and the spite;
  Ring in the love of truth and right,
Ring in the common love of good.

Ring out old shapes of foul disease;
  Ring out the narrowing lust of gold;
  Ring out the thousand wars of old,
Ring in the thousand years of peace.

Ring in the valiant man and free,
  The larger heart, the kindlier hand;
  Ring out the darkness of the land,
Ring in the Christ that is to be.

Lord Tennyson.

MY SISTER'S SLEEP.

She fell asleep on Christmas-eve :
  At length the long-ungranted shade
  Of weary eyelids overweigh'd
The pain naught else might yet relieve.

Our mother, who had leaned all day
  Over the bed from chime to chime,
  Then raised herself for the first time,
And as she sat her down did pray.

Her little work-table was spread
  With work to finish. For the glare
  Made by her candle, she had care
To work some distance from the bed.

Without there was a cold moon up,
  Of winter radiance sheer and thin ;
  The hollow halo it was in
Was like an icy crystal cup.

Through the small room, with subtle sound
  Of flame, by vents the fireshine drove
  And reddened. In its dim alcove
The mirror shed a clearness round.

I had been sitting up some nights,
    And my tired mind felt weak and blank;
    Like a sharp, strengthening wine it drank
The stillness and the broken lights.

Twelve struck.   That sound, by dwindling years
    Heard in each hour, crept off; and then
    The ruffled silence spread again,
Like water that a pebble stirs.

Our mother rose from where she sat:
    Her needles, as she laid them down,
    Met lightly, and her silken gown
Settled: no other noise than that.

"Glory unto the Newly Born,"
    So as said angels, she did say;
    Because we were in Christmas-day,
Though it would still be long till morn.

Just then in the room over us
    There was a pushing back of chairs,
    As some one had sat unawares
So late, now heard the hour, and rose.

With anxious, softly-stepping haste
    Our mother went where Margaret lay,
    Fearing the sounds o'erhead—should they
Have broken her long-watched-for rest!

She stooped an instant, calm, and turned;
  But suddenly turned back again;
  And all her features seemed in pain
With woe, and her eyes gazed and yearned.

For my part, I but hid my face,
  And held my breath, and spoke no word;
  There was none spoken; but I heard
The silence for a little space.

Our mother bowed herself and wept;
  And both my arms fell, and I said,
  " God knows I knew that she was dead,"
And there, all white, my sister slept.

Then kneeling upon Christmas morn
  A little after twelve o'clock,
  We said, ere the first quarter struck,
" Christ's blessing on the newly born!"
              Dante Gabriel Rossetti.

CHRISTMAS IN EDINBOROUGH.

I.

Sheath'd is the river as it glideth by,
Frost-pearl'd are all the boughs of forests old,
The sheep are huddling close upon the wold,
And over them the stars tremble on high.
Pure joys these winter nights around me lie;
'Tis fine to loiter through the lighted streets
At Christmas-time, and guess from brow and
          pace
The doom and history of each one we meet,
What kind of heart beats in each dusky case;
Whiles, startled by the beauty of a face
In a shop-light a moment.   Or instead,
To dream of silent fields where calm and deep
The sunshine lieth like a golden sleep—
Recalling sweetest looks of summers dead.

          Alexander Smith.

CHRISTMAS IN EDINBOROUGH.

II.

Joy like a stream flows through the Christmas
    streets,
But I am sitting in my silent room,
Sitting all silent in congenial gloom
To-night, while half the world the other greets
With smiles and grasping hands and drinks and
    meats,
I sit and muse on my poetic doom;
Like the dim scent within a budded rose,
A joy is folded in my heart; and when
I think on poets nurtured 'mong the throes
And by the lowly hearths of common men,—
Think of their works, some song, some swelling
    ode
With gorgeous music growing to a close,
Deep muffled as the dead-march of a god,—
My heart is burning to be one of those.

               Alexander Smith.

AROUND THE CHRISTMAS LAMP.

The wind may shout as it likes without;
It may rage, but cannot harm us;
For a merrier din shall resound within,
And our Christmas cheer will warm us.
There is gladness to all at its ancient call,
While its ruddy fires are gleaming,
And from far and near, o'er the landscape drear,
The Christmas light is streaming.

All the frozen ground is in fetters bound;
Ho! the yule-log we will burn it;
For Christmas is come in ev'ry home,
To summer our hearts will turn it.
There is gladness to all at its ancient call,
While its ruddy fires are gleaming;
And from far and near, o'er the landscape drear,
The Christmas light is streaming.

J. L. Molloy.

CHRISTMAS-EVE.

Alone—with one fair star for company,
  The loveliest star among the hosts of night,
  While the gray tide ebbs with the ebbing
      light—
I pace along the darkening wintry sea.
Now round the yule-log and the glittering tree
  Twinkling with festive tapers, eyes as bright
  Sparkle with Christmas joys and young de-
      light
As each one gathers to his family.

But I—a waif on earth where'er I roam—
  Uprooted with life's bleeding hopes and fears,
From that one heart that was my heart's sole
      home,
  Feel the old pang pierce through the severing
      years,
And as I think upon the years to come,
  That fair star trembles through my falling
      tears.

                                Mathilde Blind.

WONDERLAND.

Lo! I will make my home
  In the beautiful Land of Books;
Where the friends of childhood roam
  Through most delightful nooks.

I'll rent the unfinished floor
  In Aladdin's palace built,
Whose walls, to the outer door,
  Are ivory and gilt.

And the Caliph—Haroun—there
  Will pass in his deft disguise;
But him I'll know by his air
  So grand, and his eagle eyes.

And Cinderella, too,
  Will weep when her sisters whip her:
And I'll be the Prince—or you—
  Who will find her crystal slipper.

And O, what fun it will be
  With Robin the Bobbin to feast,
Or to frequently call and see
  The Beauty and the Beast.

For she and you and I
  And the Rusty Dusty Miller
Will eat of a Christmas-Pie
  With Jack the Giant-Killer.

Then come, let us make our homes
  In the most frequented nooks
Of the land of elves and gnomes,
  In the beautiful Land of Books!
                    Charles Henry Luders.

WAITING.

As little children in a darkened hall
  At Christmas-tide await the opening door,
  Eager to tread the fairy-haunted floor
Around the tree with goodly gifts for all,
Oft in the darkness to each other call,—
  Trying to guess their happiness before—
  Or knowing elders eagerly implore
To tell what fortune unto them may fall,—

So wait we in time's dim and narrow room,
  And, with strange fancies or another's
        thought,
  Try to divine before the curtain rise
The wondrous scene; forgetting that the gloom
  Must shortly flee from what the ages sought,—
  The Father's long-planned gift of Paradise.
                              C. H. Crandall.

AUNT MARY.

A CORNISH CHRISTMAS CHANT.

Now of all the trees by the king's highway,
   Which do you love the best?
O! the one that is green upon Christmas-day,
   The bush with the bleeding breast.
Now the holly with her drops of blood for me:
For that is our dear Aunt Mary's tree.

Its leaves are sweet with our Saviour's name,
   'Tis a plant that loves the poor:
Summer and winter it shines the same
   Beside the cottage door.
O! the holly with her drops of blood for me:
For that is our kind Aunt Mary's tree.

'Tis a bush that the birds will never leave:
   They sing in it all day long;
But sweetest of all upon Christmas-eve
   Is to hear the robin's song.
'Tis the merriest sound upon earth and sea:
For it comes from our own Aunt Mary's tree.

So, of all that grow by the king's highway,
　I love that tree the best;
'Tis a bower for the birds upon Christmas-day,
　The bush of the bleeding breast.
O! the holly with her drops of blood for me:
For that is our sweet Aunt Mary's tree.

Robert Stephen Hawker.

THE GLAD NEW DAY.

And why should not that land rejoice,
And darkness flee away,
When on its dim, benighted hills
Has dawned the glad new day?
For now behold the shepherds go,
The wondrous babe to see;
Ah, then methinks that all around
Was one grand jubilee!

Rejoice, ye nations blest with peace,
Let all the earth be glad;
The Prince of Peace comes down to-day,
In robes of pity clad.
Yea, thus should all mankind rejoice
On this glad day of love;
But yet, alas! how far we are
From those blest heights above!

Ah! for the time when men shall spend
This day as all men should,
When angels shall with joy attend,
And dwell among the good.
Then will this earth an Eden be,
A Paradise of love;
And all shall know the perfect bliss
Of those bright realms above.

Thomas Moore.

UNDER THE HOLLY BOUGH.

Ye who have scorned each other
In this fast fading year,
Or wronged a friend or brother,
Come gather humbly here :
Let sinned against and sinning
Forget their strife's beginning,
Be links no longer broken
   Beneath the holly bough,
Be sweet forgiveness spoken
   Beneath the holly bough.

Ye who have loved each other
In this fast fading year,
Sister, or friend, or brother,
Come gather happy here :
And let your hearts grow fonder
As mem'ry glad shall ponder
Old loves and later wooing
   Beneath the holly bough,
So sweet in their renewing
   Beneath the holly bough.

Ye who have nourished sadness
In this fast fading year,
Estranged from joy and gladness,
Come gather hopeful here :

No more let useless sorrow
Pursue you night and morrow ;
Come join in our embraces
  Beneath the holly bough ;
Take heart, uncloud your faces
  Beneath the holly bough.
Charles Mackay.

THE DAWN OF CHRISTMAS.

Acold it is and middle night:
  The moon looks down the snow,
As if an angel, clad in white,
  Carried her lanthorn so
That, going forth the streets of light,
  She made an earthward glow.

A drift enfolds the chapel eaves
  Like downy coverlet;
And, garnered into whited sheaves,
  The graves are harvest-set
Waiting the yeoman.   All the panes
  Are rich with rimy fret.

The sexton mounts the outer stair
  Where chilly sparrows cower—
And bells ring down the winter air
  From forth the snowy tower;
For, muffled deep in drift, the clock
  Hath struck the Christmas hour.

And over barn, and buried stack,
  And out the naked copse,
And where the owl sits plump and black
  Amid the chestnut tops—

The branches echo back the bells,
  Like dulcet organ stops.

For blast of wind and creak of bough
  And rustle of the frost,
And winter's inner voice—avow
  The holy hour is crossed,
And far, mysterious music sounds,
  Sweet like a harping host.

H. S. M.

BALLADE OF CHRISTMAS GHOSTS.

Between the moonlight and the fire,
  In winter evenings long ago,
What ghosts I raised at your desire,
  To make your leaping blood run slow!
How old, how grave, how wise we grow!
  What Christmas ghost can make us chill—
Save these that troop in mournful row,
  The ghosts we all can raise at will?

The beasts can talk in barn and byre
  On Christmas-eve, old legends know.
As one by one the years retire,
  We men fall silent then, I trow—
Such sights has memory to show,
  Such voices from the distance thrill.
Ah me! they come with Christmas snow,
  The ghosts we all can raise at will.

Oh, children of the village choir,
  Your carols on the midnight throw!
Oh, bright across the mist and mire,
  Ye ruddy hearths of Christmas glow!
Beat back the shades, beat down the woe,
  Renew the strength of mortal will;

Be welcome, all, to come or go,
  The ghosts we all can raise at will.

Friend, *sursum corda*, soon or slow
  We part, like guests who've joyed their fill;
Forget **them** not, nor mourn them so,
  The ghosts we all can raise at will!

                             Andrew Lang.

THE VILLAGE CHRISTMAS.

Meantime the village rouses up the fire :
While well attested, and as well believed,
Heard solemn, goes the goblin story round,
Till superstitious horror creeps o'er all.
Or, frequent in the sounding hall, they wake
The rural gambol.　Rustic mirth goes round ;
The simple joke that takes the shepherd's
　　heart,
Easily pleased ; the long, loud laugh, sincere ;
The kiss, snatched hasty from the side-long
　　maid,
On purpose guardless, or pretending sleep ;
The leap, the slap, the haul ; and, shook to
　　notes
Of native music, the respondent dance,
Thus jocund fleets with them the winter-night.

James Thomson.

WINTER.

A wrinkled, crabbéd man they picture thee,
Old winter, with a rugged beard as gray
As the long moss upon the apple-tree ;
Blue-lipt, an ice-drop at thy sharp blue nose,
Close muffled up, and on thy dreary way
Plodding alone through sleet and drifting snows.
They should have drawn thee by the high-
    heapt hearth,
Old, winter ! seated in thy great armed-chair,
Watching the children at their Christmas
    mirth ;
Or circled by them as thy lips declare
Some merry jest, or tale of murder dire,
Or troubled spirit that disturbs the night ;
Pausing at times to rouse the smouldering fire,
Or taste the old October brown and bright.

                     Robert Southey.

DECEMBER.

And after him came next the chill December:
Yet he, through merry feasting which he made
And great bonfires, did not the cold remember;
His Saviour's birth his mind so much did glad:
Upon a shaggy-bearded goat he rode,
The same wherewith Dan Jove in tender years,
They say, was nourisht by th' Iæan Mayd ;'
And in his hand a broad deep bowle he beares,
Of which he freely drinks an health to all his
　　　peeres.

Edmund Spenser.

CHRISTMAS WEATHER IN SCOTLAND.

A winter day! the feather-silent snow
Thickens the air with strange delight, and lays
A fairy carpet on the barren lea.
No sun, yet all around that inward light
Which is in purity,—a soft moonshine,
The silvery dimness of a happy dream.
How beautiful! afar on moorland ways,
Bosomed by mountains, darkened by huge glens,
(Where the lone altar raised by Druid hands
Stands like a mournful phantom,) hidden clouds
Let fall soft beauty, till each green fir branch
Is plumed and tasselled, till each heather stalk
Is delicately fringed. The sycamores,
Through all their mystical entanglement
Of boughs, are draped with silver. All the
      green
Of sweet leaves playing with the subtle air
In dainty murmuring; the obstinate drone
Of limber bees that in the monk's-hood bells
House diligent; the imperishable glow
Of summer sunshine never more confessed
The harmony of nature, the divine,
Diffusive spirit of the beautiful.
Out in the snowy dimness, half revealed
Like ghosts in glimpsing moonshine, wildly run
18

The children in bewildering delight.
There is a living glory in the air,—
A glory in the hushed air, in the soul
A palpitating wonder hushed in awe.

Softly—with delicate softness—as the light
Quickens in the undawned east ; and silently—
With definite silence—as the stealing dawn
Dapples the floating clouds, slow fall, slow fall,
With indecisive motion eddying down,
The white-winged flakes,—calm as the sleep of
      sound,
Dim as a dream.   The silver-misted air
Shines with mild radiance, as when through a
      cloud   .
Of semilucent vapor shines the moon.
I saw last evening (when the ruddy sun,
Enlarged and strange, sank low and visibly,
Spreading fierce orange o'er the west) a scene
Of winter in his milder mood.   Green fields,
Which no kine cropped, lay damp ; and naked
      trees
Threw skeleton shadows.   Hedges, thickly
      grown,
Twined into compact firmness, with no leaves,
Trembled in jewelled fretwork as the sun
To lustre touched the tremulous water-drops.
Alone, nor whistling as his fellows do
In fabling poem and provincial song,

The ploughboy shouted to his reeking train;
And at the clamor, from a neighboring field
Arose, with whirr of wings, a flock of rooks
ore clamMorous; and through the frosted air,
Blown wildly here and there without a law,
They flew, low-grumbling out loquacious croaks.
Red sunset brightened all things; streams ran red
Yet coldly; and before the unwholesome east,
Searching the bones and breathing ice, blew
      down
The hill, with a dry whistle, by the fire
In chamber twilight rested I at home.

But now what revelation of fair change,
O Giver of the seasons and the days!
Creator of all elements, pale mists,
Invisible great winds and exact frost!
How shall I speak the wonder of thy snow?
What though we know its essence and its birth,
Can quick expound, in philosophic wise,
The how, and whence, and manner of its fall;
Yet, oh, the inner beauty and the life—
The life that is in snow! The virgin-soft
And utter purity of the down-flake,
Falling upon its fellow with no sound!
Unblown by vulgar winds, innumerous flakes
Fall gently, with the gentleness of love!
The earth is cherished, for beneath the soft,
Pure uniformity is gently born

Warmth and rich mildness, fitting the dead roots
For the resuscitation of the spring.
Now while I write, the wonder clothes the
        vale,
Calmed every wind and loaded every grove ;
And looking through the implicated boughs
I see a gleaming radiance. Sparkling snow,
Refined by morning-footed frost so still,
Mantles each bough ; and such a windless hush
Breathes through the air, it seems the fairy
        glen
About some phantom palace, pale abode
Of fabled Sleeping Beauty. Songless birds
Flit restlessly about the breathless wood,
Waiting the sudden breaking of the charm ;
And as they quickly spring on nimble wing
From the white twig, a sparkling shower falls
Starlike. It is not whiteness, but a clear
Outshining of all purity, which takes
The winking eyes with such a silvery gleam.
No sunshine, and the sky is all one cloud.
The vale seems lonely, ghostlike ; while aloud
The housewife's voice is heard with doubled
        sound.
I have not words to speak the perfect show ;
The ravishment of beauty ; the delight
Of silent purity ; the sanctity
Of inspiration which o'erflows the world,
Making it breathless with divinity.

So thus with fair delapsion softly falls
The sacred shower; and when the shortened day
Dejected dies in the low streaky west,
The rising moon displays a cold blue night,
And keen as steel the east wind sprinkles ice.
Thicker than bees, about the waxing moon
Gather the punctual stars.   Huge whitened hills
Rise glimmering to the blue verge of the night,
Ghostlike, and striped with narrow glens of firs
Black-waving, solemn.   O'er the Luggie-stream
Gathers a veiny film of ice, and creeps
With elfin feet around each stone and reed,
Working fine masonry; while o'er the dam,
Dashing, a noise of waters fills the clear
And nitrous air.   All the dark, wintry hours
Sharply the winds from the white level moors
Keen whistle.   Timorous in his homely bed
The school-boy listens, fearful lest gaunt wolves
Or beasts, whose uncouth forms in ancient books
He has beheld, at creaking shutters pull
Howling.   And when at last the languid dawn
In wind redness re-illumines the east
With ineffectual fire, an intense blue
Severely vivid o'er the snowy hills
Gleams chill, while hazy, half-transparent clouds
Slow-range the freezing ether of the west.
Along the woods the keenly vehement blasts
Wail, and disrobe the mantled boughs, and fling
A snow-dust everywhere.   Thus wears the day:

IV.—o   18*

While grandfather over the well-watched fire
Hangs cowering, with a cold drop at his nose.

Now underneath the ice the Luggie growls,
And to the polished smoothness curlers come
Rudely ambitious.   Then for happy hours
The clinking stones are slid from wary hands,
And Barleycorn, best wine for surly airs,
Bites i' th' mouth, and ancient jokes are cracked.
And   oh,   the   journey   homeward,   when   the
        sun,
Low-rounding to the west, in ruddy glow
Sinks large, and all the amber-skirted clouds,
His flaming retinue, with dark'ning glow
Diverge !   The broom is brandished as the sign
Of conquest, and impetuously they boast
Of how this shot was played,—with what a
        bend
Peculiar—the perfection of all art—
That stone came rolling grandly to the Tee
With victory crowned, and flinging wide the
        rest
In lordly crash !   Within the village inn
They by the roaring chimney sit, and quaff
The beaded Usqueba with sugar dashed.
O, when the precious liquid fires the brain
To joy, and every heart beats fast with mirth
And ancient fellowship, what nervy grasps
Of horny hands o'er tables of rough oak !

What singing of Lang Syne till tear-drops
    shine,
And friendships brighten as the evening wanes!
                David Gray.

.

SIR GALAHAD.

When on my goodly charger borne
  Thro' dreaming towns I go,
The cock crows ere the Christmas morn,
  The streets are dumb with snow.
The tempest crackles on the leads
  And, ringing, springs from brand and mail;
But o'er the dark a glory spreads,
  And gilds the driving hail.

Lord Tennyson.

A THOUGHT FOR THE TIME.

In a drear-nighted December,
Too happy, happy tree,
Thy branches ne'er remember
Their green felicity :
The north cannot undo them
With a sleety whistle through them ;
Nor frozen thawings glue them
From budding at the prime.

In a drear-nighted December,
Too happy, happy brook,
Thy bubblings ne'er remember
Apollo's summer look ;
But with a sweet forgetting,
They stay their crystal fretting,
Never, never petting
About the frozen time.

Ah ! would't were so with many
A gentle girl and boy !
But were there ever any
Writhed not at passéd joy ?
To know the change and feel it,
When there is none to heal it,
Nor numbéd sense to steal it,
Was never said in rhyme.

John Keats.

BALLADE OF THE WINTER FIRESIDE.

An ingle-blaze and a steaming jug ;
   A lamp and a lazy book ;
And, deep in a doubled, downy rug
   Your feet to the warmest nook.
   And wherever the eye may crook,
A print or a tumbled tome—
For the kettle sings on the blackened hook,
   And hey ! for the sweets of home !

What though the traveller toil and tug
   Where sleety drifts be shook ?
What though i' the churchyard graves be dug ;
   And sweethearts be forsook ?
   A hearth, and a careful cook,
And cares may go or come !
For the kettle sings on the blackened hook,
   And hey ! for the sweets of home !

But—curtains down and an elbow hug ;
   A maid that comes to a look ;
A boy to carry a rimy log
   From over the frozen brook—
   And, a fig for the cawing rook,
Or ghosts in the ruddy gloam !
For the kettle sings on the blackened hook,
   And hey ! for the sweets of home !

Envoi.

And yet—or I be mistook—
　To a friend the cup should foam ;
For the kettle sings on the blackened hook,
　And hey ! for the sweets of home !

H. S. M.

A CATCH BY THE HEARTH.

Sing we all merrily
　　Christmas is here,
The day that we love best
　　Of days in the year.

Bring forth the holly,
　　The box, and the bay,
Deck out our cottage
　　For glad Christmas-day.

Sing we all merrily,
　　Draw round the fire,
Sister and brother,
　　Grandson and sire.

SALLY IN OUR ALLEY.

When Christmas comes about again,
  O then I shall have money;
I'll hoard it up, and box it all,
  I'll give it to my honey:
I would it were ten thousand pound,
  I'd give it all to Sally;
She is the darling of my heart,
  And she lives in our alley.

                H. Carey.

LITTLE MOTHER.

A GERMAN FANCY.

Little mother, why must you go?
  The children play by the white bedside,
  The world is merry for Christmas-tide,
And what would you do in the falling snow?

They sleep by now in the ember-glow,
  Hushed to dream in a child's delight,
  For wonders happen on Christmas night:
Little mother, why must you go?

The flakes fall and the night grows late.
  Oh, slender figure and small wet feet,
  Where do you haste through the lamp-lit
      street,
And out and away by the fortress gate?

It is drear and chill where the dear lie dead,
  Yet light enough with the snow to see;
  But what would you do with that Christmas-
      tree
At the tiny mound that is baby's bed?

A Christmas-tree with its tinsel gold!
Oh, how should I not have a thought for thee,
When the children sleep in their dream of
glee,
Poor little grave but a twelvemonth old!

Little mother, your heart is brave,
You kiss the cross in the drifted snow,
Kneel for a moment, rise and go
And leave your tree by the tiny grave.

While the living slept by the warm fireside,
And flakes fell white on your Christmas toy,
I think that its angel wept for joy
Because you remembered the one that died.

Rennell Rodd.

OCCIDENT AND ORIENT.

How will it dawn, the coming Christmas-day ?
A northern Christmas, such as painters love,
And kinsfolk shaking hands but once a year,
And dames who tell old legends by the fire ?
Red sun, blue sky, white snow, and pearléd ice,
Keen ringing air, which sets the blood on fire,
And makes the old man merry with the young
Through the short sunshine, through the longer
        night ?

Or southern Christmas, dark and dank with
        mist,
And heavy with the scent of steaming leaves,
And rose-buds mouldering on the dripping
        porch ;
On twilight, without rise or set of sun,
Till beetles drone along the hollow lane
And round the leafless hawthorns, flitting bats
Hawk the pale moths of winter ? Welcome
        then,
At best, the flying gleam, the flying shower,
The rain-pools glittering on the long white roads,
And shadows sweeping on from down to down
Before the salt Atlantic gale !   Yet come
In whatsoever garb, or gay or sad,

Come fair, come foul, 'twill still be Christmas-
    day.

How will it dawn, the coming Christmas-day?
To sailors lounging on the lonely deck
Beneath the rushing trade-wind? or, to him
Who by some noisome harbor of the east
Watches swart arms roll down the precious
    bales,
Spoils of the tropic forests; year by year
Amid the din of heathen voices, groaning,
Himself half heathen? How to those—brave
    hearts!
Who toil with laden loins and sinking stride
Beside the bitter wells of treeless sands
Toward the peaks which flood the ancient Nile,
To free a tyrant's captives? How to those—
New patriarchs of the new-found under world—
Who stand like Jacob, on the virgin lawns,
And count their flocks' increase? To them that
    day
Shall dawn in glory, and solstitial blaze
Of full midsummer sun: to them that morn
Gay flowers beneath their feet, gay birds aloft
Shall tell of naught but summer; but to them,
Ere yet, unwarned by carol or by chime,
They spring into the saddle, thrills may come
From that great heart of Christendom which
    beats

19*

Round all the worlds; and gracious thoughts
    of youth;
Of steadfast folk, who worship God at home,
Of wise words, learnt beside their mother's
    knee;
Of innocent faces, upturned once again
In awe and joy to listen to the tale
Of God made man, and in a manger laid:
May soften, purify, and raise the soul
From selfish cares, and growing lust of gain
And phantoms of this dream, which some call
    life,
Toward eternal facts; for here or there
Summer or winter, 'twill be Christmas-day.

Blest day, which aye reminds us year by year
What 'tis to be a man: to curb and spurn
The tyrant in us: that ignobler self
Which boasts, not loathes, its likeness to the
    brute,
And owns no good save ease, no ill save pain,
No purpose, save its share in that wild war
In which, through countless ages, living things
Compete in internecine greed—ah, God!
Are we as creeping things, which have no Lord?
That we are brutes, great God, we know too
    well:
Apes daintier-featured; silly birds who flaunt
Their plumes, unheeding of the fowler's step;

Spiders who catch with paper, not with webs ;
Tigers who slay with cannon and sharp steel,
Instead of teeth and claws ; all these we are.
Are we no more than these save in degree ?
No more than these ; and born but to com-
    pete—
To envy and devour, like beast or herb
Mere fools of nature ; puppets of strong lusts,
Taking the sword to perish with the sword
Upon the universal battle-field,
Even as the things upon the moor outside ?

The heath eats up green grass and delicate
    flowers,
The pine eats up the heath, the grub the pine,
The finch the grub, the hawk the silly finch ;
And man, the mightiest of all beasts of prey,
Eats what he lists ;—the strong eat up the weak ;
The many eat the few ; great nations, small ;
And he who cometh in the name of all
Shall, greediest, triumph by the greed of all ;
And armed by his own victims, eat up all.
While even out of the eternal heavens
Looks patient down the great magnanimous
    God
Who, Maker of all worlds, did sacrifice
All to himself. Nay, but himself to one
Who taught mankind on that first Christmas-
    day

What 'twas to be a man : to give not take;
To serve not rule ; to nourish not devour ;
To help, not crush ; if need, to die, not live.

Oh, blessed day which givest the eternal lie
To self and sense and all the brute within ;
Oh, come to us, amid this war of life,
To hall and hovel, come, to all who toil
In senate, shop, or study ; and to those
Who sundered by the wastes of half a world
Ill warned, and sorely tempted, ever face
Nature's brute powers and men unmanned to
    brutes,
Come to them, blest and blessing, Christmas-
    day.
Tell them once more the tale of Bethlehem,
The kneeling shepherds and the Babe Divine,
And keep them men indeed, fair Christmas-
    day.

               Charles Kingsley

THE BLESSED DAY.

Awake, my soul, and come away :
    Put on thy best array ;
    Lest if thou longer stay
Thou lose some minutes of so blest a day.
        Go run
And bid good-morrow to the sun ;
Welcome his safe return
        To Capricorn,
    And that great morn
    Wherein a God was born,
    Whose story none can tell
But He whose every word's a miracle.

To-day Almightiness grew weak ;
The Word itself was mute and could not speak.

That Jacob's star which made the sun
To dazzle if he durst look on,
Now mantled o'er in Bethlehem's night,
Borrowed a star to show Him light !
He that begirt each zone,
To whom both poles are one,
Who grasped the zodiac in His hand
And made it move or stand,
    IV.—*p*

Is now by nature man,
By stature but a span;
Eternity is now grown short;
A King is born without a court;
The water thirsts; the fountain's dry;
And life, being born, made apt to die.

Chorus.

Then let our praises emulate and vie
  With His humility!
Since He's exiled from skies
  That we might rise,—
    From low estate of men
    Let's sing Him up again!
    Each man wind up his heart
    To bear a part
In that angelic choir and show
  His glory high as He was low.
Let's sing towards men good-will and charity,
  Peace upon earth, glory to God on high!
      Hallelujah! Hallelujah!

Jeremy Taylor.

CHRISTMAS IN CUBA.

On the hill-side droops the palm,
  The air is faint with flowers,
In the wondrous, dream-like calm
  Of tropical morning hours.
Like a mirror lies the bay,
  And softly on its breast,
In the glow of coming day,
  The vessels sway at rest.

Through the tremulous air I hear
  The chiming of Christmas bells,
As the sun rises burning and clear
  . Over the ocean swells.
And birds with singing sweet
  Proclaim the glorious morn
When angels thronged to greet
  The Christ-child newly born.

But with strong desire I sigh
  For a frozen land afar,
Under a cold gray sky,
  Where glistens the northern star;
Where a winter of rest and sleep
  Embraces mountain and plain,
And meadows their secret keep
  To tell it in spring again.

Dearer the pine-clad hills
   And valleys wrapped in snow,
Dearer the ice-bound rills,
   And roaring winds that blow,
Than this tropical calm, and perfume
   Of jasmine and lily and rose,
These flowers that always bloom,
   This nature without repose.

Alas for the delight
   Of a distant fireside,
Where loving hearts unite
   To keep this Christmas-tide!
Where the hemlock and the pine
   Sweet memories recall,
As their fragrant boughs entwine
   Around the panelled wall.

O Christ-child pure and fair,
   Draw near and dwell with me;
Thy love is everywhere,
   On land and on the sea.
I grasp Thy saving hand,
   And while to Thee I pray,
Alone, in a foreign land,
   I bless this Christmas-day.

Helen S. Conant.

FAREWELL TO CHRISTMAS.

Now farewell, good Christmas,
  Adieu and adieu,
I needs now must leave thee,
  And look for a new ;
For till thou returnest,
  I linger in pain,
And I care not how quickly
  Thou comest again.

But ere thou departest,
  I purpose to see
What merry good pastime
  This day will show me ;
For a king of the wassail
  This night we must choose,
Or else the old customs
  We carelessly lose.

The wassail well spiced
  About shall go round,
Though it cost my good master
  Best part of a pound :
The maid in the buttery
  Stands ready to fill
Her nappy good liquor
  With heart and good-will.
20

And to welcome us kindly
   Our master stands by,
And tells me in friendship
   One tooth is a-dry.
Then let us accept it
   As lovingly, friends ;
And so for this Twelfth-day
   My carol here ends.

New Christmas Carols, A.D. 1661.

THE NEW YEAR.

Hark, the cock crows, and yon bright star
Tells us the day himself's not far ;
And see where, breaking from the night,
He gilds the western hills with light.
With him old Janus doth appear,
Peeping into the future year,
With such a look, as seems to say,
The prospect is not good that way.
Thus do we rise ill sights to see,
And 'gainst ourselves to prophesy ;
When the prophetic fear of things
A more tormenting mischief brings,
More full of soul-tormenting gall,
Than direst mischiefs can befall.
But stay ! but stay ! methinks my sight,
Better inform'd by clearer light,
Discerns sereneness in that brow,
That all contracted seem'd but now.
His reversed face may show distaste,
And frown upon the ills are past ;
But that which this way looks is clear,
And smiles upon the new-born year.

He looks, too, from a place so high,
The year lies open to his eye;
And all the moments open are
To the exact discoverer.
Yet more and more he smiles upon
The happy revolution.
Why should we then suspect or fear
The influences of a year,
So smiles upon us the first morn,
And speaks us good as soon as born?
Plague on't! the last was ill enough,
This cannot but make better proof;
Or, at the worst, as we brush'd through
The last, why so we may this too;
And then the next in reason should
Be superexcellently good:
For the worst ills (we daily see)
Have no more perpetuity
Than the best fortunes that do fall;
Which also bring us wherewithal
Longer their being to support
Than those do of the other sort;
And who has one good year in three,
And yet repines at destiny,
Appears ungrateful in the case,
And merits not the good he has.

Then let us welcome the new guest
With lusty brimmers of the best;

Mirth always should good fortune meet,
And render e'en disaster sweet ;
And though the princess turn her back,
Let us but line ourselves with sack,
We better shall by far hold out
Till the next year she face about.

Charles Cotton.

20*

A HAPPY NEW YEAR.

The old year now away is fled,
The new year it is enteréd,
Then let us now our sins down-tread
   And joyfully all appear.
Let's merry be this holiday,
And let us now both sport and play,
Hang sorrow, let's cast care away:
   God send you a happy New Year!

For Christ's circumcision this day we keep,
Who for our sins did often weep;
His hands and feet were wounded deep,
   And His blessed side with a spear.
His head they crownéd then with thorn,
And at Him they did laugh and scorn,
Who for to save our souls was born:
   God send us a happy New Year!

And now with New-Year's gifts each friend
Unto each other they do send;
God grant we may all our lives amend,
   And that the truth may appear.
Now like the snake cast off your skin
Of evil thoughts and wicked sin,
And to amend this New Year begin:
   God send us a happy New Year!

And now let all the company
In friendly manner all agree,
For we are here welcome, all may see,
   Unto this jolly good cheer.
I thank my master and my dame,
The which are founders of the same ;
To eat, to drink now is no shame :
   God send us a merry New Year !

Come, lads and lasses every one,
Jack, Tom, Dick, Bessy, Mary, and Joan,
Let's cut the meat up unto the bone,
   For welcome you need not fear ;
And here for good liquor we shall not lack,
It will whet my brains and strengthen my
      back ;
This jolly good cheer it must go to wrack :
   God send us a merry New Year !

Come, give's more liquor when I do call,
I'll drink to each one in this hall ;
I hope that so loud I must not bawl,
   But unto me lend an ear ;
Good fortune to my master send,
And to my dame which is our friend,
Lord bless us all, and so I end :
   God send us a happy New Year !
              New Christmas Carols, A.D. 1642.

NEW-YEAR'S GIFTS.

The young men and maids on New-Year's day,
  Their loves they will present
With many a gift both fine and gay,
  Which gives them true content:
And though the gift be great or small,
  Yet this is the custom still,
Expressing their loves in ribbons and gloves,
  It being their kind good-will.

Young bachelors will not spare their coin,
  But thus their love is shown ;
Young Richard will buy a bodkin fine
  And give it honest Joan.
There's Nancy and Sue with honest Prue,
  Young damsels both fair and gay,
Will give to the men choice presents again
  For the honor of New-Year's day.

Fine ruffs, cravats of curious lace,
  Maids give them fine and neat ;
For this the young men will them embrace
  With tender kisses sweet :
And give them many pleasant toys
  To deck them fine and gay,
As bodkins and rings with other fine things
  For the honor of New-Year's day

It being the first day of the year,
  To make the old amends,
All those that have it will dress good cheer,
  Inviting all their friends
To drink great James's royal health,
  As very well subjects may,
With many healths more, which we have store,
  For the honor of New-Year's day.

A Cabinet of Choice Jewels, A.D. 1688.

THE END OF THE PLAY.

The play is done; the curtain drops,
  Slow falling to the prompter's bell;
A moment yet the actor stops
  And looks around to say farewell.
It is an irksome word and task;
  And, when he's laughed and said his say,
He shows, as he removes the mask,
  A face that's anything but gay.

One word ere yet the evening ends;
  Let's close it with a parting rhyme,
And pledge a hand to all young friends,
  As fits the merry Christmas-time.
On life's wide scene you, too, have parts,
  That fate erelong shall bid you play;
Good-night! with honest, gentle hearts
  A kindly greeting go alway.

Come wealth or want, come good or ill,
  Let young and old accept their part,
And bow before the Awful Will,
  And bear it with an honest heart.
Who misses or who wins the prize,
  Go, lose or conquer as you can;
But if you fail, or if you rise,
  Be each, pray God, a gentleman.

A gentleman, or old or young!
  (Bear kindly with my humble lays);
The sacred chorus first was sung
  Upon the first of Christmas days;
The shepherds heard it overhead,
  The joyful angels raised it then;
Glory to heaven on high, it said,
  And peace on earth to gentle men.

My song, save this, is little worth;
  I lay the weary pen aside,
And wish you health, and love, and mirth,
  As fits the solemn Christmas-tide.
As fits the holy Christmas birth,
  Be this, good friends, our carol still—
Be peace on earth, be peace on earth,
  To men of gentle will.

William Makepeace Thackeray.

FINIS.

Yule's come and Yule's gane,
  And we have feasted weel ·
Sae Jock mun to his flail again,
  And Jenny to her wheel.